Etta's Fishing Ground

By

Eva Pasco

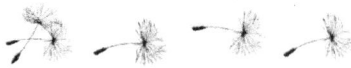

Dedication

To my dearly departed feline companions, **Misty** and **Hope**, a wellspring of unconditional love.

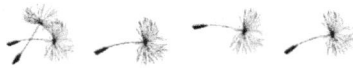

Acknowledgements

As always, heartfelt thanks to:

My mother and namesake, **Eva**, for her unwavering faith and pride in my literary accomplishments, cultivated by reading stories to me when I was a toddler.

My late father and namesake, **Pasco**, for the independent streak he instilled in me.

My sister, **Gina**, for encouraging me to pursue my dreams along untrammeled paths.

My **Beloved** on the other side, a source of light and inspiration. Until sometime tomorrow.

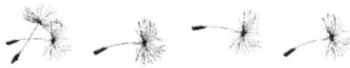

Prologue

Foster, Rhode Island—Etta's fishing ground, situated at the southeastern corner of Providence County on the Rhode Island/Connecticut state line. From the perspective of a bird's-eye view high in the sky, this rural enclave spans 51.1 square miles of land and .7 square miles of water. If you're looking to lure a trout or two, you can try your patience in tempting fate by casting your fly line across the water at any designated trout fishing spot: Green Acres Pond, Hopkins Mill Pond, and three out of the many other unnamed tributaries that feed the Ponaganset River—Dolly Cole Brook, Shippee Brook, and Winsor Brook. Keith Lawrence liked to kick-sample for rainbow trout just below Hopkins Mill Pond, but was obsessed with fly-fishing for fickle bass elsewhere along the river. Whereas most bass anglers release their catch, Keith wouldn't let go.

The town of Foster is a state of mind as much as it is a geographic entity for those who live here. Areas of dense woodland by the acre afford each homesteader plenty of elbow room between their nearest neighbors. Properties accessed by narrow driveways snaking homeward, and flanked by a tangle of trees on three sides, grant privacy. So much for swatting at an onslaught of flies and mosquitoes every summer. As for winters, "No school, Fosta-Glosta!" This public announcement, spoken like a true Rhode Islander in dropping the *er*, was heralded time and again by beloved radio broadcaster, Salty Brine, on WPRO-AM.

Amongst the population of less than 5000, there's Wyatt Cole, whose father, Mad Daddy Wayne, tried to instill in him the stoicism of supremacy. A generational mindset, it was indoctrinated in Mad Daddy from his pappy, Wentworth. He, a

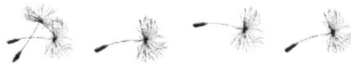

proud member of the Ku Klux Klan during the 1920s and 1930s. That's when rural Rhode Islanders and scores of middle-class white Americans across the United States relinquished their senses and souls to an organization driven to restore "true Americanism".

Xenophobia, a fear of foreigners brought on by waves of immigration, enabled the KKK to gain a foothold in Rhode Island through recruiting members by enticing attendees from all walks of life:

Jury commissioner, house painter, foreman, quarry worker, minister, attorney, weaver, mason, cashier, undertaker, harness maker, plumber, meter tester, fisherman, iceman, printer, barber, laborer, storekeeper, physician, auto mechanic. And, lumber stacker at a saw mill—*Mayflower* descendant, Wentworth Cole.

Klan meetings stoked the fire in Wentworth Cole's belly when pontificating brethren demonized non-white ethnic immigrants, condemned Communism, and denounced the evils of alcohol, birth control, and the teaching of evolution in schools. He drew inspiration from every fire-and-brimstone speech advocating reforms to reinstate the economic and political power of white Anglo-Saxon Protestants.

One of 8,000 who gathered at the Old Home grounds in Foster Center for a Klan rally on June 21, 1924, Wentworth listened with rapt attention to U.S. Senator J. Thomas Heflin of Alabama. The Klan is believed to have been responsible for setting a series of fires in 1924, 1926, and 1934 to the Watchman Institute, a school for African-American children in the neighboring town of Scituate. Although no arrests were ever made, the patriarch proudly proclaimed himself one of the arsonists. Off his rocker in his golden years, he divulged this once too often to his son and grandson behind closed doors and under the leaky roof of his cabin situated on the family tract.

Favorite son, Wayne, perpetuated the derogatory images conjured by an Overlord of the Flies who presided over a ramshackle bungalow, tool sheds on the verge of collapsing, and the rusted remains of vehicles cannibalized for their body parts. Ever ready for a cataclysmic event with a Rem 700 bolt-action rifle! A bullet-ridden No Trespassing sign, booby traps, and the omnipresence of scrap-fed, snarling mutts secured his sacred ground comprised of fifteen acres off of Mill Road where the impenetrable backwoods abutted an automobile salvage yard.

For his misconceptions and for all of the repercussions which followed, Mad Daddy's son Wyatt rued the day he came across Etta Rizzio during one of his hunting jaunts. There she was sketching on Breezy Hill, a prehistoric archaeological site which surrendered pottery remnants dated from 500 – 1000 AD. The wrenching of his heartstrings by an Eyetalian-Catholic Hippie whose dad was at odds with his, tore him apart, predisposing him to take matters into his own hands.

Remorseful thoughts haunted Wyatt while serving a sentence of fifteen years at the Adult Correctional Institute, ten years to be served in Minimum Security, with five years to be suspended for the felony of misdemeanor manslaughter.

Otherwise, the quiet town with a low crime rate would up the ante years later when a suspended police officer shot and killed three teenagers at Wilson's Auto Enterprise in retaliation against criminal charges filed for excessive force used during a traffic stop.

For better, or for worse—trespass and traverse Etta's fishing ground in Foster, Rhode Island.

Part One - Shaky Ground

Chapter 1

A head turn and double take in reaction to an innocuous, inquisitive glance of her surroundings precluded Muriel from taking another bite out of her bacon cheeseburger. Medium-well, the way she ordered it. Blindsided. Swallowing a pulpy mixture of beef and curly fries, her mind calculated the whys and wherefores which didn't add up.

Sitting across from Muriel at a booth by the window overlooking an area of the restaurant's parking lot, and oblivious to his wife's drained complexion, Obie tore into a giant roast beef. Sliced thin and piled high on a grilled bulky roll. Medium-rare, the way he ordered it. Preferring to skip the amenities of conversation during dinner, or just about any day-to-day activity with Muriel, he kept his thoughts to himself.

Gawd, how annoying!

Her shrillness went through him like a dentist's drill. At least he salvaged all of his teeth through root canals and implants, which is more than he could say for Muriel. He shivered, unhinged by the mental cruelty of her slipping under the covers after removing her dentures and depositing them in a glass on the nightstand.

Gawd, how disgusting!

Far be it from him to dispel what most of the diehards and blowhards he fraternized with thought of Muriel. *What a catch!* A financier's daughter and serial beauty pageant contestant during Nixon's administration. She could still work the room by plying her wares of rigid poise, contrived personality, brittle beauty, and artificial intelligence. Such a winning combo made her a customer-favorite, slinging hash at the State Line Diner, so named, when it moved to Foster in the '70s, until wiped out

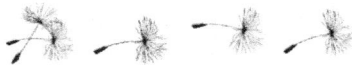

by fire on February 6, 2015. The charred remains of a local truck stop renamed Cherri's State Line Diner when it came under new management in 2010, became an eyesore, still under investigation. The date of its baptism by fire etched itself in Obie's brain because it portended Muriel's termination which impinged on a retired patrol officer's autonomy around the house.

Aw! Muriel wasn't to blame. Hell, by the time your sixties crept up on you, old age held you up like a bandit, robbing you of the goods that made you attractive and appealing to each other in the first place. Foster's Police Department alumnus, Obediah Smith, maintained his trim physique by frequenting the gym. Looked upon favorably by most females, including his old flame, Carolyn Farnum—Obie looked back, discreetly sizing up their composite sketches.

Thus far, no one compared to his wife's best friend, Etta. *Now, there was a catch!*

Hark! Muriel perforated the airspace between them by vocalizing. *Gawd dammit!* He begrudged making eye contact to acknowledge her breach of social etiquette as she craned her neck to get a better view above and beyond his head.

"Don't turn around," she cautioned. "But, you'll never guess who just came out of the bar and is walking toward the door, looking pleased as Punch!"

"You're right, Muriel. And, I've no intention of guessing either."

Before she disclosed her subject, Obie bit into the bottom portion of his sandwich. Muriel leaned forward, forcing him to look a gift set of knockers in the mouth. On their high horse, they strained against the fabric of a tank top, bolstered by a push-up bra.

"Keith!"

10

Well now! A horse of a different color!

He swallowed hard and hastily. As a result, a remnant of roast beef lodged in his throat. He guzzled most of his cola to wash it down. In the time it took to set the glass back on its coaster, Obie assumed a straight face. No need to tip off Muriel that she piqued his interest in Etta's other half. As far as he knew, the bugger was supposed to be fishing all weekend along the Ponaganset River, 12 miles away from Chelo's Hometown Bar & Grille at the Apple Valley Mall in Greenville. Muriel knew it too.

"He's with another woman!"

Aside from spasmodic choking, Obie kept his lips sealed while harboring evil intent toward Muriel for failing to fulfill his needs. Gawd, give me liberty or give her death, and I'd be pleased as Punch!

Muriel leaned back against the booth, rattled by her vision. For Etta's sake. He couldn't bring himself to take another bite, addled by her admission. For Etta's sake.

Keep your friends close. Keep your wife's best friend the closest of all, if you genuinely care for her.

The silence he so coveted between them had come with a price at Etta's expense, and grew burdensome in accordance with its discomfort. Assuming Muriel couldn't identify the other woman, he counted on her providing a physical description, either voluntarily or with prompting.

As the roast beef under his nose turned cold, he sensed the four of them approaching the point of no return in the infrastructure of their friendship and the bonds of matrimony. His dire premonition mandated he nail down stats for future reference, if needed. Obie had a feeling he would.

To his relief, Muriel found her tongue. "She kinda reminds me of Etta." Catching the implied accusation from her

11

husband's raised eyebrow, she set him straight. "It's not Etta! She's slender like Etta, but taller. She fixes her hair like Etta when she pins it up in a messy bun."

Jack shit! That's what Muriel's thumbnail sketch was worth! Gawd, could she get any vaguer?

A former officer of the law who wrote many a narrative report, he dealt strictly with factual details. For instance, when conducting a routine traffic stop, he'd run information from a driver's license through the dispatcher. With no such windfall forthcoming, Obie had to rely on his only eyewitness whose observations ran aground in generalities.

Taking in his wife's sideswept, wavy bob with mahogany streaks, he sought to uproot a significant detail from a woman who tried too hard in making herself attractive. For all of her razor-edge chic, she missed the mark with him. Unlike Etta, who threw herself together like a vintage Hippie chick and transmitted the faint scent of lavender whenever she got close to you. So, in an attempt to snag a physical trait and downplay its importance, he feigned attentiveness to the petrified slices of roast beef, while pursuing a topic of interest.

"Is her hair color similar to Etta's?"

"No, I'd say it's a honey-brown shade."

For Gawd's sake, the exact description he'd have used for Etta's.

The meager margin for error eroding, he had to set the ground rules as soon as their waitress left the tab, and before Muriel used the restroom. He intended to tailor his remark to the unwritten code of ethics among guys—your friend cheats on his woman, you take it to your grave.

When both declined dessert, the waitress threw down the gauntlet and walked away. Face-off. "Muriel, this stays between

us and goes no further. Nearly destroying Etta once in her lifetime should be enough for you!"

Jolted, her face blanched at the memory jog past honorable intentions of disclosure, implicating her as a harbinger of horror worse than death itself. True enough. But, Etta had forgiven her, and they'd been right as rain ever since.

On the contrary, Muriel had other ideas stemming from the unwritten code of ethics among gal pals—let a best friend know when her man is cheating. Before heading to the ladies room, she siphoned the dregs of her iced coffee through a straw, momentarily delaying the grim set of her lips he so duly noted from his man-on-top position on those rare occasions they had sexual intercourse.

With her eyes closed and legs semi-locked, Muriel flailed her arms as though swimming against his incoming tide, resistant to riding it with him.

He'd try to keep Muriel's mouth shut for as long as possible by taking advantage of everything the mall had to offer for enticement. When she returned to their booth, he ticked off the names of clothing shops and suggested they browse the book store, all to no avail. His last-ditch effort, "Hey, how about we see what movies are playing at the cinema?"

Muriel had her own agenda. "Let's go home. Instead of dropping off my casserole at Ethan's in the morning, I'd rather stop by this evening."

Gawd! What a lying, conniving bitch!

He could only hope Muriel would stop at their son's place and tarry with him, their daughter-in-law, and grandkids rather than paying an impromptu visit to Etta. It was just about 6:15 when Obie opened the passenger door on their Ford Escape for her. He considered the blessing of Muriel dying in a car crash, preferably on her way to Etta's, rather than on her way back.

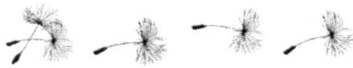

Or, best case scenario, sudden death at the onset of cardiac arrest before he got in the driver's seat.

Chapter 2

7:06 p.m.

"Hey, darlin'! I'm in over my knees. Whadda you up to?"

"Just lounging on the porch and enjoying the sunset before I draw a bath. Which nobody does better than you!"

"Darlin', whether it's scooping a tablespoon of lavender bath salts, lathering you up, or casting a fly rod—it's all in the wrist. Netted a few rainbow trout kick-sampling this morning. Got 'em on ice."

Make that five trout to be exact. The creel limit in state-owned or controlled public fishing areas like the Ponaganset River, from April 11th through November 30th. No size restriction from tip of the snout to tip of the tail.

"Tonight, I'm angling for that el—u—sive bass. Damn! My ph—one is breaking—up. Not en—ough sig—nal. We'll talk to—morr."

Cut off before Keith could tell her he loved her, or so she presumed, because he ended all of his calls with her that way. Etta still told him to be careful, and ended her call the way she always did with him, although he couldn't hear her. "I love you, my Wild One!"

At 7:09, he tucked his phone inside the front Velcro pocket on his long-sleeve, nylon fly-fishing shirt. Bug-repellant and guaranteed for 70 washes. It assured protection throughout the summer when larger insects become more active during warm temperatures and spring runoff, enticing fish to follow the horde. Likewise, whether downstream or upstream in summertime, King Neptune of the Ponaganset preferred treading water in a pair of quick-drying, nylon fly-fishing pants.

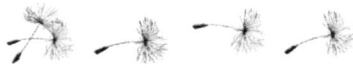

Of all those times the Smiths relaxed on his wraparound porch overlooking the backyard, as a matter of principle, Keith brought up the *dry* subject of wading wear during their most recent foursome. Not while grilling four succulent rainbow trout he gutted for their supper, which Etta had coated with salt, pepper, sugar, and fresh dill. Not in the middle of their culinary experience seated around the old rustic dining set savoring his catch, corn on the cob, and a baked potato topped with shredded cheese, bacon bits, and sour cream.

But, afterward, when Muriel and Etta cleared the glass tabletop and retreated to the kitchen to wash and dry the dishes, chugging peach-flavored wine coolers and gabbing in between swigs.

Then, Obie listened with an amused grin plastered on his face, never imagining Keith's words would stick in his craw forever.

Besieged by Foster's brash *ch-ch-ch* from katydids in competition with the incessant mating chirps of black field crickets, two hard-nosed retirees knocked back a few. That'd be Captain's Daughter, one of Rhode Island's finest home-brewed beers fermented with high-quality pilsner malt and flaked oats.

Bamboo tiki torches illuminated the faces of two silverados thrown together on account of their wives' friendship. Obie's— clean-shaven and impassive, complemented by a close trim on the sides and back of his head, which accentuated the gelled spikes on top. Keith's—unshaven and rough-hewn, complemented by a loose, wavy shag which accentuated the broodiness that attracted Etta to him in the first place.

As he had during previous get-togethers, shooting the breeze or verbally sparring mano-a-mano, Keith cast his line toward Obie, hoping to bait him into fly-fishing one of these

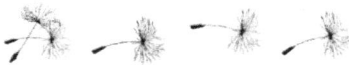

weekends. His lure of choice was shame. "Hey, whenever you grow a set of balls and decide to haul ass angling in the river, let me know, you son of a bitch!"

Gawd, the drudgery of fishing might just be the answer to his prayers for getting away from Muriel. He couldn't even tinker in the garage restoring a '65 Mustang hardtop without her hounding him for one thing or another. Only the other day, an ex-patrol officer's self-discipline stopped him from bludgeoning her to death with the ratcheting wrench he gripped in his right hand.

Obie downed the rest of his beer and gaveled the empty can on the tabletop, commanding Keith's attention. "All right, you crazy bastard! But, my customer comes first. Gimme a couple of weeks to finish the Stang, and you're on."

Keith rubbed the stubble on his chin, debating with himself over whether or not he should forewarn the guy about proper attire. He chugged the silt of his beer and crushed the empty, pitching it into a trash barrel. The die was now cast. "Believe me, you could use the time to man up. Buy yourself a pair of them nylon, river pants with zippers at the knees. You don't want to show up at the gym on the next day with nasty branch scratches tattooed all over your legs. Or, worse—the blisters of poison ivy, oak, or sumac. Me? I wouldn't be caught dead in the water without 'em!"

Lightweight enough, this fabric with benefits also kept the wearer cool and shielded the fly-fishing aficionado from ultraviolet rays by day.

Giggles heard from the kitchen disrupted his crude *manologue*. Obie noticed the understated glances Keith and Etta exchanged through the screen of the open window above the sink. Their suggestiveness only served to magnify the lack of affection and attraction between him and Muriel. Chagrined, he

averted his gaze and checked his watch. Later than he realized, he'd call the shots as soon as Muriel crossed over the threshold.

As much as Keith enjoyed keeping company with the Smiths, he and Etta's nonverbal flirtation behooved him to shut down the evening so they could make love on the cushioned chaise lounge in his line of vision. He tailored his conversation accordingly. "Before you leave, get this straight. Don't be an asshole wading in them flip-flops you got on. Aside from horrible traction, they provide no protection or support for the uneven and slippery conditions below the river surface."

Stifled by the stretch and retraction of the screen door as their wives walked the planks, and Obie cuing Muriel about heading home, Keith never finished what he wanted to say.

Essentially, Obie should step in the river wearing wading boots with interchangeable soles which allow the angler to match traction and terrain. Felt soles work best for navigating moss-covered rocks in a riverbed, albeit not foolproof by any means. As for socks: put on a polyester pair to avoid getting weighed down, while keeping the swamp-foot feeling at a minimum.

Figuring Obie for a one-hit wader looking to get away from his wife, Keith would have omitted mentioning that his wading boots should be sized one up from a standard hiking boot to accommodate wool or thermal socks in cold waters early in the season.

Priding himself with knowing all the angles in and out of the water, the notion of Obie fitting comfortably into any pair of wading boots seemed a far stretch for a guy already floundering in misery.

After the four bid each other good night on the porch, Etta's trace scent of lavender in the mix of hugs, Obie lay claim to Muriel by slipping his arm around her waist for good

measure among friends. They proceeded to their vehicle arm-in-arm as opposed to up-in-arms.

Etta and Keith, gracious hosts to the end, stood on the landing until the taillights disappeared from their winding, gravel drive. Taking Etta's hand in his, he led her to the chaise lounge. Reclined, they consummated their desire for each other under the stars. Their moans and passionate outbursts were muffled by the raucous katydids and crickets courting them in the dead of night.

Chapter 3

Etta's Wild One dug his heels in the sodden turf of Winsor Brook, one of three major brook feeders along the Ponaganset River's length spanning 12.5 miles. No other anglers in sight of the tributary, Keith Lawrence held the world by a string with a fly line and rod. With sunset imminent at 8:15 on that mid-July Saturday evening, Keith planned to hold out until dark, if necessary, on the downriver side of a dam, standing near a clump of weeds.

Smallmouth and largemouth bass gravitate toward a current. Weeds produce oxygen, thereby increasing the life potential in a body of water for fish to hide and prey on baitfish. From Keith's standpoint, his chances for sinking his hook into a bad boy looked mighty divine, blessed by the brook's gush over a natural barrier. He hedged his bet on smallmouth which preferred clearer water, especially streams and rivers with cooler temperatures.

According to regional lore of late, 6 p.m. was prime time for encountering bass within the Winsor's two-hour window of opportunity. This mitigated crossing that fine line between spending too much time in one unproductive spot and moving to another. Heck, since all designated trout waters were stocked prior to opening day of the season, and restocked, Keith hadn't bothered checking the *fatty factor*. In layman's terms, this translates to a detailed seven-day fishing forecast based on a 1 to 5 rating calculated per hour for every stream. A factor of 5 indicates the fattest prospects for hooking up.

So, having parted with his dinner companion, Keith affected a quick-change in deference to his pang of guilt for jeopardizing prime time. By 7:00, he trod ground on a full stomach, wading in river walkers with felt soles. After his

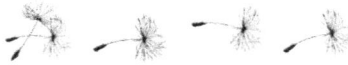

aborted phone call with Etta, he pondered the implications of seeing his accomplice in a couple of hours to work out the logistics.

His instinct told him he was making the right decision for him and Etta at this juncture in their life. He'd broach the subject with her tomorrow morning at breakfast, bracing himself for her initial reaction. If over forty years of marriage taught him more than he cared to know about withstanding life's ups and downs, Keith envisioned Etta coming to grips with the new direction in which both were headed as they approached the sunset of their golden years.

Since an angler's vision is crucial to a successful bout of fly-fishing whether day or night, Keith wore a ball cap to cut the glare of sundown reflecting off the water. Prepared for sunset, he opted for a pair of sunglasses with low-light, yellow lenses which made the environment appear brighter so he could see deeper into the water. However much these shades enhanced his eyesight, they couldn't clarify his muddied thinking which prevailed while wading in the billowing currents of Winsor Brook.

"You're just going to dump it in her lap?" his companion asked. Her hazel eyes widened in reaction at the mention of his surprise attack for making the announcement. She swept a wispy tendril of hair away from her face with a quick movement of her hand.

"It's not like I planned for this to happen, but there's no turning back or pussyfooting around it."

Empathizing, she patted his back. Sitting alongside each other at the bar, basking in the comfort of familiarity, they swigged beer and tended to their meals so he could get back to his vocation of fishing. During the course of her biting into a turkey club, and his digging into a steak sandwich, they chatted inconsequentially. Their affability belied a relationship that had

21

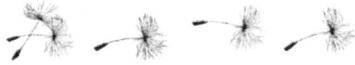

evolved from desperation on her part, and striving for self-fulfillment on his. As a result of their symbiotic bond, each had divulged confidential information to one another as the season progressed.

Rain or shine, he drew the line at roughing it in the *buff*— donning one of those neckerchiefs with UV protection over areas of skin missed by a hat. The perks of wetting a buff before wading and throughout the day provided you with your own personal swamp cooler. Nevertheless, he wouldn't be caught attaching an article of clothing he equated with an ascot some foppish Fauntleroy would don.

As the evening wore on and his mind wandered, Keith worked all the angles. He felt like Santiago in Hemingway's *Old Man and the Sea*, pitting his wits against a phantom bass, in contrast to the old man's spear-like snouted marlin. He squared his shoulders in redirecting a new cast, stripping enough line to go the desired distance.

Gripping the rod, Keith started a back cast with the rod tip near the water, lifting it smoothly as the tip went to the two o'clock position. No limp-wrist sissy, his didn't bend or break while executing a forward cast which stopped crisply at the ten o'clock position. Until the next cast, he stood sentinel, mindful of his surroundings. Mired in endurance and determination, he was entrenched in the muck of deep thought.

More often than not, thinking of Etta the way he did when flying solo, brought a smile to his lips upwelled from the depths of his heart. On occasion, tears glistened in his wizened brown eyes underscored with fine lines. A yellow lens couldn't illuminate the murkiness for him to fathom that dark place he dared not enter for fear of bringing out the worst in both of them.

Better his sleeping dog lie still, unperturbed. Every so often his sore point festered and got the better of him because of his

own reluctance to trespass and traverse forbidden territory. He had his reasons. Keith shared his dilemma with the other woman after she had confided her own alliterative trio of devastation, depression, and disorientation amidst their eye-for-an-eye trade-off session of self-revelations.

A formidable warrior of stamina with a chiseled physique, the Wild One wielded rod and reel in the rough-and-tumble Ponaganset, vigilant of the ever-changing elements in a sport beset with inherent dangers. As there aren't many days when the wind doesn't create a problem with casting technique, the odds favor getting stabbed with your own fly if you don't know where it is when executing the motion. As you can see, slipping on a pair of sunglasses has a two-pronged advantage. On the subject of slipping, a fly-fisherman must keep steadfast on his feet to avoid the perils of accidental slip-ups.

Ever since he retired, for eight months out of the year on every weekend, with few exceptions, Keith lodged at the Rainbow Trout Cabins on Winsor Road in number six. An accommodating, bare-bones comfort zone with gas heat and a cot to sleep on, the one-room efficiency had a dresser, end table and lamp, small electric fridge, propane range, toilet, wall-mount vessel sink, and a shower with hot and cold running water. The only drawback—BYO bedding, towels, and toiletries. Compared with the amenities to be had at Wyatt's former double-bunk cell at the ACI, Keith had no complaints.

The fact that he showed up at the deli when he did and spooked Wyatt into squeezing the trigger and committing murder, still rattled his brain aplenty.

The recently widowed owner gave her only long-term lodger a drastically reduced seasonal rate in exchange for taking on general maintenance and repairs during off-peak fishing hours. Fronting the string of a half-dozen cabins lined up in close proximity, presided the two-story chalet where she and

her husband had lived year-round. It was Keith's point of origin for whitewashing all cabin exteriors and painting the window trim a forest green before she put the property up for sale and moved out. Come hell or high water by the end of November.

By midsummer, the one-man marathoner sprinted his way to the last cabin in the row. Home sweet home. Before he finished the trim on number six, the property was officially on the market without the glorification of a For Sale sign no one would have seen. Secluded off a secondary road in no-man's-land, and deserted off-peak season, the Rainbow Trout Cabins had become one of Foster's best-kept secrets.

The pending private sale of Keith's sanctuary abutting his hallowed fishing ground got him thinking about real estate in Foster's redneck woods. Consequently, he did some digging and discovered properties and parcels languishing on the market past 680 days without a buyer. As inventory rose, the backlog created a less competitive market in a state whose economy was still stuck in neutral, according to the governor of Rhode Island.

These findings foretold a false lull of security for him to enjoy his slice of paradise. Then what? A prospective buyer from out of town who could afford the steep asking price might fancy bulldozing the cabins to build the family dream house, rather than preserving a hideaway for those who chased rainbow trout and pursued the elusive bass. Perish the thought. "Over my dead body!"

Keith checked his waterproof and abrasion-proof watch which indicated he should call it quits before dusk intensified to pitch-blackness. 8:46. He wanted to grab a shower, shave, and change into his last pair of clean cargo pants and one of his remaining T-shirts, preferably the less ragged of the two.

He didn't want to keep a lady waiting when he'd already told her when to expect him at her door a mite over fifteen

24

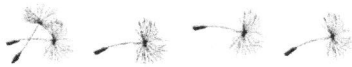

minutes ago. He anticipated nothing less than a champagne toast for celebrating life's unwritten chapter, notwithstanding where Etta stood on ceremony the following morning. A tug on the line cast aspersions over the Wild One's plan.

From what Keith could discern, he solidly hooked a fish! Keeping his cool, he let the water, resistance of the line, line elasticity, and reel drag join forces in combatting an antagonist that had to be a smallmouth bass. Landing 'em can be tough because they never give up, full of more spitfire than any other species.

Having worked up a sweat during the struggle, Keith started reeling in his trophy, careful not to snap the line on his 6-weight rod. Closer and closer and closer, pulling the rod tip up, he got a glimpse of his adversary in the encroaching darkness. The robust fish with a long, blunt snout, surfaced. Smallmouth, all right! Approximately 14 inches in length, and weighing a little over a pound, it resisted captivity. Like Santiago's marlin. Keith battled his formidable opponent while respecting its tenacity.

Already late, and at the mercy of nightfall, he reeled in the slack at a faster rate. Concurrently, his head reeled from all of his intrusive thoughts.

Tomorrow, he'd smooth-talk Etta.

Psychological mumbo jumbo undermined his better judgment. Ditching common sense, he began walking backwards to shore on uneven terrain. Whether his foot initially got trapped under a tree branch, or he slipped on a moss-covered rock, Keith lost his balance. This misstep occurred at 9:05, according to the digital annotation on his waterproof watch.

Chapter 4

Obie's wishful thinking in Chelo's parking lot failed to bring about Muriel's demise. Dead silence permeated their ride home. Up to, but not including, the dead stop at the end of a long asphalt driveway which forked to one side, laying flush against a walkway constructed from interlocking concrete pavers. Braking hard within kissing breadth of their two-car garage, he narrowly avoided plowing into one of the carriage-style doors with upper-paned windows. He put the shift lever in park and pulled out the key from the ignition.

Forcing himself to look her squarely in the eyes, he dangled a carrot in front of her nose, poised to pose a rhetorical question. "Do you plan on driving the Escape?"

She nodded her assent and held out an outstretched hand to take the bait. Both exited the SUV from their respective doors, and plodded along the walkway which widened at the entrance to the breezeway. An enclosed portal mediating polar opposite sides of refuge and residence, each pursued divergent paths away from their detached other half.

He turned the knob to a paneled side door on the left which led him into the inner sanctum of his gearhead garage. For the most part, a Muriel-free zone, if he chose to ignore *her* Lexus IS 350 sedan in the adjacent space. A present he'd gifted himself when he retired from the force became *her* consolation prize after fire destroyed the diner and wiped out her raison d'être for pasting a smile on her face.

To a degree, he's the one who got burned! Muriel could never appreciate a 3.5 liter V6 engine generating 306 horsepower and 277 pound-feet of torque tooling around the

village of Foster Center, or cruising for a parking space at Apple Valley Mall.

Eminent white pearl in color, the Lexus masqueraded as the whale, Moby-Dick. Subsequently, he imagined himself an angry, vengeful Ahab, Herman Melville's maniacal captain of the whaler *Pequod*. In as much as Ahab sought revenge on the mammal who took one leg from the knee down, Obie stopped short of murdering Muriel for emasculating him with her blatant power of disregard.

No harm done from injurious wishes or curses.

Eager to monkey around under the open hood of a vintage Mustang to restore the engine's former glory, he changed into a pair of grubby shorts and shabby tee at the ready on a wall hook. He then inserted an Iron Butterfly CD onto the drive tray of his laptop.

Gawd, if only he could relive the Sixties! He'd restore his former glory days by altering destiny to avoid striking up a conversation with Muriel in biology lab his senior year at Ponaganset High. Chalk it up to Etta who put them on a collision course. His potluck reeked of bad karma!

Opening the door to the right, Muriel entered the kitchen on the first level of their Cape Cod-style home which also accommodated a living room, formal dining area, spare bedroom, and half-bath. Upstairs, unfrequented by guests: another bath, the master bedroom, and their son's former room converted into a home office/crash pad for Obie.

More her comfort zone than his by empirical design, Muriel customized their abode according to her preference for traditional décor. Refined furnishings, symmetrical arrangements, and conservative color palettes embellished with florals, plaids and stripes dominated.

27

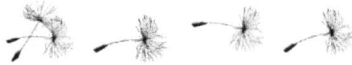

Gawd, he lost count of how many times he told her he felt like a fish out of water in their stiff and stifling surroundings. He defied her to try napping on the antique sofa with thick-rolled arms wrapped in leather upholstery.

Not one to compromise, Obie's complaints fell on deaf ears even though he paid the mortgage and financed their lifestyle. Prim, proper, precise, and predictable. Muriel's unwritten decree for imposing a sense of order through manipulation and machination served to restrain the demon she never formally introduced to her husband.

In spite of ongoing random and sporadic incidents through which Muriel's nemesis reared its ugly head, the specter retreated back to her childhood from whence it sprang after having its fill of intimidating her.

Too late to bridge the distance between them which increased with each passing anniversary, Muriel reckoned Obie wouldn't give a damn if she *had* conceded her innermost guarded secret to him. The state of their union which had disintegrated to dissatisfaction and disappointment, held itself together by a thread of dogged defiance. Both were unwilling to part with a home into which so much joint care had been lavished. He couldn't bear the thought of squandering his pension to support an ex-spouse, whereas a missus under the same roof laundered his clothes and cooked his meals.

She enjoyed the social perks of locking arms in public with a retired officer of the law. Obie never failed to generate appreciative stares from other women who found him attractive, yet beyond their jurisdiction. As far as she knew, although she couldn't be sure.

Downwind of cheesy talk at one of their recent barbecues, she overheard two of her friends giggling and gossiping about her husband and the recently widowed Carolyn Farnum. Apparently, both enjoyed working up a sweat on cycle trainers

in one another's company at Foster Fitness Center, formerly the site of Sal's Italian Deli.

"Those two look like they'd enjoy riding off into the sunset together!"

"For all we know, she rides him at sundown!"

Fine and dandy! An affair would alleviate the stress of faking headaches, pretending to be asleep when his manhood reached out to her, or provoking an argument to douse his ardor.

After freshening up a bit, Muriel reentered the kitchen and opened the fridge. Jostling an assortment of food storage containers on the uppermost shelf made it easier for her to slide out the oblong baking dish which coddled her coveted cheesy sausage-and-croissant casserole, its morning freshness assured by the seal of a red plastic lid. An audibly appreciative *m-m-m, m-m-m* escaped from her lips.

Gruyère cheese browns beautifully and adds a nutty flavor to the dish.

Sliding the chilled bakeware into an insulated carrying case for transport, more than a morsel of smugness overtook Muriel as she derived self-satisfied pleasure from her clever ploy to make an unannounced visit to Etta on a Saturday night. Muriel would not distill that smugness by poking her head into the garage to let Obie know she was leaving. Just as well. Heavy metal blared, and she didn't belong inside the headspace of "In-A-Gadda-Da-Vida".

7:32, as indicated by the digital stove clock.

Chapter 5

Despite her inclination to prepare a bath after the abrupt ending to their crackling phone conversation, Etta had an equally abrupt change of heart. As the Wild One tightened his grip on his fishing rod to initiate a back cast, she clambered barefoot along the timber-frame staircase to her studio in their sizeable rustic cabin. Originally her bedroom when she lived under the same roof with her parents, Rosalia and Sal Rizzio, she adapted it to suit her artist's soul.

That adaptation occurred soon after she fell heir to the family's misfortune during young adulthood, one of the catalysts which transitioned her coming-of-age in a hurry. Suffice it to say, the tongue-and-groove paneled walls added dimension to her workplace in their servile capacity as a gallery for displaying her sketches, each mounted to an art board.

And, what God had joined together in matrimony, let no wife put asunder. One wall exhibited Keith's skin-mounted bass specimens reeled in from the Ponaganset, ranging from 12-14.5 inches long. Keith's trophy wife preserved the legacy of his rod, so to speak.

Long before death and deviant twists of fate shaped Etta's destiny and corralled her spirit within Foster, her mother had advised her how to make the best of circumstances. Truth be known, Rosalia herself readjusted and realigned the dreams of a poetess on her Frost-like stomping ground of woods on a snowy evening.

Hence, Etta's artistic expression drew inspiration from Foster's fertile history and rural charm, emulating the subjects her mother preserved in verse through embedding poetic devices such as imagery, assonance, alliteration, simile and

metaphor. Such were the brushstrokes deftly wielded by a poet. As a result of following in Rosalia's footsteps whether climbing hills, skirting rock outcrops, sauntering along rivers and brooks, or slogging dense woodland, she named her creative enterprise *Etta's Fishing Ground.*

She picked up one of her finished sketches from a workbench and scrutinized it under the benevolence of an overhead skylight which cast waning remnants of the sun's rays over her creation. A perfectionist when it came to replicating timeworn landmarks on her fishing ground, Etta's eyes appraised the effectiveness of varying the pen strokes she used to create a likeness.

She analyzed her depiction of the Mount Vernon Tavern, c. 1760, listed on the National Register of Historic Places in 1974, a year which traversed into her past. *If well-laid plans hadn't gone awry, she'd have escaped the clutches of a rural enclave and made her bed in Greenwich Village, a haven for like-minded artists who embraced a bohemian lifestyle.*

Located on Plainfield Pike, east of its junction with Howard Hill Road, the tavern once served as a stagecoach shop on the primary road between Providence and Connecticut. The main block of the house with a gable roof was demolished in the late 19th century. Whereas, the front entrance portico featured an elaborate Federal styling, unique for its rural location, and most likely added in 1814.

The assimilation of hatching, crosshatching, stippling, cross contouring, and scribbling techniques on smooth paper reproduced the character of the edifice according to Etta's perspective. Interceding to prevent any of her detailed pen-and-ink pieces from becoming static, she used markers for applying different pressures to add dimension which rendered bold, bright colors in the process. This detail-oriented method proved

time-consuming, and in addition, necessitated she use paper thick enough to decrease the occurrence of bleeding.

A self-satisfied smirk intimated the sketch passed her visual inspection to represent January in a calendar collage, grounded with thumbnail descriptions similar in scope to the one previously shared. Toward that end, she aimed to print a prototype before heading back downstairs to take a bath and unwind until bedtime. She planned on selling her reproductions, along with stationery bundles, and one-of-a-kind framed originals—signed and dated—at the upcoming Scituate Art Festival during Columbus Day weekend.

Etta viewed her artwork as a contribution to the world beyond the grave, and on the far side of Foster. Perfectionism set aside, patrons of the art demanded excellence. Therefore, the sketches she scanned had to yield high-resolution photos, and her prints must meet industry standards to insure longevity and caliber true to the original. For posterity's sake, she set her sights on a Giclée print, one of sterling quality produced on a large-format inkjet printer.

The catch-22? Even though Etta was not your stereotypical starving artist, financially solvent due to matrilineal inheritance, it was cost prohibitive for her to use a commercial printing company. That being the case, she invested in a printer which utilized pigment-based inks, and stocked up on rag paper labelled *archival* to amp the ante in artistic impression.

As Keith pondered the straits of his bearings knee-deep in Winsor Brook, Etta fired up her Epson Sure Color P400 printer to conduct a tavern test run. She selected the desired color management option as the mode setting. Prone to bouts of eccentricity when under the spell of artistry, she engaged in her initiation ritual prior to procuring the first printout.

She patted the machine while reciting an incantation, conjuring her mother's lyricism with a smidgen of lunacy.

"Colors be true and rich in hue. No streaking, spotting, smearing, or jamming through and through. So mote it be."

Gazing at Keith's wall of trophies while the printer performed according to specifications, her eyes sparkled with love and admiration for the only man she'd ever given a piece of her heart. She envisioned him swamped by weeds while biding his time for a tug on the reel. A smile spread from ear to ear in anticipation of greeting him in the morning.

Chapter 6

While Keith postulated and Etta propagated, Muriel inched the Escape out of her driveway to make a gossip getaway with an encased casserole in tow on the passenger seat. On a mission to forewarn her best friend, a logical explanation for Keith's whereabouts never entered her mind. Nor the repercussions or retributions for dropping a bombshell based on pure speculation, however damning the spectacle before her very eyes at a fleeting glimpse.

Erring on the side of caution, she turned her head to the left and to the right in checking for oncoming vehicles on Balcom Road. An oxymoron in itself for Foster, but a necessary precaution in view of overhanging, leaf-laden branches obstructing one's field of vision. The coast clear, she turned right onto North Road the way she had an indeterminate number of times throughout the decades of their friendship. The .9-mile stretch undertaken in three minutes constituted an autopilot trek.

This one, navigated not by Muriel. Driven, instead, by her self-appointed demon who took over so his parasitic host could venture into her subconscious darkness, alone and afraid.

A spontaneous chap who appeared out of nowhere, he materialized from the slightest provocation at the behest of Muriel's cognitive reflexes to stimuli erotic in nature. Having banished his haunting apparition to a padlocked chamber in her mind again and again, he picked the lock at will and turned up unannounced to taunt her, the way he did on one of her dates with Obie. Stuck in a time warp, courtesy of Muriel, he hadn't aged a bit since she last saw him in the flesh!

Circa 1956, this clean-cut, conservative, all-American jock still styled his wavy brown hair in a side-part with tapered back

and sides smoothed in place with Vitalis hair tonic. Muriel got a whiff of its antiseptic scent, an olfactory déjà vu, exactly as she remembered from the long-distance view of a five-year-old kindergartner who once loved to read. Nor had he updated his wardrobe. Pairing the Ivy League threads of a cotton, button-down collar shirt with a raglan-sleeve, crew-neck, varsity sweater, he mimicked an acapella version of the Lettermen. *Boola Boola!*

If Muriel hadn't forbidden her mind's eye from wandering to the fly zone, she would have come across his loose-fitting, brushed cotton trousers with a sharp center crease along the pant legs. And, penny loafers, harmless enough.

And, so, he floated in Muriel's field of vision, presiding over the anointing of Obie's phallus. Her mentor nodded his approval as his 17-year-old niece gripped the base of her boyfriend's manhood with her hand. She wrapped her mouth around the engorged shaft, using an up and down motion with her lips. In due time, friction prompted her to re-lubricate by expelling a wad of saliva on its head, then resuming the locomotion to build up momentum for the outburst.

"Ahhhhhhh! Oooyeaaaah! Gawd! I'm gonna cum on your face!"

Like riding a tricycle, it all came back to her right before the gush from Obie's Fountain of Youth. Avoiding a facial, Muriel deep-throated his throbbing tumescence, and when it erupted, she swallowed squirts of semen.

Opening his eyes after spilling his seed, Obie snapped his head back, recoiling in shock at detecting Muriel's makeup smeared to kingdom cum from pleasuring him.

Given her skittishness during their necking and petting sessions in his car, or on the living room sofa at her house, he

wondered how in the world she learned to perfect the art of giving head. He didn't dare ask.

The spectral voyeur vanished as soon as Muriel paid lip-service in full. But, he'd be back, guaranteed. There he was alongside Muriel in the passenger seat, along for the ride to Etta's.

Chapter 7

"What, Honey?"

Harried trying to cram housework and dinner preparations within the meagre time frame allotted a rural, stay-at-home, busy-beaver June Cleaver. Her daughter's meek squeak frittered in the fray, dismissed and ignored. Hair, coiffed in a brushed-under bob, and a light application of loose powder compressed into her foundation, Lois Doyle deemed herself a simulated suburban sophisticate. Backwoods, but not backwards, she could blend in with the chicest of city slickers who attended PTA meetings at her son's college-preparatory high school in Providence.

Road-ready, she'd go the distance above and beyond the jurisdiction of Cucumber Hill Road once she turned the ignition key on their 1955 Chevrolet Bel Air station wagon with Powerglide automatic transmission. It was her week to carpool Muriel and a few of her classmates to the afternoon kindergarten session at Captain Isaac Paine Elementary on Foster Center Road, the only primary school in town. Following a brief rebound at home, she'd make the 45-minute drive to LaSalle Academy and bring Muriel's brother to hockey practice, a race against tardiness so Gavin could avoid his coach's verbal lashing and push-up penalty punishment.

After dropping him off, she'd pay her mother a visit at the nursing home. The last stop on the train for a widowed septuagenarian who incurred a debilitating fall when she tumbled from a stepladder five months ago during an attempt to place a star on her Christmas tree. Henceforth, Grandma Violet became an unwitting pawn in victimizing her beloved granddaughter. Dreadful, how an elderly woman's plunge precipitated a young lady's downfall.

Lois thanked her lucky stars when her younger brother offered to take care of Muriel as soon as school resumed in the New Year. The arrangement entailed meeting his niece when the bus rolled to a stop at the end of their serpentine driveway, and minding Muriel until either her mommy returned, or her daddy arrived home from work.

At first, Muriel regaled her family nonstop during the evening meal, with how much she enjoyed riding in Uncle Reggie's T-Bird up to their garage door. Or, expressed her adulation in listening to him read aloud from her favorite storybooks. By and by, when Fist began mowing the lawn in early May, she had nothing to contribute in the way of discourse. She picked at her food. Due to anxiety, Muriel skated peas back and forth on her plate, neurotic behavior generated by psychosexual association with one of her female ramparts.

Gavin seized the opportunity by monopolizing the conversation to grandstand his acceptance at Providence College, proud to follow in the footsteps of Uncle Reggie, a high-ranking senior with a promising future in the business sector. Insensitive to her daughter's withdrawal, nothing got by her daddy.

"Why so quiet, Princess? If someone's giving you a hard time at school, you let me know."

Muriel's stalwart avenger, Fist Doyle—no one called him Gordon—doted on his daughter. Founder and president of Doyle Savings & Loan, LLC, located at the intersection of Central Pike and Foster Center Road, he wielded an iron fist when lending money to folks who wanted to buy a house, make home improvements, or build on their land. An ironclad authority figure on the home front, he'd pound his fist on a hard surface for emphasis when disciplining his son, never so much as drumming a finger at Muriel, the apple of his eye.

During his adolescence, Gordon's cousin Keen from the Deep South—no one called him Dean—seized an opportunity when one presented itself. Two inseparables teetering on their teens, they wolfed down fried bologna sandwiches, standing behind the counter in the kitchen. Eager to run outdoors, Keen's mom couldn't tempt them with chocolate cake.

In a fit of rage over wrecking the tire rim on his bicycle later that afternoon, Gordon rammed his fist into the window of a barber shop and shattered the glass. Eureka! Keen, ever worried his scrawny cuz, much too quiet and reserved for his own good, would become a target for bullies, exploited and embellished the incident in front of their peers. Selling them a bill of goods named Fist, Keen got a taste of his own deceptiveness, and liked it.

Fidgeting under her daddy's expectant gaze, Muriel demurred in a noncommittal tone, her poker face giving nothing away.

Chapter 8

Preoccupied with peeling potatoes at the counter by the sink, her mother wouldn't have given a second thought if she turned tail and retreated to her room until summoned to fetch her lightweight cardigan for the ride to school on the brink of summer vacation. Instead, Muriel stood rooted in the entryway to the kitchen, trembling in fright at the knees as she raised the ante from squeak to squawk. "Mommy, I don't want Uncle Reggie to stay with me anymore."

Lois's spine stiffened before facing her daughter to acknowledge what she'd heard the first time. Squatting on ceramic tile flooring, her face at eye level with Muriel's, she clutched her daughter by the shoulders and shook her quivering body. "For heaven's sake, why not? This had better be good!"

Undermined, yet undeterred by her mother's austerity, Muriel averted her eyes away from Lois's fixed stare. Breaking free from her mother's claw-like grip, revulsion triumphed over fear. Muriel blurted the reason. "Cuz he makes me suck on his lollipop."

Stricken by her concession, Lois's facial features contracted like pleats in a deflated accordion. The blow knocked her off of her high haunches. Her bottom hit the unforgiving surface and her legs splayed out in front of her. Wallowing in a moment of truth in an undignified manner, she rallied to upright herself and rectify the situation at once, despite the wrenching pain in her lower back. Glowering and towering over Muriel from a loftier position, she grilled her hapless child. "Before we get ready for school, is there anything else you want to tell me?"

N-o-o-o!

With nary an empathetic embrace proffered by her mother, Muriel wrapped herself inside a hug. Her head lowered in shame, she studied the glazed tiles in their black-and-white checkerboard configuration, well-groomed into blaming herself for what had transpired in the living room. And, now, giving up a pinky-swear secret. After Uncle Reggie had been so nice to her right from the start when he surprised her with Zippy the Monkey, the stuffed rubber-faced chimpanzee doll she'd fallen in love with watching *Howdy Doody*.

***

Clear as a bell, then as evermore, the reverberations jangled her nerves.

As they had on numerous occasions when snuggled together, he'd read aloud to her. That day, she'd chosen her favorite Golden Book, *Cinderella*. "The mice lived in the attic with Cinderella. She made little clothes for them and gave them all names. And they thought Cinderella was the sweetest girl in the world."

Then, Uncle Reggie spread-eagled the book on the coffee table in front of the sofa, safeguarding their place. Patting her knee, he told his niece *she* was, by far, the sweetest girl in the world. That he'd grown so fond of her over their long period of time spent together. And, sometimes family members show their love in special ways.

Confused by what he meant, and about to ask, Uncle Reggie itsy bitsy spidered his index and middle fingers all the way from Muriel's lace-ruffled ankle sock to her inner thigh underneath her poodle skirt. He trespassed beyond the boundary of her panties to her lady parts. That's how her mommy referred to her genitalia each time she reminded her about proper etiquette when wearing a skirt or dress.

41

A 5-year-old during the post-war era of the hush-hush '50s, Muriel's mother kept her in the dark about her vagina's potential for conceiving and pushing babies into the world. Nor had she the vaguest idea that her lady parts had special names with their own capabilities for sexual arousal when tinkered with under the hood by fingers—and before long—a tongue.

Beyond the pale of propriety, Muriel squirmed in the discomfort of indecent behavior and gasped in horror as Uncle Reggie parted the lips of her vulva and infiltrated her dampness. His forehead pressing against hers, he peered into Muriel's eyes, wide-open with fright. The scent of his hair tonic and minty breath intermingled with the guilt trip he laid on her.

"Muriel, you're hurting my feelings by pulling away."

Muriel willed herself into a state of physiological suspension by playing possum as her predator used the tips of his middle and index fingers to stimulate her clitoris. In the twinkle of an eye, a sensation of hurtling in midair displaced uneasiness, catapulting her to Rocky Point Park. Her legs felt wobbly and her heart raced the way it had riding the Ferris wheel during its slow ascent to the top. Similarly, tipping her head back and closing her eyes, her stomach dropped during the rapid, rapturous release of tension in her nether region.

Vulnerable in the aftermath of orgasmic pleasure, she sucked her thumb while Uncle Reggie extorted a promise of secrecy. "Muriel, you can't tell anyone. Especially not Mommy, Daddy, or Gavin. Your parents would be angry at both of us if they found out what we did. And, they'd blame you!"

Bibbidi-bobbidi-boo! Forsaken by her mother, the world as she knew it turned into a rotten pumpkin.

***

Willing and compliant, she'd become addicted to the sensation of an explosion occurring deep inside her which

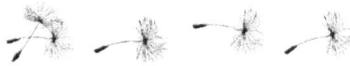

radiated from her belly button down to her pea. Having earned Muriel's confidence and broken down her inhibitions, Uncle Reggie began preying upon her by inserting his tongue inside her vaginal opening and approaching the clitoris with a lick and a promise. All told, Muriel might have become a nymphomaniac were it not for his raising the stakes by eventually cajoling her into reciprocating a tit-for-tat slip of the tongue on a serpent protruding from the unzipped gates of hell.

"Muriel, now it's your turn to do something nice for me."

A quick study, she eventually mastered the art of fellatio through administering lollipop slurps and over-the-top sucking. By letting his member hit the underside of her tongue, she quelled the gagging reflex as she aimed to please a predator who continued to push boundaries and neutralize distress. Still, her revulsion over his man scent and swallowing his seed forced her to put a stop to the dirty deed the only way she knew how.

I'll tell Mommy.

Chapter 9

On North Road, while deep in reverie, Muriel or Uncle Reggie jerked the steering wheel away from an oncoming oak whose thickset trunk surely would have gouged the lights out of her vehicle and thrown its nose out of joint. Scared straight onto the bottom of Etta's winding driveway, Muriel cut the engine. She needed a cotton-pickin' minute to piece together fragmented thoughts and perfect her post-apocalypse demeanor. After all, connivance had served her purpose well, whether moving forward along the catwalks of beauty pageants from yesteryear, or navigating the rutted roadways of life.

Certain she was out of Etta's view lest she be on her front porch, Muriel rested her head on the steering wheel still in her grip. She peeled away more layers of an onion, inciting fresh tears to brew.

***

Her mommy breathed an audible sigh of relief when she denied Uncle Reggie had done anything more. Wincing in pain whenever she twisted her torso, Lois spoke to her daughter through clenched teeth, mitigating adult depravity. "What matters is you're still a virgin, so no harm done. If anything, you've learned what a wife must do in the bedroom to please her husband. Nasty business, for sure!"

What's a virgin? And, ewwww!

Not the opportune moment to ask for a definition of the former or clarification of the latter while Lois paced back and forth, deep in puckered-brow thought. Discomfited and disappointed she'd gotten the shaft from her mother by disclosing Uncle Reggie spouted off in her mouth, she could always count on her hero.

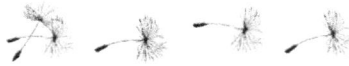

She'd leave her worry on the doorstep as soon as Daddy crossed the threshold, positive he'd do anything in order to make her troubles disappear.

Trouble is, Lois knew it too. Although she believed Fist had the comportment to kill her brother with his bare hands, he'd more than likely recruit his cousin, Keen, to make Reggie disappear. Keen, she cottoned, had strong ties with the Dixie Mafia based in Biloxi. This, she deduced from putting two and two together over the years.

As a matter of fact, Keen Doyle had no compunctions moving stolen merchandise, arms trafficking, arson, extortion, money laundering, or carrying out a contract killing for a feasible fee. In spring of 1956 he kept a low profile by heading north to Foster and freeloading off of Fist who legitimized a large sum of illegally obtained money through lucrative investments in mainstream economy. A shrewd financier, he deducted a small amount for himself in the semblance of a handling charge.

A burly, churly fella accustomed to living high on the hog in a ramshackle sty, Keen took perverse pleasure overseeing his cuz's uppity wife as she picked up after him and waited on her unwelcome houseguest hand and foot. Unbeknownst to Lois, this slacker possessed keen powers of observation worthy of his sobriquet. Too bad she hadn't eavesdropped on a certain conversation which might have tipped her off about her brother's sexual peccadilloes.

***

On Memorial Day, the smokescreen created by grilling steaks over flaming charcoal briquettes shielded two apron-tied chefs from most of the rabble-rousers engaged in merrymaking on the patio or in the backyard at Fist's expense. *What the hell! A fraction of that bogus bonus covered the cost.* Before those who wanted theirs rare enough to moo grabbed a disposable

45

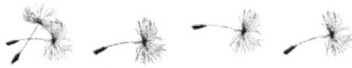

plastic plate from the wooden picnic table and moseyed on over, Keen bent his country cousin's ear.

Tugging on his shaggy beard every now and then, the born-and-bred Mississippi thespian emoted in a southern drawl, staking an unsubstantiated claim—as of yet. "Now, before you up and tell me to quit bein' ugly, I'm fixin' to give y'all a piece of my mind awwn the subject of that creased and greased brother-in-law of yawws."

Fist, who'd timed and tong-turned the first batch of steaks, produced a sizzle. He cocked an eyebrow at Keen, about to raise an argument.

"Hold your tongue, Cuz. Hear me out. Somethin' ain't right about a red-blooded American with his good looks payin' no mind to the semicircle of babes on lawwn chairs vyin' for his attention. Hopin' to get laid'd be my first guess. Instead, what's he doin'? He's on hands and knees, makin' an ass of himself horsin' around with a tyke."

"A-w-w, quit it will ya! Reggie's always had a soft spot for Muriel."

Processing the innuendo, thin-skinned Fist, distinguished by his pencil-thin mustache, narrowed his eyes into slits and laid it on the line. "If I thought for one of your cotton-pickin' minutes he was fiddling with my daughter . . ."

Keen imposed a stay of elocution, miming the action of closing a mouth by holding his fingers straight out and clamping them down on his extended thumb as though grabbing something. Sporting a wry grin, he established Fist's criminal intent. "You'd recruit me to inflict pain and make him disappear."

Fist hollered for those who wanted theirs rare to come and get 'em. Raring to go, Keen made way for the stairs to exit the

stage of the patio. "Well, I swanny! I'm gonna chat up a redhead over yonder and get me some tail. Cain't never could!"

Chapter 10

Speculation granted Lois the foresight to forewarn her brother lickety-split! So, within the meagre timespan allotted a stay-at-home mom on the go in between jaunts, she spared Reggie's life by dialing a rotary phone. Never mind that she carpooled the kids to school in a hurry and dropped Muriel off like a hot potato to do so, sparing a victim no mercy. Lois neither sought retribution on her daughter's behalf, nor demanded an apology.

He picked up on the second ring.

***

That evening, Lois minded her manners during their wholesome dinner of roast chicken, mashed potatoes, and peas. A woman who knew her rightful place at the round table among men engaged in conversation, however trivial, she waited until Gavin and Fist finished talking sports. *Boxing superstars of the '50s, Rocky Marciano and Floyd Patterson.* During the exchange with his son, Daddy Doyle duly noted from the corner of his eye, his daughter's woebegone expression.

When the opportunity presented itself for Lois to spin her rehearsed verse as previously recited to Muriel, she cleared her throat. She tipped off her accomplice by kicking her in the ankle. Numb with pain, Muriel didn't feel a thing. Her mommy's lies drifted in one ear and out the other. Gavin, gullible by hero worship, was all ears. Given that advertising boomed in the 1950s because of America's vulture culture, television's massive reach, and demand-driven consumer consumption, Fist believed his ears.

"I can hardly contain my excitement for sharing Reggie's bright prospects. One of the executives at an ad agency in San

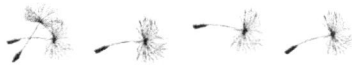

Francisco arranged an all-expense-paid trip to interview him next week. Talk about a rolling stone gathering no moss after graduation!" Her cheeks flushed crimson.

Lois paused for her fake news to take effect. She drank what was left in her water glass at one gulp in order to avoid choking on her own words. Sure enough, Gavin dropped his jaw in awe. Fist's nod of approval encouraged her to keep talking.

"Through the Cornerstone Media grapevine, Reggie heard he's their top applicant. Can't you just picture him as part of a team creating animated television ads for Speedy Alka-Seltzer, Ajax, and Frosted Flakes?" She emitted a nervous titter.

Ironically, Lois placed the fictitious ad man 1.25 miles from Alcatraz, the infamous federal penitentiary which incarcerated the most violent and dangerous offenders.

About to cross the finish line of fiction, she needn't have kicked Muriel again. "With having to make future plans on such short notice, Reggie won't be able to take care of Muriel anymore."

Lois exhaled a pseudo sigh and rubbed her daughter's back. Despite living up to her end of the bargain, Muriel's spine stiffened from the added affront of posturing for her mother.

"Hey, now! Is that why my Princess looks so sad?"

"Yes, Daddy," she mumbled, averting her eyes from his scrutiny by skating peas back and forth on her plate.

***

The Doyles moved forward without Reggie, making the necessary adjustments to accommodate Muriel during her last two weeks before school let out for the season. The bus driver dropped her off at Fist's business establishment where she stayed out of his hair until closing. Oh, how she longed to confide in her daddy to rid herself of a burden!

Once, she almost let it slip along their drive home. "Daddy?"

"Yes, Princess?"

But, she feared upsetting him beyond reason, and losing favor by disclosing her disgusting behavior. Worst of all, she worried about making him so sad for what had happened that he'd cry and never be the same. Instead, Muriel settled for telling him a simple truth. "I love you!"

Fist's eyes glistened. Without diverting them away from the road, he took his right hand off the steering wheel and reached across the front seat to pinch the apple of Muriel's cheek. "Love you more and more each day, Princess!"

Fist Doyle died peacefully in his sleep as he neared the end of his seventh decade of life, none the wiser to the criminal exploitation which took place on his living room sofa.

Oh, how she longed to tell her mommy she hated her guts!

She came so close on numerous occasions, but held her tongue. Instead, Muriel swallowed their secret which gnawed at her insides, retaliating against her betrayers by doling out the silent treatment. No one heard Muriel berate Zippy the Monkey a bad boy as she inflicted puncture wounds from head to toe with a pair of blunt-edge scissors reserved for cutting out paper dolls. No one heard Muriel rip her *Cinderella* Golden Book to shreds page by page with her bare hands.

In the privacy of her bedroom, Muriel killed—no, overkilled Uncle Reggie through the release of pent-up rage and frustration. By banishing his lingering aftereffects, she made him disappear forever. *Sort of.* Every now and then he made his presence known and gloated. Under her skin, he showed up unannounced and uninvited whenever he felt like it.

Like the first time she sucked on Obie's lollipop in the back seat of Etta's Citroen.

50

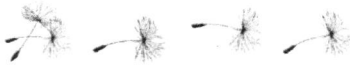

No one ever heard Muriel sass back to her mother, or badmouth her behind her back either. Come to think of it, no one ever overheard a conversation between those two, given they rarely spoke to each other. Lois never said a word to Muriel about her poor academic performance from first through eleventh grade. Barely meeting requirements to graduate from high school, she dropped out after completing her junior year. Seems Muriel's low achievement was impacted by difficulties with reading comprehension and retention, given her undiagnosed attentional deficit disorder.

Muriel never opened her mouth to protest when her mother began entering her in beauty pageants, determined for her daughter to find success unrequited by waitressing. An antidote for shoestring intelligence and lack of options, Lois saw pageants as a means for her daughter to fill in the gap prior to entering the self-fulfilling career of marriage. At best, runner-up in a few competitions, Muriel fell short in her ability to articulate ideas when answering the judges' questions pertaining to world events.

Lois Doyle died in a delirious state of dementia during her eighth decade of life, none the wiser to Muriel's deep hatred toward her.

***

Westward ho or hoax, Reginald Healy disappeared from their lives without a trace, providing no forwarding address when he sped away from Rhode Island in his Thunderbird for parts unknown. Inside the trunk, a suitcase whose contents included his college diploma. What he did with it, is anyone's guess.

If the truth ever leaked out, Keen would have left no stone unturned to find a lamb on the lam and make him disappear for real. He'd torture the bastard first, then weigh down his corpse

with concrete blocks and toss it to the fishes up a lazy river in the noonday sun.

Practice had made Keen perfect at committing unsolved murders.

Chapter 11

Either the discordant symphony of katydids and crickets, or the aroma wafting from the cheesy sausage-and-croissant casserole under wraps on the passenger seat, broke Muriel's hypnotic trance.

She wondered how long she'd zoned out after turning off the ignition and parked. Ten minutes? Fifteen? Her wristwatch indicated 7:55. Nearly 20! More than enough time to till her soiled childhood.

Discarded by Uncle Reggie, Muriel picked up the pieces of a shattered psyche by focusing on grooming herself in advance of going the distance along the steep, winding incline of Etta's driveway. Flipping on switches to the overhead interior lights, she angled the rearview mirror to better assess collateral damage. She bit into her bottom lip. *Damn!* No cotton swab at hand when you needed one! Not that her handbag left at home stowed any.

Scavenging a folded tissue from a pocket in her capris, she unfurled it and twisted a corner to ply her ingenuity. She dabbed at the inner corners of her eyes to stem the flow of oncoming teardrops. *Oh, dear!* A lethal combo of oil, sweat, and tears had caused her eyeliner and mascara to migrate south, forming dark smudges resembling raccoon eyes. She made amends the best she could with a primitive thingamajig, but failed to mete out justice. Thenceforth, a few rapid eye blinks would have to do for settling the score.

In a rush to judgment, she turned the ignition key, about to set four wheels in motion toward that point of no return Obie had alluded to earlier. As much as she abhorred her mother, Muriel parodied Lois's closed-mindedness and closed legs on

matters related to coupling and copulating. Unable to think outside the box, prudery overrode prudence as she placed the gearshift in drive. A pity it hadn't crossed her mind to tread time by extending Keith the benefit of a doubt.

In retrospect, Muriel should have followed through on her white lie to drop off the casserole at her son's place before Keith's exit wound got the best of her. Or, called it a night by slipping under the covers after removing her dentures and depositing them in a glass on the nightstand. Either decision might have made a world of difference to Etta.

Just as she never stopped to consider the catastrophic consequences of her actions all those years ago, she threw caution to the sultry breezes on a July evening. Muriel inched forward to forewarn, spraying gravel along the ascent to the crest, blind in her devotion to a best friend, and forever indebted to her.

After all, Etta had given her unconditional love and safeguarded the sordid details of her botched childhood, leaked during one of their sleepovers on a Saturday night at the semisweet age of seventeen.

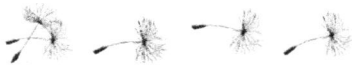

Chapter 12

1968

Both, on a high from rounds of girlish giggling. Both developed a case of the heebie-jeebies induced during Hitchcock's *The Birds*. Both, plagued by insomnia caused by binge munching on popcorn and guzzling soda.

When Sal arrived home after closing the deli, they allowed the man his due of peace and quiet by relinquishing the great room and retreating to Etta's spacious upstairs bedroom. Accompanying their trudge, more soda and fresh meatball grinders snug in their paper sleeves, warm to the touch.

In the event of errant crumbs, drips of tomato sauce, and soft drink spills, Etta pulled two pillowcases out of a bureau drawer for them to spread across their laps. Clad in their pajamas, but by no means ready to sleep, they resumed their libertine debauchery. Sitting cross-legged on top of a double bed, their incisors tore into crusty, Italian torpedo rolls to infiltrate the spicy haven of meatballs.

Speaking with their mouths full, they tore apart classmate, Carolyn Bettencourt—not yet Farnum. She had the colossal nerve in asking upperclassman, Obie Smith, to escort her to their junior prom. He said yes. She didn't have to twist his arm.

"All because you never have the nerve to go after what you want. And, *she* does!" Etta chastised, nonplussed by her best friend's lack of self-confidence despite her pageant-perfected poise on and off the runway.

Taken aback how Etta was fully aware she had a long-suffering crush on her heartthrob, yet exercised restraint in summoning her charm to wrap him around her little finger,

Muriel confessed the reason. "Why bother! Obie's lovesick for *you*! The way he stares at you in the halls and from across our table in biology lab!"

"Yeah, he does! But, he wouldn't know how to handle me, and that scares the pants off of him."

A hasty swallow of mishmash, and Muriel's jaw dropped in amazement. Taking advantage of a friend's bewilderment, Etta spoke her mind. "Well, look at me! No offense, Muriel. But, I don't fit the mold of Ponaganset High's fold. Mile-high beehives and bouffants. Or, long straightened hair. And, bobs with teased crowns!"

In reaction to Etta's accusation, Muriel skimmed the top of her beehive bob, flipped out at the ends. Sitting in close proximity, yet miles apart from each other in demeanor and deportment, a hedonistic hippie and a preened prude would bare their souls before dawn's early glow infiltrated the skylight above them.

"So, no more excuses. Go after Obie! Biology lab's your best chance to chat him up since he's always late. Plus, I intend to make that happen for you."

Logistics aside, Etta's onrush of advice brought on a wave of nausea in the pit of Muriel's stomach. "I hear Carolyn puts out. So, if you plan on sinking your claws into Obie, you'll need to do more than bat your eyelashes and wiggle your fanny. You'd better give head. It's the least you can do, while preserving your virginity."

All of a sudden, Muriel's mouth started releasing excess saliva. She felt her diaphragm contract with pulsating intensity, building pressure in her belly. Without further ado, she plucked the pillow case from her lap to serve as a provisional safety net for her sprint to the bathroom in the hall. In the nick of time, she lifted the lid to the toilet and knelt over the bowl to cast out the

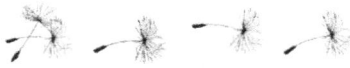

queasiness raging in her abdominal abyss, compliments of Uncle Reggie.

Her muscles went through several more rounds of contractions during the purge, necessitating she flush twice. When Muriel concluded she couldn't possibly puke another fleck of vomitus, she flushed the last few floating rejects identified as parsley flakes. Sweat seeped through every pore of her skin, though she shivered to the quick. Weakened, she crab-walked sideways along the tile floor from the bowl to the adjacent wall. Leaning her crumpled body against it, she squeezed her eyes shut in a futile attempt to vanquish a molester from view.

A timid knock on the open door forced Muriel to pry her eyes open. Etta's welcome presence striding toward her caught Uncle Reggie off guard and he fled the scene. Etta tugged a paper cup from the wall dispenser in front of the sink and filled it with cold tap water. Crouching alongside Muriel, she encouraged her to take a few slow sips. Mission accomplished, Etta placed the cup on the floor and cradled a disheveled ragdoll, rocking Muriel back and forth in her arms on the hard surface of pink and black ceramic tile, murmuring soothing terms of endearment.

Similar in pattern to the kitchen flooring Muriel studied during her mother's interrogation, all the while, wishing Lois had hugged instead of berated her, the association triggered hysterical sobbing and sniveling. Tear-streaked, she disengaged from their heart-to-heart embrace.

Making eye contact with Etta, she blubbered a woeful admission through clouded vision. "I-I know I'll have to do more than b-bat my eyelashes and walk with a wiggle, so guys won't call me a tease behind my back. B-but, the mere thought of sucking d-dick . . ."

"Nauseates you?"

Mortified her life appeared to be an open book for a self-professed bookworm who read between the lines, Muriel decided a true confession on the origin of her frigidness should take precedence above all else. Defining self-fulfillment in terms of marriage, and deeply disturbed by her sexual unresponsiveness, she feared a fate worse than death—becoming an old maid!

Somewhat composed after Etta handed her a wad of tissues to mop her tears and blow her nose, Muriel introduced her best friend to Uncle Reggie. While she plundered through every detail of his dirty deeds, Etta listened, squelching the urge to vent her outrage while Muriel exorcised a malevolent ghoul from her soul.

"He lurks over my shoulder whenever anything sexual crosses my mind. Thought I'd gotten rid of him for good after I slashed the stuffing out of a stuffed chimp and tore my storybook to shreds."

"Muriel, didn't anyone ever mention that you can't commit murder by death wish alone?"

Etta's vigorous head shake emphasized her untamed locks. Wild, voluminous, trippy tresses she often adorned with headbands of flowers or beads. "As much as I want to wring the neck of a monkey's uncle, I hate your mother even more!"

"So do I!" stated Muriel, as an undisputed matter of fact.

The abomination, aberration, and absurdity embedded in the surface tension, dispelled by Etta's gallows humor, instigated a bout of uproarious laughter causing both to double over from stomach cramping. The exertion, having taken its toll, the boho chick took Muriel by the hand and led her back to the bedroom where they climbed onto the bed and scooched under the covers.

Lying on their backs, gazing at the stars refracted from the skylight on the ceiling above them, Etta forswore one of her innermost thoughts. "I'm not interested in marriage, whatsoever. Free spirit that I am, I welcome the idea of having many lovers in my lifetime until the right guy crosses my path."

Muriel listened with astonishment, knocked for a loop by one who so readily embraced the sexual revolution which challenged the strict code of behavior her mother had ingrained in her to uphold tenets of propriety.

Respectable girls save themselves for marriage!

At long last, Muriel drifted off to sleep. But, not for long. Quite perturbed, Etta shook her with vim and vigor until she awakened in a dim-witted stupor. Granting Muriel a marginal moment to gather her wits, Etta cut to the chase without the lubrication of foreplay. "The only way you're going to learn how to loosen up and enjoy sex is by pleasuring yourself. Daily! If Uncle Reggie shows, ignore him."

A means to an end—orgasm. The following afternoon, Etta sent Muriel home with one of her own prized possessions, a tattered, paperback copy of *Candy*, an under-the-counter novel she herself read under the covers.

While Muriel had kept her up from frequent tossing and turning, perhaps coddling hellish visions of genital sugarplums, Etta took it upon herself to highlight every explicit passage in the book, piloting by lamplight. By sparing a reluctant reader the drudgery of dirty work, Muriel could literally take matters into her own hands a lot faster to get those juices flowing.

***

The remainder of their junior year coasted on dreams germinated from longing, and nurtured by wishful thinking.

Much to Muriel's relief, Tom Holden, an easy-on-the-eyes jock, asked her to the prom at the last possible opportunity to do

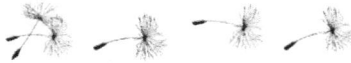

so. An accomplished belle of the ball, she worked the room which the social committee had reserved at Foster Country Club for their gala occasion. Promenading alongside her date, Muriel flaunted an ankle-length, one-shoulder, pink chiffon gown. The coveted title of prom queen eluded a junior missy who envisioned the crowning glory of a tiara perched on the laurels of her beehive. In consolation, the honor of inclusion in prom court smoothed her ruffled feathers.

Dreamy-eyed, she tried bedazzling the object of her affection when she and her partner brushed against Carolyn and Obie on the crowded dance floor during the slow number, "Cherish". Preoccupied otherwise. Muriel caught a glimpse of his hand rummaging inside the crawl space of Carolyn's black, backless gown. A sure indication she'd better limber things up to gain more flexibility in her rigid body.

The difficulty lay in following through during Etta's mandated autoerotic sessions. Besides Uncle Reggie's intrusions, she relived her childhood trauma and experienced guilt over the pleasurable tingling sensations she felt on the brink of each Ferris-wheel freefall.

Like her loathsome mother, Muriel would learn how to grimace and bear such nasty business. *'Tis better to give than to receive.*

***

For the record, Etta wanted nothing to do with attending her prom. She turned down Tom Holden's invitation each time he cornered her to ask, thereby limiting his options with slim pickings to choose from at such short notice. Comfortable in her own skin, Etta preferred the indulgence of her own company, given the alternative of jostling amongst penguins and peacocks bumper-to-bumper on the dance floor.

In accordance, she placed "Piece of My Heart" on the turntable. Pinching a speck of dust off the stylus on the tone arm, she aligned it with the outer rim of vinyl. Etta goosed up the volume to channel "Pearl"—Janis Joplin. She idolized the soul and blues singer for her rebelliousness, her thrift store ensembles, and her coarse abandon in singing about the rawness of sex, love, and life.

Shedding her apparel, Etta left a trail of undergarments, white peasant blouse, and flowing, floral skirt along the beeline to her bed, onto which she bounced in the buff. Dreamy-eyed, she began pleasuring herself to the image of her archetype flame, the one and only she'd ever give a piece of her heart to, personified by the brashness of Brando in *The Wild One*. Just before Joplin screamed her pain out of existence in the last verse, Etta transcended.

Come on, come on, come on, come on!

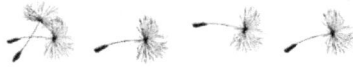

Chapter 13

Crunching gravel in agonizing slowness not to cause a ruckus, and perchance startle Etta beforehand, Muriel reached her destination in due course. At the crest, she put the gear selector in park and turned off the ignition. Weary and foggy of mind from having engaged in steep contemplation before arriving at this stopping point along a journey of deliberation, she sighed in resignation and resolution.

To her left, where the driveway curved, crouched an endangered species in the guise of a Citroen with a black roof and silver-gray metallic body. The front-wheel drive, manual 4-speed, low-rider grazed ground at 3380 lbs. In mint condition, the DS 21, four-door sedan thrived under the auspices of Etta's maternal protection ever since she adopted the vehicle, brand new during the Cold War's yesteryear of 1969. Etta joked that it bore a strong resemblance to British actor, Sydney Greenstreet, who made his film debut at the age of 62, portraying the unscrupulous Fat Man in *The Maltese Falcon*.

Muriel thought so too back then:

With all due respect and affection, Etta patted the Citroen's hood and sprinkled water from the garden hose over it. Just as Muriel surmised, eccentricity overruled, whereby Etta initiated a baptismal ceremony. "One, two three—by the power vested in me—I hereby christen thee, Sydney. So mote it be."

Based on observation, Muriel channeled the cosmic energy around them to conclude her dearest friend met the highest standards of motherhood, whatever those mote be. Damned if she knew!

A high school graduation present, paid in full from skinny dipping into the savings account set up for her by her mother,

the Citroen symbolized a means to an end. Escaping Foster. Accepted at Rhode Island School of Design, Etta tailored a 4-year undergrad program for earning a Bachelor of Fine Arts in Illustration. Thereupon, uprooting and planting herself in Greenwich Village to sprout wings and rock the cradle of an avant-garde and alternative culture.

Dreams empowered by determination and within her grasp. Until she kept company with the likes of Birch Hansford. Giving off the wrong impression to Wyatt Cole and setting off a tragedy. Falling hard for Keith Lawrence who had his own axe to grind with Birch. Before these eventualities occurred in close succession, the kismet of doom slumbered inside a faraway galaxy of Etta's mind previous to her rude awakening.

Etta's plans entailed privileged information she fed piecemeal to Muriel in the days leading up to hosting a graduation party at her home for a cross section of Ponaganset High's alumni. A latecomer who enrolled during her junior year, she could have had a rough time worming her way into established cliques. As such, Etta had no desire to fit in, preferring to orbit the fringes of society in the full regalia of a hippie attuned to ideals of peace and humanitarian reform. By and large, her classmates respected a free spirit for her genuineness and individuality. Given a laundry list of yearbook superlatives, an overwhelming consensus voted her Most Artistic.

***

Partygoers shuffled along a buffet table set up in the great room, abuzz in conversation while loading their plates with a variety of food prepared at Sal's deli. Obie caught Muriel's eye as she approached the line. He took her by the hand and led her out the front door onto Etta's porch. Cutting loose from the kickoff to a feeding frenzy, no one would notice they'd taken a temporary leave of absence. Nor miss two fish out of stagnant

water. The whole lot of recent grads had yet to row their boats and create their own ripple effect. Unlike Obie, paddling to shore along his career path in law enforcement. Unlike Muriel, up the creek without a paddle along her career path in waitressing, and walking the gangplanks of beauty pageants after she dropped out of school.

Spotting Carolyn across the room had dredged up memories from last year's post-prom hanky-panky. Paired with Chuck Farnum, she never even glanced his way. No matter. Thoughts of entering and exiting her cavity of depravity caused a logjam in his pants he needed to do something about—fast! High time Muriel stepped up her game over and above granting a beggar the favor of a hand job.

Ah, Muriel! Dim prospects and seeking the light at the end of her tunnel vision in the likeness of a future husband. Fully aware of Muriel's ambitions for him to step it up from steady boyfriend to fiancé, Obie's balls were in her court. At this stage along his upward climb, he could do much worse than marrying the uptight daughter of a successful businessman. Gawd, he couldn't do much worse if he pissed off Fist Doyle by knocking up Muriel. Initiating sex with her, null and void, he'd get his rocks off one way or another during the long, hot summer of their courtship.

In urgent need of deflating his blue balls, Obie forwarded a policeman's powers of observation, deduction, and persuasion to his frontal lobe. "Let's see if the car doors are unlocked."

In tow, and to Muriel's dismay, a tug on the handle opened Sydney's back door. "After you, Muriel."

Lying down on the back seat to avoid detection worked to Obie's advantage for leading Muriel's upper torso in a downward direction. As soon as he had Muriel right where he wanted her, and his full-fledged member danced before the eyes of his beholder, Uncle Reggie turned up sight unseen by Obie.

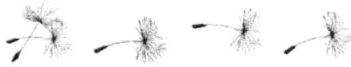

Coming to grips upon discovering that smudges, streaks, and smears had wreaked havoc with Muriel's greasepaint, Obie did what he could to rescue a damsel in distress, bordering on magic. He whipped out an iron-pressed, folded square of a handkerchief from the back pocket of his jeans, and opened it in half vertically. "Give it a few hawks, Muriel. I know you got what it takes, girl. Again."

After Obie removed most traces of Muriel's makeup mishap from her face by means of spit-and-swipe, he had the prescience of mind to suggest they lower the back windows to air out Etta's car. Then, they made their getaway from the sunny side of the seat into the house, inattentive to the formation of cumulus clouds, precursors to an ominous thunderstorm whenever unstable weather factors colluded.

To Obie's relief, no stealth was required on their part. Everyone had deserted the great room, eliminating the need for either one of them to concoct a flimsy excuse as to their whereabouts. From out back on the far side of the porch, brays of laughter and bluster dominated the decibels detonated by the Doors' "Light My Fire".

Muriel made haste to cleanse her face with soap and water in the bathroom before joining the others. Obie fixed himself a plate of food from the dregs of satiety before swaggering into a hotbed of activity, cocksure of many more blow jobs until he'd score the full monty on their honeymoon.

Lightning and the acoustics of thunder awakened Muriel from a late night's slumber hard to come by. Still not fully recovered from the trauma of sword swallowing, she thrashed about as though tempest-tossed on the high seas. The storm's strong winds and propensity for the accompaniment of heavy

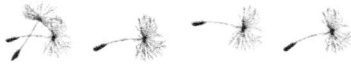

rain jolted her into taking action. At an arm's-length distance on the end table next to the bed, squatted Muriel's pink Princess phone. Via the lighted touch-tone dial, she pushed Etta's buttons.

A light sleeper, Etta heard the quiet bell ringer on her own turquoise Princess. She picked up the receiver after two ringy-dingies and funneled Muriel's brisk apology for the wake-up call. "When Obie and I left the party, I noticed Sydney's back windows rolled down halfway. Was wondering if you remembered to close them. It's about to pour."

Etta wracked her brain, but drew a blank on cranking. "Funny. I don't remember opening the windows on account of the weather forecast."

After a rudimentary exchange of pleasantries to end the conversation, Etta stepped into the pair of scuff slippers lying in wait for her when she got out of bed.

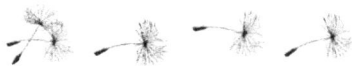

Chapter 14

With no time to wallow in the mire any longer than she already had, Muriel stepped out of her vehicle. She steadied herself on uneven terrain before rounding the nose of the Escape to grab hold of the thermal carrier on the passenger seat. Mounting stairs to the porch, and a hair's breadth away from the front door, the countdown for hesitation had run out. There she was, a fingertip shy of pressing the doorbell and about to set the night on fire.

One ringy-dingy.

Tickled pink with the prototype print of the Mowry Tavern illustration, Etta placed it inside a file folder. She tidied up the studio and closed the door on her way out. About to draw a bath, wishing Keith had laid it out in lavender for her, she fantasized about him lathering her twin peaks and silken valley as she lit a cluster of aromatic candles on the corner ledge at the foot of the bathtub.

A single, intrusive ding-dong drowned further wistfulness along those lines, foreshadowing all good things coming to an end. Bounding barefoot to the bottom of the stairs and into the great room, Etta caught the time on the fireplace mantel clock—8:07. She parted the ruffles along a pair of unbleached muslin curtains on one of two windows flanking the front door. Casting a side-glance through her makeshift portal, she discovered Muriel on the porch, much to her surprise, never suspecting a motive in disguise for precipitating her demise.

A bearer of alms, Muriel might have procured a better outcome if she'd cradled a concealed weapon inside the insulated carrier for all the incidental damage she'd inflict from the wag of her tongue. *As she had once before.*

Despite full exposure of both bottom screens on the double-hung windows, she never heard Etta's creaking footfalls along the hardwood expanse leading up to the rustic pine door. Caught off guard by its abrupt opening, and dumbstruck by Etta's messy bun, a poignant reminder of the other woman and the purpose for her visit, Muriel lost her tongue.

Annoyed rather than delighted to see Muriel, the purpose of her messy bun a prelude to soaking in the tub and pleasuring herself to "Piece of My Heart" with her man in mind. Etta mustered a smile and feigned glad tidings. "H-h-hey, hey! What have I done to deserve some lovin' from your oven on a Saturday night? Come on in before the mosquitoes have a feast."

Etta stepped aside for Muriel to cross the threshold into the great room and forge on ahead to the kitchen while she shut the door behind them, closing them in for a kill. Preoccupied with unzipping the carrier she set on the counter, and removing an object of pretension, Muriel found her tongue.

"Thought you and Keith might enjoy my cheesy sausage-and-croissant casserole for tomorrow's breakfast." Any footing she thought she'd regained for striking up a conversation on the subject of Keith slipped away.

"Just this morning, hadn't you mentioned baking a casserole for Ethan?"

Muriel's face bore the same glazed expression it had whenever teachers or pageant judges posed questions about current events that stumped her stupid. Squirming in embarrassment, Etta regretted casting aspersions on Muriel's altruism as soon as the words escaped her lips. Looking directly into the eyes of a deer in the headlights, she beheld their red-rimmed puffiness, upstaged by the aberration of smeared eyeshadow and clumped mascara. She didn't pry.

From the whirlpool of conjectures swirling inside her head, Etta hazarded a guess that her bestie and Obie hit another snag in their turbulent marriage. So, wanting to get out of the house, Muriel deviated from her original intention and came up with a cheesy excuse to ring her doorbell. Circumstantial evidence, leading Etta to believe marital discord was the reason behind an unexpected visit, paved the way for her to bridge the gap between them. She embraced Muriel in a hug, followed by an appeasement to temper her insensitivity.

"Whatever your change of heart, you can bet your sweet bippy, Keith and I will dig into your casserole at breakfast!" Etta did the honors of placing the baking dish inside the fridge, the newbie Pyrex now surrounded by her glass gals and Keith's aluminum amigos.

Never crediting Muriel with the capability for crafting a clever, calculated ploy, Etta's congeniality got the better of her desire for self-exploration, while the draft from the open door on the fridge cooled her horniness. "If you're not in any hurry, how 'bout a belt for the road?"

Just what Muriel needed to loosen up. As she had on numerous occasions, or on no occasion at all, she pulled out her self-appointed chair from behind the roughhewn, farmhouse table and occupied it.

"Shall we have our usual?" Etta asked, leaning against the fridge, arching her brow.

Chapter 15

Presiding at opposite ends of the table, the two munched on miniature cheese crackers and downed peachy-keen wine coolers from the bottle. Knocking back their carbonated alcohol down the hatch, time was running out before awkwardness crept up on them.

Having no intention of offering a chaser, Etta sought to terminate the visit through jargon, testing the validity of her homespun theory of relativity. "If you and Obie aren't doing anything tomorrow night, come over for dinner. Sure as death and taxes, Keith is going to grill the rainbow trout he's got on ice at the cabin."

The gift of gab provided Muriel flint to blowtorch the night. "Yeah. Sounds great! When did he make the catch?"

"Early this morning, would be my guess."

Rivulets of perspiration pooled in the hollow of Muriel's cleavage. "When did you last talk to him?"

"About an hour ago. Why?"

"Just curious. What's he up to?"

"What else!"

Indeed! Muriel kept an untoward remark to herself, moistening dry lips with a flick of her tongue. *He could have called her from anywhere in the company of the other woman. Somehow, she had to establish Keith's whereabouts.*

Etta excused herself to run upstairs and snuff the candles.

Intermission for the persecution.

In dire need of remedying a parched throat before she choked on her own words, a throwback yielded nothing more than a few drops. Muriel freed her sticky buns from the chair, grabbed a drinking glass from one of the cabinets above the sink, and filled it with tap water. Shaking in her shoes and sloshing her way back to the table, she was unmindful of the splatter which landed on the tile floor, so preoccupied with kindling a presumptive allegation.

***

The time to hesitate is done for.

Aware she'd overstayed her welcome, Muriel stood when Etta re-entered the kitchen. Weak-kneed over the prospect of launching a preemptive strike, she gripped the top rail on the sturdy chair. "What should I bring tomorrow night?"

"You get a pass for the casserole. But, if you're up to knocking yourself out—I'm thinking Keith would stake his claim for peach cobbler."

Muriel, quick on the uptake. "Why not give him a call and find out."

"Trust me. I know better than to break his concentration when he's in the muckety-muck. Besides, his phone signal went kaput."

Uh-huh! Now or never, legs shoulder-width apart and knees slightly bent, Muriel tightened her grip and cast her line. "So, how can you be sure he was fishing then—or, right now?"

Like the smallmouth bass Keith wrested with as they spoke, Etta's resistance surfaced. "Just what are you getting at?"

The truth. The truth of the matter pinpointed Keith leaving a restaurant with another woman earlier in the evening. What she couldn't pin down, reeling from the shock of discovery, was

whether or not he'd slipped his arm around her waist. He must have.

"A couple of hours ago, I saw Keith leaving Chelo's with his arm around another woman."

Gobsmacked!

Etta paced back and forth, breezing past Muriel who wallowed in muddled thinking. An incriminating testimony pigeonholing her husband a lying cheat cavorting around town, robbed her of the ability to speak. In the throes of losing a grip on reality, her heel made contact with the slick spot on the floor, give or take a few minutes before Keith lost his balance wrangling bass.

To Muriel's horror, Etta took a pratfall onto the tile, grimacing in pain. She stooped and extended a helping hand, but quickly withdrew the offer upon peering into pupils dilated in anger directed at her. Etta's reproachful glare bore an eerie similarity to her mother's when she fell from grace coming to terms with the darkness of a man's heart. The major difference—Etta's rebuke tore at her innards.

Through gritted teeth, Etta spoke. "Go!"

Blinded by scalding tears, Muriel grabbed the insulated carrier off the counter and fled, speeding away from the scene of a crime.

***

Grappling with emotional anguish and physical pain, Etta propped herself up on her elbows to relax her spine. She took it from there with deliberate slowness. Back on her feet, and fostering the belief her lower back pain was the result of a sprain and nothing more, she hobbled to the island in the center of her kitchen where she'd left her phone.

The call went straight to voicemail without ringing, yielding zilch. The dilemma of hypothesizing whether Keith turned his phone off, or it didn't receive a signal, rankled her. According to the glowing 9:08 on the digital stove clock, the dictates of logic put him in his cabin by now, instead of where he was.

Had the Wild One actually gone fishing and retired for the night? Or, was he elsewhere, shacked up with another woman? Morning couldn't arrive soon enough for her to ask him when he got home.

Meanwhile, Etta festered with hostility. If Muriel hadn't taken off, justified or not, she'd have doled out double damnation for her infraction in the past, and her accusation of the moment. She'd have throttled the bitch until her smudged and swollen eyes popped out of their sockets. Not having that luxury at her disposal, she opened the door of the fridge for a viable alternative.

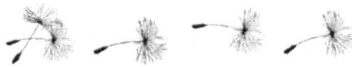

Chapter 16

During Muriel's absence, Obie took over the crash pad where he aimed to hide out for the night. The closed door in and of itself established the unwritten ground rule, Do Not Disturb, for a certain thickheaded and headstrong passerby on her way to their bedroom. Showered, shaved, and in his skivvies, he lounged on the only comfortable seat in the house. An upholstered, swivel rocker-recliner he had put his foot down for when push came to shove.

So angry with Muriel, the closed door hushed any sounds of her pending return home after sticking her nose where it didn't belong. The barrier precluded him from jumping down her throat when she did. His long-range plan included turning up the volume on the set to tune out any grooming rituals a prima donna ministered in the adjoining bathroom before retiring to bed. What's more, Obie's audacious adjustment blocked Muriel's convulsive sobbing into her pillow once she had turned in for the night.

For Saturday night's salvation, he chose to watch one of his DVDs from *The Tonight Show* collection as an antidote for curbing his foul mood. The iconic episode of Johnny Carson and Betty White playing Adam and Eve going through history's first divorce proved prophetic rather than comedic.

Muriel's made my life a misery, all right! Till death do us part. A hex best dispelled by divorce to allay my murderous thoughts.

The ornate, bell-style ring emanating from his mobile phone on the end table at precisely 10:25 made him jumpy. He reached out to grab hold of the device at such an unlikely hour for a social call, apprehensive over its substance.

Flinging aside diabolical thoughts of Muriel departing this world to meet her maker, Obie exhaled a sigh of relief when he discovered the caller wasn't his son opening up a can of worms. *Whew! Man!* His buddy, one of Foster's six patrol officers in the department, downplayed his angst, or so he thought. The two had planned to meet for breakfast on Sunday to shoot the breeze.

Obie hoped to Gawd he wasn't calling on account of a last-minute schedule change for his five days on, three days off. Cancellation portended the dreaded sit-down with Muriel at the kitchen table over whatever she stirred up—victuals or vitriol! Moreover, a shrill sergeant's honey-do list of household chores she'd rattle off for him to get cracking on before sundown.

"What's up, Ray?"

Apparent from the tone of his voice and the omission of smack talk—official business. "Obie, I'm over by Winsor Brook."

About to question the whys and wherefores, Ray—Officer Patterson—addressed the situation, demonstrating his adeptness at communicating in a clear, concise, and confident manner without pulling any punches. "This is a courtesy call out of respect for your friendship with the Lawrences."

Obie's toes curled, his knees locked, and his shoulders squared in readiness for the shoe to drop. "I was dispatched to Winsor Brook over by the Rainbow Trout Cabins after the proprietor made a 911 call, reporting a drowning. As the investigating officer at the scene, I'm waiting for the medical examiner to officially determine the cause, manner, and time of Keith's death."

The patrolman backed off, granting a former crime-fighting comrade the wherewithal to recover from a swift kick to his

gonads. *Right on that count!* At first, the context hadn't permeated Obie's steel-trap mind.

Thrown for a loop when the nitty-gritty finally took hold of him, his knees buckled and he keeled over. Exhibiting symptoms of shock, his skin paled and he experienced shortness of breath. Summoning the vestiges of impeccable conduct demonstrated during his career in law enforcement, he gathered his wits to pull himself together for Etta. He hoisted himself up from the carpet. Obie's capacity to extend empathy and compassion for another superseded all else. Staggering on his feet, he spoke up. "I'm on my way."

Intending right along to let Muriel sleep undisturbed so he could sneak out the door in the morning after a shower without uttering a word to her, he had previously gathered underwear, a short-sleeved pullover, and cargo shorts from a chest of drawers in the master bedroom. There they were, draped over the back of his desk chair and ready for wear. He skipped the clean undies and proceeded to don his outerwear in an absentminded manner, deep in thought about Keith.

Ball-busting bastard has to drown!

Obie pinched the bridge of his nose, struggling with the traumatic incident. About to slip into a pair of flip-flops off to the side of the recliner, Keith's haunting words on the topic of traction dissuaded him from being an asshole. Barefoot, he opened the door to make a quick getaway, sensing Muriel's olfactory presence from the scent of her fragrant soap wafting throughout the hall, having originated from the unoccupied bathroom swathed in darkness.

Undetected, Obie padded down the stairs, onto the breezeway, and into the garage where he snatched the key for the Escape, dangling from a hook on the wall adjacent to the door. He could at least count on Muriel putting things in their proper place. Rummaging for a halfway decent pair of shoes

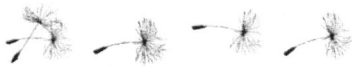

lined up on the cement floor along the back wall, he force fed his feet into a grass-stained pair of athletic sneakers still armed with deep enough grooves on their soles.

His gait, compromised from cramped toes, exacerbated his wretchedness to the point of grousing out loud. "Damn it, Keith! You're killing me!"

Lumbering to *his* vehicle, Obie noted the hood was still warm from Muriel's round trip. Once inside, he started 'er up and backed onto the driveway where it forked to one side. He gunned her in drive without slowing or braking, fishtailing onto Balcom Road and heading north toward Central Pike. He banked a right onto US 6-E. Goosing the gas, he aimed to traverse the 5.7-mile span well under an allowance of 11 minutes without jeopardizing his own safety.

Traveling at breakneck speed along dark, deserted backroads in the boonies on a midsummer night when the moon waxed the sliver of a crescent, illuminating at only 5 per cent, Obie's thoughts raced ahead of his destination. He intended to stay at the scene just long enough to hear the medical examiner's pronouncement.

Counting on Ray to cut him some slack by leaning on the Sarge, he'd accompany his former colleague for the in-person notification of breaking the news to Etta. His presence might soften the blow. By the same token, he'd cool his heels to ascertain just how much punitive damage Muriel inflicted during her visit, if any at all, for implicating Keith in committing adultery.

If so? Gawd!

As much as Obie dreaded bearing bad news, his sphincter tightened at the prospect of going home to Muriel afterward. The brutal murder of a harridan not an option, he anticipated

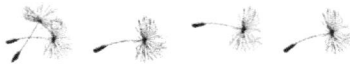

bracing himself for an assault of high-pitched squeals from a cornered rat once he got through browbeating her for meddling.

He veered left onto Rams Tail Road, the former site of a thriving textile mill built in 1813, officially designated as haunted in the 1885 Rhode Island State Census. Destroyed by fire, the barely visible ruins of its foundations were now overgrown with weeds, and purported to stir up sensations of unease and eeriness.

Be that as it may, haunted surroundings hadn't caused the hairs on the back of Obie's neck to bristle. No siree! After a left onto the Old Danielson Pike which turns right to become Winsor Road, and bearing a left to stay on Winsor, he squinted from the blinding glare of headlights beaming on high from every vehicle in the vicinity. All of them, except for Keith's truck, were conspicuous for their positional correctness. They had been parked against, rather than alongside one of two low-slung segments of the bridge connected to a viaduct. The concerted effort to illuminate the woods cast a pall over the grim scene.

This veritable Festival of Lights resurrected an unholy night when he was the investigating officer dispatched to the scene of a heinous crime at the deli. Flashbacks from hell provoked an involuntary shudder. Gawd, he blamed himself for not slugging Muriel and ending their marriage for showing her face when she did outside a skating rink slippery with blood.

Shoulda, woulda. But, couldn't. On account of Muriel's pregnancy! How she conceived in the first place boggled the mind based on unfavorable odds she'd consent to a catch-as-catch-can roll in the hay.

Far be it from Obie to fall out of line and defy regimentation. He wedged the Escape into the last available space, tight as a tick. Like his predecessors, he threw the gearshift in park, leaving the motor running and high beams on.

Before squeezing his body out of the partially opened door on the driver's side, Obie had the foresight to grab a can of insect repellent from the glove compartment. He fortified himself against prevalent mosquitoes and ticks in preparedness for tramping into the valley of death.

Chapter 17

Stepping over the guardrail into the entangling maze of brambles for his trek to where Keith lay in repose, Obie struggled to stay upright as he loped along a slope to the low-lying area below. His priority to avoid tumbling headfirst into a bed of prickly brush undermined the bloody scratches his bare legs sustained. Barbs snagging his britches propelled an erratic descent to the ground.

Adding insult to his multiple injuries, a ghostly visage of Keith brandished a wry grin in mockery of a foolhardy wayfarer out of his element plundering through a briar patch wearing knee-skimming shorts. The dead head metamorphosed into a hoarse whisperer who taunted him with words boomeranging from a barbecue on the subject of proper environmental attire.

"You don't want to show up at the gym on the next day with nasty branch scratches tattooed all over your legs. Or, worse— the blisters of poison ivy, oak, or sumac. Me? I wouldn't be caught dead in the water without 'em!"

River pants. Forewarned is forearmed. Wisdom wasted on the rash and reckless! Too late for heeding practical advice on donning long pants for a walk on the wild side, he begrudged Keith the last laugh. But, not the last word! Obie shook his fist and wised off at a devil's advocate. "Jiminy Cricket! Caught dead in the water with your boots on too!"

Grief resurged inside of him for a formidable sparring opponent. Tears be damned! Obie focused on his trudge to the bank of the brook on uneven terrain through more dense undergrowth which flayed the skin off of his open wounds. Encroaching on the outer perimeter referred to as the third tier for restricting immediate access, Obie's ill-fitting pair of shoes

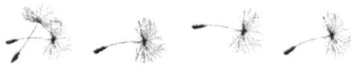

had not only chafed the back of his ankles, but blistered the tender skin in retaliation for wear and tear. A sorry sight for sore eyes, he bypassed nonessential onlookers, mainly the press, who'd entrenched themselves along the periphery.

Plodding onward, face recognition and a nod from Ray just yonder, permitted Obie to barrel past the second tier. This inner perimeter served as a command post for backup personnel positioned a short distance from the core. On his last legs tromping through underbrush, skinned alive by thorns and thistles along his valiant footslog, he arrived at Keith's finish line. There, he respectfully stationed himself outside the jurisdiction of a yellow ribbon tied around some old oak trees, at a vantage point for speculating about the departed.

In keeping with a sappy song, Obie mulled over whether or not Keith had remained faithful and devoted. *Had he honored the one he rightfully belonged to when he drew his last breath on earth?*

The forensic pathologist and her assistant never looked up from their crouching, post-mortem probe of a corpse garishly illuminated by Officer Patterson's flashlight.

Gawd! As for determining Keith's cause of death? After all those years of putting up with the ornery bastard, he still hadn't figured him out! Close-mouthed, except for pulling his own weight at social gatherings, had this man of slight build decomposing before his very eyes, hidden any secrets?

The luminosity afforded him a ghoulish view of a guy he believed had every reason to die with a smile on his face. One of those reasons, Etta. Instead, Keith's stiff upper lip twisted into the curl of a sneer, suggesting something troubled him when the Grim Reaper tapped his shoulder.

Given his own twist of fate to stare death in the face during the line of duty many moons ago, he now peered into Keith's

eyes which had started to sink into the skull. From his devout Catholic upbringing, Obie inferred the occupant had vacated his discolored vessel in spirit form, taking flight along a soulful journey to new digs in the heavenly exosphere. Once St. Peter opened the pearly gates to admit Keith inside God's abode, he'd have an eternity to cross-examine his soul.

While those he left behind dealt with his remains in the middle of nowhere!

Obie's brooding on Keith's behalf ceased and desisted when Officer Patterson motioned for a patrolman on standby in the second tier to approach. The investigating officer passed on the torch to his temporary replacement so he and Obie could step away and confer out of earshot in the wilderness. In short order, the medical examiner would document her findings on the Pronouncement of Death form before sealing Keith inside a body bag and rolling him over hill and dale to the van for transport at the lab morgue. There he'd lay, pending arrangements with the next of kin's designated funeral home or crematorium.

Despite no airtight indicators, the doc had rounded the bend in formulating her assessment for time of expiration, hinged on when the person was last known to be alive, and factoring in various changes incurred from the onset of death. In that regard: after the heart stops beating, *algor mortis* occurs, whereby body temperature typically drops 1.5 degrees Fahrenheit per hour. Accompanying the death chill, blood starts to pool, staining the skin a dark purple during this stage of lividity, wherein the lips and nails tend to turn white.

***

Out of the limelight, and far enough away from those encamped, the commanding officer and retired patrolman strategized their post-mortem stage of morbidity which involved the dreaded, dreadful task of death notification. The legal

batting order for who's on deck regarding next of kin is defined as the spouse. By the playbook, notification is done in pairs, and one of them should be in uniform.

By default, Officer Patterson would be the lead man in uniform who'd deliver the news in a straightforward, compassionate manner. At Ray's request, the Sarge had granted permission for Obie to string along in providing support and monitoring the survivor for any adverse reaction. Hence, the need for adhering to police protocol by arriving with two vehicles in the event of medical transport for the bereaved.

Having dispensed with the brass tacks, Ray seized the opportunity to brief his former partner in crime on a breach of etiquette which ran afoul of a cardinal rule.

No one is allowed to touch anything at the scene until a coroner or medical examiner gives the okay.

"When I got here, the scene had already been tampered with and sorely compromised. According to the distraught wisp of a woman who made the discovery at approximately half past nine, she pulled the deceased out of the water and dragged the body to where it is now. Get this. She admits to plucking a bass from the reel line, extracting the hook from its mouth, and putting it in the ice cooler Keith had placed on the bank. I didn't ask what possessed her to act in such a manner, chalking it up to aftershock."

Obie shook his head in disbelief. Baffled even more by what gnawed at him, he raked his fingers through his spiked crop of hair. "What in Gawd's name ever possessed her to look for Keith in the first place?"

The officer flipped through pages in his pocket notebook. Pinpointing where he'd jotted down name and address of the so-called witness, he read aloud pertinent details from his notes with utmost deliberation for Obie's edification. "Judith Grant,

83

the widowed proprietor of Rainbow Trout Cabins who discovered the body and reported a death, stated she became overly concerned by what hadn't seemed right to her when nine o'clock rolled around.

"When I asked her to explain further, she related that the truck belonging to the deceased was not parked in front of his lodging, which appeared to be in complete darkness. She claims to have waited no more than ten minutes before getting in her vehicle and setting out to search for him."

While processing the officer's explanation, Obie's index finger rested vertically along his cheek, and the thumb supported his chin, indicating he harbored skepticism. His thoughts surfaced outright. "Okay, given the period of time you mention, this places your witness at the scene within a matter of minutes. There are three brooks and any number of unnamed tributaries along the Ponaganset, lending itself to a wild-goose chase. It tells me your witness must have known Keith's whereabouts from the get-go."

"Unless the medical examiner rules Keith's death a homicide, it's not in my purview to hypothesize or delve further. If you want to chat her up, off the cuff, she's over by the reporters where I requested she remain until it's feasible for her to leave the vicinity. And, haul bass!"

Obie cringed in protest against the flimsy stab at humor. The investigating officer returned to his command post, leaving him to simmer in his own speculations. Impelled by curiosity, he about-faced himself in the direction of the third tier. Squinting, he perused from afar, peering through the haze cast by high beams. Searching the crowd for the aforementioned Judith Grant, his arresting gaze fixated on the object of its projection. In spite of the distance between them, Muriel's jack-shit description nailed Mrs. Grant as the other woman she'd spotted with a dead man walking.

Observed dabbing at her eyes with a tissue, construed a gesture indicative of grief. The retinal snapshot bolstered his hunch in suspecting the proprietor's emotional attachment to her lodger. How her affinity for Keith oscillated in magnitude on the Richter scale from platonic to passionate warranted exploration, especially if Muriel stirred a hornet's nest at the Lawrence residence.

Keep your friends close. Keep your wife's best friend the closest of all, if you genuinely care for her. And, keep any plausible rival for her husband's affections close as a fresh shave.

Because he genuinely cared for Etta, Obie intended to do just that when the opportunity presented itself. Meantime, he wended his way back to assist with Keith's send-off. Once zip-sealed inside a body bag, lifting usually involves four people in moving a cadaver of average size and weight onto the stretcher. Ray, Obie, and two other officers from the second tier made the transfer.

In a monotone, the pathologist summarized Keith's exit strategy, estimating time of death as having occurred between 8:00 and 9:00 p.m. "Cause of death for this sixty-seven-year-old white male is accidental drowning, resulting from a fall in which blunt force trauma to the cranium was sustained, rendering him unconscious."

Gawd! Keith's death sentence!

Chapter 18

Those deep-rooted in the outlying sectors began matriculating wither thee and thou goest. One of them, Artie Dufresne, emerged from the third tier, exercising a purpose-driven stride toward a newsmonger's primary sources before they disbanded and dissipated. Noting his rapid transit, the responding officer and medical examiner braced themselves for the old-school investigative reporter toting a ballpoint pen and steno pad. Tagging along behind the legendary newsman about to retire, the camera operator trying to keep up with him. Without a doubt, Rhode Island's iconic Artie contributed to a local news channel's stellar reputation in the New England area.

However brief, two men of might acknowledged each other with a nod, telepathically transporting themselves to the bloody crime scene at Sal's Italian Deli when Obie was a fledgling officer. On the move toward different ports of call, their averted gaze broke the disturbing connection between them.

Obie redirected his tunnel vision to focus on the woman trampling through the woods toward Keith's ice cooler, a gift horse for him to exploit. When she breached the distance, he moved forward, aiming to charm his way into her good graces. "Mam, let me help you with that."

Befuddled, bedraggled and begrimed as a result of her exertions during the witching hour of Keith's death, and vulnerable from the affront of a stranger's intrusiveness, she tightened her grip on the handle. He espied wariness in her eyes. An enchanting green, they cast him in an unfavorable light. "If you're an off-duty police officer, I've already given my statement."

He disgorged a baseless chuckle, hoping to put her at ease. "Way off! I retired from the force a few years ago." He extended his arm to initiate a handshake. "Obie Smith, a close friend of Keith."

"I'm sorry for your loss. Judith Grant. Judy." Relaxing her guard, she freed her right hand to engage in a social formality. Having relinquished her proprietary hold on the cooler, she took him up on his offer. "I sure could use your help toting this barge."

Obie's smile widened into a broad grin as he took the bait for rescuing a madam in distress. Their eyes locked. With a raised eyebrow and trace of a smile, she unleashed her dry humor. "Looks like you could use first aid. I'm offering."

"That obvious?"

Gawd! Due to the urgent face to face with Etta, he'd have to pass on a golden opportunity to scrape at the surface of an unsubstantiated suspicion. For damn sure, he'd get around to asking her what the hell she intended to do with Keith's catch of the day before they parted ways and nurtured their disparate bleakness.

"There's somewhere I gotta be."

She nodded with understanding. In solemnity and relative silence, they journeyed through the darkness. Those who'd already made their getaway had deprived them of illumination afforded by the high beams. He spotted one of the officers from the second tier driving Keith's pickup, presumably back to the cabin.

Out of habit, he'd leave the doors unlocked with the key in the ignition. A man of faith, Keith believed the rotted-out fender wells on his Dodge Ram deterred thieves from boosting his truck.

87

Retracing their steps on unforgiving turf, and trudging along the incline to the guardrail, Obie winced in pain from the barrage of barbs piercing his festering flesh. Stealing a surreptitious glance at her now and then, he detected the quiver of her lips, hinting at stoicism for resisting an urge to cry. It renewed his curiosity as to the nature of her relationship with Keith.

Sharing the burden of hoisting a cooler laden with ice over the guardrail, two pallbearers lifted the provisional casket for a bass. Obie thought this would be a good time as any to question her obsession with possession. He didn't need to. When their panting subsided, she bespoke justification for dragging a burden worth its weight in gold, delivering a sucker-punch to his mindset.

"Godspeed, Obie. Give a fisherman's wife her due."

Frozen in his tracks, slack-jawed, he stood like a hapless deer transfixed in her headlights. Mesmerizing orbs shimmering with tears held him in captivity. For that fleeting moment of immobility, he drew an imaginary line to accommodate the shifting sand of his perceptions in comparing two women of similar appearance. Setting aside the difference in eye color, as well as acute variations in height and hair shade, he discerned a major distinction between their heart of hearts.

The Etta he beheld, often enough, kept her truest, innermost feelings well-hidden under a veneer of composure. With death knocking twice on her door, he understood her cautious walk along a tightrope lest she plunge headlong into a downward spiral.

And, now, all bets were off cuz third time's a charm!

The other woman? Somewhat guarded and frugal with words, he sensed transparency. If eyes are indeed the gateway to one's soul, Judy's allowed him a sneak peek inside of hers.

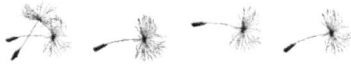

Before she drove away in her shiny red pickup, Obie hedged a bet on gaining a stranger's trust based on his gut instinct. Out of his element in uncharted territory without pencil or paper, he improvised.

Grabbing his wallet from a back pocket, he rummaged through it, and offered her a one-dollar bill through the open window on the driver's side. "I'm hoping you can meet me halfway by coming up with a writing implement to jot down your phone number. At some point, I'll need to make arrangements with you to get Keith's belongings."

Enthroned inside the cab with the engine running, she reached for the glove compartment, procured a pen, and complied with a scribble. She passed the buck through the open window on the passenger's side. "Next time, you won't have to be such a glutton for punishment. Unless you prefer walking."

Chapter 19

Nyuk nyuk nyuk! Happy trails until we meet again.

She sped off, leaving him in the lurch to summon his mental forbearance. Inside the Escape, he gripped the steering wheel. Factoring in acceleration, he figured on maintaining his record for under 11 minutes to backtrack along Foster's deserted roads. Given the situation, Obie predicted he'd take a turn for the worse onto Etta's driveway before Ray rounded the bend.

One of the last to leave the promontory, he departed Winsor Road for Old Danielson Pike. While revisiting his interaction with the other woman during the course of his drive, an impudent grin surfaced in the midnight gloom.

When it came to covering more ground with her, Judy Grant left a lot to be desired.

Deep in thought while navigating from here to there, he snapped out of his pensive mood. Much to his amazement, he had already veered left onto Foster Center Road which cropped up out of nowhere, horning in on his trance. A cue for him to clear his head of clutter, since only half a mile remained before he'd bear right onto North Road. Not much of a leeway to perfect his pitch for serenading Etta in harmony with his other half.

Like Rudolph, the red-nosed reindeer, a flashing red cherry on the rooftop of a squad car on his tail, confirmed the lead investigator's welcome presence in the doleful darkness. In the flash of an eye, both took that hairpin turn onto Etta's winding driveway, giving credence to misery loves company. Their urgency amplified the crunch of gravel. Grating enough to startle Etta awake in the event nary a creature was stirring, not

even a mouse. On the contrary, an influx of light filtering through the screen on one of the open windows in the great room, afflicted him with disquietude.

Familiar with the lay of the land, he cozied up alongside Sydney at the curve, bequeathing Ray the straightaway. Upon opening the door of his vehicle, Obie shook his mind free of the cobwebs entrapping him with Muriel who had performed a backseat blow job at his bidding. Leaving her specter behind to stew in his plum pudding, he and Ray strode up the porch steps.

Between twilight and dawn, Etta's doorbell had rung twice. This time it tolled for Keith. The door flew open from an abrupt yank on the other side, undermining the best-laid plans of mice and two men.

***

Still squeamish from the repercussions of shock wrought by circumstances surrounding Keith's death, Obie's stomach roiled in reaction to an aromatic abomination wafting from the rafters. And, from Etta herself.

Best guess, she hadn't slept a wink, pulling an all-nighter without a shower or change of clothes. Horror of horrors, flecks of yellow matter speckled her tank top and pedal pushers. Plenty more particles reeking of vomit nested in her lopsided bun, an unraveled shamble of tangles. Unnerving him even more, if at all possible, her blue eyes were dark storm clouds, their pupils dilated with malevolence.

The hideousness of Obie's legs broke the hostility of her pernicious stare. Taking full advantage of Etta's downcast eyes, Officer Patterson closed in for the kill. "Mrs. Lawrence, may we please come in?"

Struck by another incongruence, with more forthcoming in rapid-fire succession, Etta stepped aside without voicing alarm, or asking why Obie and a uniformed police officer came calling

in the wee hours of the morning. When passing over the threshold into the great room, the stench of rot grew more pervasive with each footfall inside its stronghold.

A discreet glance hazarded by two sleuths uncovered the source of foul play radiating from the kitchen. Judiciously, without diverting attention from their undertaking, and careful not to spook the lady of the house, Officer Patterson suggested he and Etta sit down on the sofa. Obie wondered if his own facial flesh had assumed a pastiness matching Ray's whiter shade of pale.

In stark contrast to the malice she'd displayed earlier, Etta deferred, taking a load off her feet with the malleability of a marshmallow. Oblivious too. Obie suspected the ravages of mental exhaustion from a fallout. Of far-flung cheesy sausage-and-croissant casserole!

Facing each other, the lead man got to the point. "Mrs. Lawrence, I'm sorry to tell you that your husband died late last night in a fishing accident. Keith was knocked unconscious by a fall and drowned."

Affording the widow across from him a moment of silence to absorb heartbreaking news, he braced himself for an assortment of typical reactions. Fomenting inside the murky waters of the dead pool: screaming rampage, passing out, denial, or stunned silence.

Not falling too far from the apple tree, Etta exorcised her misery through a bloodcurdling wail compatible with denial. "N-o-o-o-o-o!"

Then, upon pummeling the bearer of pall with blows to his chest, Obie moved in to intervene. Pinning Etta's arms behind her back, he granted his teammate a leg to stand on in front of the sofa. Undeterred, she scissor-kicked her legs, targeting Officer Patterson's scrotum with her bare feet. Ray sidestepped

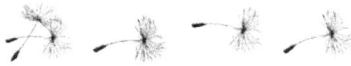

the affront and grabbed hold of both ankles, restraining, but not subduing a warring dervish by any means.

Bucking authority at both ends, Etta writhed in anger and aggression, spewing expletives and cussing them out. She retaliated against Keith's death by refuting their claim until her protests vanished into thin air on the wings of self-induced laryngitis. Wilted from debilitating fatigue which had gotten a running start in the kitchen, both men relinquished their grip on her assault weapons. They eased her into a supine position on the sofa, propping two pillows behind her head.

Heavy-lidded eyes riddled with weariness riveted on Obie, excluding Officer Patterson from the gist of her understatement. Bearing the brunt of her scrutiny, Etta's unflinching gaze had the power to fell him like an axe. Her concession, strained from the loss of her voice, and downplayed for secrecy, made him want to wield an axe at Muriel. "A little after nine, I tried getting through to Keith on his phone to ask him something."

He balled his hands into tight fists, white-knuckled with rage.

Gawd! He might have known Muriel had been the driving force behind the stink which had either preceded, coincided, or shadowed Keith's arrival at his suite in the celestial palace.

Officer Patterson cleared his throat, succeeding in drawing Etta's attention his way. He offered to make a phone call to the clergy, which she declined. Neither she nor Keith attended worship services at the local parish of St. Paul. Aware the couple had no family, Ray anticipated his friend would endorse the suggestion of asking Muriel to stay with her.

Etta bristled. Sparing Obie potential embarrassment in clamoring for an excuse and stammering through one, she snapped, "No. I prefer to be alone."

Out of consideration for both, Obie rose to the occasion. "Ray, you go on home and catch a few winks. I'll stay awhile to pick up the slack. And, to keep an eye on Etta."

Reluctant to turn tail and run, Obie reassured the dedicated officer he'd be fine. Seeing Ray to the front door, he mumbled, "No need for the two of us to pull KP duty."

Chapter 20

As soon as Ray backed onto North Road, Obie followed his nose into a hotbed of fermentation brought about by casserole carnage. In the clutches of the great room, Etta spooked him. Sitting upright, ramrod straight and raring to go, she bushwhacked him. "Was the other woman Muriel said Keith had his arm around when they left Chelo's together, with him when he died?"

In all likelihood, that poor bastard wouldn't have drowned if she were! Gee, Muriel never mentioned Keith had an arm around his companion. Is that what she implied when she said Keith "looked pleased as Punch"?

He scratched the backside of his head and neck, buying him pause for thought. Obie decided to run with the truth as he knew it. "Now, looky here! Swearing by all that's holy, *I* never saw Keith with another woman. Furthermore, he was alone when he died."

Unappeased, she lashed out. "Fully aware of how you avoid Muriel at all costs, maybe you never saw Keith with another woman because your back was toward them, and you didn't bother to turn around!"

Obie flashed his palm to stop her from running off at the mouth in petty vindictiveness. "Before things turn butt ugly on us, not another word!"

"Fair enough. For now." That said, Etta backed off and collapsed against the pillows, relapsing into a comatose state.

Before her eyes closed of their own volition, and sleep snowed her under, Obie set the stage. "I'll be here for a while." Holding his arm out with fingers folded, he pointed a

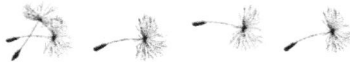

hitchhiker's thumb toward the kitchen. She flinched. "I'll lock up on my way out, and come back around nine tomorrow to help you with the funeral arrangements."

On the brink of dozing off, one of Etta's innermost thoughts surfaced as an ultimatum, sending shivers up and down his spine. "At all costs, keep Muriel away from me. If you know what's good for her!"

Swell!

***

The widespread mess all around him had Muriel's handwriting on the walls in the throes of her signature dish strewn everywhere. Mapping out a strategy inside the trench of stench while bone-weary, dying for a shower, and in need of first-aid, Obie devised a plan of attack for his restoration project. First, he'd start at the top by purging the cabinet doors of leprosy.

He lugged a stepladder from the broom closet and grabbed a spatula out of one of the drawers, yielded by trial-and-error spelunking. Climbing to the topmost crosspiece on a sturdy workhorse, he espied Muriel's Pyrex baking dish on the kitchen island rather than the floor where he expected to find it. This peculiar discovery, which included the spoils of war pockmarked with craters, led him to deduce Etta used her bare hands to dig up hunks of casserole which she hurled willy-nilly.

As for the missing devil-red lid, Etta made short work of prying it off and pitching it in the wastebasket. Unseen and unsought by Obie, the lid escaped detection during his avalanche of aftereffects.

From cabinets to walls, then on to counters, furniture, fridge, stove, and floor—Obie scraped, scrubbed, and swept up the residue from a grime scene, which he disposed of in the wastebasket. Tying the ends of the inner liner, he pulled out the

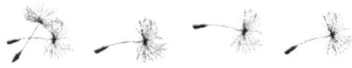

bag and stuffed it into a trash barrel on the porch. For all of his toil and trouble, swabbing surfaces with an all-purpose cleaner removed every trace of evidence and replaced an offensive odor with a refreshing pine scent.

In essence, he merely defrayed the whiplash of a ripple effect with far-reaching consequences caused by Muriel dishing the dirt. The stove clock winked him a 1:50. Before Obie locked up and left, he had unfinished business to take care of. Two things, in and of themselves. Separate nonentities, each would profoundly affect those sucked into a whirlpool eddying from ill-effects.

Of utmost importance, the casserole coffer. He chiseled the crud cemented to its bottom and sides, then fed the slop to the garbage disposal. He scoured the vessel of vile with a soap pad, aware that his thorough cleansing couldn't wash away Muriel's mouthy transgression.

He'd leave the empty receptacle on their kitchen table for her to discover in a few hours. In his frame of mind, pleased as Punch in launching a pre-emptive strike to catch her off guard so he could initiate and negotiate from an unfair advantage.

To gain the upper hand, he counted on Muriel sleeping like a rock in the Ponaganset's riverbed when he got back.

Of utmost concern, a fine-finned friend. In all good conscience, he couldn't stash the bass in Etta's freezer.

Gawd! No telling what she might do, considering her anger and resentment toward Keith. Instead, Obie emptied the ice trays in the freezer, pouring the cubes into a plastic bag. *At all costs, he'd preserve the integrity of Keith's bass.*

Careful not to awaken Etta, he let himself out with his baggage. He stood on the front porch, pressing buttons on the remote key fob, and inhaling deep breaths of fresh air until the rear cargo door sprung open for him to stow the glassware.

With reverence, Obie lifted the lid to the cooler and anointed Keith's bass with ice for safekeeping.

Behind the wheel, coasting to the bottom of Etta's driveway, and without braking, he turned left onto Balcom Road. Within a few minutes, he'd reach his place of residence where he never felt at home.

Chapter 21

Obie counted on Muriel getting her much needed beauty sleep until seven so he could plant evidence, jump in the shower, and get some shut-eye until showdown. A glimmer of light through the kitchen window sabotaged his scheme.

Still in his favor, which no jolly good fellow could deny— the element of surprise. Up for grabs, who'd speak first? And, who'd have the last word?

Crossing over the threshold into the kitchen, he stopped short of grandstanding a display of bravado upon confronting a sacrificial lamb. Slumped on one of the spindle-slatted chairs tucked in close to the table, Muriel nursed a cup of tea and nibbled at a wafer with absentminded abandon. She had just about depleted the sleeve from which she extracted it from.

Attired in a nightgown, her hair in disarray with cowlicks resistant to taming, she lifted her head up and looked him in the eye. Had her eyes wandered where they seldom ventured, below the beltway, she might have addressed Obie's torn flesh and granted him a stay of elocution. The hollows of Muriel's eyes, darkened, by what he speculated had surfaced from lack of sleep over a blowout with Etta, swayed him to put his peeves on hold. With an arm crooked behind his back, he concealed the empty baking dish and turned the other cheek. Shuffling toward the stairway, Obie had as much chance as a wax cat in hell for escaping into the spare room with his prize possession.

Cornered by a fishwife!

Muriel pounced with combative shrillness, self-assured at having cornered a rat. "Where have you been?"

Questioning Obie's whereabouts originated from a midsummer morn's trip to the bathroom at 12:23. The open door to his oasis got the better of her curiosity. Peeking inside, rather than stumbling back to bed, Muriel stared into a black hole.

During the waiting period, Obie's absence did not make her heart grow fonder. Not in the least. The more she pondered the situation while sipping an orange pekoe brew, nibbling, and keeping a weather eye on his homecoming, her imagination ran amok. Jumping to conclusions without supporting evidence, Muriel held Carolyn Farnum accountable for her missing husband.

She felt both relief and rancor from overindulging in another one of her suspicions involving his old flame. From time to time, she squeezed her eyes shut to block out a fanciful glimpse of them entangled in the nasty, wasty stuff Obie couldn't get her to try.

***

In keeping with tradition, Obie should have ignored Muriel's outburst and distanced himself from her. Turns out, his brush-offs had preserved and prolonged their marriage past due. Dog-tired and dragging, his machismo wouldn't let him bow out of a fight. Not this time!

Obie backed away from the stairs, champing at the bit to give as good as he got, once and for all. Refraining from bashing Muriel's brains in, he kept the Pyrex ovenware hidden to accommodate his malicious intent. Towering over Muriel's low profile, he amplified his contempt. "Where? Have? I? Been? You want to know where I've been?"

He paused to gauge the effectiveness of close-range intimidation, losing self-respect for tyrannizing Muriel nose to

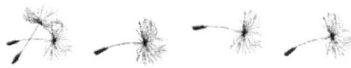

nose even when she had it coming to her. "At Etta's! That's where I've been!"

Jolted! At an impasse for words, Muriel cudgeled her addled brain, trying to make sense of something out of order. Her one-track mind still in the gutter, she sputtered disbelief and derision. "At E-t-t-a's? *No wonder she didn't seem all that eager to see me.* What m-m-monkey business do you two have going on after dark?"

Appalled by Muriel's accusatory turn of phrase, Obie hit back with no holds barred. Pent-up rage executed a sweeping motion of his arm from behind which resulted in a lowering of the boom on the table with brute force. Stealth, be not proud! As expected and intended, Muriel flinched, a shade shy of jumping out of her skin.

While she cringed and cowered in fear, Obie took an unfair advantage. "Yeah, at Etta's! Cleaning up your mess! Thanks to what you brought to her attention last night, she tried calling Keith to hear his side of the story, but couldn't get through. Beside herself, she went on a rampage in her kitchen."

Out of necessity, Obie paused for Muriel to swallow the bitter pill he administered. In point of fact, she had an adverse reaction from staring into the glass enclosure, peering at a mirage of Etta in her kitchen when she landed on her butt. Muriel's eyes misted over as she relived the anguish of her departure at Etta's insistence. And, apparently, this covert Sicilian message Obie delivered, may have signified the death of their friendship.

"As I was saying, Etta couldn't get hold of Keith," he reiterated. "Because, in the meantime, he drowned fishing in Winsor Brook. Which is what brought Officer Patterson and me to Etta's in the first place."

By pure luck of the Irish, Obie moved away from Muriel's territory in the nick of time. Every ounce of tea and morsel of wafers she'd consumed backfired into the trough under her nose. Befouling Obie's sour disposition even more, the color and consistency of her regurgitation bore a freakish resemblance to the slop he'd scraped into the garbage less than a half hour ago. He suppressed the urge to dry-heave.

Woozy, but resolute with groundless self-conviction, Muriel bolted upright from her chair, expelling fetid breath in Obie's face. "I'm heading over there to comfort Etta!"

Shuddering from the funk of their close encounter, he placed both hands firmly on her shoulders. With a gentleness he didn't know he had left in him, he guided Muriel back onto her seat. His telltale heart convinced him it'd be the last time he'd ever lay a hand on her. He mustered compassion. "In a roundabout way, Etta made it clear she doesn't want to see you."

By proxy, Etta had the last say.

Muriel crumbled like a broken wafer. Stench aside, he couldn't stomach looking at her any longer. Nor could he justify sleeping under the same roof with her. Foregoing a shower, and hightailing it without a change of clothes and toothbrush, Obie locked the kitchen and breezeway doors behind him. He got back inside the Escape. In need of a freezer to preserve Keith's bass until its homecoming, he knew where to find one at an ungodly hour.

Come to think of it, he could use a crash pad and temporary lodging while he figured things out.

Taking a chance, Obie navigated his way back to Winsor Road toward the Rainbow Trout Cabins.

Part Two - Breaking Ground

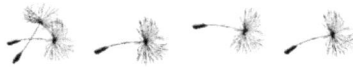

Chapter 22

A glimpse of Etta during adolescence in the Sixties:

"Girl, you're rockin' it!"

Etta rolled her eyes at the lame wordplay, considering.

Rosalia had surveyed her daughter's sketch of a stone wall with an approving eye. An opportunistic glance stolen during a poet's pregnant pause to evaluate the verity of her first verse on their mutual subject of interest in the wooded area surrounding Borders Farm.

Rambling wall

A farmstead's boundary zone

Withstanding the onslaught of elements

Save for boulders rolled

By deer coursing hurdles

High as a man's thigh

***

Come to think of it, Etta rolled her eyes a lot lately. No doubt, under the long-distance influence of her classmates at St. Mary Academy – Bay View, an all-girls, Catholic school in Riverside, attended since kindergarten.

As familiarity tends to beget complacency, Etta took for granted her sharp mental acuity manifesting itself in superior academic achievement. She made the honor roll her freshman year! Yet, none too eager for September to roll around to put on her uniform and test the waters of tenth grade.

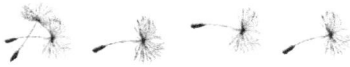

Nevertheless, Etta had formed an inextricable bond with other girls whose parents could also afford the steep yearly tuition. By no means, a stipend to purchase salvation, the fee secured the privilege of enrollment in a first-rate institution whose instructors strived to impart a holistic education that valued social responsibility and global awareness.

Other than spending summers in Foster cavorting with her mother, Etta preferred the sanctuary of the academy and the camaraderie among her elite classmates. Outside its hallowed walls too, during weekends and school breaks. Attending parties at one another's homes, Etta socialized with friends of friends. Boys were in the mix. Whenever Birch Hansford sallied forth in her direction, her heart beat faster and her belly released butterflies.

Consorting with la crème de la crème of the in-crowd, she'd tally-ho to downtown Providence in the vicinity of the Strand and Majestic theaters. Whether or not they actually took in a movie proved inconsequential. The pack preferred to emulate the lifestyle personified by the lyrics to "Downtown," Petula Clark's international hit song topping the charts in '64. On that account, they socialized with other teeny-boppers who lingered on the sidewalk, within earshot of the acoustics from traffic in the city.

On more than one occasion, the lobbies provided an escape hatch for victimized, vulnerable vixens whose wild abandon under the harsh glare of enterprising neon, garnered unwelcome attention from many a n'er-do-well. More to the point, if Etta or any of her soulmates had received Holy Communion in a state of grace at mass, they kicked piety to the curb in the context of free-for-alls most Friday evenings.

Despite shucking their uniforms, Bay View's bevy of babes comprised an oxymoronic choir of conformists in rebellious alliance with others cloned from the Mod subculture. Strutting

the sidewalk to the beat of Carnaby Street in trendsetting mini-skirts at mid-thigh, they fell prey to the whims of designer, Mary Quant, Queen of Tarts. These damsels became gape bait, recipients of toots from horny drivers whose overheated passengers rolled down their respective windows to caterwaul lewd remarks reserved for call girls.

Berets tilted at a cocky angle reinforced a false bravado. As did dragging on cigs, sending mixed smoke signals to rabble-rousers from the wrong side of the tracks, clad in outdated leather jackets. Swaggering up to them, a posse of passé greasers parroting lingo behind the eight-ball, fixing to score at a game of dirty pool.

In heaven's name, before things escalated to a feverish pitch, parents arrived curbside to squire their high-and-mighty hides in regal rides. The adults, under the false assumption their angelic daughters were part of the throng exiting the theater at the conclusion of *That Darn Cat!* Or, *The Sound of Music.*

At odds with the motorcade, Etta's mom drove a '50 Ford Woodie wagon. Perfectly acceptable to the inner circle of winners who interpreted the anomaly an artsy-fartsy eccentricity indulged by the daughter of none other than Oliver Taversham, New York real estate mogul. A person of affluence who graduated from Pembroke, an Ivy League college, she humbled them in her presence. Rosalia humored them in hers, grinning and bearing their deference with ill-disguised amusement.

Hence, orbiting inside her own concentric circle, oblivious to highbrow haughtiness, Etta had yet to make the acquaintance of Muriel. Until the flying fickle finger of fate aligned their stars, precluding Etta to transfer from St. Mary's Upper School to Ponaganset High during her junior year. Meanwhile, on borrowed time, she embraced the cosmopolitan metropolis embedded in the all-girls academy.

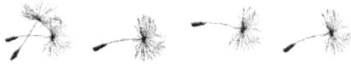

Many a bold and brassy lassie amongst the diverse bunch, they collectively embodied a smorgasbord of ethnic, cultural, and religious backgrounds. A smattering of international students, along with those hailing from cities and towns throughout Rhode Island, southeastern Massachusetts, and northeastern Connecticut filed into their classroom bright and early, ready to rock on.

Familiarity also tends to beget contemptuous behavior. Let's face it, girls just wanna have fun at each other's expense. Volleying cheeky and snarky retorts became one of their favorite pastimes on school grounds. Etta had no qualms paying the irreverence forward, inside or outside the womb of Bay View.

***

Witty word exploitation set aside, Etta countered her mother's phrase of praise with a scowl of skepticism, discerning a disparity between her artistic rendition and reality. Rosalia put her pen and spiral notebook out to pasture on their chosen patch of blended grasses abutting the vegetable gardens and hayfield, heretofore grazed and trampled on by foraging cows.

She disengaged from a cross-legged sitting position, rising to the occasion to scoop Etta in her arms for a one-sided hug. Brushing aside wayward corkscrews with the tip of her nose, she bared the flushed apples of Etta's cheeks, smoothing the way for dispersing slurpy smooches. To Rosalia's delight, Etta endured, rather than wriggled out from under the clutches of a sticky situation.

The oppressive heat generated by the sun reaching its highest position above the horizon, behooved them to disengage and grab lunch at the deli. Relinquishing her hold, Rosalia discreetly appraised how puberty had endowed Etta with a smaller waistline accentuated by curvier hips, thighs, and derriere. The madras plaid shorts she wore showed off a pair of

long limbs, tanned and muscular from their frequent jaunts off the beaten path.

Freezing out Etta's anatomy, Rosalia sanctified her approval. "You've a keen eye for detail like Nonna."

Etta's eyes lit up at the comparison to her maternal grandmother, Viola Taversham, née Gianni. A compliment she neither expected, nor felt she deserved, put a feather in her cap. Whenever she and Momma got away to visit her grandparents at their brownstone rowhouse in Brooklyn Village, Nonna allowed her to stay in the parlor during a sitting if she promised to keep *silenzioso come un topo.*

Upholding her end of the bargain to remain quiet as a mouse served to hone Etta's powers of observation, whether for artistic adroitness or sizing up people. With her hand on her hip, Etta postured a mocking bird, refuting her mother's claim. "Seriously, Momma? Nonna is a portrait artist. I'm sketching a shitload of dead rocks!" she protested.

Rosalia arched a brow in disapproval. "Shitload! A breach of etiquette tolerated by the Sisters of Mercy for sake of argument during discussions?"

"Like hell! They'd shit a brick!" Etta retorted with vulgar intent. Rosalia rolled her eyes at her daughter's impudence. In jest, she anointed the tip of her forefinger with a flick of her tongue. Aiming for Etta's forehead, Rosalia traced a sign of the cross in the center of a frown line.

Sweltering, the two began gathering the tools of their respective trades in preparation for returning to their point of origin. Home. A short distance from the farmstead, their mountaineer-style log house on North Road, presided at the summit of the sloping acreage surrounding it. Staring out one of its front windows, as she often did, Etta would envision a dark, handsome stranger on his motorcycle spiriting her away from

the confines of Foster. Her very own Johnny Strabler from *The Wild One*.

Not as simple an undertaking for Etta, she welcomed her mother's assistance with getting her show on the road. In order to achieve that purpose, they sorted various pens, nibs, and markers for stashing inside a pencil case. Mind you, not just any pencil case. Etta's had several compartments. With the utmost of care, she secured her pens inside mesh pockets, arranging them in rainbow formation. Far less discriminate with her markers, she tossed them haphazardly inside the large, central pouch.

While packing, Rosalia picked up the slack in their unfinished tête-à-tête. "Nonna blends the physical and spiritual traits of each person she paints into a telling portrait. She knows the importance of capturing the essence of her subject. An artist's impressions are far more important than precision alone."

Since her mother never minced words to appease her, Etta retreated from self-defeat like the glaciers that melted across New England, dumping a shitload of rocks in their wake. The most common—granite! True survivors of a rough-and-tumble journey, they resisted rounding and smoothing. Massive, hard, and tough! These properties made granite the heart and soul of stone walls in New England.

"If you say so, Momma!" Etta's telltale blush belied her off-handed tone.

The devil's in the details! Etta's discriminating eye guided her deftness in superimposing grainy texture and emphasizing granite's subtle striations of pink, gray, and white. By figuratively extracting blood from each stone in her field of vision, she captured the spiritual essence of historic grandeur which a callous artist might have overlooked.

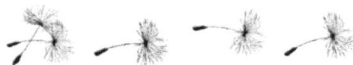

Rosalia slipped her bare feet into a pair of multi-strap, leather sandals in sunshine yellow. With greater difficulty, Etta wedged hers into a pair of white, grass-stained sneakers she hadn't bothered to untie when kicking them off. The struggle afforded her mother the wherewithal to drain the dregs from their water thermoses and stow everything they brought with them into a knapsack. She put her arms through the straps and hoisted the lightweight bundle on her back with a few seconds to spare before Etta bounced to her feet.

"Come on, Momma! Let's go! I'm starving!"

"Well, slap me silly!"

Etta feigned compliance. She twisted her features into a menacing grimace and mimed the delivery of a blow with the palm of her hand, stopping short of striking Rosalia's cheek. In a heartbeat, Etta put her arms around her mother's neck and hugged tight, reluctant to let her go.

Rosalia deflected the onset of sentimental tears by summoning her deadpan humor. "To what do I owe this outburst of affection?"

They peered into each other's eyes, both fathoming the deep adoration one radiated toward the other. "Don't you know, Momma? You're my rock!"

Chapter 23

Zippedy-doo-dah!

A couple of rolling stones gathering no moss, Etta and Rosalia Rizzio blazed their homeward journey on a sultry afternoon. Neither the wiser to what loomed ahead in their horizon, the ignorance of bliss propelled their purposeful stride along North Road.

A pity the sudden onset of a severe headache was dismissed rather than deemed a force to reckon with. It might have prevented the chain of events precipitated in its wake.

A mesh canopy of leaves interwoven by overextended tree limbs on both sides of the corridor shaded two wayfarers. Slight, sporadic breezes hindered them from throwing caution to the wind in totality, as proliferate vines of poison ivy encroaching onto the verge of the pavement behooved them to exercise vigilance. Keeping their distance from triads of tapering leaflets necessitated wending a course in the center of their barren road which meandered through the middle of Foster's nowhere.

Appreciative of nature's bounty, the mother-daughter duo dispensed with idle chatter, preferring to heed protocol of the wild. Swept along by euphoria, they hearkened to the warble of a bird, hum of a bee, or flit of a butterfly on their fishing ground, an idyllic sprawl inviting artistic imaginings and improvisation.

When confronted by their steep gravel driveway, pondering fell by the wayside in condescension to the vigorous workout required of them. Leaning slightly into the slope and shortening their stride, they scrambled to the crest, taxing and strengthening abdominal, gluteus, and leg muscles in the

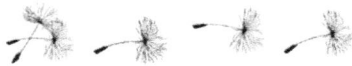

process. Accustomed to treks of this temperament, neither throbbing nor soreness in their calf muscles accompanied the exertion. Other than a spate of perspiration, they reaped the benefits of endurance, along with enhanced flexibility and agility.

At the crest, on their left where the driveway curved, squatted Sydney's predecessor. Rosalia's workhorse, the aforementioned '50 Woodie wagon, accommodated their arrival with its windows cranked all the way down. Her pride and joy rolled off Ford's assembly line at the advent of an era when Elvis reigned as king of rock n' roll and Lucille Ball held sway as queen of comedy.

A college pre-graduation gift from Rosalia's dad, Tavvy, so-called by those who loved him and those he loved in return. He, a self-made millionaire who rose to eminence from the conquests of pioneering the Brownstone Revival by buying and renovating pre-Civil war houses in Brooklyn Heights.

Etta swiped the sweat from her brow with the back of her hand. More refined, Rosalia blotted beads of moisture along her upper lip with a crumpled tissue retrieved from the side pocket of her Bermuda shorts. Without further delay, she opened the unlocked paneled door on the driver's side and pitched her knapsack on the back seat before taking the wheel.

Etta had already assumed her position on the passenger side, an eyewitness to the dreamy expression her mother displayed, subdued and secretive at that, whenever she approached the maroon and maple maven. Preferring to honor her mother's contemplations, Etta refrained from giving in to the gnawing hunger of curiosity.

Rosalia backed the wagon onto the straightaway. Then, maneuvering the gearshift to neutral, she rode the brake to the end of the gravel. Not a breeze stirring from the boughs above, Etta suggested they make their own. "Peel rubber, Momma!"

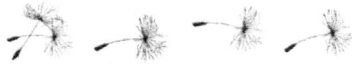

Despite the Woodie's 100-horsepower V-8 transmission, Rosalia drove the half-mile stretch to Foster Center Road at 25 mph. Perturbed, but undismayed, Etta revved up her vivid imagination, consistent with tooling around town alongside her mother.

"So, Momma. Do you think we'll come across a handsome hitchhiker this time?"

*One of many parodied probes consistent with correlating Rosalia's wagon to a similar one driven in the '47 film, **Dark Passage**. Stashing her oil paints and canvasses in her Ford Woodie after painting landscapes, Irene Jansen picks up an escapee from San Quentin.*

Etta absorbed the romantic nuances from every old movie she and her mother watched together on rainy days.

"Surely, you jest! Aren't girls your age fantasizing about getting swept off their feet by Prince Charles and whisked away to England?"

Etta rolled her eyes. "Momma, that's s-o-o far-fetched! Try Ringo Starr."

Etta had the right of way in supposing her mother's faraway gaze beheld a pleasurable vision for her eyes only. And, with probable cause.

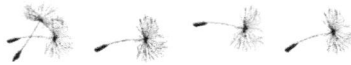

Chapter 24

On the cusp of Rosalia's graduation in the looming, blooming spring of 1950:

Pembroker, Rosalia Taversham, flourished at Rhode Island's prestigious coordinate women's college at Brown University before it merged with the good ole boys' institution twenty years later. At Pembroke, her spirited nature blossomed with poetic licentiousness, thriving on Thoreau's transcendentalism.

Well-versed in articulating her burning desire in front of a mirror to strengthen her resolve, a young woman's fancy turned to thoughts of springing.

To hell with dull duties of domesticity! Constricted by society's narrow expectations for middle-class white women at the conclusion of their formal education. Marriage. Homemaking. Raising a family. Foregoing personal pursuits of happiness. Not my idea of the American Dream by a long shot!

Rosalia's plan to shun gender rules and roles of her generation formulated when Tavvy asked his daughter what she wanted at the forefront of marching into the sunset to the tune of "Pomp and Circumstance".

A Ford Woodie Wagon would do nicely, thank you!

In comparison to the Nash-Healey Roadster her dad suggested, the Woodie outfoxed it in spades for bolstering her mid-summer objective. A liberal arts degree up for grabs, Rosalia had her heart set on packing her belongings and heading for the steep rolling hills of San Francisco. The cinematic foreplay in *Dark Passage* isn't what tickled her fancy for

wanderlust. Nope. She sold her soul to the beatnik ambience of North Beach, the anti-Christ of conformity in life and literature.

Rosalia figured on a hiatus in Brooklyn to grant herself ample time for breaking the news to her parents. Instead, embarking on a lark of frolicking set her wheels in motion elsewhere, causing well-thought-out plans to go haywire.

Hankering for a meatball sandwich put her in charm's way.

***

From an omniscient viewpoint, slouched back on the bed and propped on her elbows, Rosalia's insightful third eye critiqued the calm, cool, and collected contentment of her collegiate cohorts. Confined, they were, inside a dorm room on a Friday evening, outnumbered by potted plants pinch-hitting for drapes. Sultry and smoldering, Rosalia's long, chestnut curls accented with bumper-bangs, glorified a style worn by pin-up model, Bettie Page.

And, transparent as the voluptuousness she exposed in all her vainglory, Helen exercised squatters' rights in her domain, wearing only a bra and panties. Sitting behind her desk, talking on the phone, she raked her fingers through a mousy-brown pixie with soft, wispy bangs. Chunky legs extended, she had propped her bare feet alongside a typewriter with sticky keys. Recuperating from regurgitating a term paper, it rested on the scarred surface upon which Helen stubbed out her cigarettes, one after another.

Obvious to Rosalia, who had no intention or inclination to eavesdrop, their preoccupied hostess was chatting with her fiancé. Apparent by the terms of endearment discerned in between record changing by the other two. A time-consuming transaction which worked in Helen's favor and had worn Rosalia's patience thin.

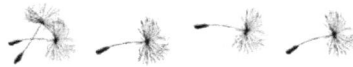

On hands and knees, *they* rummaged through their pooled resources of scattered vinyl, all newfangled 45 rpm records introduced by RCA Victor last year, phasing out the 78. Each suggestion for spinning a popular or country & western hit on the *Billboard* chart invited amicable disagreement.

"Some Enchanted Evening." "I'm So Lonesome I Could Cry." "Texarkana Baby."

They:

Joan, who appeared more matronly than she ought to on account of her poodle cut arrayed with tight, permed curls.

Gloria, the most glamorous among them, and the least academically acclimated or innovative, drained every last drop of sensuality from Rita Hayworth, the top pin-up girl during World War II. It stood to reason, she duplicated the color and hairstyle worn by the temptress, a la Gilda, dying hers a fiery red, and pin-waving her long locks. More than willing to go the distance in wide-leg trousers and monochrome flats, Gloria channeled the screen siren's sultriness.

Looking to cash in on her makeover in Hollywood, regardless of its casting-couch contracts, she and Rosalia had been fine tuning their joint travel plans.

"A Room Full of Roses." "There's No Tomorrow."

Pissed off by the evening's spin, or lack thereof, Rosalia waited for Helen to cradle her conversation before delivering an ultimatum. After all, their soda bottles stood empty, and their fair share of cream cheese on crackers wouldn't hold them for the night. More to the point, Friday night beckoned the warm-blooded to trot hot on the town.

She needed to act fast before their world revolved around Frankie Laine's "Mule Train," Helen's pathetic pick which put an end to the tongue-of-war.

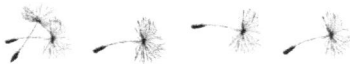

Rosalia took a flying leap off the bed.

Startling her friends, she used the element of surprise for intimidating them to do her bidding. "Listen up, bitches! Helen, grab a skirt and cardigan. You two, put your saddle shoes on. Clippety clop your cabooses over to my station wagon. I'll be waiting with the motor running, five minutes tops. Last one in is a rotten egg!"

She made a deliberate show of checking her wristwatch on the way out. "Crunch time starts—now!"

Mouths agape at the sudden shift in plans, they ran circles around themselves and each other to comply. Helen, at a disadvantage, charged her clothes closet, invoking Stooge-Curly slapstick. "Woo-woo-woo-woo-woo!"

"Has anyone seen my left shoe?" yelled Joan, frantic.

Gloria bolted for the door. "See ya later, alligators!"

***

In the glimmer of the utility pole's street light reflecting off of her compact mirror, Gloria applied a fresh coat of orange-red lipstick, a shade her movie-star muse glided on her lips. She had settled where she normally did, on the passenger side, riding shotgun in awe and amusement at Rosalia's proficiency for shifting gears. Helen situated herself in the back seat behind the wheeler. With bated breath, all three focused their attention on the arched double doors of the Hall, still closed to the world at large.

When they espied Joan, a bat bursting out of hell scaling the steps, Rosalia pretended to leave without her by easing away from the curb. All three howled with mirth. Winded, Joan tugged on the backdoor handle and slid onto the seat, opposite Helen. She berated them for their perverted sense of humor, while enduring their taunts, one voice shy of a barbershop quartet. "Rotten egg! Rotten egg! Rotten egg!"

117

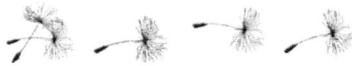

Rosalia set off, goosing the gas.

"Pray tell, where was it?" asked Gloria, craning her neck to get a glimpse of Joan behind her.

"Under the bed, of all places."

"Mind if I ask where you're taking us?" inquired Helen.

"Now that I have my own set of wheels, we're going to try the Capisci Deli on the Hill. I'm dying for a meatball sandwich!"

"O-o-h! Federal Hill!" exclaimed Gloria. "Away from Pembroke's comfort zone."

Rosalia pulled over to the shoulder of the road, toying with her passengers. "Any complaints?" She peered at Gloria, then peeked at her backseat charges through the rearview mirror.

"Not if the alternative is for conscientious objectors to walk all the way back," groused Helen.

"None at all!" replied Gloria.

"I'm in," said Joan, "I'll have me an Italian grinder."

"There she goes again, talking dirty!" quipped Helen.

***

Wisecracks prevailed throughout the remaining half of their 1.4-mile pilgrimage from the affluent East Side to Atwells Avenue in the Federal Hill neighborhood, an *Italo-Americani* community with an abundance of ethnic restaurants to choose from.

Short of a united front, their shouts upon discovering the deli's lighted window sign reverberated as an echo. "CCCapppisscccci DDelliiii!"

Rosalia swung around to the private parking lot in the back of the restaurant. In no time flat, four doors opened and

slammed shut behind an eagerness to sample authentic Italian food off-campus.

***

A foodie's paradise! One of the staff sliced a mixture of meats and cheeses to build Joan's cold sandwich on fresh-baked bread, right before her eyes. Hot sandwiches topped with roasted peppers or mozzarella were heated to perfection, including Rosalia's meatball grinder, the driving force behind their patronage. An assortment of prepared sides: polenta salad; pasta, rabe, and sausage; pasta with arugula; veal and peas; sausage and peppers; broccoli and mushrooms teleported Rosalia back to her mama's kitchen.

She'd frequent the hole-in-the-wall deli often enough, bringing up the rear with various combinations of Helen, Gloria, and Joan. Until they declined to accompany her for one reason or another. Excuses. Rosalia knew her sidekicks were on to the handsome deli worker who had eyes for her ever since Gloria invited him over to their table near closing time. So be it!

L'appetito vien mangiando!

As appetite comes with eating, Rosalia's appetite for Sal Rizzio grew whenever they broke bread together at the Capisci Deli. Each head-to-head and heart-to-heart conversation broke down barriers and deepened their connection to one another. Sooner than later, their chemistry reached a boiling point. Tempered, in a way, by Fist Doyle who had a hand in tempting fate. Theirs.

119

Chapter 25

To some extent, Sal Rizzio got off easy when it came to serving his country. He was fifteen when the Imperial Japanese Navy Air Service launched a surprise military strike against the American naval base at Pearl Harbor on December 7, 1941. This hostile act led to the United States' formal entry into World War II, inciting many a red-blooded American to burst at the seams with patriotism. Sal, who numbered among the gung-ho, jumped at the chance to fight for his country, and if need be, die while defending democracy.

Left in the lurch to bide his time, droves of young men who qualified, along with those who dropped out of high school and lied about their age, registered at their local draft board for immediate induction into one of five branches of the U.S. Armed Forces.

Any wartime draftee or volunteer in the Army of the United States who survived combat could expect to stay put in war-torn Europe for the duration of the conflict, plus six months. Some soldiers recruited in 1940 didn't come home until 1946!

On the other hand, recruits like Sal who enlisted or were instated in '44 or '45, got out in 1945. When he signed up for the Navy on his eighteenth birthday in June of '44, the Battle of Tinian had been fought and won between July 24th and August 1st of that year. Soon afterward, this Northern Mariana Island became an important base for further Allied operations in the Pacific, namely the launching pad for dropping atomic bombs on Hiroshima and Nagasaki in Japan. Toward that purpose, Uncle Sam had plans for Salvatore P. Rizzio.

After completing three weeks of boot training at Camp Allen in Norfolk, Virginia, Sal was shipped to the Advanced

Base Depot at Quonset in Davisville, Rhode Island. Home of the Seabees, this Navy unit helped build bases and other infrastructures in the Pacific. There, Sal's battalion underwent six weeks of advanced military and technical training before deployment overseas.

Tinian, no island paradise!

Navy construction battalions comprised of 15,000 Seabees bulldozed the ground they walked on, transforming North Field into the busiest airport in the world for the war effort. Working for more than 45 days and nights, often under fire, their coordinated manpower built six 7,900-foot attack runways, barracks, an administration building, oil storage facilities, weapons depots, an air-conditioned bomb assembly building, and two bomb-loading pits.

Sal's unit bored into middle earth, digging a Marianas trench known as Atomic Bomb Pit. No. 1, notorious for loading Little Boy, the 4-ton uranium bomb dropped on Hiroshima.

***

Back in Rhode Island on Providence soil where Sal's parents put down roots after emigrating from Italy three months before he was born, an unsung hero did an about-face. Sal turned his back on the woes of war in order to get on with his life. This meant coping with the trauma of cheating death when others in his unit didn't. He also had nightmares of Little Boy vaporizing 80,000 in an instant.

Not a religious man per se, in short order of his homecoming, Sal made a visit to Holy Ghost Church, the Catholic parish on Atwells Avenue, within walking distance of the second-floor tenement he rented above the deli. In the off-hours of an empty house of worship, Sal knelt before the statue of St. Joseph in a posture of prayer, and choked out heartfelt

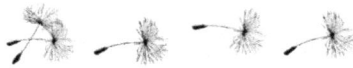

words. "Thank you, Jesus, for sparing my life! I will not take it for granted."

As the statistics for body bags stack up, 416,800 USA military sacrificed their lives for ideals the Allies upheld. Many years later, Sal would stare down the barrel of a gun, sacrificing his life for no apparent reason whatsoever.

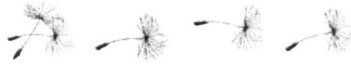

Chapter 26

Setting aside the Italian grinders Sal bestrewed with precision-sliced provolone, capicola, and salami—garnished with lettuce & tomatoes, and drizzles of olive oil and vinegar—he had his own winning combination for begetting success. Initiative, motivation, and perseverance groomed Sal to achieve the ambition of owning and operating his own deli. Preferably outside the borders of Federal Hill, away from the established and well-patronized Capisci Deli. His line of thinking encompassed eliminating competition, while respecting his employers, a husband and wife team, who took him under their wing by mentoring him in every aspect of the business.

A quick study, hands-on Sal received provisions through the back door, prepared foodstuffs in the kitchen, took inventory, and ordered dwindling supplies from local vendors. Ample practice honed proficiency, increasing Sal's eagerness to spread his wings while the *gabagool* was hot. So, a few years after his honorable military discharge, he had socked most of his earnings away in preparation for untying the bib apron strings binding him to a neighborhood institution. Taking into account his reputation as a ladies' man with a penchant for gallant spending on dinner and flowers, Sal still had more than enough moolah to invest in his dream.

A mutual hunger for success formed an alliance between two strange bedfellows. Fist, a friendly fella who liked to chew the fat with customers and staff at his favorite deli, obtained permission to leave a stockpile of business cards on the counter. The financier indulged his epicurean appreciation for fine Italian delicacies sandwiched on a bed of crusty bread by frequenting the Capisci Deli more often than usual as of late. A venture from Foster to Providence provided him a good excuse

to get away from his wife. Lois's mood swings during her early stage of pregnancy with their second child drove him batty.

A miracle, if you asked him, based on their touch-and-go tumbles in the hay coinciding with confirmation of the first impregnation twelve years ago.

***

One of Gordon Doyle's calling cards, ripe for Sal's picking off the counter, provided incentive for backing his objective with a plan. Insisting he call him Fist, the loan originator invited Sal to follow him on over to one of the tables in the rear of the deli. Sal obliged. He sat across from his host, straddling a bentwood chair. With his legs firmly planted, and his arms resting on its frame, Sal craned his neck forward to pick Fist's brain. His well-thought-out questions provided fodder for forthcoming feedback.

Meanwhile, mentally strategizing a soft sell against the backdrop of a red-and-white checkered, vinyl tablecloth, Fist tucked into his oven-warmed chicken cutlet sandwich. Topped with roasted red peppers and melted mozzarella, Sal had prepared it to specifications with perfection. In between bites, Fist brandished a napkin to wipe crumbs off of his mustache.

Soon, the money man steered his potential client toward a business proposition beneficial for both of them. A sure thing for Fist. An Italian deli practically next door to Doyle Savings & Loan, LLC, and a handsome profit margin on the interest his borrower paid on a loan. For a wary venturer, a plausibly lucrative investment in uncharted territory.

Now, to convince a doubting Thomas without yanking his chain. "As for Foster being in the boonies, no dispute there. You can't see the forest for the trees with a population under two thousand. But . . ."

He leaned in, and for emphasis, pounded his fist on the table, causing patrons to flinch and turn their heads. He lowered his voice to a conspiratorial whisper. "Folks like me who want a decent sandwich have to leave town or slap their own together at home. A slice of baloney between two slices of white bread. You follow me?"

In his mind, Sal had followed the trail of breadcrumbs leading him to believe a deli established far away from the main drag eliminated any competition. He nodded his acquiescence, though remained impassive until Fist sweetened the pot.

"Just so happens, in Foster Center—an ideal location, by the way—there's a beauty shop for sale. From what I hear, Grace Bettencourt's in a family way, and eager to sell." Fist arched his brow to accentuate the positive. "Wouldn't take much to throw in a counter or two, would it now?"

Sal rubbed his chin, mulling over a proposal warranting further investigation rather than flat-out dismissal. Fist, not one to allow indecisiveness to ferment into inertia, cut off caution at the pass when ascertaining Sal's day off. "It won't cost a penny to look at the property, would it now? How about my meeting you here on Sunday afternoon, and we take a drive?"

Figuring he had nothing to lose, Sal went along with the idea.

***

In a matter of weeks, the two became steadfast friends for life, however long its duration for each man. Sitting across from one another at Fist's desk in his office, the financier drew up the paper work for Sal's loan. Factoring in his client's sizable out-of-pocket down payment for the future home of Sal's Italian Deli, Fist calculated payback on the principal and interest rate.

While Sal finished adding his signature on the designated dotted lines, Fist took the liberty of pouring a dram of Irish whiskey into two shot glasses.

What Sal didn't know right off the bat would end up killing him!

***

Fist, who drummed up business by fostering the town's rural charm and wholesomeness, prevailed over the wiles of Wayne Cole. A redneck fixing to purchase the salon and convert it to Cole's Rod & Gun Shop, he needed manhandling. Far from calling on Cuz Keen to inflict bodily harm on Wayne, or make him disappear, Fist relied on diplomacy.

"See here, Wayne. A firearms shop slam-bang in the middle of town is all wrong! Mark my words, you want such an enterprise on a backroad with privacy for comings and goings. Not to mention, plenty of land with no obstructions for shooting the breeze."

The numbskull had enough horse sense to withdraw his offer on the property, while nurturing deep resentment toward an Eyetalian intent on setting up shop in his town, damn it! Wayne did his utmost to sabotage business by throwing his weight around likeminded louts.

***

Sal and Fist raised their glasses in the air. "My friend, may your troubles be less and your blessings more. Furthermore, may plenty a hungry belly come to Sal's Italian Deli," toasted Fist.

Heads tilted back, both gents swallowed their shots of liquid fire down the hatch.

Chapter 27

Mindful of the daily grind to and from no man's land, and taking into consideration Fist's defamation of Foster's harsh winters, Sal bit the bullet. One might joke, the chair his tushie sat on at Doyle Savings & Loan, LLC had yet to cool off. There he was, right back at the drawing board, pen poised to sign along the dotted lines on a land loan for a tract of wilderness off of North Road.

In for a penny, in for a pound. The near foreseeable future predicated Sal would need a construction loan to build his cabin in the woods. Before the felling of the first tree, Sal had already fallen hard for someone he wanted to keep his home fires burning.

***

Love at first bite!

Sal muttered those four words to his daughter during the first leg of their grief-stricken ride home from the cemetery. Well-nigh sealing his wife's entombment with the epitaph he'd chosen for her half of their double headstone. Although Etta refrained from rolling her eyes, it struck her as a line of bull.

For good reason.

The long-range plans her mother had disclosed during their private jammies' sessions fell short of mentioning her father at all. Worse, her mother glossed over the details of their courtship with a synopsis befitting one of those Cozy romance novels. It didn't take a mathematical genius to figure out the close call between their wedding anniversary and the date of her birth.

Scrapping all the malarkey, Etta preferred her own line of ghoulish thinking, tainted by Sister Mary Catharine's imposed

summer reading list which included a selection of Poe's short stories. Dead at age thirty-six, the epitaph, *A Premature Burial*, made more sense.

Oh, she had no misgivings her parents loved each other from the exchanged glances she observed from afar. Often enough, the muffled grunts and squeals transmitted through the walls of their bedroom adjoining hers, gave proof through the night it was so.

Out of the question, ever, any inquiry on her part to dig up their past. On that closed subject, Etta buried her head in the sand then and there inside Momma's station wagon. A discreet glance at her dad, wallowing in mournfulness and plaintiveness at the wheel, convinced her to back off. Etta focused straight ahead during the last leg of the journey to their new phase in life.

The quiver of a smile she detected on her dad during a fleeting glimpse suggested he called to mind a remembrance justifying those words engraved in stone.

The entire truth of the matter wasn't for her to see.

***

Truth of the matter:

"Pull up a chair, broadside—why don't you!" The gals scowled at Gloria's coarse insinuation.

Like a moth attracted to a flame, Sal took the fiery redhead up on her invitation, a common man eager to pit his wits against an elite, educated foursome. Initially stricken by Gloria's beauty, his attraction withered on the vine, having seen enough of Rita Hayworth pinned up on his locker at the barracks.

Sal's attention strayed to Rosalia as she took the first bite of her meatball grinder. Proficient in sizing up women with a sidelong glance, he got a gander of the goodies from bosom to

brow line, and liked what he saw. A gentleman who respected women, he minded his manners while he imagined running his fingers through her cascade of tawny brown curls.

Belying the demureness of downcast eyes which came with the territory of sinking one's teeth into thick crusty bread to penetrate mashed meatballs, Rosalia sneaked a peak, however limited in scope, at Sal's face. Jutting out in topographic relief, an aquiline nose with a bump on its ridge. Quite an affront to her line of vision!

Biting one side of her lower lip to stifle an outburst of laughter at his expense, tomato sauce dribbled along her chin. No laughing matter! Self-conscious under Sal's casual scrutiny, Rosalia grabbed her napkin and dabbed at the trickle.

Looking upward in the act of making amends, she felt her cheeks flush from the rising temperature of discomposure which had nothing to do with swiping the sauce. 'Twas how he held her hostage with his gaze when they locked eyes. Floundering in the depths of his pensive, brown beholders, Rosalia averted her crystal blues to save herself from drowning.

Falling head over heels for a total stranger didn't fit into her grand scheme of things. Not with March just about over and graduation in mid-May. Soon as feasible, she'd put her shoulder to the wheel, gearing up for a road trip with Gloria.

Careful not to bite off more than she could chew, sandwich and self-imposed sanction, Rosalia held herself in check during their conversation, despite Sal's swashbuckling grin which threatened to undermine her efforts of impartiality. Trying her best to distance herself from him, she'd nod at her pals, attempting to draw them into their discussion. They pretended not to notice.

As sandwiches dwindled, and dialoguing died down, Rosalia took it upon herself to dissuade Sal from sinking his

even grillwork of choppers into her any further than he already had. On their way out, over the acoustics of wood scraping along tile from pushing their vacated chairs in place behind the table, Rosalia dropped a bombshell.

San Francisco!

At last, she'd gotten a rise out of one in particular. Gloria played right into her hands, batting eyelashes at Sal while disclosing her supporting role to substantiate Rosalia's claim. "Oh, yeah! And, I'm riding with her as far as L.A. This small-town girl has big dreams of becoming a Hollywood star, you betcha!"

Sal stopped himself from dousing the fiery redhead's starry-eyed scheme to cash in on her beauty. It wasn't his place to bring up the naked corpse, cut in half and drained of blood in '47, nicknamed "The Black Dahlia".

For all of her scheming, Rosalia's bombshell failed to detonate.

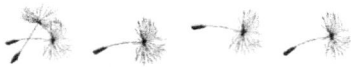

Chapter 28

The only ticking time bombs set to go off were the loud pops of champagne corks at various parties Pembroke grads and gatecrashers planned on attending after the commencement ceremony the Sunday before Memorial Day. In three weeks. This timespan somewhat coincided with the advance notice Sal had given his employer.

Though neither admitted it to each other, both dreaded the countdown. Rosalia tossed and turned in bed at night, sawing wood against her own grain. Sal paced the floor in his apartment, formulating a strategy to counteract erring on the side of caution the way he had whenever they sat across from one another. Broadly speaking, the other women in their presence hampered his romantic overture of asking Rosalia out on a date.

Catch as catch can, he had the pleasure of Rosalia's company all to himself twice. Several calendar squares in between their table talks discouraged him from jumping the gun with a cool cucumber who had her heart set on joyriding to Frisco. In any case, copping the cavalier attitude of nothing ventured, nothing gained, Sal's bravado gave him the green light to move forward.

Backing his foolhardy decisiveness, Sal's schnozzola sniffed out Rosalia's body language. A connoisseur of women, he interpreted each gesture as a telltale sign he meant more to her than she let on. When he touched her shoulder, she leaned into him. She laughed at his offhand remarks, funny or not. Twirling a curl around her finger, she came across as flirtatious. Above all, she listened to what he had to say with rapt attention, expressing her concern over the hazardous driving conditions he'd have to grapple with along Foster's primitive roads.

Lightening up, she dropped him a line, giving credit where credit was due.

Whose woods these are I think I know.

His house is in the village though.

Down to the wire, he vowed to act on the feelings in his bones and those in his heart the next time she came into the deli. Pike's Peak or Bust, he'd lay it on the line, hoping to either postpone or prevent her from chasing a poetic pipe-dream.

Third time's a charm.

Until he could do just that, he paid a visit to the Providence Public Library and borrowed *The Poetry of Robert Frost*.

***

"Are you sure you won't change your mind?" asked Joan, poking her head through the partly opened door to Rosalia's room, and espying her friend lying in bed with the bedcover tucked under her chin.

Gloria had commandeered their evening by suggesting they take in a movie at the Avon Cinema, a theater inside the Brown-Pembroke beltway of College Hill on the East Side. She nudged Joan out of the way, peering in to sweeten the pot. "Tickets for *All About Eve* are half-price for seniors."

Gloria stepped aside for Helen to add her two cents worth. "Can't you give it the old college try?"

"Nope. I'm going to sleep off this headache. You bitches enjoy yourselves and fill me in tomorrow." Rosalia turned the other cheek and closed her eyes.

At that, Helen shut the door with painstaking civility to deaden the click of the doorknob. The trail of Joan's voice penetrated the sealed tomb. "Just as well. The bags under her eyes are suitcases!"

Payola for the sleep-deprived!

Perceiving no further flurry of activity in the hall, Rosalia kicked her way out from under the quilt. Vaulting out of bed, scantily clad in a bra, panties, and knee socks, she had some unfinished business to address as soon as her feet touched down on the carpet. She made a mad dash to the closet, plucking preselected, steam-ironed clothes off of hangers. Originally pegged for the movie theater, she intended this outfit to set the stage for her charade.

On cue, she grabbed a pastel-pink, button-down blouse with a round Peter Pan collar. Its long sleeves demanded single-handed dexterity from a nervous wreck to button both wide-wrist cuffs on the fly. From the other hanger, she snatched a pair of black, gabardine, wide-leg trousers with a flat front. She wiggled and waggled her fanny into them, battling the bulge of tucking the blouse inside for a tailored fit. Put together, she stepped into black-and-white oxfords, tying the laces into straight bows.

Up to speed, Rosalia peered at her reflection in the mirror above the dresser, frowning in disparagement at the crestfallen face of a Basset Hound. Averting her gaze away from the darkness overshadowing the hollows of her eyes, she wielded a hairbrush to smooth down flyaway curls. Satisfied, she proceeded to blend a dab of pink rouge on her upper cheekbones for contouring. Done, she glided a tube of Pink Dawn along the plush pillows of her lips, and blotted them with a tissue she crumpled and discarded into a wicker wastebasket by the dresser.

On a roll, Rosalia seized hold of a black, chunky-knit sweater draped over the back of her cushioned desk chair. Bracing for the chilly night air, she threw it on and jammed her arms inside the sleeves, dispensing with buttons in her frugality to scram. For her accessory after the fact, she abided by the

round, crocheted, drawstring purse her mother had gifted her. Used only on special occasions, she removed it from the bottom dresser drawer and handled the keepsake with gentleness.

No sooner had Rosalia flipped the light switch off, the door slammed from behind without hitting her on the way out.

The die was cast!

Chapter 29

One door closed, and another with a high-pitched squeak, opened for Rosalia to enter the deli. Jumpy, in comparison to her three chums who had settled themselves in their cinema seats. Munching popcorn, they took in the opening scene where narrator and theater critic, Addison De Witt, presents the Sarah Siddons Award to Eve Harrington.

The only reason Rosalia faked a headache and showed up on the premises at all, hinged on decorum in saying good-bye to a newfound friend she'd never imagine coming across again, respective of their divergent paths. The Sword of Damocles, in the guise of well wishes, dangled over her head by a metaphorical thread, emboldening her initiative.

Words were left unsaid during their last buzz session when Sal shoved off for an inrush of customers. These, she repeated verbatim over and over in her mind through bouts of restlessness, and past her bedtime for a full fortnight. For an airtight swan song, she drummed up a little white lie, enhanced by dressing the part to smooth her way for exiting stage left.

By the looks of it, quicker than she thought. Behind the counter, she caught sight of Sal in the act of doffing his apron and paper hat. He ran his fingers through dark hair, tamping down displaced strands over a mop top, long and slicked back with pomade. In the habit of keeping tabs on the door whenever its vibrato announced someone's patronage, his heart skipped a beat in anticipation of tempting fate.

Feeling the warmth radiating from Sal's broad grin which glimmered in his eyes, Rosalia weakened at the knees, obliging her to overcompensate in order to steady her gait moving toward the counter. Sal rounded the bend to the other side,

refraining from scooping her in his arms. He kept his cool. While addressing Rosalia, he motioned with an index finger for his replacement to step forward. "What can Tony prepare for you?"

Would Sal leave her high and dry again? Was he in a hurry to pick up a hot date? Why on earth should she care?

Her stomach clenched at the mere thought of food. Her mind raced to steer their conversation to a terminus of amicable departure. Stepping aside to make room for a customer closing in behind her, she let Tony off the hook. "Nothing for me, thanks."

Tony's quizzical expression presented an ultimatum for her to explain herself. Blushing, she stammered through the ad-libbed truth. "Ac-c-tually, I chanced touching base with S-s-al. Looks like I got here just in time."

Sensing her embarrassment, Sal shot Tony a withering glance to dissuade a cut-up from giving Rosalia a hard time by dishing out a suggestive remark. Since Rosalia's fancy threads insinuated she had big plans that didn't include him, Sal deigned to impose his power of dissuasion, no matter what she had up her sweater sleeve. First order of business—isolate a damsel in distress—on his terms.

"How 'bout we move out of the way and get a table in the back corner?"

Just so happened, the only one available placed them where Fist exerted his influence over Sal. Fancy that! His second order of business demanded he lead like a man in making the right moves. Before Sal implemented his cat-and-mouse power play, curiosity got the best of him.

"You, okay?"

So, her under-eye bags were that obvious!

"If my Bette Davis lamps are flipping your lid, I've been staying up late cramming for finals," she lied, about to add one more before hitting the road. "Anyway, heading in this direction, I thought I'd stop by to wish you —"

Sal refused to hear what might have come next, making his move to lead Rosalia astray, pouncing on her own cue to improvise without compromise. "Glad you did! I was about to make a break for it before dark to check up on my new digs," he blurted. "Why not come along for the ride! For sure, we'll work up an appetite after breathing in Foster's country air."

In a flux of abeyance, Sal's heart thumped.

Sounds tempting, but I've made plans to meet up with the crew for a night on the town. According to her well-rehearsed script.

In her own flux of abeyance, Rosalia flubbed her lines. Following the dictates of her heart, she cast her fate to the wind along curved roads with potholes. "I'd like that. From what you've told me about those rocky roads to no man's land, we'd better take my wagon."

Chapter 30

Handed the keys, Sal unlocked and swung the wood-trimmed, passenger door open for Rosalia, standing behind it until she settled in. Coming around to situate himself on the driver's side, Sal adjusted the seat to accommodate a compact Italian of slight build, who, at five-foot-nine, towered over Rosalia by nine inches. Once out of the parking lot and onto Atwells Avenue, he fine-tuned the rearview mirror.

Before Interstate 95 made inroads in Rhode Island, two-lane highways and secondary roads paved the way for travel. A little after five when they got their head start along a 21-mile journey, it would take the better part of an hour to get there. Working in their favor, a 7:53 p.m. sunset on that May evening, allowing them a little leeway for exploring their surroundings before showdown.

During the drive, Sal steered their conversation to the ever-changing scenery in front of the windshield. The last thing he wanted was for Rosalia to rewind what she started saying back at the Capisci Deli. No matter how much finesse she'd drum up to soften the blow at the finish line, it all boiled down to one thing.

So long, pal!

Going along for the ride, in a manner of speaking, Rosalia held up her end in keeping their lengthy commentary running to suspend disbelief in impending doom. The notion of backpedaling to verbalize a foregone conclusion forced her to swallow the lump in her throat.

***

Based on the remnants of natural light remaining, and the existence of streetlights versus their nonexistence, Sal's thoughts swerved in a different direction from where he originally intended to go. Instead of proceeding to Sal's Italian Deli in Foster Center, he took the right leading to the outback of North Road. That 2-mile, 4-minute deviation along the road less traveled would alter the course of their lives.

He maneuvered the station wagon off of North Road's narrow artery and coasted into the rutted clearing a ways, mowing down stray brush which snapped and crackled under the wheels. He left the gearshift in first, pulled the handbrake, and switched off the ignition. Facing Rosalia, he beamed with pride. "If you can visualize it, that there open stretch in front of us, is my cabin in the woods."

Her eyes twinkled with merriment. "Yeah, with a stretch of my imagination, I can see your curtains billowing in the breeze."

Sal let out a guffaw. With a sheepish grin, he met her gaze. "I admit these woods are dark and deep. And, I've got miles to go before I sleep—inside my cabin!" He took pleasure in her slack-jawed astonishment. "What? You think a deli man don't know poetry from pastrami?"

Rosalia felt the heat of embarrassment flushing her cheeks. "N-n-o! Not at all!" she protested. "You're like my father. A self-made man capable of doing anything you put your mind to. In fact—you amaze me!"

Overcome with emotion, Sal interjected humor to keep his voice from breaking up. "Self-serving too! Thanks to your touch of Frost that day, I hoofed it to the library and signed out one of his books. Opened it and actually turned the pages!"

Rosalia's reaction catapulted his heart over the moon. Her eyes glistening, she placed her hand over his. "And?"

"I'm into it. For a poet, that guy has a realistic way of depicting rural life in New England so it doesn't come off as bullshit."

She made a mental note to do a reality sweep for dung deposits in her own poetic compositions.

Sal interlaced his fingers with hers. "Ready for a grand tour of the grounds? Come on. Let's get out and flex our legs."

***

As Sal led the way a single step ahead of her, Rosalia exercised caution navigating her way around the booby trip-traps of exposed tree roots and bulldozer ruts throughout the steep gradient. He pointed out a pile of rough-hewn timber, some of which, he'd already chopped into logs and kindling. At the mercy of his contractor, several designated oaks marked for death, splotched with fluorescent pink aerosol, awaited a chainsaw massacre. It had to be done in preparation for grading soil around the cabin's foundation and leveling a yard around its perimeter.

Awed by the surrounding wilderness awash in verdant green, Rosalia relaxed her vigilance and tripped over a protruding root, venting a startled cry. Sal spun around as she pitched forward like a tree. He grabbed her by the arm, inches before smashing the ground headfirst and eating dirt. Within kissing distance of Sal's mud-streaked, penny loafers, Rosalia wondered why he'd subject his Sunday-best, shoe-shined leathers to such harsh conditions.

Unless, he fibbed his way to Foster from the get-go, willing to sacrifice his soles to the ground he walked on. A pot calling the kettle black, she couldn't fault Sal for a ruse she'd fully embraced when suggested.

Attributing Rosalia's unsteadiness to a forestalled fall, Sal's chivalric reflexes prompted him to put a protective arm around

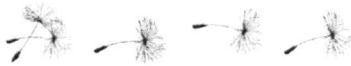

her shoulder as they picked their way through the underbrush in heading back to the wagon. Platonic enough. Up to when he had second thoughts about opening the door for his leading lady, coming up with an idea that rivaled his ploy to postpone parting ways.

He leaned his arm against the doorframe. When Rosalia turned to face him, he moved in close. She moved in closer. Sal's lips blazed a trail of kisses along the bare skin above the neckline of her blouse, his breath warming the soft contours of her throat and igniting a fever in her loins.

The wanton sensations Sal stirred inside her tore down the invisible barrier she'd fortified through resisting romantic involvement. His heart at stake, Sal stepped back and peered into Rosalia's eyes, probing their depths to detect a heat index on a par with his. Otherwise, with courtesy and deference, he'd open the passenger door for her and backtrack to Providence, distancing himself from someone whose heart didn't measure up to his, and licking his wounds to boot.

Rosalia's gaze radiated a mutual burning desire, giving Sal a taste of victory right before his lips brushed hers with a soft kiss. Then another. In unison, they varied the pace and pressure of their kisses, until Sal upped the ante by grazing Rosalia's lips with the tip of his tongue. When she reciprocated, Sal stepped back and cupped her chin in his hand. An overture overlaid with tenderness, he asked, "Any objection to us taking a back seat?"

Stroking his cheek with the back of her hand, she replied, "None whatsoever."

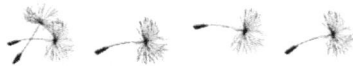

Chapter 31

Rosalia shimmied her bottom along leather upholstery, leaning her back against the door behind the driver's seat. Sal closed the opposite door, confining them inside their make-do passion pit. He discarded a lightweight shirt jacket, one of those boy-next-door, Van Johnson types with an elastic waistband and flap pocket on the chest. Rosalia followed suit, easing out of her bulky sweater as Sal stripped down to his bare torso. Furthering himself along, he undid the buckle of a skinny, alligator belt looped around the waist of close-fitting, crisp, cotton-wash trousers. Needing more wiggle room to accommodate an erection making headway, he unzipped his fly.

Out of respect for the only woman he ever idolized, in contrast to the accustomed dime-a-dozen dames, Sal led like a man in laying the preliminary groundwork for their sacred rite of passage. Genuflecting with one knee on the floor in cramped quarters, he began taking matters in his own hands. Slowly unbuttoning and removing Rosalia's blouse, he afforded her the grace period to sprawl along the back seat with a modicum of comfort.

Disarming her with the sort of dexterity that comes with practice, Sal then unhooked and slipped off her bra, draping both garments over the front seat. His eyes feasted upon the splendor of Rosalia's breasts, their nipples erect. But, his peepers didn't tarry for long! Hornier than a toad, she put an arm around his neck, pulling him toward the vortex of her lofty peaks.

Sal took her up on the invitation, caressing the tops, sides, and bottoms of her breasts. Writhing in pleasure from his ministrations, Sal advanced to circling each areola with his finger. Encouraged by Rosalia's moans, he flicked his tongue at

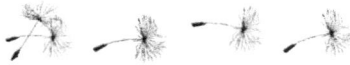

one of her erect nipples, the rhythmic thrusts of a serpent spearheading its way to alternately licking and sucking on each bullseye.

Unsure of Rosalia's compliance with the Catholic Church's condemnation of going all the way before marriage, and without a spare condom in his wallet, Sal thought he'd blaze a trail with his tongue toward the Promised Land. All the better, if she orgasmed. He'd consider himself blessed if she reciprocated a blow job before they called it a night in commemorating their formerly nondescript courtship.

Wrong!

Rosalia's eager beaver demanded penetration! Especially after Sal nibbled on her collar bone. Impenitent, she felt no remorse or regret for having sex more times than she could count with Lenny Weintraub, a senior med student at Brown. With Lenny ready to roll on a condom when primed, they'd scratch the surface of each other's itch, in what amounted to a gymnastic fait accompli devoid of lovemaking and leaving much to desire.

Along the back seat of a Ford Woodie wagon, double indemnity took effect: a surge in her vaginal tide and succumbing to love at Sal's first bite.

She'd be darned if she'd admit it during a touch-and-go situation.

While Sal busied himself topside, Rosalia took advantage by accessing the open door of his trousers and trespassed into his undershorts. Groping and grasping, she grabbed onto, what felt like to her, a thick and stiff hunk of salami. Gliding the pads of her fingers on her left hand up and down her find, she freed a hot-throb from captivity, distracting Sal from forging ahead with his original game plan.

Putting a lull to good use, she lowered her britches and undies to her ankles, leaving no doubt in Sal's mind as to their wayward direction on a deserted road. Or, whether Rosalia was a devout Catholic. Up for the task in more ways than one, he dropped his drawers to his ankles. His manhood at full mast, Sal thought it only fair to mention, "I don't have a rubber, so I'll pull out."

Until he took that plunge, Sal still didn't know for sure if Rosalia held onto her virginity, but thought it impolite to ask. When she fished a vial of vegetable oil out of her purse and handed it to him, he had his doubts, but couldn't care less. For him, sex with Rosalia constituted a labor of love, despite abandoning foreplay. Quivering with excitement, they maneuvered themselves into the missionary position.

***

At first dip, Sal's extremity simmered in a hotbed of pulsations. The tingle created a ripple effect, prompting him to speed things along at his end to sate a mutual hunger. Deeper. Faster. Harder.

Panting and groaning accompanied their synchronized locomotion of thrusting and swiveling. At the 5.4-minute benchmark, Rosalia felt a stiffening and twitching inside her. Despite putting herself at risk for an unplanned pregnancy, she wanted him to flood her with his warmth. Before Sal could pull out, she grabbed his butt, pushing him in deeper.

"I want you to come inside me!" she expelled in a throaty growl.

Up against a wall with no way out, Sal erupted, shooting a hot stream of semen against Rosalia's bedrock, hitting the A-spot she didn't know existed within her confines. Pleasurable shock waves shook her to the core, releasing an orgasmic tide, something she'd never experienced with Lenny. Wrinkling her

nose, and clenching her toes, Rosalia cried out in ecstasy. "O-h-h, Gah-h-h-ddd!"

Baptism by fire!

Chapter 32

Without uttering the four-letter word signifying what each felt inside their hearts toward one another, they trod lightly during the lull leading up to Rosalia's graduation. Sal didn't want to set off any tripwires. Instead, he curried favor by treating his beloved to movies and occasional meals. Their stomping ground, Angelo's, serving authentic and affordable Italian comfort food since 1924. Nearing the end of their rope, Camille's, a swanky Rhode Island dining landmark since 1914, the purported favorite haunt of New England crime boss, Raymond L.S. Patriarca.

Eateries of diverse ambience, both were within short walking distance of Sal's flat above the deli on Atwells Avenue. Culminating most of their evenings, they made love in Sal's bed. Standard procedure during their blissful stretch, Sal slipped on a condom to corral a bucking bronco that had escaped from the barn only once.

Habit-forming, Rosalia relished waking in their entanglement of limbs, reluctant to leave Sal's side at dawn to drive back to her dorm. Or, for that matter, loath to leave him altogether. In retrospect, pursuing a poet's pipe dream struck her as a scatterbrained scheme whose rhyme and reason lost ground to romance. But, lately, the frequent need to urinate forced her to disconnect in the middle of the night and tiptoe to the bathroom, a blameworthy source for tiredness, in conjunction with overthinking.

***

Down to the wire of their cohabitation, Sal pulled out all the stops before they finished breakfast and Rosalia took off for Pembroke. Lacking an appetite, she toyed with her oatmeal,

unable to shake the haze of malaise that made her feel so sluggish. Observing the absentminded trenches dug with her spoon, and fretful she'd forego eating to sabotage his plan, Sal forged ahead through spontaneous combustion.

During one of their timeshares, Etta thought her mother's disclosure far-fetched, reeking of conduct unbecoming for her plainspoken and pragmatic dad, ill-disposed to flights of fancy.

"Desperate times call for desperate measures," her momma had replied.

Sal rose from the chair opposite Rosalia, scraping its legs on the worn linoleum, grandstanding in unison with the screech. "I'm in the mood for Puccini!"

Diverted from going stir-crazy with a spoon, Rosalia looked up, waggling her brows. "Frost? Now, Puccini? I've been sleeping with a Renaissance man!"

Leaving nothing to chance, Sal had put Puccini in his place the night before. He moseyed on over to the record player in the open living room. Turning it on, he picked up the arm and placed the needle on the outside groove for "Musetta's Waltz" from *La Boheme* to sweeten his plot.

With his heart in his mouth, Sal padded barefoot to the kitchen. He knelt in front of Rosalia, reached for her hand, and laced his fingers with hers. "Don't you know I've fallen in love with you for the rest of my life? Don't you know I was yours when you took the first bite of your sandwich and sauce dribbled down your chin?"

Without pausing for effect, or allowing for his declaration to penetrate, Sal let go of Rosalia's hand long enough for him to slip a diamond on her ring finger. "I want you to scrap your plans and marry me!"

Moonstruck, Rosalia sobbed and threw her arms around his neck. When she loosened her hold and peered into his eyes, hers

glistened with tears. Time to own up. "That night, in the back seat, when you nibbled on my collar bone, it was love at first bite!"

"Does that mean yes?"

Whatever the logic behind Rosalia's rendition, Etta felt shortchanged by a glossed-over version of her parents' courtship waltzing to Puccini. If her momma conveyed sketchy details solely to reinforce the significance of her birth name, so mote it be on the subject of Musetta.

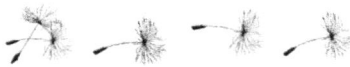

Chapter 33

Feeling the worse for wear, belied by the buoyancy of walking on cloud nine, Rosalia tore into Helen's dorm, their unofficial headquarters for gatherings. As agreed upon during their last powwow, the bitches had checked in before graduation rehearsal. While three of them were in the midst of kibitzing, Rosalia flashed her engagement ring under their noses. Doing so, she plugged a dam of torrential conversation, startling them from uttering another word. For a few seconds. Collectively, they gathered their wits and mobilized to dispense a round of hugs.

The most timid of the sisterhood, and the first to find her tongue, Joan stepped forward. "I'm so happy, I could cry! And, a little jealous you found a good man to support you."

Helen shot Joan a look of contempt. "Remind me to knock some sense into you later! On how to use a college degree for opening doors without having to spit and polish a man's knob for financial security."

While Joan fidgeted with embarrassment, Helen turned to Rosalia, shaking her head in disgust. "And, *you*! When you're married to Sal, maybe he'll cool his meatballs so you can get some sleep. You look like hell!"

Rosalia scrunched her fingers into a tight fist and shook it in Gloria's direction. "One untoward remark out of you—right in the kisser!"

Taking a threat at face value, Gloria raised her arms in surrender to the space between them. "A-w-w! Don't be sore. Helen's on the rag. She told us so herself this morning. That means she's not responsible for her reactions. Right?"

Gloria's withering glance meant to cower Helen into recanting, only served to embolden her resolve. "If I had any decency, I'd take it all back. But, I meant what I said to Rosalia and Joan. And, Gloria—you're gonna get yours too! 'Cause I don't mince words with those I love."

Also feeling the pinch of mood swings and emotional sensitivity in anticipation of her period, Rosalia burst into tears. They all did.

"Come on," quivered Helen. Group hug before we walk out the door and raise hell during procession practice! Let's shake on it."

***

Unbeknownst to Gloria, she'd undertake the walk-on role of her lifetime. Humming "Put the Blame on Mame," the song she'd shimmy and sway to when padding barefoot in her terry robe, fresh out of the shower, was mere child's play.

Not this time. Abandoning shtick, Gloria tightened her belt and headed for Rosalia's room, wanting to square things and assure her pal she harbored no ill will over the San Francisco shake-up. The trickle of parents coming into town over the next couple of days to attend the graduation ceremony for Pembroke's Class of 1950 motivated Gloria to knock on her door. No telling when there'd be another opportunity.

From the far side of the partition, a muffled retort, "Go away!"

Gloria had no intention of disappearing around the corner. She jiggled the knob on the unlocked door which opened for her to witness Rosalia sobbing headfirst into a pillow. And, discover her diamond ring by a set of keys on the stark surface of a desk bared for next fall's resident.

At a loss for words, Gloria pitter-pattered to the bed and rubbed Rosalia's back. Lifting her head and turning a tear-

streaked face toward an intruder, she shrieked an earth-shattering revelation.

***

Feeling more exhausted than warranted from marching in a mock procession, Rosalia dragged herself to her room. She called Sal, letting him know she'd come by the apartment when he finished his shift, rather than join him for a bite at the deli. She voiced her need to crash and sleep off sluggishness, implicating the distance covered during rehearsal.

Before diving on the bed, discomfort from sensitive, swollen breasts goaded her into rummaging for the wall calendar she'd packed away in a box for transport to New York. Smitten with Sal and addle-brained, one day blended into the next leading up to graduation. She'd lost touch with keeping her eye on the red checkmark designating the onset of her period.

How she'd welcome an onrush of bloodletting for some relief!

Slayed by the whereabouts of a red flag, Rosalia dropped to her knees, cradling her head in disbelief. Nine days late! Evident from the logic of hindsight, she concluded her ornery horniness in the back seat of a station wagon occurred during her fertile days.

The likely outcome of reckless ramifications reverberated in her skull, numb to all else. So-called pregnancy tests, non-existent back then, Rosalia relied on her own biorhythms and female intuition as burdensome proof that her overwhelming maladies went above and beyond a late period.

She tugged the quarter-carat diamond ring off her finger, tossed it on the desk and flung herself onto the bed. Through an onrush of scalding tears, she vowed to make good on her promise to stop at Sal's. To break off their engagement! She

didn't want a marriage proposal expedited by a man's moral obligation.

***

Mind-blown! Gawping, not on account of Rosalia's admission, but because of her cockamamie reason for calling it off with Sal. Gloria ransacked her brain for a pearl of wisdom to dispense, hoping she'd inspire a change of heart. Coming up empty, she settled for an impact statement. "Sal never would have asked you to marry him in the first place if he didn't love you unconditionally."

Unmoved, Rosalia narrowed her focus on Gloria, her eyes shutting of their own volition. "Come back in an hour to wake me."

She butted her head against the pillow and conked out from the narcotic effect of exhaustion. Waiting in the wings, Gloria stood by Rosalia's bedside, making darn sure she'd fallen asleep before setting the wheels of a Ford Woodie wagon in motion. Swiping the keys and ring off of the desk, she absconded on tiptoe out of the room, closing the door behind her without registering a sound.

Charging down the hall and into her room, Gloria grabbed the same blouse and pair of slacks she'd peeled off before her shower, and threw them back on. Mindful of trickling time, she ran from the dorm at reckless speed, nearly pitching forward and tumbling down the stairs. Hustling to the station wagon with the key ready to spring the lock, Gloria asked the saints above for guidance in overstepping her bounds.

Chapter 34

Steering her way to Sal's place was a no-brainer, considering its familiar location. Getting there proved problematic for a novice driving a wagon powered by a flathead V8 engine with a 3-speed transmission. From watching Rosalia in action, she got the hang of accelerating and decelerating gears in sequence.

When the steering wheel juddered, Gloria stepped on the clutch and shifted. All of the jerking and jolting along a journey to alert a jilted lover jangled her nerves. Increasing her agitation, the frustration in parking the wagon parallel to a curb. Engaged in the repetitive calisthenics of plying her torso and upper arms to browbeat a brute into submission, Gloria worked up a sweat and suffered sore muscles from wrenching the wheel back and forth. Several inaccurate alignments resulted in stalling for lack of coordination.

For all of these laborious efforts, her curbside calibrations missed their mark, leaving the wagon vulnerable to a sideswipe. The least of Gloria's concerns in her race against time, she peered into the rearview mirror to check for any vehicles coming from behind. None approaching, she released the door handle, planted her feet onto Atwells Avenue, and hit the ground running until she reached the top of the second-floor landing.

***

Thrown off guard by tenacious pounding, conduct unbecoming for Rosalia who had her own key, Sal yanked the door open. He stepped back before the caller's follow-up blow smashed his nose. Taken aback at discovering the brazen

bombshell darkening his doorway, Sal's jaw dropped, rendering him speechless.

Taken aback at the abrupt appearance of Rosalia's suitor, shirtless and sculpted, Gloria's mouth opened and froze. Within arm's reach, she had no trouble envisioning what Rosalia was up against in Sal's bed. Snapping out of a self-induced stupor, she fished the ring out of the breast pocket on her blouse and levelled it with Sal's gaze of disbelief.

"If you're keen on marrying Rosalia, you'll need to propose again." Thunderstruck on his threshold, Gloria sliced through the silence with rapier wit. "If we hurry and make it to Pembroke before the hour's up, you can wake your slumbering Briar Rose with a kiss."

Reverting to the last conversation he had with Rosalia helped to clarify his confusion. Somewhat. "Let me grab a shirt."

Sal be nimble; Sal be quick! Sal turned up unbuttoned and untucked.

"Come on! I parked Rosalia's wagon next to the curb. Sorta!"

When they reached the bottom of the stairs, Gloria dangled the keys in front of him. "You'd better take the wheel because I don't have a driver's license."

***

Sal commandeered the Woodie, navigating it through a series of tree-lined side streets, careful not to exceed the speed limit or run a stop sign. Coming across enough surprises for one evening, with yet another whopper to rack up, he couldn't chance getting pulled over for a traffic violation. Racking his brain, Sal tried to come up with a plausible reason for Rosalia's sudden change of heart.

Stumped, he appealed to Gloria. "Mind giving me a heads-up so I can work my angle?"

She offered nothing. "That's for you to find out from Rosalia."

He thought as much, and admired a friend's loyalty. For the few remaining roads not yet taken, Sal kept a stiff upper lip and Gloria remained tight-lipped.

Once inside the dorm, and destined to part ways, Gloria addressed the issue. "Good luck, Sal. You're gonna need it!"

Instead of buckling at the knees, determination lengthened a purposeful stride to win back his future bride.

***

As quietly as Gloria slipped out of Rosalia's room at the top of the hour, Sal slipped in a few minutes shy of waking his sleeping beauty at her behest.

Dead to the world!

No matter how he'd rouse her, Rosalia would be in for a rude awakening. Preferring to wait in the wings rather than startle her, Sal picked up the desk chair and placed it next to her bed on the side where she lay sleeping. Sitting it out, he kept vigil, peeking every now and then, at the vision of loveliness in front of him.

Holding the engagement ring between his thumb and forefinger, Sal gazed into the miniature, round diamond as though it were a crystal ball capable of dispensing semantics for a secondhand proposal.

Sal's beating heart stilled. Rosalia stirred.

Her eyes fluttered open. Deluded from sleep drunkenness, she took in her immediate surroundings. An unforeseeable

glimpse of Sal jarred her awake. She bolted upright in bed. "What are you doing here?"

"A friend of yours came to get me."

Mentally narrowing the list of suspects down to one through her brain fog, Rosalia challenged him. "Gloria? She doesn't have a car, let alone a driver's license."

"You might say she borrowed your wheels and improvised."

Rosalia glared into space, appalled at Gloria's gall to hijack her station wagon. Aghast after the fact, she broke into a cold sweat from apprehension over the punch line a go-between may have delivered making a house call.

Sal raised the diamond ring at eye-level as collateral for a confrontation. "Is there something you've been meaning to tell me?"

Under duress from the ambiguity of Sal's reproach, Rosalia hyperventilated. Woozy, with the lean-to of a headboard to fall back against for moral support, she mentally groped her way in the dark, trembling as she sought clarification.

"Would I be parroting what Gloria already told you?"

"Other than advising me to propose again, she gave away nothin'! Believe me, I asked."

Rosalia's split-second reprieve of relief swerved onto foul territory. "Save your breath!" Cutting it close to the bone, "Sure as death and taxes, I'm pregnant! Furthermore, I will not allow the parent trap to shame us into rushing down the altar so we can squeak by public disgrace, only to suffer the consequences of misery afterward."

Rosalia dissolved into blinding tears, granting Sal a blessing in disguise for him to absorb the shock and man up in a minute. Furthermore, he felt squeezed to come up with the right

156

words to say, knowing all too well their potential to redefine their relationship forever, for better or for worse.

Pulling a tissue from the box on her nightstand, Sal sopped up Rosalia's deluge of tears. Beads of sweat formed on his upper lip. "Sooner or later this was bound to happen, even if we hadn't planned on it."

Despite her stubborn resistance, Rosalia restrained herself from interrupting Sal's soliloquy. "But, it did. As the result of an act of love. And, I can guess where." Bolstered by her passivity, Sal bared his soul. "To be honest—I've gotten cold feet just thinking about your parents sinking their dough into the lavish wedding they never had for themselves. Parading down the aisle in a monkey suit for hundreds of spectators isn't the wedding ceremony I had in mind when I proposed to you the first time. A quickie in front of a judge is more to my liking.

"Now, as for my proposing again. I can't top Puccini on a bended knee. So, Rosalia, whaddya say? You gonna marry me, or what?"

Convinced of Sal's sincerest intentions, she caved. Comparable to the aftermath of Sal's first proposal, Puccini or no Puccini, Rosalia threw her arms around his neck.

"Is that your second yes?"

She leaned back and peered into his eyes with adoration. "It's my final!"

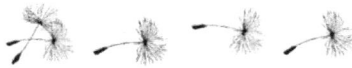

Chapter 35

The ritual of turning their tassels on the occasion of Pembroke's commencement ceremony not only symbolized the recognition of earning a degree, but stoked separation anxiety among the bitches. The winds of change, about to blow, would scatter them in separate directions, but not before the official pronouncement of Rosalia and Sal as husband and wife three days hence.

***

During the remains of Graduation Day, in the shadow of introducing a fiancé to her parents, Rosalia's mother shepherded her away to reopen their interrupted conversation in private. Team planners, the shrewd tycoon capitalized on his wife's distraction to size up a prospective son-in-law they knew next to nothing about other than Rosalia's biased opinions of Mr. Wonderful.

Sal expected and respected the maneuver from an overprotective father who loosened his tie to diffuse the rigidity of an interrogation and put him at ease. Furthering that objective, Oliver Taversham conducted his thorough cross-examination while smoking a pipe. Dapper and distinguished with slicked, side-swept hair, heavy on the gray, he upheld Albert Einstein's notion that pipe smoking contributes to rendering a calm and objective judgment in human affairs.

An enjoyable, drawn-out process, the art of manliness infused with relaxation, enabled him to find out what he needed to know in twenty minutes. Moreover, Sal's steadfastness and unflinching candor garnered approval from the self-made millionaire who'd gone out on a limb in his twenties to achieve financial independence.

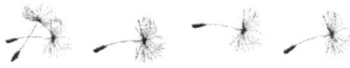

He admired Sal's self-reliance to strike out on his own when his parents relocated to Italy to care for his paternal grandmother. An eagerness to enlist in the Navy demonstrated ethical responsibility. The feather in his cap, betting heart and soul on the success of Sal's Italian Deli in the boondocks of Foster.

Sensing a pioneering spirit matching his own, Oliver took an immediate liking to his beloved daughter's intended, and insisted Sal call him Tavvy.

Standing in good stead, indeed!

***

Close to wrapping up the evening before tying loose ends knotted with tension, Rosalia and Sal maintained facades of geniality within the elegant, pastel-pink confines of Joe Marzilli's Old Canteen where he'd made dinner reservations for four. The simple matter of crossing Atwells to his apartment for nightcap Brandy Alexanders and full disclosure played into his decision. They'd only just begun to peruse their menus, exhorting Sal to parody Frost in his thoughts, originating from the anxiety he and Rosalia shared.

Soon plunging into a shitstorm, dark and deep,

There'll be miles to go before anyone can sleep.

By outward appearances, the foursome had immersed themselves in studying the menu offerings. All except Tavvy, preoccupied with the cover, and twisting the tips of his salt-and-pepper, handlebar mustache, had opened theirs. Rosalia kicked off her saddle shoe and rubbed Sal's ankle with her stockinged foot, playing footsie under the table. Although Sal blushed, he assumed a poker face and put on a show of scanning dinner options.

"H-m-m, according to the cover, this is the oldest family-owned Italian restaurant in Rhode Island. How 'bout that, Honey Bun?"

Scrutinizing several selections under the seven-course dinner section, Viola looked up and peered into her husband's deep-set, blue blinkers through cat-eye frame glasses embellished with rhinestones. Her trendsetting choice of eyewear coincided with women gaining a sense of independence post-World War II.

She humored him. "Giving credit where it's due, Sal knows how to pick 'em—an upscale restaurant and a classy lady for his bride!"

A slight Italian accent tempered her proficiency in speaking impeccable English, honed by a bilingual and cultured upbringing in the Old Country previous to her family's immigration to New York, post-World War I. Her father, Luigi Gianni, bless his heart, was one of the diplomats negotiating for territory if Italy entered the war on the side of the Allied Power, and the Allies won. Turns out, during the sit-down for drafting the Treaty of Versailles in 1919, Italy received less territory in Europe than had been promised, and none overseas.

Unlike the hordes of poorer, uneducated immigrants arriving in New York during the Roaring '20s, Lucky Luigi's punctilious wordsmithing and a magistrate's letter of recommendation paved his way to glory in the Appellate Division of the Supreme Court. Appointed Clerk/Executive Officer, each week he deposited a sizeable amount of his substantial salary into a savings account at a bank on Madison Avenue. An eagle's nest egg accrued.

All well and good until the Crash of '29! The mass panic to withdraw deposits until the banks had no money to lend caused thousands of financial institutions to fail. Luigi Gianni never

160

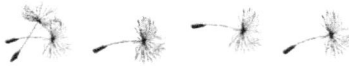

saw a red cent of his savings. But, far be it from him to jump off a bridge or fling himself out of a window.

Viola plied her artistic flair for pennies on the dollar to help her parents make ends meet during the lean, mean years. Pretty as a picture herself! During the early spring of 1930, she attracted the likes of a self-assured, young man with ambitions. Pounding the pavement with holes in his soles, and a wad of scrounged $10 gold certificates in his wallet to invest in real estate, Oliver Taversham would soon architect his fortune. Not before he married Viola with her father's blessing in a wedding ceremony lacking the finery the Giannis had been accustomed to in their heyday.

Still easily sidetracked by his wife's buxom beauty, Tavvy raised his wine glass, beseeching the others to do the same as he proposed a toast. "To our daughter and future son-in-law. May you both hold onto each other along your journey together, leading up to and throughout marriage, in sickness and in health."

Dewy-eyed, they clinked glasses with one another, echoing Viola's sentiment, *"Alla tua salute!"*

To your health! Contrariwise, Rosalia felt sick to her empty stomach for justifiable reasons, compounded by additional distress. Her bottom lip quivered. Sheer willpower quashed the tremors, suppressing an onset of tears from ruining their doubleheader dinner in celebration of her graduation and engagement.

Deflowered before one's wedding day failed to make the grade for desirable traits a classy lady upheld. Soon enough, before a rooster crowed at the crack of dawn, she'd open the floodgate of anguish for all. Heartsick, she shuddered over bursting her parents' bubble from distorting their perceptions of her polished perfection. Wise to Rosalia's inner turmoil, Sal

squeezed her hand and whispered into her ear, "Hey, we're in this together."

None the wiser, her parents smiled at each other, attributing their tête-à-tête to canoodling and whispering sweet nothings. Not one to forestall, in or out of the boardroom, Tavvy took the initiative. "So, what has everyone decided?"

***

The assortment of desserts culminating a seven-course dinner reflected their unique temperaments: chocolate chip cannoli, tiramisu, spumoni, and ricotta cheese pie. Stuffed from the steady consumption of appetizers and entrees, they fawned and dawdled over polishing off every morsel of their sweet pleasures by engaging in frivolous chatter. In that regard, Sal spoke more than his fair share, pinch-hitting for Rosalia who busied herself spooning claret sauce over spumoni, softening the layers to mush.

Tavvy decided to hold onto his peripheral observation of his daughter's abstinence from animation for the short duration remaining, probing when warranted. More than meets the eye, he came to a Hamletized conclusion. *Something is rotten in the state of Denmark!*

Noticing Tavvy was wise to Rosalia's misery, and not one to prolong his own agony or hers any more than necessary, Sal placed his napkin and utensils face down on his plate, a subtle signal for their attentive waiter to leave the tab. Rosalia looked up from her neglected puddle of spumoni and mustered cheer. "Before Sal and I drive you two back to the Biltmore, we'd like you to come up for nightcaps."

Her mother demurred. "Your father and I have had a long day, and it's getting late. I want to be bright-eyed and bushy-tailed for tomorrow's downtown shopping spree."

Tavvy overrode his wife's objection based on his objective to delve below the surface of Rosalia's aloofness. "Poppycock! What's your hurry, Honey Bun? We're staying in the city for a few more days. You'll have ample opportunity to shop until you're footsore. So, there's no reason for us to give these kids the bum's rush. Is there?"

Settled.

Tavvy also knew better than to undermine Sal's generosity by insisting on picking up the tab. Preferring to choose his battles wisely, he reckoned there were bigger fish to fry for appropriating his Midas touch.

Chapter 36

Stepping away from the sidewalk in front of the Old Canteen, Rosalia and Sal held hands crossing the asphalt gangplank to the opposite side. The Tavershams followed close behind, exercising greater caution climbing the steep staircase to Sal's apartment. In back of his moving target, Tavvy took note of his daughter's surefootedness along the dimly lit passageway which smacked to him of overfamiliarity.

Once inside the sparsely furnished living room, the New York socialites sat at opposite ends of a lumpy sofa while their hosts tended to libations in the open kitchen. Over the din of spilling ice into a cocktail shaker, Sal hollered into the intervening area. "Chocolate shavings or nutmeg sprinkled on your Brandy Alexanders?"

Viola expressed her preference, raising her voice to be heard above the din. "Anything other than nutmeg is sacrilegious!"

Tavvy concurred. "I'll go along for that ride."

During the shake-up of cognac, crème de cacao, cream, and ice, Tavvy conducted a psychic reading of Sal's flat. His wide-range perusal seized hold of threadbare upholstery on the sofa and chair. The marred surfaces of an incompatible end table and coffee table also corroborated the minimalist, mismatched décor of a bachelor.

Atypical—not a speck of dust on wood grain polished to a high sheen. A vase filled with fresh flowers cozied up to a lamp on the end table. *Heavens to Betsy, both on a doily!*

Bug-eyed, he gawked at frilled curtains on the window in the pantry, his eyes protruding above and beyond their periscopic boundaries. *Starched ruffles. Well, I'll be darned!*

Tavvy felt himself getting hot under his starched, white collar from implications barreling into his chest. Viola, a portrait artist with an observant eye for incongruence, drew the same inference. Sidling closer to her husband, she whispered, "I wonder who Sal's decorator is!"

"And, who's his maid? Honey Bun, let me steer the wheel on this one."

***

A few tentative sips into past-their-bedtime tipples, Tavvy's vexation steered the drift of his discourse into a hairpin turn of phrase directed at two unwed lovebirds nesting under the same roof. His penetrative stare encompassed Rosalia who sat on the armchair across from the sofa, and Sal who knelt beside her for lack of a throne.

"So, unless you two have something else in mind, we're ready to set the wheels in motion for planning a gala October wedding at Grace Church."

Hallelujah! As the sacraments fly, Rosalia's ceremonial stomping ground: Baptism, First Communion, and Confirmation. God willing, at least five months along by then! Her stomach flip-flopped over her parents' proposal of a fairy-tale wedding.

Grateful for her father's opening statement to fess up, she pinched Sal's shoulder, emboldened to dispel magic illusions, despite the quiver in her voice as the stroke of midnight approached. "The way things stand—it will be better if you and Mama plan for a christening, instead."

Rosalia's news advisory sucked the air out of the room. Regaining an awareness of conscious thought, Viola bit her

165

hand in a feeble attempt to stifle a cry. Tavvy raised an index finger, prefacing an elocutionary execution.

The four of them were in for the long haul, staying put in the living room. Sal rubbed the back of his neck, marking his words. *And, miles to go before we sleep!*

Chapter 37

Slight of build, but not one to trifle with, Tavvy wagged his finger back and forth like the pendulum swing of a metronome. He ad-libbed in laying down the law to two tongue-tied whippersnappers who dared not contradict his non-negotiable terms. Every once in a while, his stern-faced sergeant-at-arms alongside him, nodded her head in the affirmative. A short, bouncy poodle cut dyed in reddish-brown henna, softened the harsh effect of her posturing.

"We expect to wave our good-byes from the train to a lawfully wedded couple. Which means expediting a shotgun wedding within three days. Just so happens, a district court judge in this great city owes me a favor for giving him some real-estate investment advice."

Tavvy stalled his train of thought to fill the bowl in his pipe with tobacco and tamp it down. Putting the stem to his mouth, he took a few draws, moving a match in a circular motion over the tobacco until evenly lit. The distraction somewhat appeased his disgruntlement.

On track, his sidekick conducted her own manifesto directed at Rosalia. "However you work things out to choose your maid of honor—by mid-morning, at the latest—swing downtown by the hotel for me, tagging her along. The three of us will be off-rack shopping inside Shepard's, Peerless, and the Outlet. Tired or not, from lack of sleep!"

She glanced at Tavvy, who winced from the jab of her pointed look. Clearing his throat, he turned his attention to Sal. "You need to pick a best man within the same time frame. Come by the hotel for me tomorrow morning as well. We're taking a walk to the jeweler's for wedding bands."

Hoarse from strategizing his plans for two starstruck lovers, Tavvy emphasized footing the bill. The grimace plastered on Sal's face laid bare an intolerable affront to his pride. Of similar build, and not one to cross, Sal was about to protest.

Tavvy waved him off. "Pipe down, Son. As advised by your future mother-in-law, according to traditional etiquette, the bride's family pretty much pays for the whole shebang. Compared to expenses for the original wedding we had in mind—not yet factoring in costs to accommodate out-of-town guests—you can rest assured we're getting off easy."

No longer holding her emotions in check, sobs wracked Rosalia's core. Tears rolling rampant down her cheeks and obscuring her vision, she sprang from the chair and lumbered forward to embrace both parents in a single chokehold. Following in her footsteps, Sal stood close behind, gripping his beloved's shoulder. Their laying on of hands established a familial bond.

Rosalia faltered, "I'm . . . I'm sorry . . . for disappointing you and M-mama! And, I don't want to s-sound ungrateful . . . b-but," she hesitated, "before the stork delivered its telltale signs, Sal and I had in mind a simple ceremony without f-fanfare."

Cheek to cheek, Viola's tears intermingled with her daughter's. She pulled away, initiating a chain reaction severing their trinity. Rosalia and Sal straightened to their full stature. Still seated, Viola met Rosalia's gaze. Flustered with emotion, her voice cracked. "Your dad and I wanted to err on the side of extravagance to overcompensate for our poverty during the Depression. For our wedding, I wore the nicest dress off the rack from my closet."

Misty-eyed, Tavvy scrambled to his feet and stood in front of them. Reaching out for his daughter's hand, his fingers laced with hers. "And I borrowed an ill-fitting suit with droopy

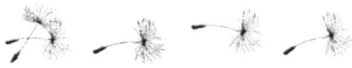

shoulders and baggy pants." He winked at Sal. "Now that I'm a man of means, I probably wouldn't have looked any better wearing a custom-fitted, tailed tuxedo."

"No, Tavvy—you wouldn't. Downright ridiculous, if you ask me!"

***

An exchange of vows sealed with a kiss before Tavvy's pigeonholed judge, would take place without razzle-dazzle three days post-graduation inside the Capisci Deli. The best place Sal could come up with on such short notice, Tavvy backed his suggestion. Asserting himself, he made it advantageous for the proprietor to close his establishment that evening and set up a buffet resplendent for a wedding reception to accommodate twenty. Just about half as many were expected.

And, who might they be?

The judge. Four key players. Three bitches—outspoken and accounted for.

Not so funny, Sal's predicament to find a guy to stand up next to and slightly behind him during the civil wedding ceremony. Tony volunteered. "May as well show up to eat what I'm gonna cook."

Tony, off the clock. His bashful wife who'd offer little to further the conversation

***

In contrast, Rosalia found it difficult to choose a maid of honor when three contenders vied for the heavyweight title. She found it endearing her best friends postponed their own getaway just long enough to attend her wedding. They'd foregone their original travel plans with parents, choosing to share a room at the Renaissance, downtown.

169

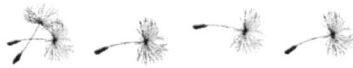

Fraught with anguish over making a decision, Helen suggested the impartiality of drawing straws. "Whoever draws the shortest one out of Rosalia's hand, wins. Then, it's put up or shut up!"

Joan, turning on her heels to leave the room, announced, "I'll scrounge up a straw from the lounge."

A cursory glance at Gloria's crestfallen demeanor was all it took for Rosalia to make things right. "Joan. Never mind!"

She let go of the doorknob.

"There'll be no contest! If Gloria hadn't taken off in my station wagon to get Sal, there's no telling how things might have turned out."

"You'd deprive me of envisioning Joan running around like a chicken with her head cut off, grasping at straws? I doth protest!" mocked Helen.

Gloria recouped her brazenness, a mischievous grin spreading from ear to ear. "Put up or shut up! Remember?"

Helen relented. "I suppose there is such a thing as honor among four women who are thick as thieves."

Before Rosalia and Gloria set out for the Biltmore, in what boiled down to the final curtain on acts of buffoonery, all held hands. Smiling, laughing and romping, the foursome sang "Ring around the Rosie" until they all fell down, kicking their legs in the air and howling with mirth.

Chapter 38

No way near a simple and straightforward shopping spree, by any means, they had tried on more than a few dresses apiece at each store, critiquing every prospect for fit and figure flattery. Other than refueling at the lunch counter in Woolworth's, one of the original five-and-dime stores, the gals pounded the sidewalks from late morning until sundown.

Conversely, the gents had plenty of time to fritter in the hotel lounge after their smooth transaction of securing 14-karat gold. Sal left Tavvy behind, driven by the importance of being earnest in entrusting the wedding bands to his comedic best man before Tony's shift ended at the deli.

Meanwhile, the gals continued to cover the same ground, bandying about in a haphazard grid pattern bearing a resemblance to the cat's scratch stalemate in tic-tac-toe. A tolerable expedition if you're traipsing in saddle shoes. Agonizing, in the low, thin kitten heels Viola wore. 'Twas the pointed toes that did her in.

***

There, sitting in a wingback chair, Tavvy smoked his pipe, hunkering down to read the newspaper from front to back. Periodically, he pulled his fob watch out of the left pocket in his vest, impatient for the long overdue bridal party to show. A recurring grumble in the pit of his empty stomach calibrated a famished stage of hunger. The evening plan involved dinner for four, which couldn't occur soon enough, and both girls staying overnight in the Taversham's suite.

Although the horse had already been let out of the barn, Rosalia's parents persuaded her to honor the ancient tradition

of the groom not seeing the bride the night before their wedding.

The intensifying volume of babbling from familiar voices led Tavvy to abandon his newspaper. Three prodigal shoppers advanced toward him. As expected, the outbursts from two exuberant young ladies overrode their mindfulness of staid aristocrats who preferred quietude inside the stuffy inner sanctum of the hotel.

Taken aback by the spectacle of his wife lagging in the rear and limping along, Tavvy rushed toward her. The furrowing between her brows conveyed to him the intense pain through which she labored. He relieved her of her pocketbook and shopping bag which she'd refused to relinquish to Rosalia or Gloria, persisting with an inordinate display of pride.

"Honey Bun! What in tarnation?"

"Mama mia! My feet are killing me! I'm not budging tonight, so I suggest you call the concierge for room service recommendations."

Arm in arm, he escorted Viola to the elevator. "I'll request that the chef prepare a horse to my specifications."

***

On the QT in the suite, Gloria had rung Helen to apprise her of the bridal party's color palette. In much less time than it took for the notorious shopping trek, two whirling dervishes acquired the finishing touches for puttin' on the Ritz, hours before the wedding. Expediting matters on their way into the local florist shop that morning, Helen menaced Joan with her sardonic wit. "On account of my allergies, let's make it quick. We'll get out a lot sooner if I do the talking and you nod your head in agreement."

On their way out, Joan prevailed—for once. "Well, I never thought I'd live to see Helen Chandler speechless! I assume all

that head bobbing up and down were nods of approval for my brilliant choices."

"Achoooo!"

"I think you just hailed our taxi."

***

In advance of the civil ceremony, Helen and Joan jammed several tables together to simulate one oblong surface. They placed a chair at each end, and arranged others along both sides of the table, allowing for enough elbow room between guests. A white, oversized rectangular tablecloth extended to the floor, camouflaging shoddiness, while complementing the centerpiece comprised of lavender and white carnations, delivered on the fly, as promised.

In a rare display of vulnerability, Helen sought reassurance from her accomplice. "Promise me you'll move this sucker far away before everyone sits down."

"Relax! Consider it done."

Amused, Sal fussed with his tie. "Sit tight. Tony's on his way to the Biltmore now."

His best man had borrowed Rosalia's wagon to chauffer the bride, her parents, and maid of honor in a conveyance with ample room.

***

Belle of the banquet, Rosalia stunned in her bridal dress, snared off the rack from upscale Shepard's at the corner of Westminster and Clemence Streets. She sashayed toward Sal in a lavender, three-quarter sleeve, below-the-knee dress. A veil overlay of off-white lace embellished with sprigs of lavender glorified the earthy, flowering herb. By far, Rosalia's favorite floral. The skirt twirled whenever she twisted her torso, animating the blossoms as though stirred by a breeze.

173

Befitting a pinup wannabe, Gloria showed off her curves in a straight-up lavender, snug-fitting sheath wiggle dress which charted the swivel of her hips as she flitted about. She snatched that hot number off the rack at Peerless, on the corner of Westminster and Union Streets.

Rather than upstage or clash with the bride and maid of honor, Viola settled for sensibility, snagging her outfit at the Outlet on Weybossett Street, a pigeon toe from Westminster. She cast a shadow in pearl gray, conservatively attired in a coatdress. Similar to the shirtwaist dress, its bodice morphed into a long coat instead of a shirt. Even the oversized buttons and larger collar resembled those found on her outer garment.

***

As the evening drew to a close, guests toyed with remnants of food on their plates, too full to take another bite, or one more hit of wine. The laying down of utensils and tapering off of conversations ushered in a transitory awkwardness for bidding farewells. Up until this juncture, Viola had kept her unshod, stockinged feet well-hidden under the drape of the tablecloth. Toe blisters did not bode well inside cramped quarters.

While trying to maintain a dignified bearing, her tootsies sought the low-cut vamps she had kicked off without a care for their flight path.

Sal approached his in-laws. "If you two are ready to call it a night, I'll drive you to the hotel. This way Rosalia can tie up loose ends with the girls before I swing by for us to drop them off at the Renaissance."

"What do you say to that, Honey Bun?"

Flustered, "Give me a minute." Viola disappeared, crawling underneath the makeshift banquet table, retrieving her pumps midway down the alley. Slightly disheveled, she emerged, dangling the pair from her fingers. "My wedding favors."

Flabbergasted over his wife's predicament, Tavvy vented his frustration. "Fiddlesticks, Honey Bun! If you can't bear putting on shoes, how in the world do you expect to walk around the excavation site tomorrow?"

Looking into her darling husband's eyes with the utmost adoration, she rubbed the back of her free hand along his cheek. "Mio caro, I'll be fine wearing your slippers."

***

Helen was the first to pull away from a malingering hug bejeweled with glistening tears. Once more, and for old times' sake, she demonstrated pragmatism. "Figuring none of you bubbleheads thought to bring anything other than your hanky to a wedding, I came prepared."

She delved into her handbag, retrieving pencils and a pocket-sized notepad from which she tore off four sheets. "Jot down your name, telephone number, and address. Then pass the papers around until we're all accounted for. On your mark, get set, go!" The surface of the table humored their indulgence.

Overseeing the swap, Helen addressed the future. "Now, we make a pact to stay in touch for the rest of our lives."

Gloria elaborated, "Especially during holidays."

"Birthdays too," insisted Joan.

"Let's not forget milestones," Rosalia added.

"And, hot messes!" emphasized Helen. "Speaking for three of us, we expect to find baby pictures in our mailboxes around Valentine's Day."

They put their hands together, one on top of the other, in confirmation of their solidarity. The high-pitch squeak of the door announced Sal's return.

***

Not a fair-weather friend among them, the bitches honored their pledge throughout the years. They maintained a steadfast friendship through the medium of phone, photos, and penning letters stamped from Rhode Island, Illinois, Wyoming, and Nebraska.

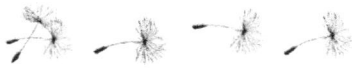

Chapter 39

Tavvy paced the perimeter of the clearing, his hands clasped behind his back. Pensive, he drew his own architectural conclusions for laying the groundwork, keeping an eye out for the future. Deep in thought, he held off on adding a footnote to his wife's unsteady gait as she navigated potholed topography wearing his leather slippers in size nine. Despite crooking elbows with Sal and Rosalia on each side of her, Viola's dainty feet overstepped their bounds, leaving behind one or the other clodhopper to retrieve and reinsert a left or right.

None the wiser, or so she thought, Tavvy turned around and trudged toward them. He squared his shoulders and leveraged his focus on Sal and Rosalia. "Good-sized parcel of God's green earth. Nonetheless, if that plot represents square footage of the cabin—your homestead's worth diddly-squat!"

Viola cringed. Quick on the draw, the aggrieved party opened their mouths to fire a retort. "Before you two interrupt, let a well-intentioned man have the ground floor and listen to what I have to say."

Sal yielded, "Fair enough, Tavvy."

Less agreeable, Rosalia nodded, muting words from rolling off the tip of her tongue.

"Now that you're in a family way, and if the good Lord wants—the pitter-patter of more tiny feet—your dream house needs realistic adjustments. So does the yard."

Tavvy paused to reap the full effect of a reality check hitting both of them smack between the eyes in the mode of dumbfounded stares. Viola stood her ground, reluctant to lose

her footing for dispensing a hug to her husband. "That's my Tavvy!"

His smile penetrated her soul.

Begrudging the twosome any opening to speak their mind, Tavvy plowed through, addressing Sal. "From the looks of things, your contractor's dragging his feet." He winked a conspiratorial smoke signal. "Like your mother-in-law."

Discomposed, though far from nonplussed, "Nothing gets by my Tavvy, does it?"

Eager to keep a captive audience corralled in his corner, tenacity prevailed. "Kids, in the race against time, yours truly has your best interests at heart. So, it's imperative I settle the account with your developer and hire the big guns to build a functional home with ample living space—with your input for layout, of course. Consider it a wedding gift."

If Sal intended to object, he needed to comfort Rosalia, who had dissolved into tears over her dad's generous offer. Viola seized the moment to sweeten the pot. "A house isn't a home without the amenities of furniture, appliances, carpeting, and window treatments. Of your choosing, and installed before moving in, of course."

Overwhelmed by the unexpected windfall heaped upon them, both hit the dirt in each other's arms, Rosalia sobbing uncontrollably and Sal choking up with emotion.

Tavvy squeezed his wife around her middle. "Honey Bun, you and I make such a formidable tag team, we brought them to their knees! And, they'd better not lollygag any longer, or we'll miss our train."

Viola stroked his cheek. "Mio caro, we'll get to the depot a lot sooner if you carry me across the threshold of these tree roots and into the wagon."

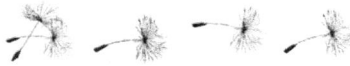

Standing on the platform at Providence's Union Station, waiting for the outbound train to New York, the four of them exchanged endearing words reinforced with hugs. While Rosalia and her mother embellished their private conversation, Tavvy took Sal aside.

"Son, on my word of honor, I'll never interfere in your line of work. I won't flap my trap to offer advice. Nor will I bankroll a venture on the verge of collapse, should that ever happen— God forbid. Some lines just aren't meant to be crossed, out of respect for another man's territory."

"Thanks, Tavvy. Understood and appreciated."

Both men sealed the deal with a firm handshake and back slaps as the train crawled to a stop on its track. The Tavershams boarded. Viola tottered in her worn, everyday street-shoes she'd slipped on before exiting the station wagon.

Procuring a seat facing the terminal, they huddled in front of the window, waving last-minute good-byes suiting their dispositions. Tavvy proffered a staunch palm-wide wave. Viola flaunted a vigorous side-to-side wag.

Peering inside the railcar from where they stood, the newlyweds reciprocated. Rosalia's send-off wave resembled her mother's. Sal swayed his forearm back and forth, slow and steady, redolent of his durability for facing adversity.

The train soon gained acceleration and disappeared from view, leaving the young couple behind with their whole life ahead of them, neither the wiser to its short duration.

Chapter 40

It was not an easy nine-month term for Mr. and Mrs. Salvatore Rizzio, by any stretch of the imagination. A volley of morning sickness, tiredness, headaches, and lower back cramps blighted Rosalia throughout her early stages of pregnancy. The latter stage picked up the slack, afflicting her with leg swelling and heartburn. For the most part, she endured these symptoms with all the stoicism she could muster out of consideration for Sal, whose entrepreneurial endeavor tested his durability. Without factoring in travel, his typical day began at nine o'clock, preparing foodstuff in readiness for opening his door at 11:00 a.m., and closing at 8:00 p.m.

A man of few words, he spoke fewer still when he got home an hour or so later, not to burden his wife. Exhaustion, accounted for—Sal, for the most part, minimized or muzzled any pickles he might have found himself in. The kind without solution.

His dwindling bank account and her bottomless trust fund fed a money-hungry enterprise. From an operational standpoint, Sal's culinary skills and Fist's word-of-mouth marketing brought in a trickle of locals to the tables or take-out counter. Most of these folks, in turn, spread the word around their sparsely-settled town of 1613 residents, the official count recorded in the 1950 census.

That mentioned, since the deli's grand opening, the amount of customers on any given day proved far less than the imaginary sheep Sal counted to induce sleep. Tossing and turning, he also impaired Rosalia's chances for getting a good night's rest.

A little more than two months down the road, Sal implemented drastic measures to increase prospects for greater stability and steadier revenue to override inconsistent proceeds from easy-come, easy-go walk-ins. Out of desperation to succeed, he drummed up efforts to make a go at catering, focusing on pockets of wealth in the greater Providence area.

Parlaying money obtained from selling his car, supplemented with Rosalia's allotment, Sal purchased a catering truck which he reserved for use primarily on weekends. Taking over the station wagon for his daily commute, in no way, impinged upon Rosalia's freedom of movement, pregnancy notwithstanding.

The location of their temporary lodging was within walking distance of the neighborhood markets in Providence's Little Italy. A moot point considering Sal brought home the bacon, toting pre-cooked vittles from the deli. As well, the Pembroke graduate who forfeited spiriting herself away to San Francisco's Little Italy in the North Beach neighborhood, an epicenter for the Beat Generation, didn't miss a beat. Not one to wallow in the consequence of spilled semen, Rosalia put her nose to the grindstone, writing poetry during Sal's absence.

***

"You're joking!"

"Tony, you're the comic. I'm being straight. Figuring you got another mouth to feed on the way, I thought you could use the extra bucks on weekends as my set-up man. Don't think about it too long. Tell me your decision before I'm outta here."

His ultimatum delivered in-person at the Capisci Deli, Sal turned his back and walked toward the door.

"Hey! Gimme a sec, will ya! All right! Yeah! We'll talk. Soon as I palm off an eggplant parm to my customer."

Sal obliged, waiting for Tony at the infamous back table, chuckling in the corner over another one of his best man's jokes pawned off on a customer.

"So, this woman tells her doctor she's got a bad back, right? The doc says it's old age. Not convinced, the woman tells him she wants a second opinion. Without hesitation, the doc says, 'In my second opinion, you're annoying too!'"

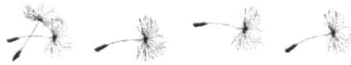

Chapter 41

When December rolled in, it began to feel a lot more like Christmas for the Rizzios. During that seventh month of Rosalia's pregnancy, marking the beginning of her third trimester, Sal's long shot started to pay off in bookings. By then, catering became the bread and butter for financing his gourmet gamble. It enabled him to secure a livelihood and pay the bills without sheepishly relying on his benefactress for a cash advance. Signed contracts locked in nearly every Saturday and Sunday afternoon or evening. More often than not, Fridays and sporadic weeknights too.

Birthdays, christenings, bridal showers, fundraisers, bar mitzvahs, graduations, funeral repasts and other causes célèbres, whether joyous or somber, require food to pacify a crowd. Tasty cuisine and superlative service whisk together a lasting impression for creating a memorable event. In every sense of the word, Sal's Italian Deli had the chops to fill the bill.

For all intents and purposes, beneficial to both, Tony hitched his rump to Sal's lunch wagon. Business thrived with a crackerjack qualified to handle the demands of setting up shop at a client's home. Besides earning extra cash on the side, Tony fine-tuned his comedy routines by cracking an occasional joke on the job to break the ice.

"Hey, I got this friend at the deli who tells me an onion is the only food that can make you cry. His theory backfired when I picked up a grapefruit and threw it at his face!"

Sal's right-hand man made an exception for funeral luncheons, keeping his alter ego in check.

After roughly twenty years, and three trucks later, Tony hit the brakes on moonlighting for Sal. With two self-supporting

adult children, his day job at the Capisci Deli sufficed. Seniority guaranteed a fixed work schedule which granted him the freedom to pursue steady nocturnal gigs at comedy clubs.

Like a bolt from the blue, a drifter on a '65 Harley-Davidson Electra Glide stopped at Sal's deli. Out of options, and at the end of his rope, he foresaw himself putting down roots in a godforsaken town. The Help Wanted – Inquire Within sign hanging from the storefront window, offered the scraggly biker a slim prospect to shake a stick at his rotten luck. In walked Keith Lawrence.

We've more miles to go before this breach of etiquette.

***

With a few weeks to spare before Rosalia and Sal moved into their rustic log house, it appeared their life—by gosh, by golly—bore symbolic semblance to a hunky-dory sleigh ride. Until Sal rounded the bend to Foster Center, shocked at the sight he beheld on a merry, mid-month morning. Through the windshield of the wagon, he espied the storefront window of the deli. Fractured, its jagged shards had mutated the glass into a grotesque jigsaw puzzle of fragile infrastructure.

A surge of adrenalin jettisoned Sal out of his vehicle after he had jerked the handbrake and killed the engine with the gearshift in first. He bounded to the front of the building, reaping a small measure of comfort when the door hadn't budged from his tug on its handle. Right away, Sal reckoned his property had been vandalized rather than burglarized. All the same, jitteriness caused him to fumble with inserting the key in the lock.

Once inside, Sal eyeballed the joint anyway. Nothing out of place. Had it been a case of nighttime breaking and entering with intent to commit a felony, the burglar would have been sorely disappointed. Without fail, Sal emptied the cash register

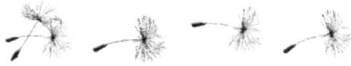

drawer at closing time, whether its compartments teemed with green, or coddled chump change.

Referencing one of the telephone numbers on an index card thumbtacked next to the black, wall-mount phone, Sal rotary-dialed the police station. During his less than five-minute wait for an officer to arrive, he dialed Fist's office.

***

Not shocked in the least over what Sal had to say, nor at a loss for pointing a finger at the hooligan who inflicted deliberate damage, Fist still took it hard. Guilt gnawed at his insides.

Sure, forewarned is forearmed. And, he had good reason to predict something ugly coming down the pike. Shared this premonition with his Thursday-night poker buddy, Chief Bretton, who couldn't prevent a crime of this nature from happening. Said so himself. It's not likely that tipping off Sal would have amounted to an ounce of prevention either. Short of Sal hiring a pistol-waving goon to provide overnight security.

Closemouthed on the subject itself, Fist also refrained from regurgitating a slew of profanities Cousin Keen would have surrendered on the spot. "I'll be right there, my friend." Slamming a fist on his desk diverted parboiling rage. When his beast had retreated, he snatched the car keys off a peg on the wall.

Not one to dawdle, Sal grabbed the telephone book off a shelf underneath the counter. He rifled through the yellow pages for the listing of his insurance agent. That's when he chanced upon a thug's calling card.

***

The Foster Police Department's skeletal staff efficiently enforced laws within the jurisdiction of the sparse and scattered population it served. Irrespective of a sergeant and patrol

officer, in-house, sipping coffee and nibbling on doughnuts, Chief Boone Bretton was raring to dispatch himself at the scene of a crime after the fact. The bearded mountain of a man with ample girth who volunteered his services to portray Santa at charitable events, squeezed behind the wheel of a cruiser. His heavy foot pressed the pedal to the metal, and he burned rubber to get there.

A frequent flyer to Sal's deli at lunchtime, he took a liking to the guy, as did most who met him. Of greater importance, the incident justified throwing his weight around for instilling the fear of God in a person under suspicion.

Standing outside, Sal bore witness to the chief careening into the lot and slamming on the brakes. A heave-ho empowered him to extricate his bulk out of the cruiser's snug fit. Stingy on social graces as a result of the pox on his establishment, Sal cut to the quick. "Hey, Chief! I left something of interest intact for you."

"Well now, let me have a look see."

The door had closed behind them by a whisker, when Fist pulled up to the curbing and parked. He decided to wait inside his sedan rather than poke his nose into an investigation. So much the better for conducting a one-on-one conversation with Boone before paying his respects to Sal in private. Fist hunkered down on the front seat, passing the time flipping through several black-and-white Kodak moments he'd tucked inside the plastic sleeves of his wallet.

***

Chief Bretton pulled out a handkerchief from his back pocket to scoop up a copper-plated BB off the tile floor. He studied the specimen as might a prospector who stumbled upon the rare find of a gold nugget. Pleased, he snickered, much to Sal's exasperation.

186

"After I nip this in the bud once and for all, I'll be back at noon for a chicken parm."

"Mind telling me who's on your radar?"

"Someone you don't want to know."

***

Coinciding with Boone's exit from the deli, Fist rolled down the window of his prestigious Buick Roadmaster to get the lowdown. The chief leaned in. "Heading to Wayne's place. The son of a bitch may not eat crow, but I can almost guarantee he'll back off when I show him a bullet from the crime scene."

"You're going to wage war on a booby-trapped battlefield against a trigger-happy roughneck without proof of culpability?"

Boone snickered, affecting more confidence than he felt. "But, I've got enough bluster to call a madman's bluff based on other illegal activities I surmise he's involved in on the side."

"The odds in your favor for driving away from the fairgrounds of hell—alive—are . . ."

"Next to nil! Told Sal I'd be stopping in for lunch at my usual time. If you don't get a call from me at the station by noon . . ."

"I know the drill."

***

When Fist entered the premises, Sal had already made progress slicing and dicing vegetables on his staging area of a butcher-block tabletop. "Howdy, my good man! Sitting ringside in the front seat of my car, I was admiring the abstract mosaic embedded in your storefront window."

Without looking up from his chopping block, he replied, "Chief Bretton seems to know the artist's identity."

187

"Believe you me, Boone's proven track record in the field of law enforcement puts to shame his poker-playing strategies. You may as well fix me a grinder to go, seeing you're way ahead of yourself on the onions."

"Sure thing, Fist."

"Gotchya to look up, didn't I?"

Fist reached inside one of the inner pockets of his jacket, retrieving a cigar with a pink band. Beaming, he presented it to Sal. "Can't contain my joy over the birth of my daughter!"

Lois Doyle's history of high blood pressure worked in tandem with her vaginal lockdown whenever Fist had made sexual overtures in their marital bed. Her obstetrician had advised a C-section, and scheduled her delivery date at Providence Lying-In Hospital in advance.

Upon arrival, Lois was administered a regional anesthesia and antiseptically prepped for the procedure. At 3:25 p.m., on December 8, 1950, Muriel Ann Doyle was surgically removed through incisions in her mother's abdomen and uterus. She weighed in at 5 pounds 8 ounces.

To prevent infection, Lois received instructions to avoid sex for six weeks. When informing Fist of their fornication fast, she added two more weeks for good measure.

Chapter 42

In contrast to the greased-lightning speed at which Chief Bretton arrived at the deli, he drove with sluggish caution along North Road. On the way to his dreaded destination, he passed by the new home belonging to one of Wayne Cole's secluded neighbors. As far as the eye could see, several commercial vehicles formed a queue on the driveway. The Rizzios' rustic mansion, visible to passersby through threadbare tree branches, stuck out like a sore thumb. Boone chuckled at the irony of its proximity to Cole's dilapidated compound.

Seemingly of its own accord, the cruiser slowed to a crawl as the driver navigated rugged terrain of the netherworld. Easy-peasy for the monster tires on Mad Daddy Wayne's predatory wrecker looming ahead. But, Boone had no intention of infiltrating any further, preferring not to raise the hackles on the chained hounds from hell.

Even the hell-bent, unpruned trees formed a sinister alliance of ill will toward trespassers. Out of the entanglement of branches, coming into the light, one of the devil's own snot-nosed, knee-high spawns. Running as fast as his little legs would take him to his maker, a knit cap practically pulled the wool over the youngster's eyes. His stray ash-blond curls spilled onto the collar of an oversized, hand-me-down parka. Over the years, Boone lost count over how many tykes the warlord had sired. His last-born son, Wyatt, belly crawled to the finger-smudged storm door his daddy had just opened to let his brother in before he stormed out.

Wayne Cole had already spotted an adversary on his property, beating his son, Wendell, to the punch in warning him. Dressed the part of a loony in his outer attire of coonskin

189

cap, red-plaid woolen jacket and hunting boots, the lord of the manor strode toward the cruiser, none too pleased.

To Wayne's credit, he hadn't barreled out of his hovel with a shotgun in the crook of an arm.

Boone concluded if he'd been a civilian without the protective logo on a marked police vehicle, Wayne would have greeted him with a bullet fired into his brain. Harboring that thought, his mind traveled down a dark path of plausible scenarios for Wayne to cover his tracks:

Digging a shallow grave in the bowels of the woods to dump his body. Towing the cruiser to the auto parts & salvage place in town, where he worked. Gutting it for useful parts, then crushing the shell.

His flesh puckered with shivers from horrific speculation. Grateful for the stay of execution, Boone killed the engine. He unfastened his holster which was attached to a wide, leather Sam Browne belt supported by a strap extending diagonally over his right shoulder. Figuring he may as well neutralize the battlefield on god-forbidden soil, Boone forfeited his handgun-in-a-holster to the passenger side of the front seat.

In the meantime, Wayne had stationed himself outside the driver's door, forcing Chief Bretton to squeeze his body through a space of limited jurisdiction. When he emerged from his cocoon, the loon spat a plug of chewing tobacco aimed a tad shy of one high-gloss, black steel-toe. Although the heat of anger had risen to his collarbone, the chief chose to ignore an anomaly, preferring to expend his energy for the greater good of mankind during the holiday season.

Wayne narrowed his eyes in suspicion at the authority figure who towered over him. "Since you drove past two No Trespassin' signs on my private property, you got a warrant to be here?"

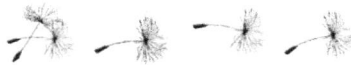

Standing too close for comfort, Boone got a whiff of Wayne's rancid breath, and a gander of the brown tobacco stains on his choppers—those still standing at allegiance. "Seeing I've entered your property solely for the purpose of speaking with you, I don't need one."

Fact is, it's a mistaken belief No Trespassing signs can keep police off private property without a warrant. Courts have consistently ruled against the complainant. Hey, no need to disgruntle a person of interest any more than he had.

For the indeterminate duration of their exchange, the clean-shaven chief contrived to stay one step ahead of the scruffy redneck.

"Well, seeing, I ain't got all day—spit it out, will ya!"

Poor choice of words, Boone thought. "Keep your cool now. Gonna reach into a back pocket for my handkerchief where I've placed a token from a crime scene you ought to see for yourself." He unveiled the BB. "You're lookin' at the projectile from the fore-end of a Daisy Red Ryder which shattered the town deli's storefront window."

Just as he'd predicted, Wayne didn't bat an eye. His reaction, an insolent smirk accompanied by a squirt of tobacco juice on the ground. "Betchya most red-blooded American males in Foster and their grown sons have themselves a Daisy."

"Regardless. You're my only suspect, hands down! Ever since the zoning board was unanimously against your opening up a guns and ammo shop in Foster Center, you've had a hard-on for the deli. And, everybody knows you're a bigot, notorious for mouthing off racial and ethnic slurs. I hear Sal Rizzio's your prime target."

Not in the least perturbed, Wayne stood his ground. "Maybe in your line of work, you heard of the First Amendment respectin' freedom of speech."

191

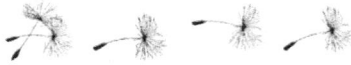

Oh, how sweet it is! The taste of victory at the end of his dance with the devil. Sooner than he expected.

"In my line of work, if one's freedom of speech can be tied to causing direct harm, even a shred of physical evidence contributes to building a behavioral composite."

Wayne's arrogance continued to blaze a trail down the primrose path. "You're buildin' yourself a castle in the air with birdshot."

"All the same, I'm saving this souvenir as a down payment for holding you accountable should another hate crime against Sal occur."

Boone inserted the BB into the vertical rectangle of his handkerchief, then folded it into a square which he wedged inside the back pocket of his trousers. Mustering austerity, he locked eyes with Wayne's evil orbs and tore into him. "By the hairs on your chinny chin chin, it behooves you to toe the line. Maybe you heard it's illegal to manufacture moonshine for personal consumption and distribution. The feds or locals wouldn't need a warrant to barrel past your No Trespassing signs, should you ever give me probable cause to make a phone call."

No surprise, the tough nut to crack didn't move a muscle, nor shift the focus of his eyes elsewhere. To Boone's satisfaction, however, the color drained from Wayne's face. Perhaps the surprising disclosure tied his testicles into a knot.

"Now, if you'll step aside, I'll get into my vehicle so we can both move on with our day."

***

Much to Fist's relief, Boone called him from the station before zero hour, preempting the financier from playing lead detective had the situation warranted. Even so, nursing anxiety

192

over a friend's conceivable demise had predisposed him to chew the inside of his lower lip and draw blood.

Working up an appetite from standing outdoors in the cold, Boone dialed the deli, ravenous to rectify his hunger pangs. "Sal, fire up the oven and start breading those chicken cutlets. I'm on my way."

***

Throughout the lifespan of Sal's Italian Deli, no further infractions disturbed its daily operations. Thanks to Chief Bretton who made a threat he was willing to carry out. By and by, the chief retired to Florida for the perks of no tax on income and a low cost of living.

Post-factum, Wyatt Cole entered the deli, up to no good. Spooked by the slam of a door, he shot Sal to death. Wyatt's Mad Daddy never knew what hit Sal, having taken leave of this world beforehand, courtesy of lung cancer.

We've more miles to go before Sal is laid to rest.

Chapter 43

A hard taskmaster and astute coordinator, Tavvy prevailed in getting his way with the artisans he hired to complete Rosalia and Sal's dream house in the woods. In advance of occupancy, furniture filled their future living quarters. According to each room's function and décor, the accoutrements of curtains, drapes, swags, or valances adorned the windows.

Thrilled to have a roof over their head without the yoke of a mortgage around his neck, Sal delegated any and all decision-making for interior decorating to Rosalia. She usurped her authority with glee, voicing her preferences to Viola, who did her best to accommodate all of her daughter's requests.

Shortly after the New Year, the couple made their grand entrance into their forever home. They walked the runner, protective of the parquet flooring, leading them to the great room. Tavvy and Viola brought up the rear, tugging their luggage.

During the last stage of Rosalia's pregnancy, Sal voiced his apprehensions about leaving her alone for hours at a time in the hinterland of North Road. He convinced his in-laws to take up residence at the oversized cabin to see Rosalia through her pregnancy, and provide in-home help after she gave birth. The Tavershams were jubilant at the prospect.

The waiting and not knowing, exhaustion, and body soreness increased Rosalia's appreciation for everyone's intervention on her behalf. Viola delighted in running the household while her daughter rested in ramped-up readiness for going into labor. Tavvy salivated over the opportunity to acquire property in the capital city, and oversee construction of residential and commercial developments.

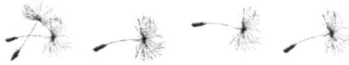

Their standby operation ran like a well-oiled machine in granting Sal and Rosalia peace of mind.

**

Coming upon a week or so after Valentine's Day, in the latter part of the day at an hour before closing, Tavvy pulled into the deli's deserted parking lot with perilous abandon. He braked the station wagon hard, jolting his two passengers. Viola gripped the dashboard to steady herself. Sitting behind Tavvy in the back seat, the partition of leather cushioned Rosalia's sudden lunge forward.

Although Viola had reassured her husband that Rosalia's labor could last anywhere from four to eight hours, his adrenalin rush was in overdrive. Tavvy hurled himself out of the wagon, slamming the door behind him with the engine running. He heard none of the inflammatory remarks targeting his erratic behavior.

He scurried to the storefront door, wrenched it open, and barged in. His eyes darted a nervous glance around the dining area. "Sal! Where are you hiding?"

Prickling from the urgency in his father-in-law's tone, and surmising the reason for it, Sal abandoned scrubbing the butcher-block workhorse. He scooted out front, on high alert.

Tavvy, relishing his role of messenger, "From the look of things, you're gonna be a dad before the rooster crows. So, close up shop. Rosalia could use some company in the back seat."

Having expelled a thrifty amount of words, Tavvy turned to leave, ready to take the wheel and pop the gear in reverse for their getaway. Taken aback at finding Viola in the driver's seat, he stammered, "Honey Bun! What's the big idea?"

Nonplussed, Viola rolled down the window partway. "During your absence, the two of us decided you will no longer

195

endanger the lives of your passengers and unborn grandchild with reckless driving. Now, go around and get in."

A domineering tycoon in the boardroom, and henpecked husband who did his wife's bidding, Tavvy yielded, falling into line. "Balderdash!" he muttered.

Meanwhile, Sal hastened to tie up loose ends. Taking long, deep breaths to calm himself, he dipped into the contents of the cash register drawer and scooped each handful of loot inside a till-drawer bag. He threw on his jacket, killed the lights, and locked the door on his way out.

With difficulty, Rosalia slid along the seat to open the car door for Sal and his till. Scooting to make room for him, she stifled a giggle. Settled in, he cozied up to his wife and held her hand, while exchanging brief greetings with his mother-in-law as she backed away from the curb.

"Am I the only one who noticed Sal's apron hanging below his knees?" Rosalia inquired.

On a mission to reach Providence Lying-In Hospital under cover of darkness without mishap, Viola focused solely on her driving. Tavvy peered over the front seat. "Well, now that you mention it."

***

Determined to soothe everyone's frayed nerves during the time it would take to travel from Foster to the outlying area of Providence, Tavvy turned on the radio. Billy Ecstine's operatic, bass-baritone voice serenaded them with "My Foolish Heart."

In adoration, Sal gazed at Rosalia and patted her belly. Moving closer, he murmured in her ear, "We're back here where it all started."

Their lips met for a tender, lingering kiss which Viola espied through the rearview mirror. She took her eyes off the

196

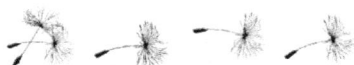

road for a split second to smile at Tavvy. Sight unseen by Honey Bun who returned her focus to the dimly lit road ahead, he smiled back.

Chapter 44

Relegated to the waiting area, far from the maddening cries in the labor room, Tavvy and Sal tripped the lamplight's fandango, wistfully speculating whether Rosalia would give birth to a boy or girl. Having been there and done that, tears stung Viola's eyes as she wrung her hands during a moment of déjà vu crackling with doom. Her fleeting premonition abounded with accuracy.

Standard procedure during the Fifties for vaginal childbirth, one of the nurses injected Rosalia with a one-size-fits-all hypodermic cocktail of morphine and scopolamine for pain management.

Hardy har har!

The small amount of morphine invariably failed to deliver its promise for preventing pain, but had the tendency to cause psychotic behavior which necessitated the use of restraints. Accordingly, Rosalia and the other two screaming meemies bashing their heads, clawing at themselves, and thrashing wildly alongside her in the torture chamber, were shackled to their padded beds. Bound for the duration of labor, they'd lie in their own vomit or feces until delivery, should intestinal discomfort dictate.

***

A groggy and disoriented Rosalia awakened from Twilight Sleep. A state induced by the scopolamine which had anesthetized her to the point of unconsciousness, it erased any memory of her having given birth. She also had no recollection of pain, or pickling in her own excrement.

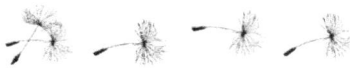

At 2:17 a.m. on February 20, 1951, Rosalia's obstetrician used forceps to remove the baby from her vagina. Since the drugs infiltrated the placenta and depressed the central nervous system, newborns were unable to breathe normally. Hence, Dr. Mulholland held Musetta Rose upside down and tapped her bottom to stimulate a cry and bring oxygen into her lungs. She weighed in at 5 pounds and 1 ounce.

Consequently, still under the influence of absurdity, Rosalia felt ill at ease when the nurse placed her blanket-swathed newborn in her arms and left the two of them alone to get acquainted. Even after studying her baby's wrinkled face, and gliding her forefinger over its tightly-clenched fists, Rosalia felt detached. Unfathomable, considering the labor of love it took so Musetta Rose could make her grand entrance into the world.

Depending on a number of factors, the maternal bond between mother and infant can take hours, days, weeks, or even months to develop. The motley crew creeping into Rosalia's room, as though walking on eggshells, would activate that symbiosis through zany antics.

Sal, woozy from the intoxication of newfound fatherhood, stared speechless at the tiny bundle his lovemaking had created. He kissed Rosalia's forehead.

Tavvy's elbow nudge and gentle urging emboldened him to hold his daughter. "Son, go ahead and claim what's half yours."

With tentativeness and tenderness, Sal reached out to accept his beloved's gift. Viola and Tavvy then flanked both sides of the bed, each gripping one of Rosalia's hands. The sight of Sal rocking back and forth on the balls of his feet, fawning over their baby, began to melt Rosalia's standoffish heart.

When the two locked eyes, hers glistening with tears of endearment, Sal announced his first parental decision. "My

sweet, I don't suppose Puccini would object if we call our Musetta Rose—Etta. Whaddya say?"

Rosalia nodded with enthusiasm, her face aglow.

Viola took her cue and walked up to Sal. Tapping his shoulder, "Mind if I cut in and have this dance with Etta?"

Parting with his daughter, Sal lay down alongside Rosalia on the bed, a vantage point for both of them to observe two besotted grandparents. After waltzing the newborn around the room, Viola sat on the visitor's chair, rocking her grandchild in her arms. Intent on lulling Etta to sleep, she lilted "Rock-a-Bye-Baby" in Italian.

"Ninna nanna, ninna oh Questo bimbo a chi lo do?"

As newborns have the nearsighted visual capacity to focus on faces by zeroing in on the eyes, Etta's grandpa undermined her nonna's efforts to close them. Hovering less than a foot away from the infant's line of vision, he hooked a thumb in each ear and waved his fingers at Etta. Tavvy didn't anticipate the rollicking laughter he'd evoke from three adults getting a load of his buffoonery.

***

No laughing matter, Rosalia developed uterine fibroids. These benign growths caused heavy menstrual bleeding, chronic pelvic pain, and impacted the movement of sperm which rendered her infertile. Medical decorum of the Fifties dictated she undergo the widespread, straightforward solution of a hysterectomy.

A sorrowful time for Sal and Rosalia, the innocence of a three-year-old harbored only glee in her heart when her grandparents turned up for an extended, post-op stay. Etta squealed in delight as Grandpa Tavvy chased her around the great room, oinking in pursuit.

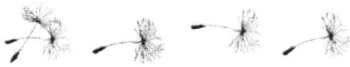

Part Three - Losing Ground

Chapter 45

When all traces of her dad's sliver of a smile had vanished during their drive home after Momma's funeral, Etta thought the coast clear enough to infiltrate the silence between them. "Too bad the bitches aren't joining us for lunch."

***

Tony, who had yet to sever his ties to Sal's apron strings, took it upon himself to singlehandedly prepare foodstuff at the deli which was closed for bereavement. Arriving before daybreak, and grateful for the solitary confinement, he turned up the heat for cooking a full-course Italian meal to go. For their first course, he put together an antipasto. Up next, escarole & white bean soup. His main dishes included lasagna, eggplant with roasted peppers, and veal piccata. For dessert, Tony whipped up a batch of cannoli—tubular shells of fried pastry dough filled with ricotta.

Cutting it close, he arrived at the Rizzios' rural retreat, thinking he had a bit of leeway to set up before the grieving party returned. Spotting the Tavershams' late-model Caddie parked where the driveway curved, nixed that assumption.

He sure as hell wouldn't need Sal's spare key to let himself in. It also appeared he needn't bother to ring the bell either. Sal's mother-in-law opened the front door before he stepped out of the catering truck. She stood on the other side of the threshold, waiting for him to draw near.

No laughing matter to joke about!

Wheeling a food-pan carrier filled with chafing dishes up to the first checkpoint for his task at hand, Tony glanced at a marked woman, singled out by swollen eyelids. When standing

opposite her outside the entry, and much too close for comfort, he stammered his condolences.

"Mrs. Taversham, I'm so . . ."

Interrupting, "I know you are. Contrite words can only go so far. Say no more."

Trolleying on tenterhooks past her toward the dining room, Viola's voice trailed behind him. "Hope you don't mind my taking the reins for setting the table with fine china and silverware. And, contrary to what we originally thought, the girls won't be coming."

Having sworn his comedic devil to civility, Tony abstained from replying, *"Oh, yeah? What about our two guests of honor? I don't see them around either."*

Viola's afterthought unnerved him. "We left the cemetery ahead of Sal and Etta so they could have their privacy at the gravesite."

We. Meaning her other half had to be someplace along his green mile to the dining room. The missus had already shot down his sincere efforts to convey his deepest sympathies, traumatized as he was over the whole thing himself. So, what could he possibly say to Rosalia's father?

The rustling of an open newspaper gave away Tavvy's whereabouts in the great room. The morning edition concealed his identity behind the jurisdiction of its widespread pages, the way he'd intended. He hadn't read a word, and didn't plan on it. Puffing on a pipe, he assumed his bogus posturing to build a wall for keeping out trespassers.

Tony figured as much. Try as he might, pushing onward to his destination without disturbing the patriarch, Tavvy peered over the edge of his newspaper.

Curses! Squeaky wheels sounded an alarm.

Siphoning his last vestiges of dry humor, he called Tony on the carpet. "Hark! Who goes there?"

His anxiety, somewhat appeased, Tony rolled with it. "Hey, is that a set-up for a knock-knock joke?"

Tavvy put the newspaper down. He looked Tony dead in the eye. Tony stopped in his tracks, leaning against the food carrier for support. "My good man, Honey Bun and I know you're hurting too. So, you don't have to come up with clever remarks when your heart isn't in it."

Well-played, Tavvy. Well-played.

Tony's comedic devil, his alter ego, made a run for it, absconding with his cojones. Heaving with sobs, his knees caved. In an instant, the Tavershams rushed over, surrounding him with hugs and spilling their own comforting words.

Chapter 46

Gathered around the dining table, partaking in a post-funeral reception, the skeleton crew of mourners kept their innermost thoughts to themselves. Lest any of the adults say something emotionally upsetting to provoke a fresh onslaught of tears, each weighed their words. All of that pussyfooting around grated on Etta's nerves.

"Not a single one of you have mentioned Momma! If the bitches were here, I'll bet they'd have had plenty to say about her!"

"In front of a minor? Censored for sure," proclaimed Sal.

***

A collaboration of bitches:

Lack of candor vs. outspoken valor.

Before their rental ride from downtown Providence to Foster, the bitches steeled themselves with caffeine and blueberry muffins at the coffee shop in the Crown Hotel where they had stayed overnight. Seeds scattered far and wide, the four could never coordinate a time and place to meet. Although they parted ways after Rosalia and Sal's nuptials at the Capisci Deli, they stayed in touch with regularity as pledged.

However, the increased odds of probability existed for fudging facts when penning letters, and feigning cheer while conversing over the phone. Reducing the odds for falsities, glossies projected glaring truths to behold. Sealed inside plastic sleeves of an album, each insertion chronicled their transformation as they ripened on the vine.

Ever-changing hairdos, fluctuating waistlines, and infringing wrinkles left little for the imagination to ponder.

Joan fell short of transparency. It took a funeral pilgrimage to discover the reason why inside their suite as they got ready for bed. When Joan emerged from the bathroom wearing a long-sleeved nightgown on a midsummer night—squeaky-clean, her face devoid of heavy-handed foundation—Helen and Gloria got the picture. In livid color. Blue and purple, to be precise.

Joan scurried to slip under the covers in her own double bed. Reaching for the lamp on the nightstand, Gloria intercepted her from turning it off. "How did you get those bruises on your face?"

Prefaced with nervous laughter, "Carrying a basket of laundry down to the basement, I lost my balance and tumbled. Hit the cement floor, face-first, I did." She followed through in pressing the push-button. "G'night. Don't let the bedbugs bite."

Helen and Gloria slipped under the covers in their double bed, each supine at the opposite side. Before Gloria hit the push-button on their lamp, she and Helen expressed mutual disbelief through the sign language of arching their eyebrows.

***

Sipping refills at the secluded table Helen requested, she took the initiative in conducting an unpleasant probe. Emboldened by Joan's long-sleeve blouse on a sultry day, she charged ahead. "By the way… we're not buying into that bedtime story you told last night. Suppose you tell us how you really got those bruises on your face. And, the others you're covering up."

Caught off guard, the color drained from Joan's face. Pancake pâté camouflaged the blanching which stunned her to silence.

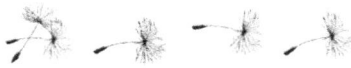

Helen hammered away. "Well, seeing your tongue is in a knot for the moment, I'll tell *you*! Correct me if I'm wrong. You're married to a brute who beats you to a pulp!"

Denial, not an option, Joan scraped together a feeble defense. "Only when he loses his temper."

Helen threw her arms in the air. "O-o-h! And, how often does he go apeshit?" She snorted in Gloria's direction, "Howdy, pardner! Anything you want to get off your chest?"

Put on the spot, Gloria spared Joan a second round of humiliation. "As a matter of fact, I do. Going apeshit just once is one too many times!"

"Spoken with true conviction!" Helen clapped her hands above her head and swayed. "Can I get an amen?"

Defeated, Joan slumped in her seat.

Seeing no use in beating a dead horse any further, Gloria soft-pedaled. "From what I gather, he's the sole breadwinner, strapping you financially and calling all the shots because of it."

"Please don't tell us you love him and never thought of leaving," challenged Helen.

Joan bowed her head, unable to look them in the eye head-on. "I've nowhere to go. Coming from a family of staunch Catholics who believe divorce is a deadly sin, they've turned their backs on me."

Helen shook her head. "Murder is next to godliness! Hope you realize, sooner than later, your luck of the Irish is going to run out."

Joan wept into an embroidered handkerchief she pulled out of her handbag. Gloria signaled the waiter for second refills of coffee. Helen waited for the denouement of tear dabbing before taking Joan's life into her hands.

"Woe is me! A mother hen's work is never done! If I'm going to take you under my wing, you'll need to go the distance. Follow me?"

"This, I gotta hear!" blurted Gloria.

Joan, hedging, "It depends."

"On what? You don't have any children to consider. Just yourself." Helen triggered a fresh onslaught of tears.

Barely coherent between sobs, Joan relinquished her weighty secret. "My child would have been close to Etta's age. I mis-c-c-ar-ried three months along. Stuart had no g-grounds to claim he wasn't the father of our baby. One day, he w-w-orked himself into a rage over it."

Helen felt a chill. Gloria felt faint. Joan's crying jag granted her bewildered companions a breather to gather their wits.

Blotting her face dry, Joan added, with a firm voice and fixed glare, "Soon afterward, I had an IUD inserted without him knowing about it. I'll be damned if I'd ever give him the son he so desperately wants!"

Helen cleared her throat of cobwebs and began to negotiate, improvising as she went along, "Your indignation and bitterness got you off to a running start—jogging in place—going nowhere. If you value your life—leave!"

"How? He never gives me enough money to siphon and save. I don't have two dimes to rub together after grocery shopping."

"With the clothes on your back, and those in your suitcase, you're coming home with me to Seward, Nebraska. No time like the present to start divorce proceedings. You're welcome to stay for as long as you need until you can support yourself through the education you've squandered. I'll convince one of

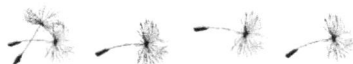

my five kids to share their room. Bearing in mind the stories I've told them about you, it won't be easy."

"Oh, Helen! You say the sweetest things!" Joan leaped from her chair on the opposite side of the table and hugged her heavyset savior.

When Joan let go, Gloria's Cheshire grin and scheming enterprise diffused Helen's onset of tears. "What are you doing?"

"I'm putting the finishing touches on checks for each of you to spend as needed. Sure as God made little green apples, Rosalia would have written one of them herself if she were here."

In receipt of Gloria's largesse, each protested her lavishness.

"Being married to a doctor might make you a rich bitch—but, really? Three zeros?" argued Helen.

Joan objected, "This is far more than I deserve!"

"You can't put a price on friendship. Now, shall we head up to the room to fetch our luggage and check out? I think Rosalia would nod her approval for us to get off our fannies so we won't be late for her funeral."

Chapter 47

As though Rosalia were there in person egging them on over dessert, mourning transposed to mirth. Viola and Tavvy held nothing back in sharing their daughter's childhood shenanigans.

"Darn tootin' I was angry, Honey Bun! Adding insult to injury, both of you howled mercilessly when I fell over." Grateful for turning the tide in their table talk, the twinkle in his eye belied indignation. "Perhaps my counting to ten will grant all of you laughing hyenas enough time to compose yourselves."

Taking unfair advantage of her dad when he dozed off in his favorite armchair, Rosalia tied his shoelaces together. Crouching from behind, she waited for him to awaken and take the fall for her prank.

"Great story, Nonna! Wonder why Momma kept that one from me!"

"Well, after my stern talking-to about the cruelty in finding humor through someone else's misfortune, your momma saw the error of her ways. Expressing remorse, she begged my forgiveness. Considering the outcome a lesson well-learned, I never brought up the subject again. Nor did your mother, as far as I know."

"Off subject—if you'll excuse me, I'd like to clear the main course and wrap leftovers," Tony interjected. "While I eavesdrop."

Determined to delay her family from excusing themselves to retire in their respective rooms, Etta rallied with smugness, sure she'd outdo her grandparents. "Bet you two never knew

that after Momma graduated from Pembroke, she planned on driving to San Francisco—with Gloria!"

Open-mouthed, Tavvy turned to his wife. Unfazed, Viola knocked her granddaughter down a peg. "I surmised as much when I spotted a roadmap buried under her bras. A mother's occupational hazard when tucking folded laundry inside bureau drawers."

In eye-popping astonishment, Tavvy took issue. "Honey Bun! You didn't think it prudent to bring me up to snuff?"

"Mio caro," she trilled, stroking his cheek. "No. On the weak foundation of a hunch, I saw no point in causing you to blow a fuse. Like you are now."

"H-m-m," he retreated, sheepishly rubbing his chin. "Now that you mention it—all these years later—I'm getting the picture. No wonder she turned down a roadster and insisted on a station wagon."

"Even though Momma's adventure didn't pan out, that wagon's boss for tooling around," chirped Rosalia.

*No way, would she give up her secret of equating Momma's wagon with the one in **Dark Passage**.*

"Define *boss,* young lady."

"Oh, Grampa! *G-r-o-o-v-y!*"

"That's supposed to clarify things for a time-warped gent?" he joshed.

"Anyways," Etta continued, streaming her thoughts, "Someday, I'm going to spread my wings."

Sal, who, for the most part, presided over dinner with a solemn gaze, redirected the flow of conversation. "Before you take off on any flight of fancy, your education comes first. We'll talk more about this. Later," he emphasized. "And, come

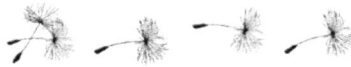

to think of it, there's one other thing weighing heavily on my mind."

Discomfited over Sal's timing, Tavvy and Viola bowed their heads. Thrown for a loop by her dad's firmness, Etta thought it best not to antagonize him further while they were both saturated with grief. However, the temptation to mouth off proved too great.

"Anytime you need to talk about female stuff or boys—that's where Nonna comes in," advised Sal, seemingly determined to get it off his chest at the table.

Summoning a fragment of spunk with a smirk, "Was that one of the heavies?"

"In addition to, and of equal weight." His penetrating glare discouraged any more unsolicited comments, effectively wiping the smirk off her face.

She lowered her eyes, muttering, "I'll keep it in mind, Dad."

Watching Etta wilt from the atmospheric pressure, Tony interceded on her behalf. "I'll set you straight about boys right now! Finding a decent fella who's a man of his word is like looking for a needle in a haystack."

"Well-spoken, Tony!" Viola championed, glad for the diversion. "Etta, look around. You and I are fortunate to be in the presence of great men."

Etta, also appreciating the abrupt conversational spin, backtracked to amend and appease. Turning to her dad, "Momma told me she was right in following her instincts *that* day. Whatever she meant. And, choosing you over a pie in the sky."

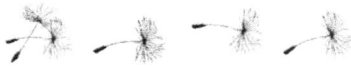

Sal's disposition sweetened. Well aware of what Rosalia meant, a vivid flashback of their diversionary drive and lovemaking in the back seat crossed his mind.

"She said that?"

"Lots of times."

Less demonstrative than Rosalia for displaying the affection he harbored within his heart for Etta, he broke with precedent and reached over to envelop his daughter in a tight embrace.

Chapter 48

The retreat to their respective quarters underway, Etta listened for the clicking of the door to her grandparents' guest bedroom next to hers. Catching snatches of Grampa's consoling murmurs convinced her they'd stay put for a while. While her dad and Tony talked shop in the great room downstairs, Etta had all the clearance she needed to sneak undetected into the other adjoining bedroom where her parents slept.

The scent of lavender wafted from the sheets on the four-poster bed, its lightweight comforter folded to the foot. Etta supposed she'd check with her dad before changing the bed linens. While traces of her mother's scent lay in repose, Etta climbed onto her half of the bed.

She didn't stem the flow of tears rolling down her cheeks, tasting their sorrowful saltiness. Through blurred vision, her mind meandered through a mist of melancholia which led her back to the point from which it originated:

Before dawn's early light encroached upon her bedroom, Etta awakened with a start.

"Rosalia! Wake up! Rosalia!"

Her father's reverberations penetrating through the wall roused her brain from its stupor of sleep. Alarm, stimulating a surge of adrenalin, Etta kicked off the bedcovers and rushed next door, turning the knob and charging in.

"Dad!"

Hovering over Momma, Sal faced his daughter and barked, "I already called the police station. An ambulance should be here any minute. Hurry downstairs and unlock the door!"

If ever there was an occasion to obey her father without question, this qualified. Frightened, her legs turned to rubber, impeding progress in vaulting from the top of the landing to the bottom of the stairs.

Unbeknownst to Etta, her dad sent her on a fool's errand to prevent her from catching a glimpse of her mother's lifeless form.

She still hadn't come to terms with her Momma's swift and sudden passing connected with heading to bed earlier than usual that evening on account of a severe headache. The coroner determined Rosalia's cause of death resulted from a ruptured brain aneurysm.

Surrounded by vestiges of lavender, Etta concluded, right then and there, her momma's signature scent would become hers too. There, poised on the filigree, mirrored vanity tray on top of the dresser, beckoned a nearly-depleted bottle of Yardley English Lavender Eau de Toilette. With reverence, she picked it up. Squirting her wrist and allowing the fragrant spirits to settle a bit, she took a deep breath to inhale the olfactory essence of her momma.

Deciding against putting the bottle back where it belonged because she couldn't bear to part with the memento, Etta stuck it inside the pocket of her funeral dress. Nonna had approved of the simple, boatneck, sheath dress in black, elegant in its simplicity. Etta doubted she'd ever wear the garment again for its somber and stark association with her mother's death. She couldn't wait to slip out of it.

But, first, snatch what she came for and get out, sight unseen, so she wouldn't have to explain her motive to anyone. Etta tugged the handle on the stubborn bottom drawer of the dresser until it opened wide enough for her to grab hold of Momma's photo album. Cradling the leather-bound keepsake to

her bosom, she approached her bedroom with stealth, and nursed closing the door behind her.

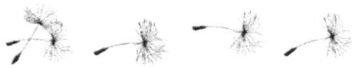

Chapter 49

Mission accomplished, Etta let her hair down by removing the hairpins which held a contrived, unkempt upsweep in place. Complying with Nonna's suggestion, she had gone the whole nine yards for presenting a conservative package. Shaking her head and raking her fingers through a thick entanglement, she liberated unruly curls to tumble past her shoulders.

The trade-off in slipping out of a dress and slipping into pajamas offered a measure of comfort for sitting on the bed with the album on her lap. Turning back the pages of time, she started at the beginning of the hefty tome she and Momma revisited often enough. In fact, they had perused the most recent inserts a week before her leave-taking.

By the grace of every tale her mother told in correspondence with each glossy along their progression from black-and-white to color, Etta came to adore the bitches. Meeting them for the first time, she felt the mutual love each one radiated through their consoling hugs accompanied by words of compassion during the civil ceremony and at the gravesite.

***

Etta gazed at one of Helen's college snapshots, replaying the scenario her Momma had shared. That'd be the incident where Rosalia commandeered a boring Friday evening right after Helen ended a telephone conversation with her fiancé. Most times, Momma pointed out, Helen called the shots. From what Etta had observed through their brief acquaintanceship, her mother hit the nail on the head.

The autumn after graduation, Helen Chandler married John Winters, the Nebraskan love of her life whom she'd dated during high school. They appropriated most of the income from

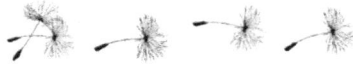

his veterinary practice and her nursing career toward raising their five children. Whatever accrued in discretionary funds, they used for renovating the old, drafty farmhouse John had inherited from his folks.

Seeing Helen in the flesh confirmed what the forward march of snapshots revealed. She had packed on the pounds. All the better for throwing her weight around, Etta mused. A thumbs-up for Helen's tousled, mopsy hairstyle which she'd considered an improvement over yesteryear's college pixie.

***

Etta channeled her focus on Joan, whom at first, came across starched and secretarial during their encounter. Peanut-brittle thin. Frosted with makeup. Not a hair out of place in her flipped bob. High-buttoned propriety. Despite outward appearances, Joan's timidity corroborated Momma labelling her a shrinking violet.

Rosalia had canonized Joan a saint for putting up with their teasing. Momma also confided how Joan gave her the impression she enrolled at the elite college with an ulterior motive. Foremost, earning a degree while searching for a suitable husband on the grounds of Pembroke's adjunct Brown University campus. Instead, Joan Sullivan went back home to Cheyenne, Wyoming without lining up any romantic leads whatsoever.

Indicative of the 1950s, a woman's academic achievement did little to alleviate discrimination in seeking employment. Betwixt and between the drivel inside one of Joan's infrequent letters to Rosalia, she disclosed how fortunate she felt to have landed a supervisory position at a utility company. Overseeing dozens of secretaries in a typing pool, Joan kept tabs on the speed at which her subordinates pounded the keys transforming shorthand to words.

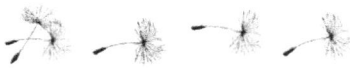

Every Friday evening after work, she forsook the conduct of a rigid forewoman to socialize with a bunch of single typists at the Wigwam Lounge in the Plains Hotel. One such Friday, she happened to catch the roving eye of an insurance salesman tipping back the dregs of Irish dry stout from a beer stein. The revolving bar stool he perched on proved ideal for looking over women gathered around the campfire of candlelit tables.

For sure, Joan's respectable attire would earn his mother's approval should he decide to traipse the stepping stones leading toward marriage. Faith and begorrah! Stuart O'Rourke got off his high horse. Unsteady on his feet, he ambled toward Joan's table. Distracting her with enough smooth-talking blarney, she welcomed his advances and agreed to another martini.

Whether Joan had been aware of any warning signs during their courtship, or chose to ignore them, she appeared starry-eyed standing next to her strapping, Peterbilt husband in the wedding photo Momma preserved for all posterity.

**

Etta stifled a yawn, fighting fatigue wrought from all the trauma compacted within the span of a week. She persevered in determination to rekindle her memories of Gloria, some grounded in Momma's anecdotes, and others she'd fantasized. Idolized for commanding an adventurous spirit akin to her mother's, Etta heroicized Gloria, her favorite bitch.

A far cry from those days of embracing Rita Hayworth, Gloria still set the bar for exuding glamour. Her red hair, styled in a mod blowout, achieved both the classiness of a bob with flipped ends, and the dishevelment of Bardot in all its teased glory. Gloria had no qualms flaunting her shapely legs in an above-the-knee mini dress, albeit in funerary black.

Etta recalled asking her momma point-blank whether she thought Gloria might have pursued her Hollywood dream if she

hadn't bailed on her. Without flinching, Momma said, "Falling in love has a way of sealing one's fate by smashing all preconceived notions to pieces." Then, Momma, perhaps feeling the need to get herself off the hook, filled her in on Gloria's detour, miles away from any euphemistic casting couch.

Since Rosalia and Sal's post-grad, marriage ceremony detained her from accompanying her parents on their flight home to Illinois, *Gloria was up shit's creek*, Momma's exact words.

Just so happened, one of the Brown hangers-on who wanted to experience the seaside of Newport before departing Rhode Island for good, got wind of Gloria's predicament. Heading back to his native state of Oklahoma, he could barrel through Illinois, no problem. Besides, he'd welcome the company for conversation to pass the time.

And, in no hurry with the summer ahead of them, he'd apply the brakes and pull over to get their kicks taking in the roadside attractions along Route 66. Together, hours on end, in the front seat of a '47 Mercury convertible with the sun bearing down on them, familiarity might have bred contempt. Au contraire!

Omitting any sordid details to Etta, and no doubt, sparing Gloria of the same, Rosalia nipped her story in the bud, paraphrasing content from one of Gloria's letters. "During the last leg of their journey, digging into a stack of buckwheat pancakes drenched in maple syrup at the Rooster Tail Café, Lenny Weintraub proposed to Gloria Maguire."

That Lenny!

On a full stomach, and chock-full of luck, a passerby notary public solemnized their marriage in front of the 15-foot-tall Man of Steel in Metropolis, Illinois. All this, minutes before

Lenny pulled in the driveway and tooted the horn to smoke Gloria's parents out their front door.

In the due course of time, Dr. Leonard Weintraub established a successful dermatology practice in Peoria. Familiarity breeding even more devotion between them, Lenny hired his wife for the office manager position. With her parents overseeing child care, Gloria had the presence of mind to run a tight ship for her captain and join him for lunch.

***

As evening shadows skittered across her room, a rap on the door curbed Etta's sigh of ecstasy exhaled in adulation of Gloria. "Your nonna and I are heading down for a snack. Figured we may as well grab a bite while Tony's still around to dish it out. Care to join us?"

Although more tired than hungry, Etta craved the comradery. Breaking bread together never failed to bring out the best in all of them. "I'll be there in a minute!"

After bestowing a kiss on one of her momma's glossies, she closed the album and stashed it under her bed for safekeeping until next time.

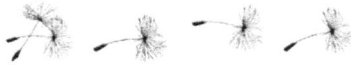

Chapter 50

As the simmering summer days of July rolled to an end, Etta grew more resentful of her dad's tight leash on her whereabouts. For that major reason, hanging out in the city with Bay View's crème de la crème of the in-crowd no longer held curb appeal for her. Also a bummer, several of the pack were vacationing abroad. Others retreated to their summer home, either on Long Island or Martha's Vineyard.

Strutting the sidewalk outside the theater, Etta kept a wary eye out for her dad. She didn't put it past him to career around the corner in Momma's wagon before the movie ended. More dreadful, the thought of him dropping her off and parking far enough away within spying distance from the theater.

Who was she kidding? Etta knew darn well her dad wouldn't last more than five minutes. If he discovered her lingering on the sidewalk under garish neon signs, sending out mixed signals to the honking stream of traffic, she'd suffer his scourge of public vilification.

All good things, including hedonistic and heedless frivolity, must come to an end. And, quick! Truth be told, there'd be no turning back for Etta once Sal made up his mind for her.

***

First and foremost, Etta's education.

Sal and Etta neared the finish line of their late-night supper. Wielding a four-pronged attack, they speared grilled steaks drizzled in garlic butter sauce, herb-grilled potatoes, and thick strips of seared zucchini. Lack of conversation, chalked up to savoring their delicious meal on the section of the wraparound porch overlooking the back yard. Escalating in proportion by

the minute, wind gusts prefacing a thunderstorm hitherto forecasted.

Intending to outwit Mother Nature and avoid the mishap of getting drenched in the sideswipe, the two hustled. Sal moistened a steel wool pad to clean the grill prior to securing its lid. Etta cleared most trace evidence of dinner from the rustic table, hewn from solid acacia wood, Selected by Rosalia for its durability, it weathered the elements many more years after her death. Sal's too.

Etta's dexterity in handling a stack of plates topped with glasses and utensils enabled her to whisk everything to the kitchen by way of the screen door. Once inside, she unloaded the teetering tower onto the counter by the sink.

Retracing her steps over the threshold and onto the porch, she sponged and towel-dried the vinyl tablecloth which Sal helped her to fold. While he snuffed the tiki torches, Etta dashed inside seconds ahead of her dad. No sooner had the screen door closed behind two fleers, thunder pealed and the sky unleashed its fury.

***

Etta thought it downright odd and out of character for her dad to horn in beside her at the sink. Picking up the slack, he dried whatever she'd wash and plunk in the dish strainer. Furthermore, he returned all tableware to the rightful drawer or cupboard from which Etta had retrieved them.

Until that evening, Sal had never breached the strict code of conduct for an old-school Italian. Lowering his standards to undertake what he thought of as women's work made Etta jittery, raising her suspicion of an ulterior motive.

Ready to throw in the towel, Etta draped the damp cloth over one of the dowels on a wall-mounted drying rack. Without so much as a preface, Sal electrified the air. "With Momma not

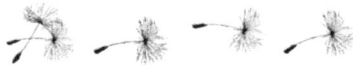

around to drive you back and forth to school, I enrolled you at Ponaganset High."

Disbelief coursed through Etta's veins. Anger roused her from a daze and resuscitated the ability to think on her feet. "Just like that?" she retaliated with a snap of her fingers.

"Of course not!" countered Sal. "It involved my hunting down your birth certificate and immunization record. Rummaging through your wallet, I got lucky and found your Social Security card."

Etta felt weak in the knees.

"Bay View will forward your transcript. The easy part was showing proof of residency."

She slumped to the kitchen floor, feeling her father had hung her out to dry. From a compromised position, Etta sputtered her indignation. "D-dad, how dare you s-n-noop in my wallet without asking permission! You v-v-iolated my p-privacy!"

Chagrined, Sal raked his fingers through his thick crop of hair, seasoned with gray. "Awright, maybe I overstepped a little," pinching his thumb and forefinger together. "But, you weren't around that day, off somewhere with Nonna and Grampa."

"Still! That didn't give you the right!"

Etta picked herself up from the floor. Standing face to face with her dad, she confronted him at close range. "And, the colossal nerve of arranging a school transfer behind my back!"

Gesticulating, she waved her hands and arms around in anger, chewing him out. "I'm not stupid, Dad! I know transportation was going to be a problem, and already surmised I wouldn't start my junior year at Bay View. If you had any

consideration or respect, you'd have discussed this with me beforehand."

Dropping her arms by her side, Etta clenched her hands into white-knuckled fists. Tears stung her eyes, but she wouldn't allow them to fall on his watch.

"There! You just said so yourself. An unavoidable situation. Why belabor the inevitable by discussing a done deal?"

Etta brushed past her dad in a huff, charging up the stairs.

"Whoa! Hold on a minute!"

Halfway to the sanctuary of her room, Etta spun around and glared at him.

"There's someone I want you to meet."

"Suppose I'd rather not?" she challenged. "Hope you didn't make any arrangements."

Sal tilted his head at a cocky angle and smirked, irritating her to no end. "What do you think?"

Assuming an assertive pose, Etta placed her hands on her hips, her upper eyelids raised in a dare.

"Tomorrow."

"O-o-o-h!" Etta seethed.

Sal stood at the bottom of the landing. Arms folded across his chest, he watched his daughter stomp the rest of the way to her room. He chuckled when he heard the door slam behind her. The spittin' image of his beloved Rosalia, in appearance and attitude, Sal's heart swelled with love and pride for their Musetta Rose.

Expressing how he felt toward her—not in so many words, or outward displays of affection.

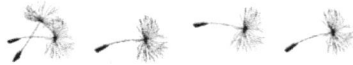

Chapter 51

Embarking along those roads less traveled.

Issued her driver's license when she turned sixteen in February of 1967, Etta was still a novice behind the steering wheel at the end of July. Foster, one of two towns in northwestern Rhode Island, invariably snowbound at any given time from late autumn until early spring, prevented her from wresting the wheel from her momma. You may recall the local radio broadcaster's frequent double-header announcement, "No school, Fosta-Glosta."

Come rain, sleet or snow, Rosalia forged their way from the backroads of Foster to the main thoroughfares of Riverside unless the academy cancelled classes. The occasional slipping and sliding on black ice put a damper on Etta's eagerness to navigate.

On a few occasions during Rosalia's last summer on earth, she allowed her daughter to go *steer crazy*, the term she coined for Etta taking over the wheel. With Rosalia in the passenger seat, Etta inched along those tricky backroads toward one of their Frost-like stomping grounds in the woods. Since both preferred walking to their destinations whenever feasible, Etta lacked the confidence she might have gained from regular practice runs that summer. At any rate, death killed the furtherance of pleasurable pastimes and prospects which might have been.

***

Biting her bottom lip, and with a viselike grip on the steering wheel so it wouldn't slip past sweaty palms, Etta set out for the deli. Her dad's tomorrow, mutated into today with noon fast approaching. A stickler for punctuality, her dad

expected her to arrive on time, preferably a few minutes early. So he said before leaving for work that morning.

"It's a set-up!" so she said.

"Keep an open mind, would you please?"

Also attuned to his daughter's anxiety in taking to the road on her own along the half-mile, deserted stretch, Sal made a lighthearted attempt to calm her nerves. "Whether or not there's another car behind you, play it safe and use your blinkers."

Etta rolled her eyes. "You mean turn signals."

"If that's what you want to call them. See you soon."

At first, feeling lost without the compass of her momma's encouraging words, an aura of peace gradually filled her headspace. No doubt in Etta's mind, Rosalia hovered in spirit alongside her, nodding approval at how she hugged the road. Etta dared to take one hand off the wheel to brush away a tear. "Thank you, Momma," she said aloud.

Rounding the bend to her destination, she rode the brake until rolling to a stop, kissing the curb aligned with the front door of the deli. Here against her will, Etta had her own best interests at heart, determined to exemplify her best behavior moving onward. Or, else.

***

A tug on the door to open it broadened Etta's view when her eyes adjusted to the filtered sunlight inside. Stepping over the threshold, she stifled the urge to let loose a contemptuous snigger at the expense of her dad's honorary guest.

A beehive flip hairdo coiffed her in place at one of the bistro tables. Sitting tall, she projected a morally upright posture. Awash in a pastel, short-sleeved over-blouse pegged

her a strait-laced conformist upholding archaic traditions of the right-wing Establishment.

Led by the grace of God and her dad's insistence she be there, Etta strolled in wearing frayed bell-bottom jeans and a floral, bubble-sleeve blouse a tad short of midriff to pass her dad's muster. A rolled-up bandana wrapped around her head suppressed an uprising of anarchistic curls from rioting in the humidity.

The distance between them abridged, they locked eyes. Hers, brown, and reflecting doe-eyed amazement. Etta attributed it to her off-center appearance, at odds with the general population in an outlying area far from the eclectic capital city. Perhaps. But, on second glance, Etta detected the unexpected, which caused her to wince in shame and swallow the threat of bitter laughter. They glistened with warmth, as did her welcoming smile.

About to say something, their guest's father sauntered away from the counter where he'd been chatting with Sal, slicing and dicing in earnest on the opposite side. "Have you two introduced each other yet?"

Etta, pleased to witness another dad getting the eye-roll treatment. "Daddy, you didn't give me half a chance."

Sal came around to the front, wiping his hands on the dish towel he carried with him. At the sight of his daughter, he beamed with delight and winked. "Well, whaddaya know! Looks like you made it here in one piece after all."

Etta grinned, construing the wise crack as high praise from her dad. She cut off their tender exchange to follow through on her self-made promise to display impeccable manners. Addressing the gentleman standing next to her, who, mere days ago, had offered his condolences at Momma's funeral, "Hi, Mr. Doyle."

Acknowledging Etta with a quick, one-sided hug, Fist bandied a greeting. "Hello there, young lady! Etta, this is my daughter, Muriel. The apple of my eye."

Although Muriel fidgeted in embarrassment, her eyes bespoke of adoration for her daddy.

Sal, still standing in front of the counter, observing the goings-on, partook in the exchange. "Muriel, my daughter, Etta. A thorn in my side."

Covering her mouth, Muriel failed to suppress a giggle at the expense of her hostess, and blushed. "Sorry, Etta. I didn't see it coming."

"Oh, my dad is full of spur-of-the-moment surprises, one right after another." Sal wore his amused expression well, unfazed by Etta's goading to get his goat, rather than feeding it more impudence to gloat.

Fist changed the dynamics with his declaration. "Well! Someone has to get back to the office. But, not before I grab my order to go."

Sal went around back to fetch the wrapped and bagged large Italian grinder. Returning to the dining area, he hustled to the social gathering, and handed over Fist's lunch.

"Princess, give me a call when you want me to come by and get you."

Not to be undone by her dad, Etta cooked up an impulsive decision of her own. "If no one objects, I don't mind driving Muriel home."

Muriel's unbridled endorsement to ride in a classic vehicle earned her father's reluctant approval. "I suppose it's okay. So long as you ease up on the chatter so Etta can pay attention taking those sharp curves."

In an instant, Etta regretted her hasty suggestion. She'd gotten her dad to lose the shit-eating grin, all right. But, she didn't like the way his eyebrows scrunched together and his forehead wrinkled. She'd only succeeded in forcing him to sober up in a hurry with worry.

Etta responded with an antidote from her father's own medicine chest. "Dad, I promise to focus on my driving and use my blinkers even if no one's behind me."

"Now you're talkin' my language."

***

Back to business as usual after Fist left, Sal rallied for his cause. "I was in the middle of fixing an antipasto for Muriel when you barged in to interrupt me. What can I get you?"

"Make it a double! No anchovies."

"That's what Muriel said. Chop chop!" Sal disappeared around the corner to cleave cured meats, cheeses, artichoke hearts and vegetables on the butcher-block table.

Chapter 52

Dining in the ambient light streaming through the deli, polite conversation had yet to approach animated lift-off. Muriel's third forkful of antipasto proved itself an accelerant. Sucker-punched by the pepperoncini she bit into, the combination of vinegar brine and heat index instigated a choking fit. Unsuccessful in blinking back the tears running down her cheeks, Muriel let 'em roll. Hastening to put out the fire, she hosed down her throat by siphoning diet cola through the straw in her glass. Attempting to restore her composure, she used her napkin to dab at tear-stained cheeks.

Etta cross-examined Muriel over the acoustics of throat clearing. "I can tell you're a pepperoncini greenhorn. Unless you're a masochist, you can slide the other two on my plate so they don't go to waste."

"Wow! I didn't see this one coming either! So, that's what you call those things!" She took another sip in fortification of full disclosure. "As a matter of fact, this is my first antipasto. I usually have a garden salad for lunch. One of the strict regimens I follow to keep in shape for beauty pageants."

While she dipped her fork in a pepperoncini-free zone, Etta dwelled on the correlation between poise and pageantry which corroborated the untouchable twinge she'd perceived from Muriel at first glance. "Twitchin' and bitchin'! Man, that's gotta involve an awful lot of dedication and discipline! What else do you do to stay in shape?"

While Etta speared a pepperoncini and slice of salami, Muriel replied, grateful for the interest. "Oh, I practice my tap dancing routines in preparation for the talent scoring segment."

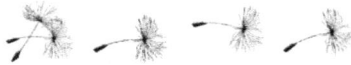

A quip surfaced from out of nowhere. With a swipe of her tongue, Etta maneuvered the contents of food in her mouth to the side pocket of her jaw to give it voice. "Sword swallowing. Now, there's a talent for judges to sit up and take notice. A cut above the rest, huh?"

Etta washed the masticated contents out of jowl storage by slurping regular cola from her straw. Then, going in for the kill, lancing more than she could chew from her plate, Etta paid little else any mind. Therefore, none the wiser in having slashed Muriel's innards to ribbons from inducing a tremulous psychosexual reaction associated with deep-throating Uncle Reggie's pork sword and swallowing his scum.

Swimming against the floodtide of memories, Muriel grasped at her straw. Gulping the remains of her soda, she waded through her mind for something to say that would transport her to the present. She came up dry.

Sal, keeping an eye out for the girls to see how they were getting along, wanted to pat himself on the back for suggesting to Fist their daughters should meet. He noticed Muriel needed a refill, so headed on over with a pitcher of soda. Topping off her glass and inquiring how both of them liked their meals, he then left well enough alone to fulfill his duties as chef and cashier for the paying customers straggling in.

The subtle intrusion broke Muriel's trance, and Etta's subsequent inquiry rousted her away from a nightmarish childhood. "So, what prizes are up for grabs if you win first place?" While reluctant to probe further, inquisitiveness triumphed over reticence. "Have you ever? You know—come in first?" Prepared to listen intently, Etta fortified her fork with sustenance to mince and mash.

If only Muriel possessed the means to answer the judges with as much aplomb. "Well, speaking from my experience as a contestant in pageants sponsored by local festivals and fairs,

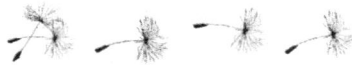

you could get a sash with the winning title on it. Or, a trophy. Savings bond. Maybe a tiara."

Suspending her loaded fork in mid-air, Etta awaited Muriel's second-tier response. The suspense rivaled that of a cliffhanger.

Prefaced with a self-conscious titter, "No title. Yet. Runner-up a few times. After I finish our junior year and quit school, my mother plans on entering me in the Miss Rhode Island competition. Then, she'll take it from there."

Stupefied by such an unheard-of declaration, and unable to take the next bite, Etta put her fork to bed on a cushion of lettuce. "Q-q-uit? Aren't you even the least bit interested in getting a high school diploma?"

Muriel dipped her fork into uncharted territory on her plate, determined not to let tears emerge over the spilled semen of yesteryear, culpable for souring her academic performance. When Muriel did reply, Etta hit upon her faraway glaze as though her mind had ventured elsewhere. Out of thin air, Etta pinpointed Timbuktu.

"Really. It's in my best interest to drop out. Since first grade, I've been in danger of failing, and passed from one year to the next by the skin of my teeth. Except for repeating fifth grade."

Etta didn't know what to say. Thinking an awkward subject closed, she picked up her fork and inserted its contents into her gaping mouth. Wrong.

Picking up steam, Muriel ran off at the mouth. "Anyway, even if I never win a pageant title, it's something to do before marriage. My mother told me, that as a rule, men prefer beauty over intelligence when it comes to choosing a wife."

She stopped short of mentioning what else her mother told her. *"When you're married, it's best to lie still during the dirty*

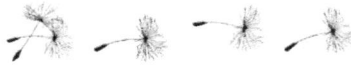

deed so you don't prolong the agony. This way you don't encourage your husband into thinking he's got to do more nasty stuff."

Stabbing the last pepperoncini, along with a wedge of tomato and artichoke heart, Etta shoveled in the grub. Chewing restrained her from retaliating in anger. For God's sake, her own macho honcho of a dad put his foot down when it came to her prioritizing a college education. "Even though you already know too much for your own good," he said.

As for dating, more than once, he admonished her with a faraway stare Etta christened Poughkeepsie, "Remember— when playing with fire, you burn your bridges behind you, so there's no turning back."

Etta's body heat intensified the scent of lavender she'd applied before leaving the house. She sensed the energy of her mother's indignation through the runoff of perspiration in her cleavage

Muriel also delved into her antipasto with gusto, giving chase to an appetite intensified by true confessions. Her rapid arm movement reminded Etta of a fiddler's elbow, in light of how she embraced women playing second fiddle to men.

In the thick of dipping and nipping antipasto, Muriel nursed second thoughts about laying any more of her soul on the line to someone she'd just met. Despite foreseeing the development of a strong and steadfast friendship between them, Muriel decided to table the topic.

Her face assumed a dreamy expression as she and Etta polished off the rest of their antipasto in a lull of quietude. Taking a breather to quench her thirst in slurping what remained of her cola, Etta glimpsed the neither-here-nor-there vacancy sign of a mind in exile. For crying out loud, riding a giant tortoise on the Galapagos Islands, for all she knew!

Muriel had lost herself in thought. *She had until the end of her junior year in high school to grab the attention of an upperclassman she'd pined for as long as she could remember. Gain his confidence. Get him to fall under her spell and ask her out. Go steady.* Etta interrupted her dream stream when she suggested they help out her dad by stacking their plates and utensils before taking to the road.

Even though he had never cast a second glance in Muriel's direction, she decided the only man she'd ever give her hand in marriage to was Obie Smith.

***

Gabbing past due in the front seat of the Woodie on the Doyles' driveway, both girls had ditched any misgivings about kicking off a friendship. From that day forward, they established a lifelong alliance despite their differences. And, despite those occasions where Etta restrained herself from throttling Muriel in reaction to an acid reflux of exasperation.

Lifting the door handle to let herself out, the rarity of a brilliant idea crossed Muriel's mind. "Tomorrow afternoon, my mother and I could swing by to pick you up on our way to the dance studio. That is, if you'd like to watch my routine."

Lois stepped away from her stakeout behind an end pleat in the open drapery on the living room window.

Wide-eyed with enthusiasm, Etta jump-started their chumming around together. "You bet! Can't wait! Call me. Toodle-loo." Having already exchanged telephone numbers, Muriel would dial her up within the hour. As their friendship progressed throughout summer, Muriel accepted invitations to tag along on Etta's sketching jaunts traversing her fishing ground.

***

From what Lois picked up on during the drive to the studio, and from sitting alongside the Rizzio girl while her daughter performed, she didn't like one bit. Why, if she had her druthers, she'd put the kibosh on a friendship with potential to corrupt the morals she had taken great pains to drum into Muriel's head so she could land a proper husband to support her.

Instead, Lois Doyle sucked it up on account of Etta's affluent pedigree on the Taversham side of the family. Prestige by association was worth the perks of name-dropping at backyard barbecues. Besides, her husband thought the sun rose and set on Sal Rizzio. She didn't dare instigate one of his fist-pounding episodes by bringing up her prejudices to him.

Nope. After all these years, Lois finally convinced Fist to come around to her way of thinking in their marital bed. They no longer did the nasty-wasty once a week. If, at all. How, when, where, and who her husband did the dipsy-doodle with outside their home was none of her business. Each night when Lois lay herself down to sleep, and prayed to the Lord her soul to keep, she gave thanks for small blessings.

Chapter 53

As Etta's friendship with Muriel flourished, she felt so much better about switching schools. In all verity, she looked forward to starting classes at Ponaganset High. Without letting her dad in on it, Etta thought the transfer from Bay View was the greatest thing since toasty garlic bread. Not having to don a uniform from Monday through Friday, a perk in itself, also granted a new lease on life for embracing her bohemian rapture. However, atypical for the grassroots of Foster.

Other than throwing a good-bye kiss at a shot for scoring big with Birch Hansford, she had no hang-ups stepping outside the circle of cronies she'd consorted with at the elite academy since kindergarten. Getting down to the nitty-gritty, Etta likened their circle to a corral enclosing high-horse fillies who pranced to the beat of the mod subculture. Whereas, she strained at the seam to embrace the eclecticism of mix-and-match, shabby chic outside the city limits of their downtown escapades. She now welcomed leaving behind the confining exclusivity of friendships forged through privilege.

Take Muriel, horse of a different color, altogether. An enigma she couldn't figure out if she cared to try. Yet, for all of Muriel's stiff carriage, her stodgy mannerisms, and her rigid viewpoints, Etta could never imagine accusing her of snobbery. Thinking back on some of those occasions spent in each other's company, Muriel proved herself down-to-earth, warmhearted, and affable without exception.

The world-shattering event of Momma's death may have blown her off course, but she had Muriel's friendship to thank for snapping her out of the doldrums. True, those in her social circle had reached out to her during those dark days. However,

their own discomfort and awkwardness in conveying condolences only augmented her despondency.

So, forced by her dad to take the road not yet taken in the town she'd been born and bred, and not minding in the least, Etta initiated the phone chain for bidding farewells. She touchtone-dialed her turquoise Princess and made the connection for severing a connection.

Chummy-wummy Alison Perry answered on the fourth ring.

The ringleader whom Etta counted on to dispatch her message forward, happened to be a direct descendant of Oliver Hazard Perry, an American naval commander born in southern Rhode Island.

***

What Sister Mary Catharine had yet to cover during their American history lesson that day, got waylaid when Alison raised her hand and Sister called on her.

Alison stood up beside her desk, stretching her willowy figure into a statuesque supposition of superiority. She tossed her straight, brown locks over her shoulder and brushed the Marianne-Faithfull bangs away from her hidden peepers. The adjustment enabled her to peer into the whites of her classmates' eyes. "I'll have you know that during the war against Britain, my distant cousin Oliver supervised the building of a fleet in Erie, Pennsylvania."

Sucking in a deep breath, she exhaled the rest. "For leading the American forces to victory in battle, he earned the title, 'Hero of Lake Erie,' and won a Congressional Gold Medal."

Self-assured of victory in having captured everyone's attention, Alison failed to notice stifled yawns from the peanut

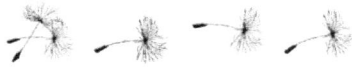

gallery. Blinded by the glaring headlight of pride, she buggered on. "Guess where the medal is now?"

Expecting an onrush of raised hands vying for the privilege of hazarding a guess, she canvassed the room. Not one volunteer. Realizing she'd created her own lake fog without any prospect for adjusting her sails, a quiver tugged at her bottom lip. The shade of red enveloping her face deepened in proportion to the humiliation oozing from her pores in each prolonged second.

Squirming in Alison's misery, Etta contemplated raising her hand to surrender a guess as to where, oh where, Cousin Ollie's fakata medal hung out. Offhand, the Smithsonian.

Too little, too late.

Before Etta had a chance to thrust her hand into the air at full mast, Alison talked herself out of the red through the heroic action of answering the question she posed. "Well, I'll tell you. The medal hangs from a hook on a wall shelf in our den, next to all of my dad's trophies."

Judging by the stone faces around the room, no one gave a shit. The next wave of embarrassment stiffened Alison in place at the center of attention, stirring Etta to action once and for all. For lack of anything better to come up with, she applauded. Clapping awakened the girls from their passive resistance. Everyone joined in the hootenanny, including Sister Mary Catharine.

Not even eye-sweeping bangs blinded Alison to the mission of mercy which allowed her to save face by the skin of her teeth. From that day onward, she cozied up to her savior, rearranging Etta's pecking order in her chain of command. Whoop-dee-do! Etta never felt beholden to anyone, nor duty-bound to a hierarchy of hornets contesting for the status of queen bee.

**

239

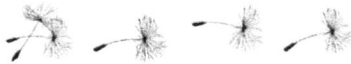

After a preliminary back-and-forth of sweet nothings transmitted through the mouthpiece on their phones, Etta delivered the news to Alison. Taken by surprise, a momentary respite of silence hovered between them, broken by the sound of sniffles Etta heard at the other end.

Alison's words, music to Etta's ears, had a nasal timbre to them. "That sucks!"

A crying jag got the best of her. Faltering, she excused herself to grab a tissue. Etta heard the trumpeting of one long and two short toots. The emotional preamble granted Alison a breather to summon her wits about her. That she did, usurping her leadership role for a nobler cause, rather than the usual high jinks she masterminded.

Her comeback spiel, not any more eloquent. "E-t-t-a, I can't do this right now. When I grab hold of myself, I'll phone the others and plan a get-together." Breaking down again, she fumbled, "I'll be in touch, okay? Oh, and I'll call Birch too."

The last thing Etta wanted was to use her departure as a ploy for playing up to a hard-to-get kind of guy. "N-n-o! N-n-n-o! Don't bother."

Dead silence posed no resistance to her plea. Alison had already severed their connection.

Chapter 54

Hail, hail, the gang's all here. The usual suspects, barring those still vacationing elsewhere. Alison had pulled off a coup. In organizing a farewell party, she made sure each invited guest honored their commitment to show up at The Swirl, a swinging ice cream parlor in the downtown theater district. In attendance that afternoon, besides the Queen Bee and her second-in-command: Karen, Patricia, Lynn, Madge, Phoebe, and Julie.

More of an emotional occasion than anticipated, Etta did her best to play it cool. Hugs and well wishes from each partygoer upon their arrival caused her vision to blur with tears. Through the watery film, everyone blended into the meek-pink wallpaper featuring a sprinkles motif.

To her relief, things took an upswing when Madge pushed the jukebox button for "I Want to Hold Your Hand." Competing against the Beatles at their own warped rate of speed and surging volume, they drowned out the Fab Four. After considerable hemming and hawing, each of them resolved their separate dilemma for choosing a sundae.

Then, the inevitable last-minute changes. A wonder, Sarah, their frazzled server didn't free herself from the albatross tied around her neck, and discard the pink, ruffled pinafore apron to make a fast getaway. Instead, she stuck with it, crossing out and scribbling final judgments on her pad.

After Sarah turned on her heel and had distanced herself from their table to fill her tall orders, Lynn, dense as they come, piped up. "I don't understand all her confusion. Every one of us ordered sundaes with nuts and a cherry on top."

***

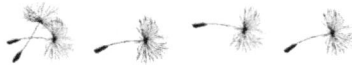

Appreciative of having secured a seat facing the door, Etta cast a glance there every now and then, on the lookout for you-know-who. Wishful thinking. Maybe Alison never called Birch in the first place. Not that she'd ever ask her. Or, maybe, he couldn't be bothered. She didn't blame him for shunning a girlie ice cream fest.

In an ironic twist of fate, Karen push-buttoned "My Guy," which courted Etta's thoughts as they delved into the sundaes Sarah jockeyed in front of them. In a rapid onset of brain freeze, she got a taste of Birch playing the field.

Conversations frozen in abeyance, they dipped long-handled spoons into deep-throated glass troughs. A myriad assortment of ice cream flavors and toppings gratified the lot of them. Similarly, each individual brought their own personality traits to the table.

***

In so many blinks of an eye, you could hear the sound of spoons scraping glass bottom. Alison winked one of hers at Phoebe, a premeditated signal of meaning. Behind a pair of tortoise-shell cat eyes, Phoebe winked back. Ducking under the table, she resurfaced with a gift bag. Clanging her spoon against her dessert glass, she waited until everyone gave her their undivided attention.

"Etta, we put our heads together and came up with a parting gift each of us autographed so you won't forget us." Incriminating the others with a sweeping glance, "And, since I was the only one brave enough to get it, I'm the one handing it over."

Julie authenticated the report. "Phoebe failed to mention I went with her. Even though I stayed outside, I peeked through the door to make sure she didn't chicken out."

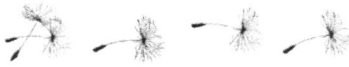

Patricia and Karen, backup vocalists, vouched for Julie. They had gone along for moral support, taking in the view from where they stood across the street.

Etta, the only member in the spoiled-brat pack not in on the joke and giggling, felt uncomfortable. Phoebe stretched her arm across the table and parted company with the bag. While everyone awaited her reaction, Etta ransacked the tissue paper until she struck pay dirt. Now, in on the joke, she giggled with the rest of them.

In her hands, nested a 1965 paperback edition of the dirty book, *Candy*. Inside the front cover, and spilling over onto the title page, her school chums had penned personal notes using their Sunday-best cursive handwriting illustrative of the Palmer method the nuns strictly enforced.

***

Outside The Swirl, mingling in the parking lot, they hugged and dispensed tearful good-byes. Instead of staring straight ahead along her walk to the Woodie, Etta turned her head to look back one last time, and regretted doing so. An invisible line had been drawn in the windblown sand covering the asphalt, severing her from the in-crowd.

Huddled together in the solidarity of their Penny Lane threads, the mod squad had formed a closed circle to conduct a private conversation which no longer included her. Etta shuddered and stepped it up to increase her distance from a defining moment.

In truth, she had given them a piece of her heart when she materialized channeling Janis Joplin in the outfit she chose as her mission statement for the occasion. Seeing they'd glossed over her short skirt with lace tights, and a blouse with wide bat-wing sleeves adorned with layers of beads, spoke volumes. Perhaps the feather earrings blew their mind.

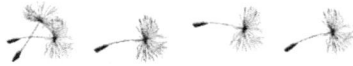

"Hey, Etta! Wait up!"

Turning her head to acknowledge a blast from the past, she discovered Alison bounding toward her. Etta cooled her heels.

"Blazing hell! Are you on your way to a fire?" she panted. After catching her breath, "I didn't want to say this in front of the others, but Birch had to caddy today. He said to tell you, 'Ciao.'"

***

Etta slid in on the driver's side of the Woodie and turned the ignition key. There was no turning back from venturing along the fork in the road leading her away from familiar faces. Other than the lasting impressions her friends inked inside a dirty book.

Whether the naked truth, or a tale about caddying, she advised herself to forget Birch Hansford due to the unlikelihood of their crossing paths ever again. So, she thought.

Chapter 55

Taking advantage of the sunlight streaming through the great room, Etta plied her markers to enhance coloration and to integrate subtle details in the drawing she had sketched the day before on her fishing ground. Muriel had accompanied her on their .3-mile hike to Jerimoth Hill, the highest point in Rhode Island, squatting at the dwarfish elevation of 812 feet. Freedom to roam the backwoods up to the summit would be prohibited in the 1990s by a homeowner whose driveway formed the only path leading the way in. To emphasize his point, "The Madman of Jerimoth Hill" either threatened hikers, held them at gunpoint, or fired shots over their heads if they defied his No Trespassing signs.

Of no concern at the tail end of August in 1968.

Etta looked for the brown Jerimoth Hill sign, east of Pole 212 along the south side of Route 101, Hartford Pike. She parked Momma's wagon in the small parking area across the road from the trailhead which marked the entrance to a narrow clearing. From their point of origin, she and Muriel hiked along the right-hand path directing their way to the summit.

Having worked up a hearty appetite trudging to their destination, they sat themselves down on a sprawling, rocky outcrop at the high point. Lest there be any doubt, a federal geodetic survey marker indicated as much: Jerimoth Hill Register Elev 812 '. Without fanfare, they spread the lunches Sal packed for them on their granite tabletop. Italian grinders on torpedo rolls. Pepperoncini rings withheld from Muriel's.

"If your mother could see you tearing into a grinder instead of nibbling a garden salad!" nudged Etta. A figment of

her imagination sketched a tight-tush thumbnail of Lois with a few warts on her face added into the bargain.

"I shudder to think!" Muriel replied with her mouth full.

They chased their last bites swigging from cans of grape soda, both of them prudent in saving the rest for quenching their thirst on the way down.

A belch preceded Etta's artistic endeavor of sketching an unobstructed view of evergreens and underbrush in her field of vision. Muriel painted her nails. Since both ground plans required focus, absence of conversation enabled them to hear breezes rustling in the pine trees.

So absorbed in finishing the sketch while the scene endured in her memory, Sal's inching from behind and peering over her shoulder, caught Etta unaware. For cripes' sake, she could feel him breathing down her neck.

Point-blank, her dad unnerved her for trespassing in her work-zone. As a rule, he never did, respecting their mutual agreement to lay eyes on her sketches when she presented him the finished piece of art. Alarm bells went off inside her head. She rose from the desk chair. Tool of her trade in one hand, Etta was about to square off.

Sal raised his hands in the air, conceding a screw-up. "Before you get on my case, what I gotta say shouldn't wait for tomorrow."

"Can't it wait until later today? You've interrupted my flow of thought," Etta chastised, with no attempt to hide her annoyance.

"It could. But, in the long run, you'd prefer the light of day."

Growing more irritated, Etta shook her marker at a menacing rate. "Well, Dad—spill! I'd like to salvage what's left of today's sunlight to finish my sketch."

"Fair enough." Warming up, "I want you to know how proud I am at how you've handled transferring to a new school." He winked. "Me thinks I deserve some credit owing to setting up a lunch date with Muriel."

Etta put the marker down, tabling her aggression. She surrendered a half-grin to her dad. "I'll give you that. Having a friend will take the edge off walking into a snake pit on my first day. But, where's this leading, I want to know?"

"More to the point, I took care of the other thing weighing on my mind since after the funeral. As of tomorrow morning, Momma's wagon will be on its way to an auto museum in Newport where it'll be exhibited and preserved for many years to come."

Like a Shelby Mustang in the Woodie's Ford family, Etta's rage accelerated from 0 to 60 in seconds, predisposing her to kick her dad in the shin for raking her over the coals yet again. Except, the emotional turmoil etched on his face dissuaded her from inflicting bodily harm. Instead, she launched a verbal assault.

"How could you be so cruel? You know what Momma's wagon means to me!" she yelled, instigating a shouting match between them.

"What! You don't think I have memories and feelings attached to that wagon too?"

"Not really! Momma and I were two peas in a pod tooling around town. When was the last time you sat in that wagon, huh?"

"About an hour ago. All right?"

Sal's response put a dent in their vitriolic exchange, piquing Etta's curiosity and slamming the brakes on her anger. "What for?"

"To relive the past, that's what! Aw, you think you know it all, but you don't know the half of it!" Choking up, he turned to walk away.

Furious that her dad intended to abandon her with unfinished business between them, Etta landed into him before he disappeared from sight. "Dad! Get in here! You can't just leave me hanging without an explanation."

Sal retraced his steps, leading him right back to their nose-to-nose confrontation in progress. At war with himself, he rubbed the scruff on his jawline, unsure how to proceed. Hoarse from emotion, he decided to follow up a half-truth with the whole truth. "I already told you about the last time I sat in Momma's wagon. The first time I was there, you were conceived in the back seat. So, contrary to what you thought— Momma and I were also two peas in a pod."

Before taking his leave for Etta to mull over his confession in private, Sal dangled the keys to the Woodie in front of her. "If you intend to relive your own past in broad daylight, now's your chance."

***

Blinded by tears, but not blindsided by her dad's revelation, Etta stumbled her way out of the great room, onto the front porch, and down the steps to where the Woodie rested on its laurels at the bend in the driveway. She opened the door on the passenger side and slid onto the front seat the way she always did whenever Momma took the wheel for their outings.

For goodness' sake, the close proximity of her birthdate and her parents' wedding anniversary always led her to the same conclusion. Such that, premarital intimacy resulted in a

248

pregnancy warranting their rush to wed when they did. Her dad may have let the horse out of the barn to get through to her, but their horsing around was none of her business. Nor was her birthplace.

While daylight still remained, she had more important business to tend inside Momma's wagon. She caressed the woodgrain dash and circumnavigated her hands around the steering wheel. She palmed the leather seat. Through closed eyes, Etta committed the wagon's shiny interior to memory for those sight-unseen days ahead.

"Well, Momma. A little birdie told me where the seed was planted for me to grow inside your womb. Maybe you thought I didn't notice your dreamlike trances, but I did."

Etta laid her head on the driver's side of the front seat, reliving the past between them begotten inside the Woodie's womb.

***

Quid pro quo, Etta sneaked up behind Sal in the great room. During her absence, he settled back onto the sofa to watch a rerun of *Gunsmoke*. Although caught unaware, he didn't flinch when Etta began rubbing his temples.

"Dad?"

"H-m-m?" he acknowledged, without deflecting his attention away from the western.

"Think you'll ever marry again?"

"Nah! I happen to like my own cooking. Never heard you or Momma complain, did I?"

"Nope. You know, without Momma to keep the peace between us, we're going to make each other's life a living hell."

"You can't bend minds of steel."

The following morning, Sal and Etta presented a united front. Liking arms, they stood at the top of the driveway, neither uttering a word as the back end of the Woodie disappeared from view altogether.

Sal broke the somber silence between them. "Got everything you need for the start of school tomorrow? If not, you can borrow my car to make a run into town."

His brazen remark catalyzed the desired effect of getting a rise out of Etta, pulling them both out of a funk. "The less I'm seen driving a Chevy Biscayne—anywhere—all the better!"

In a lather over her predicament, Etta stormed up the porch steps, fuming. Sal stayed behind, granting his daughter enough leeway to build up a head of steam all the way up the flight of stairs and into her bedroom. When he heard the faint slam of a door, Sal let out the bellow of laughter he'd suppressed, grateful for the spunky daughter who made his life worth living.

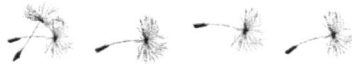

Chapter 56

Making his way to the front door, Sal did an about-face. Out of the corner of his eye, he caught a glimpse of Etta decked out in all her independent glory.

Poking around inside the drawer of an end table, he came across a surplus stash of coupons saved for a rainy day. "If you're not going to change into something more conservative, you'd better put these in your handbag."

"What the heck am I my supposed to do with these?"

"You're a smart girl. You'll figure it out." Sal breezed out the door, in a hurry to start slicing and dicing at the deli before it officially opened.

For her debut at Ponaganset High, Etta carried out her plan to go for broke in piecing together an outfit representing her true identity. Using attire as a barometer for measuring peer pressure, she'd soon determine whether the student body accepted or rejected her based solely on outward appearance.

Until gauging major attitude, Etta put her best foot forward stepping into the back seat behind the driver. She sat opposite Muriel, inside Fist's brand new Cutlass sedan. The maneuver required she hike up her long, wraparound cotton skirt with lettuce-trim hem. When she did, Fist and Muriel got a peek at Etta's brown leather combat boots laced to the ankle. She came by those at a military thrift store.

The flash reminded Fist that his daughter had on a pair of oxblood penny loafers. It bowled him over how two girls different as night and day became best friends in no time at all. He teared up, grateful for Etta in rescuing his Princess from the clutches of her domineering mother. He came out ahead too.

For volunteering to drive Etta back and forth to school, Sal insisted on treating him to a free lunch every day.

Nevertheless, he had a fashion statement to make before transporting precious cargo from North Road to the regional high school on Anan Wade Road in North Scituate. An early start granted him flexibility to digress in advance of their 17-minute ride spanning 10 miles. Fist twisted his torso to accommodate dishing out rhetoric to his backseat passengers.

"You two are lucky I'm not school superintendent because I'd mandate wearing uniforms. Muriel, your knees are showing and your mountain of hair is sprayed so stiff it could trap flies. Etta, if you're not dressed in a gypsy Halloween costume, the joke's on me!"

"Daddy, how rude!" retorted Muriel, taken aback.

While Etta wanted to give Mr. Doyle a piece of her mind for his insult, she held her tongue out of respect for a decent enough guy who happened to be Muriel's father and her dad's close friend.

Seeing the damage written all over their faces, Fist backpedaled his way out of holy hell. "Well, if that's what you girls call dressing for success nowadays, I hope the academic year gets off to a good start for both of you."

According to the dress code specified in their school handbook, Muriel and Etta skirted the rules. Since skirts were required to touch the floor when girls kneeled, all Muriel had to do was unroll the waistband to avoid receiving a demerit from any hawkeyed teacher patrolling the corridors for such an infraction. Although floor-length dresses and skirts were also prohibited, all Etta had to do was roll up the waistband on hers to pass inspection.

***

Ponaganset's student body piled out of school buses and passenger vehicles. Seeking out friends, they gathered together in diverse formations of comradery across the concrete entryway and front lawn. Lost in a sea of unfamiliar faces, Etta suffered a momentary relapse, longing for the comfort zone of Bay View. At least she knew where she'd stand along the periphery of the old guard's circle of jet-setters.

Sensing her unease, Muriel shifted her shoulder bag and notebook, placing an arm around Etta and leading her to a group of juniors she hung around with. "Hey, everybody! I want you to meet Etta, a real nice kid I became friends with over the summer."

These birds of a feather wore pleated, knee-length skirts in dark colors, or plaid. Like Muriel, a couple of them had bared their knees. Most chose white blouses with round, Peter Pan collars to pair with their skirts. These outfits reminded Etta of the regulation uniform she chucked, along with life as she knew it.

Although their hairstyles differed, excessive hairspray glued every strand in place. The group, a cross section representing the general female population of Ponaganset High, sported: beehives, pouffed bouffants, flicked-up bobs, geometrical and asymmetrical Sassoon cuts, pixies, and the flipped-under, bubble bob Muriel favored. Those who didn't fit the mold, grooved to the flower power of long, poker-straight hair, either with a center-part or full-fringe bangs.

While latching onto snatches of private conversations going on at once, and interjecting where and when feasible, Etta scanned the scattered groups of boys. An extinct specimen at Bay View, the only interaction she ever had with the opposite sex occurred at social events on weekends or during school vacations.

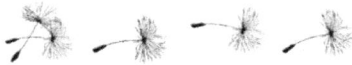

In her opinion, none could compete with drop-dead gorgeous Birch, despite most sporting similar Beatles' mop-tops, and finding many easy on her eyes. Under the impression her surveillance went unnoticed, she cringed when one locked eyes with her. Neither of them averted their gaze until he elbowed the guy standing next to him.

To Etta's embarrassment, they sauntered toward the huddle, their path aligned with her territorial claim on grass. Both blazed the grins of conquistadors. The one she first laid eyes on—tall, blond, having an athletic build and self-assured saunter, addressed her—by name. His dark-haired friend, also of athletic stock, stood by, taking in the scenery.

To Etta's horror, their intrusion disrupted dynamics, cutting off conversations mid-sentence throughout the gabfest. Soon, other curiosity seekers lumbered away from their outlying congregations, advancing like zombies foraging for fresh flesh.

"So, you must be the Rizzio girl." Without benefit of affirmation, he continued uninterrupted. "When I stopped by the deli last week, your dad mentioned a far-out hippie chick would be coming here."

The sudden impact of her dad's audacity to infiltrate every aspect of her life skyrocketed Etta's spunk. "Fair warning, maybe?"

Laughter in a variety of modes erupted all around.

"The name's Obie. This here, is Tom."

Several more introductions flew back and forth among the hodgepodge of students who surrounded a fashion rebel. Thinking on her feet while she had the opportunity to win over receptive hearts and minds, Etta unsnapped the flap on her distressed leather shoulder bag with tassels. In doing so, her gaze landed on Muriel, an elbow's poke away.

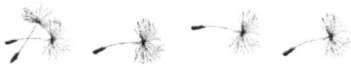

There it was again! An out-of-body, dreamlike state projecting Muriel's mind miles away from where she stood. She may very well have vacated to the Galapagos Islands. Etta had a hunch Obie or Tom sent her there, although neither of them seemed to notice Muriel's presence.

Of secondary importance at the moment, Etta clawed her way to the bottom of her bag, a grin daring to surface at her dad's hell to pay. Oh, she figured it out all right! And, it would cost him!

"Hey, thanks for the warm welcome! Whenever you're in the mood for Italian take-out or dine-in, just present this discount coupon to my dad."

From out of nowhere, arms jutted toward her to grab what Etta had to give until she ran out. Puffed up for having orchestrated her own acceptance at Ponaganset High, she had her dad to thank for his clout in Foster. Otherwise, her momma's lineage might have worked against her in these here parts, rather than for her, the way it had at Bay View.

Disheveled from all the jostling, Etta was saved by the bell. Everyone broke rank to enter the building through front doors held open by faculty members greeting students. Sensing Muriel's low spirits, Etta linked arms with her heading to homeroom.

***

Etta changed her clothes and sat behind her desk in the great room to start her homework. While engaged in the juggling act of balancing an equation, she heard the familiar slam reverberating from the door on her dad's uncouth Biscayne. She couldn't wait to see the expression on his face when she told him how much business she had drummed up for the deli at his expense.

***

255

Etta gave her dad a run for his money until every voucher had been redeemed. Whenever Sal bellyached, she'd point out that he had walked straight into his own trap. Heck, it's not like Sal needed to work in the first place, before or after widowhood.

Although Etta never told him, and wished she had before it was too late, she admired her dad's strong work ethic. He prided himself in diligence and determination to become a successful entrepreneur without relying on her momma's wealth for solvency. Through perseverance, amiability, goodwill, and top-rate culinary skills, Sal achieved his American dream within the sparsely settled countryside. Other than Mad Daddy Wayne Cole's unsuccessful plot to run him out of town, business flourished.

So, up until Sal's bitter end, he and Etta continued to outwit each other throughout her growing independence under his watchful, blind eye. What he didn't know wouldn't kill him—yet!

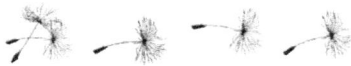

Chapter 57

Etta graduated from Ponaganset High with honors paving the way for acceptance at the prestigious Rhode Island School of Design, tuition funded by her inheritance. Scholastic accolades aside, she deemed her finest accomplishment that of matchmaker extraordinaire. True to her word, she had kept her promise to Muriel for altering the composition of Obie's romantic chemistry in biology lab. From Etta's inaccurate observation at her graduation party, the steady couple seemed crazy for each other. After all, she had caught sight of Obie leading Muriel by the hand to sneak off somewhere together.

Muriel's guest appearance reminded Etta her senior year had sucked without her best friend around. Incentive in itself to focus on excelling for the payout of ranking in the top 5th percentile of her class.

***

While stringing Obie along through oral pacification during their courtship, Muriel aspired to waitressing at the State Line Diner. Thanks to her daddy putting in a good word to the owner, Muriel was hired on the spot without filling out an application. Got to hand it to Fist who exercised his power of persuasion in exemplifying the creed, "Anything for My Princess".

Treading the slippery slopes of wedding preparations and beauty competitions, Muriel had her hands full. She perfected her pageant strut on the job, balancing plates of stick-to-your-ribs food along her arm, heading to any or all four tables at one end of the diner. Grace under fire on Fridays, Muriel's frenetic heel-and-toe kept her body toned and strengthened as she served

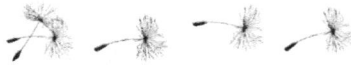

fish-and-chips to the never-ending stream of customers filing in. According to the locals, a fish dish second to none.

For darn sure, Muriel needed stamina to live up to her mother's expectations for every last-ditch effort until sudden death came to pass. Lois had lined up several low-on-the-totem-pole beauty pageants, stopping short of her daughter's wedding. It stood to reason, she recognized Muriel's' limitations, so overturned the decision to fill out an application on her behalf for the Miss Rhode Island USA pageant.

Overseeing Muriel's strict diet regimen, critiquing her dance rehearsals, perfecting her makeup, coordinating her shoes with her catwalk gowns, and taming flyaways on her polished hairstyle were all in good prime. But, all for naught! No matter how intensely Lois grilled Muriel with potential interview questions, she froze on her feet in front of the judges.

Her daddy suggested she read up on current events for better preparedness in backing her opinions on controversial subject matters. Muriel wanted to please him in the worst way, but lacked the ability to focus on the printed word or retain information. Women's rights. Gay rights. Environmental concerns. The ongoing Vietnam War.

Sheesh!

And, as much as she wanted to oblige Etta more than she did Obie, Muriel couldn't bring herself to decipher or enact the underlined passages in *Candy* without feeling sick to her stomach. Heaven forbid, she rummage through her own pot o'gold. Still and all, she kept up the multi-faceted pretense of putting up and putting out.

She tap danced to her mother's puppet strings. She dazzled her customers with contrived cheer. She deep-throated Obie's shaft and managed to suppress the gag reflex.

Until Lois pulled the plug on a contender making a public spectacle of herself, Muriel sought refuge through the conduit of friendship under the cover of darkness during late-night hours. No matter who initiated the phone call, she and Etta stayed in touch despite their different pursuits and lack of leisure. Complicating matters, Muriel had been less than honest with Etta about her dim prospects for taking the crown in any one of those beauty charades.

***

Although Etta sensed evasiveness, she didn't pry. She saw no need to excavate below the surface and unearth Muriel's moral high ground any more than she'd already tried, with too little success.

However much Muriel skimmed forthrightness, Etta made up for in vagueness when sharing particulars about her freshman year. Those particulars, strictly academic. "I'm really diggin' my three-D project involving paper manipulation."

Etta found herself drawn to a student in her second-semester, three-dimensional, illustration course. Sloan's blonde, curly mop-top and blue eyes summoned the solid image of Birch Hansford whom she deep-froze during her ride home from The Swirl. Out of sight, out of mind. Until a stand-in thawed the ice in her veins.

Even as Sloan led her to his dorm room, she knew neither he nor Birch could ever slake her untamed desire for a rebel along the parallels of Johnny Strabler to whom she remained faithful on each occasion she pleasured herself. Although Sloan was Etta's first hookup, he didn't have to do the grunt work of rupturing a hymen she'd already broken during one of her self-stimulating marathons.

Outweighing her eagerness to experience the sensation of a hot, throbbing penis embedded inside her vagina, were her

259

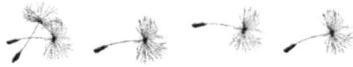

apprehensions for contracting a sexually transmitted infection. Or, worse—an unplanned pregnancy. As for using a contraceptive, Etta was plumb out of luck until 1972 when the Supreme Court's landmark decision, Eisenstadt v. Baird, legalized birth control regardless of marital status.

She put her worries away when she saw Sloan slipping a condom on his erect member. Much to her relief, he suited up every time they shagged. As freshman year sprinted to the finish, both parted company with their friendship still intact. Like Lenny who served his purpose for Rosalia, Sloan had served his for Etta. Without spilling his fertilizer, he led her to greener pastures.

***

Winding down their telephone conversation past midnight, Etta substituted vagueness with brutal honesty in answering Muriel's question pertaining to current affairs. "Nope. Not seeing anyone."

For pity's sake, if she hadn't primed her own well pump!

"Maybe it's high time you reciprocated an interest in Tom," suggested Muriel.

Tom Holden. She not only turned him down when he asked her to their junior prom, but spent most of her senior year dodging his advances to arrange a date. In two weeks, she'd lock arms with him in their united front of best man and maid of honor strolling down the bridal path at Muriel's garden wedding in her backyard.

"Tom's nice. But, he's not my spice."

One of the few times she'd ever expressed gratitude to her dad, she thanked him for planning to ride out the whole Doyle-Smith shebang in the capacity of distinguished guest, closing the deli so he could attend. Tony would cater the sumptuous buffet Sal provided for free, a gesture to pay his respects to Fist.

Flat-out, Etta had told him of her intentions to stick by his side like glue as a means to dissuade Tom's misplaced affections. To which he responded, "And, you take offense whenever I mention you're a thorn in my side!"

Muriel backed off. They terminated their connection with affectionate repartee and air-kissing.

Chapter 58

Muriel Doyle's day of reckoning took place on a sun-dappled Saturday of Memorial Day weekend in 1970, two years before Watergate scandalized a nation. Nuptial blessings endowed, the newlyweds shared a kiss of bliss to seal their fate. Foregoing the traditional head table and formal receiving line, guests rushed toward the couple who stepped outside the gazebo, holding hands. And, like the flow of free champagne served by a bartender who presided over the open bar, conversation bubbled amongst family and friends surrounding the bride and groom. Mingling at length, they were reluctant to settle in at their assigned seats just yet.

Before Fist joined the swarm of celebrants and exercised his official hosting duties, he took it upon himself to survey the scene and commit it to memory. Looking slick and dapper, the father of the bride wore a light gray suit with coordinating tie and patterned pocket square in lavender. His attire complemented the bridal party's color scheme Muriel had chosen to favor Etta's partiality for the flowering plant. Misty-eyed, Gordon Doyle's gaze alighted on the apple of his eye, his heart swelling with pride. To the best of his knowledge, a blushing bride never looked more radiant than his beloved Princess.

Out of the loop, Fist had no idea that his daughter's radiant complexion had softened in intensity from the deep shade of scarlet it had borne. A reaction attributed to Muriel's highly agitated state an hour before he walked her down the aisle runner to the gazebo. While Lois fastened the strand of borrowed pearls she'd worn at her own wedding, around Muriel's neck, she dispensed dowdy marital advice from a bygone era.

"Tonight, when your husband climbs on top of you to take what's his, pretend you enjoy it. The sooner he's in, the sooner he'll pull out to roll over and fall asleep."

Already emotionally stressed over First Night, Muriel's adrenaline kicked butt, thus increasing the action of those capillaries carrying blood to the surface of the skin. Parboiled scarlet! Because, contrary to despising her mother and dismissing her dour news brief, Muriel had arrived at the same conclusion days ago. The best one she could come up with to undermine her waking nightmare of the ménage à trois she envisioned once Uncle Reggie's phantom slid under the covers with them—Fake it until Obie makes it.

***

Undermining Fist's sentimental musings, his sighting of Keen holding a glass of foolproof Southern Comfort, cutting across the lawn and closing in on him. The genuine affection Fist lavished on his cousin made up for his wife's undisguised abhorrence toward a regular houseguest she considered a no-count peasant.

"Hey, Cuz!" Keen elbowed Fist in the ribs. "From the looks o' this weddin', I reckon you must be livin' in high cotton! Been talkin' with Sal. That guy's awright."

"Best friend a man could have!" Fist replied without equivocation.

"His daughter's pretty as a peach!" noted Keen.

"Aren't lonely, rich widows more your type?"

"Damn straight, they are! I got principles! Ain't no perv, that's for sure!" Keen recommended, slinking along the road to hell paved with his good intentions. "As the creek rises, I find it mighty strange that brother-in-law o' yours ain't nowhere to be found on these grounds. Where's he been holed up all these years? And, why?"

Fist gave Keen his undivided attention. "Muriel's never so much as mentioned Reggie by name. Not even Lois. As far as I'm concerned, he's out of the picture. For the record, if I had the slightest inkling of what you're driving at, your services wouldn't be necessary. I'd have killed the bastard myself with my own bare hands!"

Keen patted him on the back. "Bless your heart, Cuz!"

"Now, seeing you're holding up a glass half-empty or half-full, your call . . . Why don't you get yourself a refill? While folks are starting to line up for the buffet, I'm going to get myself a hug from Muriel."

***

Chatter diminished among those who'd scored their heaping plates of food ahead of other guests in the procession along the buffet table. Overpowering the sound of cutlery scratching porcelain, the off-and-on rumbles of thunderous laughter erupting in response to Tony's comedic material. "Hey! If I'm pushing the eggplant parmigiana, it's because I wouldn't recommend any of the other stuff. Capiche?"

When every guest had taken their assigned seat, Fist proposed a toast, bellowing his gratitude to Sal's Italian Deli. He insisted Sal take a bow for the delicious spread, and for Tony to take a load off his feet while everyone ate to their heart's content. The crowd went wild, honoring both with a standing ovation.

When all the commotion subsided, Etta and Sal, along with all other guests, picked up their forks and delved. To the dinner date sitting across from her, Etta proclaimed, "Dad, you and Tony are hot stuff!"

Sal grinned in appreciation. "Officially, this is Tony's last catering stint. He's taking off to find the footlights in comedy

clubs. But, he'll pinch hit until I find a replacement, and he's going to train the new hire."

"You two have been a team for so long, that I find it sad."

"I'll tell you what's sad. Tony assured me he'd drop by the house, unannounced, like always."

Etta slapped his hand in reproach. "Even though you're joking, it's not funny."

"Hey, since I'm doing you a favor keeping Tom away, how about making me a Help Wanted sign in return? I'll expect nothing less than spectacular from an art major."

"Consider it done," Etta replied. "Oh, you're not off the hook yet. Your biggest challenge is keeping Tom at bay on that dance floor over yonder."

***

Etta and Sal, along with the other two bridesmaids and their dads, granted Muriel and Fist a head start for the traditional father-daughter dance inspired by the deejay's spin of "Daddy's Little Girl". When Al Martino crooned, *you're at the end of the rainbow*, they joined the slow dance in progress on the portable platform.

Following Sal's lead by moving backward on her right foot, then left, Etta spoke to her dad with a gentleness that jarred his composure. "You know, even though we rarely see eye to eye on tons of stuff, you always have my back. Like today. That's one of the many reasons I love you."

Etta rested her head on her dad's shoulder. Unable to say much without shedding tears, Sal maintained their rhythm. While swaying a forward half-box, he murmured, "That's because you're daddy's little girl." He stroked her curls, regarding his daughter a treasure he cherished, as specified in the last verse of the song.

Walking off the dance floor together, Sal managed to steady his voice, adding, "So, you were saying—there's more than one reason you're keeping me around?"

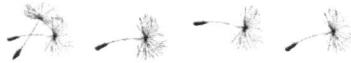

Chapter 59

Etta came up with a sign that exceeded her dad's stringent requirements for perfection. In addition to bold lettering used to create an attention-grabbing headline above the job description, she embellished her handiwork with a colorful sketch of an antipasto salad.

Boy, that antipasto sure looks appetizing, if I do say so myself!

When Etta paid a visit to the deli and presented the poster to Sal, he stared at it, bug-eyed. Rounding the corner to stand on the customer's side of the counter, he slapped his daughter on the back. "You done me proud!" Addressing the eat-in diners, "My talented daughter. Thanks to my cooking, she's not one of those starving artists."

Etta arched her eyebrows in preface of a reprimand. "Dad, when you get back to where you belong at the chopping block, I'll hang it in the front window."

Besides enjoying their meals, smiles and chuckles indicated the customers were eating up the free entertainment. Sal played along. "Going. I'll have a broader view to let you know if it's crooked. Or, upside down."

***

Born to be wild, Keith Lawrence mounted his '69 Harley-Davidson Electra Glide, a present to himself when he fulfilled his military obligation in the Vietnam War after a 12-month deployment. Having enlisted to avoid the pitfalls in store for Uncle Sam's expendable draftees, he was required to serve only three more years in the inactive reserves.

Eager to distance himself from Brooklyn, Connecticut, the Harley's electric starter cut him some slack for not having to kick-start the big-ass, V-twin engine. A rebel's godsend. Though the curb weight of more than 700 pounds somewhat hampered performance, Keith had no problem overcoming road friction heading east on US 6-E.

Wearing a denim jacket and jeans may have shielded him from potential scratches and scrapes. Of little consolation, the highway responded in kind to Keith riding roughshod on asphalt, embedding dust and dirt in his unkempt mane of hair and scruffy beard. When he'd ridden halfway from hell along the 6.6-mile stretch to Foster, being of sound mind, he attested—*I can ride . . .*

Soon as Keith was honorably discharged from the army, he sowed his wild oats. Indiscriminate in choosing the women he slept with on a first-come-first-serve basis, one of them bit him on the butt with a paternity suit.

But, I can't very well hide.

He didn't have to. Soon enough, he'd head back to where he fled from and emerge the victor in an out-of-court settlement. The proof was inked on a crumpled motel receipt. A forgotten scrap of truth shoved in his pants pocket scared the living daylights out of a wretched liar, more than enough for her to throw in the towel.

For now, he'd try to line up menial, part-time work in this neck of the woods to earn a fast buck. More in line with his capabilities and his druthers, Keith hoped to secure gainful employment at the sawmill on Plainfield Pike.

Of course, he'd need to find a place to crash for the night, or longer, if the accommodations suited him. Accustomed to the fleabag motels he stayed in when he got back to the states, he didn't fancy himself a connoisseur of domiciles. And, if the

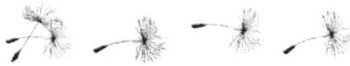

army taught him anything, neatness and efficiency topped the list. He packed all of his worldly possessions inside the Harley's hard saddle bags. Namely: jeans and shirts, underwear and socks, a pair of work boots, toiletries.

First things first. A bite to eat. Keith veered off the Pike and onto the State Line's parking lot. He'd chat up the waitress to find out if they could use a short-order cook. Regardless of the feedback, he'd order a burger—medium-well with the works—and, a side of fries.

Rough around the edges, but always a gentleman, he leveled his eyes on the name tag pinned to her uniform, situated at the upper shelf of her breast. "How's it going, Muriel?"

She rewarded him with a congenial smile and poised her pen, ready to write down his order. Wedding band or not, in his mind, Muriel's put-together package shrink-wrapped her in the likeness of a mummy. Well-preserved. Finding her dramatic make-up, coifed hair, and overpowering perfume a turn-off, he abandoned his foolproof strategy of warming up the babes with a flirtatious approach.

Keith got to the point before Muriel's pen did. "By any chance, are you guys hiring?"

Thinking the windblown fella a destitute vagabond, Muriel, for once in her life, demonstrated the ability to think on her feet. "We're not. But, the owner of the town deli is looking to hire a set-up man for his catering service."

Seeing the stranger tipped his chin up to meet her gaze, Muriel supplied directions to Foster Center. Without faltering, she steered him from the Pike onto Rockland Road, and from there, to Sal's Italian Deli. "Darn! If you're fixing to catch Sal, he closes the deli at six on Thursdays."

According to Muriel's estimation of the fifteen minutes it would take him to get there, Keith had better get going. Hungry

as he was, he wouldn't be ordering that burger and fries after all. Muriel surmised as much, tucking her pad and pen inside a pocket on the skirt of her uniform.

As Keith bolted for the door, she shouted after him, "It might help if you tell him Muriel sent you. Sal and my dad are best buddies."

Keith turned around to acknowledge her kindness with a shake of his head and mumbled his thanks. Unforeseen and unfathomable to both, Muriel would become one of the puzzle pieces fitting snugly into the configuration of his life, industrious in destroying what he held dear based on speculation.

***

Coasting to a stop in front of the curb outside the deli, Keith couldn't help notice the Help Wanted sign on the storefront window. Its super-sized, surreal, Picasso antipasto piqued his hunger even more. Through the glass on the door, he glimpsed a guy wet-mopping the floor. Assuming, it must be none other than Sal, he dismounted from his bike, walked up to the door, and yanked the handle.

"Don't step any further!" bellowed Sal. "Last thing I need is for you to slip on wet tile and sue me. I'm getting ready to close. You can grab a bite at the State Line over on the Pike."

"Just came from there. Muriel sent me. Are you Sal?"

"I am," he replied, eyeing the disheveled trespasser who had stopped dead in his tracks inside the doorway.

"Sal, I take it that's not your art work on display."

Finished with the last task of the day, Sal parked his mop inside the bucket. "No, it isn't. My daughter, the aspiring artist, whipped that up. "If Muriel sent you here, you didn't stop by to discuss art. Am I right?"

Impatient to get his show on the road, motivated by hunger and the need to find lodging, Keith cut the small talk. "According to the sign, if you're willing to train—I'm game to learn. I take it, you haven't hired anyone just yet. Am I right?"

Sal scrubbed his chin in contemplation of a comeback. He had already written off the few who'd inquired within. Based on his judgement, they'd never measure up to Tony. Now, this ballbuster struck him as the least likely applicant of all.

"Plain and simple, long hair and serving food don't mix. You'd have to wear it tied back, or God forbid—cut it. Most of all, you'd need to crack a smile once in a while. Could you do that?"

"If it's in my best interest," Keith replied.

"Look, I can't give you an answer off the top of my head right now. I'm on my way out the door you're blocking. Are you hungry?"

"Starving!"

"Whaddya know—a straightforward answer! I always bring home the leftovers I cook, so you're welcome to join my daughter and me for supper. That is, unless you have an aversion to chicken parm and ziti."

"Oh, man! Are you crazy?"

"That's what I thought. Who knows, company at the table might intimidate my outspoken daughter into being agreeable. While breaking bread, we might even learn your name," ribbed Sal.

"Could be," said Keith.

"Seeing you'll be following me to North Road for all of four minutes, I hope that bike of yours can keep up with a Biscayne."

271

Keith hit back, "If I put the squeeze on the front brakes."

Chapter 60

In anticipation of her dad's arrival with food straight out of the oven for their evening meal, Etta had set the dining room table at opposite ends for the two of them. She sliced half a loaf of Italian bread and placed four thick slices in the basket at the center of the table. She proceeded to fill their tall glasses with iced water. Sal's gregarious shout from the entryway preceded his presence. "Add another place setting. We have company."

Before she put down the pitcher, her dad and his guest entered the dining area. "This is my daughter, Etta."

Caught off guard by the guy her dad dragged in, his unflinching brown eyes knuckling her under, Etta liked what she saw. About to say hello, Sal's exuberance cut her off. "Now, is as good a time as any to tell us your name."

Momentarily awestruck by the rough-and-tumble stranger, like unpredictable New England weather, Etta turned on a dime and lashed out at her dad. "Wait a minute! You invited someone, whose name you don't know, to dinner? Is he homeless?"

"Don't be ridiculous!" Sal shouted, his temper flaring. Turning to his guest, "Forget what I said about company intimidating her into being pleasant."

Boring his eyes into Etta's once more, this time with a hell-bent glint of mischief, "The name's Keith Lawrence. And, I *am* homeless. Just temporarily."

Further exasperated, Etta piped up. "Gee, Dad! The stakes are even higher you brought a serial killer under our roof!"

Desperate to diffuse the situation and get dinner started, Sal tried to appease his irate daughter. "Lest you forget, I know all

the ins and outs of butcher knives." Pointing to the chair on his left for Keith to use, "Park it. Make yourself at home."

In a jiffy, Etta made up another place setting, sliced more bread, and began heaping generous portions of chicken parmigiana and ziti on their plates.

Just warming up, not even hunger could dissuade Keith from sparring with a fiery temptress. "Serial killer? You betcha! I can't give you an exact body count for the number of Viet Cong I slaughtered during ground-assault raids and sniper attacks."

Her face blanched whiter than boiling pasta. Sal, ready to pounce if she started hammering Keith with her dove position against the war, Etta backed down. "You were just following orders. Let's eat."

On a whim, Sal rose from the table to grab a bottle of Merlot from the wine fridge. Etta then fetched three goblets from the hutch and situated them to the right of their water glasses. Sal filled each one, pouring his heart out in the process. "My Seabee unit stationed in the Northern Mariana Islands dug the pit for the uranium bomb dropped on Hiroshima. War is hell! Let's leave it there and enjoy my cooking."

***

The blast detonated by heated words discouraged civil drivel during dinner. Polishing off their meals discouraged discord and minimized discomfort. Throughout the sit-down, Keith and Etta sneaked wary, sidelong glances at each other. Every bit aware, Sal glared daggers at his daughter.

Aiming to restore cordiality by eliminating a source of hostility, Sal broke through the barrier of silence toward dinner's demise. "Keith, why don't you and I talk shop on the porch? Etta, looks like you're stuck with KP duty."

"That's nothing new," she countered.

Sal winked at Keith. Wagging his finger at Etta, "Oh, I beg to differ, young lady. There was that one time you washed and I dried. Remember?"

Etta stared him down. "I sure do! You set me up!"

"A set-up man!" interjected Keith, his lips twisting into a wry grin, gunning for Etta.

"Hey, my daughter got you to smile! If you really want the job, you're the new set-up man."

***

The basic requirements of a set-up man discussed and dispensed with sitting across from each other on cushioned loungers, Keith and Sal took in the June twilight, steeped in their own thoughts. While attuned to the raucous sounds produced from birds either alighting on branches or passing through, Sal spoke his mind. "So, what's this I hear about your being homeless?"

"Yeah. I was getting around to that. Do you happen to know of any motels in the area?"

Sal turned his head from side to side, indicating just how far-off Keith pitched his probe. "You gotta be kidding me! Hospitality out here in the sticks? There's the no-frills, frontier Rainbow Trout Cabins over on Winsor Road. You'd have to supply your own towels, toiletries, and *fine* linens for a cot. I know for a fact the proprietor isn't there at this hour. Tell you what . . ."

Chapter 61

Acting in her own self-interest after clearing the table and doing the dishes, Etta left those two on the porch to fend for themselves. The etiquette both parents instilled in her dictated she poke her head out the screen door and give a holler that she had a fresh pot of coffee brewing. Even so, stubbornness defied her to cap off the evening with caffeinated social grace.

She put up with her dad's impertinence because she gave as good as she got in every one of their verbal duels. But, she took umbrage at the impertinence of a total stranger who delighted in goading her to lose her temper. Most disturbing of all, she felt a carnal attraction to the rolling stone who pressed all her buttons with a blink of his eye. He had all the hallmarks of the unattainable, celluloid Wild One who gathered no moss as he mounted his bike and drifted from one town to the next, breaking hearts along the way.

By some fluke, a composite of the man in her autoerotic fantasies rode into Foster and happened to be relaxing on her porch. As a consequence, the torch she carried for Johnny Strabler burned out because a movie icon couldn't hold a candle to the flash, or flesh and bones, of Keith Lawrence. Of the notion love sledgehammers you only once in a lifetime if you're lucky, the odds for laying eyes on him ever again to cross-examine his allure seemed highly improbable.

Unless, she swallowed her pride and stepped onto the porch to mouth words without a ring of truth to them: *"Nice meeting you."*

When hell freezes over!

Etta switched off the light above the kitchen sink and stomped along the stairs, itching to reach her bedroom.

Barricading herself from the outside world by closing a door behind her, Etta sloughed off her clothes. She deposited the detritus of an embroidered, off-the-shoulder peasant blouse, along with tattered cutoffs and undies, in the hamper. Padding around the bedroom in her bare skin, she pinned her hair up and gathered essentials to set the ambience for indulging in a long, hot bath laid out in lavender. Toting an embodiment of the pale, purple flower's fragrance in a bottle of bubble bath and a scented candle, she headed down the hall toward her private bathroom.

An ultrafeminine retreat formerly shared with her momma, they had collaborated on creating a tranquil haven by repainting the beige plastered interior walls of the rustic bathroom in ivory. Etta stenciled a smattering of lavender sprigs, interspersing them on the background and brushing sage green through the leaves and stems. To complement the pink tiles in the flooring, she stippled pink, lavender, and deep purple on the flowers in each sprig. An affront to Sal's masculinity, he staked an exclusive claim on the downstairs bathroom which suited all three of them just fine.

Ever since his wife's tragic death in the master bedroom, Sal rarely set foot on the second floor, preferring to make his bed on the sofa in the great room. Apart from the guest room her grandparents shared during their extended visits which never seemed long enough, Etta generally had the entire suite to herself for romping in the buff if she so chose.

After their recent week-long stay, Nonna and Grampa headed back home the previous morning. For that reason, she had no inhibitions leaving the bathroom door ajar as she filled the tub with hot water for a steamy bubble bath. When full and frothy, Etta tested the waters with her big toe, gradually immersing herself up to her waist in the bubbly. For a brief

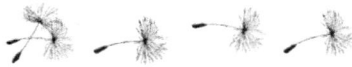

interlude, she filed Keith Lawrence in a mind-over-matter folder at the forefront of her brain so she could focus on a short-term summer setback.

Tomorrow's change of venue called for putting together a Jekyll-Hyde transformation, an imposition brought on by her Grampa's adherence to the golden rule of doing unto others when they're between a rock and a hard place.

**

The favor:

Ever since the last day of spring semester in late May, Etta luxuriated in the freedom to do as she pleased. Late to bed and late to rise at eight. Sunbathing on the porch. Traversing her fishing ground to sketch Foster's landmarks and historic buildings. Cocooned inside her comfort zone, she envisioned enjoying much of the same from mid-June until the start of classes after Labor Day.

The whimsical notions of a carefree, wealthy heiress went awry with a hand-me-down phone call from Tavvy who'd bent her dad's ear with his proposition. Still gripping the receiver to the wall-mount phone in the kitchen, Sal stretched its cord taut in walking the distance to the bottom of the stairs. Smoking Etta out of her bedroom, he yelled, "Hey! Hurry on down! Grampa's holding the line for you!"

Etta charged down the stairs and snapped up the phone, curious about Tavvy's urgency to speak to her right away instead of waiting until he and Nonna got back from golfing. A read on her dad's expression set her off. "Your evil grin tells me something's up with you two!"

Sal shrugged his shoulders, turned on his heel and headed for the great room, blowing air to the tune of "Whistle While You Work".

278

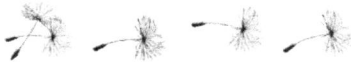

Seething, Etta took a deep breath to compose herself before addressing her grandfather. "Hey, Grampa! What's up?"

So it goes:

"You first, Etta. Do you have anything scheduled for the next two weeks?"

To the point, Tavvy conducted a telephone conversation much the same way he managed a board meeting, expecting an upfront response to a simple query. Anyone who hemmed and hawed could expect a severe tongue-lashing. No exemptions.

Intimidated, Etta blurted, "Not that I recall."

"I thought as much. Which is why I'm counting on you to help out a friend of mine who's in a bind."

Etta slumped to the floor, assuming a better position for absorbing the full impact yet to come. Whatever her grandfather expected of her, she'd do it out of love and respect without giving him any lip. Not so with her dad, whom she also loved and respected to the moon and back, but had no compunctions locking horns with. Putty in her Grampa's hands, she listened without interrupting his shot to deliver the ball on the green.

Tight with the general manager of Foster Country Club whom he fraternized with often enough during his stopovers in Rhode Island, Tavvy empathized with his friend's predicament. As disclosed over lunch at the tavern, a retail clerk who operates the pro shop, gave short notice for time off on account of family obligations.

Appreciating a native Rhode Islander's tips for generating lucrative real estate leads in unfamiliar territory, and a firm believer in reciprocating favors, Tavvy tapped a human resource. "I assured him he could count on my smart-cookie of a granddaughter to run the shop for two weeks."

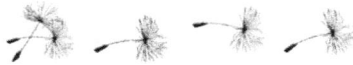

Stripped of any bargaining power to protest, Etta surrendered with a lack of inflection. "When do I start?"

Peeved at her monotone, "Are you asking out of eagerness or resignation? Friday. I'll spell out the details when Nonna and I get back after our lunch."

Etta stood, wobbling on her feet as she cradled the phone. Making matters worse, Sal peeked around the corner and badgered her with another toot of "Whistle While You Work".

***

Soon thrust into the maelstrom of country club subculture through no desire of her own, Etta solemnly swore she would wholeheartedly embrace the duties of a pro shop clerk. This, she professed as her grandfather enveloped her in his arms during their good-bye hug. Throwing in a wrench, she added, "Whatever those are, Grampa."

Of all the details Tavvy disclosed, the most important one he left unsaid, albeit subtly implied, she'd have to dress the part.

Lounging in the bathtub and soaking up thought, a rueful grin spread across her face as she imagined the old guard attending the Ivy League universities they'd applied to. Followers of fashion, rather than innovators, she envisioned them as neat, tailored, and understated preppy protégés wearing nautical stripes, pastels, or plaids. Just the steam-clouded vision she needed to hold onto for her conservative makeover.

Etta mentally ticked off the clothes she'd get ready for tomorrow's outfit. Remnants about to be resurrected from their burial chambers represented a social life laid to rest when she left Bay View behind. In order to sustain the charade for two whole weeks, she'd have to break down and forage inside Abercrombie & Fitch for collegiate-inspired casualwear.

Satisfied she'd pull off the first day, Etta proceeded to mix cleansing with pleasure. She turned the knobs on both faucets,

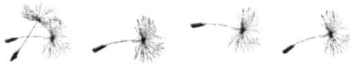

adjusting temperature and flow to reheat the tepid bathwater, and to accommodate her libido. Positioning herself beneath the stream, in the twinkling of an eye, the gush produced an orgasmic rush induced by erogenous thoughts. Johnny Strabler was a no-show, stepping aside for Keith Lawrence to emerge from the file folder at the forefront of her brain.

Chapter 62

Out of bed much earlier than usual and already showered, Etta slipped on, what she considered, phony finery. After putting the finishing touches to her disheveled updo, she stepped out of her bedroom in white canvas sneakers rather than huarache sandals.

Walking past the master bedroom, she noticed the bed's untidy, slept-in look which could only mean her dad spent the night there. Puzzling enough. Before heading downstairs, she took a detour inside to make up the bed, and got a whiff of coffee and bacon streaming from its downstairs origin. Odd. She and her dad fended for themselves in the morning to suit their own schedules. He preferred toast and coffee. She charged her batteries with oatmeal and orange juice.

Skedaddling down the stairs, and following her nose into the kitchen, an involuntary gasp escaped her lips. Peacocking a wet head of hair, Keith Lawrence sat at the farmhouse table, tearing into a slice of toast and digging into a plate loaded with bacon and ketchup-stained scrambled eggs.

Standing in front of the stove, Sal turned his head in acknowledgement of her dramatic entry, and intervened to avert a potential showdown. "Sit down. Yours is just about ready."

Astounded, Etta cut loose. "Dad, what's he doing here?"

"I'll let him explain. Unless, you want your eggs burnt."

With one hand on her hip, and a heap of defiance, she locked eyes with those of their guest. Her steely-blue gaze didn't faze his brazen browns which reflected amusement at her indignation. He took his blessed time to explain, affecting a deliberate drawl. "Yeah, well . . . since it was too late for me to

make a run for the Rainbow Trout Cabins, your dad offered to put me up for the night."

Thoughts of having fantasized the rough-and-tumble drifter while writhing in the froth shortly before he made his bed on the sofa in the great room below, stirred her innards. Woozy, she sat down in a hurry. Since her dad always presided at the head of the table, Etta lay claim to the chair directly across from Keith. He inhaled her subtle fragrance, enamored with the scent of lavender wafting from her pores. She inhaled his shower-fresh soapiness, enamored with the scent of morning manliness wafting from his pores.

Sal plunked down two more plates on their placemats, and discouraged further altercation. "Let's buckle down before our food gets cold."

Keith levelled his eyes on her as she spread jelly on toast, then tucked into her scrambled eggs with gusto. "What's up with the polo shirt and plaid skirt?" he asked, poking fun.

Etta rolled her eyes. Talking with her mouth full, she appointed Sal her spokesperson. "I'll let my dad explain."

Miffed, he shot her an accusatory look. "In case you hadn't noticed, I'm trying to strike while my food is still hot." Addressing Keith, "The hippie chick is doing her grandfather a favor by filling in as a temp at a country club pro shop for two weeks. End of discussion."

For the remainder of their short-lived breakfast, its tempo set by places to go and people to greet, the percussive tapping of forks on stoneware serenaded their thoughts. Sal's pertained to the work cut out for him at the deli. Keith's, eagerness to come by lodging on Winsor Road, ever grateful for the leg up, thanks to Sal supplying him with a pillow and bed linens. Etta's, keenness on making a favorable first impression with the general manager of Foster Country Club.

Before they parted ways, Etta's discreet cross-examination of Keith confirmed his undeniable allure. In her unforeseeable future with him, she'd take great pleasure in raking her fingers through his wavy hair as she leaned in for a kiss.

Keith's discreet cross-examination of Etta confirmed more than a physical attraction to the handful with an independent streak. In his unforeseeable future with her, he'd take great pleasure in kissing the nape of her neck as he removed the bobby pins holding her hair in place.

Chapter 63

If Etta thought she'd twiddle her thumbs temping from nine-to-five at the pro shop, Earl McGregor, the general manager, proved her wrong from day one. Impeccably attired, he turned up in a pair of creased, gray chinos. Although she didn't want to dwell where the sun didn't shine, she'd bet money the placket of his well-tucked, navy-blue golf shirt with the Foster Country Club deer logo, lined up with the fly on his trousers.

She figured him to be in the same age bracket as her Grampa, schmoozing through their sixth decade of life, trim and fit. Etta thought his choice of hairstyle strengthened his magnetic field for attracting the footloose, gimlet-swirling socialites prone to tying one on after a round of golf.

Crowned with a thick crop of snow-white, wavy hair, which he parted on the side and combed over, Mr. McGregor perfected Dean Martin's Rat Pack look. And, without the handicap of a wedding band, he just had to be the ladies' hole in one on a par 5.

A handshake and brief exchange of pleasantries behind them, he got into the swing of things, teeing off with a broad overview. "Basically, you'll greet customers and collect payment for rounds of golf, lessons, and merchandise. Since you've never had to work a day in your life until now, I'll give you a rundown on operating the cash register."

Taking offense at a condescending attitude, Etta interrupted his spiel. Jutting out her chin, "Mr. McGregor, contrary to what you may think, I've operated a cash register at my dad's deli. And, balanced receipts and payments at the end of the day."

Seldom. Sal didn't want anyone messing in his kitchen or pillaging the spoils of his till.

One unwavering glare to another, Earl McGregor reacted. "Your grandfather said you were a spunky lass. I reckon that was a forewarning. You just talked yourself into being in charge of closing out the cash register."

"I'd be glad to." Then, Etta had the moxie to tell him it looked like she had a cushy job on her hands.

In the twinkling of an eye, Mr. McGregor dispelled that notion. "In addition to the basics, you'll schedule tee times and private lessons. You'll be responsible for restocking empty shelves. Before closing, you're to spray clean the display cases and make sure the merchandise is neatly arranged the way you find it now."

Red in the face from feeling foolish at shooting off her mouth, but not about to grovel in humility, Etta nipped it her way. "Guess I won't have to pack *War and Peace* to fend off boredom."

For all she knew, Mr. McGregor's pinched features were the result of biting his tongue in an exercise of self-restraint. She wondered if his speech delay had anything to do with taking a deep breath and counting to ten. "Shall we get on with our tutorial before we open shop?"

"By all means. While you're showing me the ropes, you may as well throw in a refresher course on the cash register."

***

Etta kept her composure and rose to Mr. McGregor's expectations of a pro shop attendant. She followed his cardinal rule of setting tee times ten to fifteen minutes apart for every group starting at the first hole. Per his instructions, she allowed a two-week lead time for scheduling as many as a couple dozen tee times. He had stressed that with twenty groups, she'd need

three to four hours of tee times to fit the whole group in. She must have worn down the erasers at the end of several No. 2 Ticonderoga pencils from making numerous corrections to coordinate data on spreadsheets.

Pretty much exhausted at the end of her work day, Etta kicked back when she arrived home. After dinner, she and her dad stayed out of each other's hair in the great room. He, watching television. She, putting the finishing touches on a sketch of the Woodland Meeting House, a 130-year-old restaurant and tavern, purportedly a brothel in the nineteenth century.

Careful not to tip her hand for revealing an avid interest in Keith Lawrence, she played it cool. Without missing a stroke in plying her marker, she asked, "Hey, how's the new set-up man doing?"

Without looking away from *Laugh-In*, "Better than I thought! Thanks to his teacher. Tony's even gone so far as getting him to smile on the job once in a while."

Etta harrumphed. Sal directed his focus away from the set and stared down his daughter to hone a point for her benefit. "Far from being the shiftless drifter you thought he was, the guy has two jobs."

She looked up. Keeping her feelings in check not to blow her cover, "Okay, so I underestimated his work ethic."

"Got himself hired at the sawmill. Says he's staying put at the cabin for now, and has taken up fishing." Sal renewed his absorption with the rapid-fire, sketch comedy show.

While coloring, Etta mulled over the information, deeming it newsworthy of a reference in the *Funk & Wagnalls Standard Encyclopedia.*

***

Toward the end of Etta's second week at the pro shop, she had a better handle on juggling her responsibilities. Mr. McGregor checked in on her with far less frequency, and commended her job performance when he did. Restocking a shelf behind the main counter on a slow afternoon, Etta turned around to face front when the shopkeeper's bell on the outer door jingled.

At first glance, both customer and clerk did a double take. He spoke first. "Holy smoke! For someone who never has to work a day in your life, why are you standing behind a counter?"

Again, the presumption of entitlement associated with her lineage. "My grandfather put the squeeze on me. He's good friends with the general manager who was in a bind when the real clerk had a family emergency. So, here I stand."

Confident, bordering on cocky, like most of the pros she'd met, he trod on their past acquaintanceship along a trail that had gone cold. "Sure as hell can't be the pay."

For someone who infatuated her in bygone days, she found his remark off-putting. Birch Hansford, even more handsome than her freeze-framed image of the lanky teen, had matured into a man of athletic build. His dirty blond mop-top was longer and unrulier, more in line with the Rolling Stones. Squinting in the sun had scored wrinkles under his dreamy, blue eyes, wizening them into hardened agates.

Then, as now, those eyes never sparkled at the sight of her, indicating his lack of attraction from square one. Now, unlike then, she felt no stir of sexual excitement, despite standing across from him and getting a beguiling whiff of sandalwood and musk from his cologne.

"What brings you to a country club on the far side of Blackstone Boulevard?"

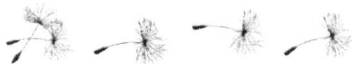

"I'm playing in the charity tournament next week. Thought I'd fine tune my game by copping a feel for the green. Today, the front nine. Tomorrow, if the rain holds off—the back end."

Smart! The first nine tees meander through farm country, while the latter nine run through rugged elevation changes.

"By a stroke of luck, I won't be here next week to get embroiled in that shindig," Etta informed him.

While Etta rang up his sale of the green fee by pressing keys to record the amount, she glimpsed Birch's hangdog look. "Hey, it shouldn't take me more than seventy-five minutes to play a round. Close enough to when the shop closes. How 'bout we grab a bite at the tavern before you take off?"

Oh, how the passage of time stings the toes and bites the nose, she thought to herself. "Factoring in your wait time of fifteen minutes, and the unknowable skills of the players ahead of you . . ." she faltered.

"Yeah," he said, crestfallen. "Bumping into you like this reminded me of things I'd left unsaid between us. Only, I couldn't say them then. Humor me. Let's meet somewhere to catch up."

"If you're a glutton for Foster's terrain, may I suggest my father's deli? We can grab a picnic lunch and head out to one of the scenic overlooks. How does that grab you?"

"You're on!"

They set a date for after the tournament. Etta scribbled directions to the deli from the starting point of Providence. Through no fault of theirs, an innocent venture would become the tipping point for a violent end.

Chapter 64

Enjoying a quiet evening on their porch, partway through a dinner of spaghetti and meatballs with a tossed salad, Etta thought it wise to bring up the subject of Birch Hansford. A cautionary measure might curb her dad from grandstanding false speculations to entertain patrons at the deli while she and Birch waited behind the counter for their takeout.

Twirling her spaghetti with a spoon, Etta sought assurance. "Do you solemnly swear not to make any dumbass remarks tomorrow?"

Sal, wedging his fork into a meatball, "Do I strike you as dumb? From the little you told me about this guy, he's all wrong for you."

Taking issue, Etta challenged him, "Like, you know who's right for me!"

"Plain as the nose on your face, you already figured it out for yourself."

Etta felt the flames of embarrassment licking her cheeks. Rather than dig herself into a hole by denying his implication, she changed the subject.

***

In the back of beyond, Birch looked out of place standing behind the deli counter. His preppy attire of wrinkled chino shorts, faded designer polo shirt, and grass-stained boat shoes reeked of a low-profile, moneyed lifestyle. At odds with the lunch crowd in the dining area who worked hard for a living, he culled their attention, rubbing them the wrong way.

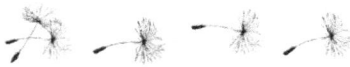

Standing alongside him in toe-thong leather sandals, Etta's outlandish flower-power, bat-sleeve top and ragged denim shorts didn't rattle them in the least. The locals embraced the eccentricities in one of Foster's born and bred. After all, she was an artist. And, one whose sketches of historic landmarks showed off the town in a favorable light to tourists who purchased her work from A Bee's Buzz.

Sal, peering out at the sea of faces plastered with quizzical expressions, thought he'd better change the scenery by grandstanding, after all. "Are you sure you can take the heat of pepperoncini on your grinder? I shudder to think of my daughter reviving you with mouth-to-mouth resuscitation when you collapse in a choking fit."

Chortles and guffaws cleared the atmosphere of toxicity.

Before Birch had a chance to wing a comeback, Etta remarked without considering the implications. "Birch can handle hot stuff, okay?"

The diners lost their composure, their raucous laughter off on a tangent she never intended. Turning around to face their onlookers, Etta didn't see the side door to the kitchen open, nor who entered Sal's sacred ground. Preoccupied with gaining the upper hand, she marshaled a sheepish grin and offered a dismissive wave. Birch gestured a thumbs-up.

Sal hastened to bag their sandwiches and drinks so they could make their getaway while the uproar subsided. Fat chance. On his way out the same door he entered, rolling a service cart loaded with transport pans, Keith fanned the fire, fueled with speculation. "So, you're hot stuff, huh?"

Although unseen by patrons, they heard his remark. Like Tony, his catering mentor, Keith had a comedic effect. Sal handed Etta and Birch their provisions, shouting to compensate

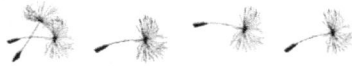

for the second fit of laughter. "Be on your way and don't look back."

***

But, she did.

Before Etta opened Sydney's door on the driver's side, she sneaked a peek at Keith loading the catering truck. She hadn't expected him to turn around in the split second she intended to look away.

But, he did.

During their brief interlude of staring each other down, her perceptive abilities picked up an unfavorable psychic reading.

Spot-on! From the moment Keith drove out of the parking lot in broad daylight, until the evening he drowned in Winsor Brook, speculations clouded his thinking. Unwarranted, but conceivable.

Shaken, Etta opened the door and got behind the wheel, upset she'd blown any chance she might have had with Keith because of misspoken words and a misleading impression.

"Do you mind telling me what just happened in there?" pressed Birch.

Etta rolled her eyes, exasperated with herself. "I put my foot in my mouth. That's what happened."

He forwarded a gentle poke to her arm. "Maybe so. But, given the chance to speak, I would have said *I* liked hot stuff. Either way, they would've been gunning for us."

"No doubt."

"Your dad's something else! Wish mine had a sense of humor."

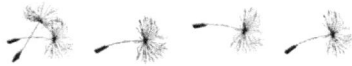

Bearing in mind the dead weight of Birch's words, Etta turned the ignition key, gearing Sydney for their drive to the woods off of Route 6 and Rams Tail Road, peeling out of the lot.

Chapter 65

Had Birch raised any objections over picnicking at a historic site verified as haunted, according to the 1885 State Census, she would have headed toward Foster Farm instead. To her delight, he voiced his eager approval for day-tripping to the ruins of Ram Tail Mill, named after the sheep's wool its machinery spun and wove into woolen cloth.

Acting in accordance to her capricious nature, Etta forestalled mentioning the specter of Peleg Walker haunting the grounds where remnants of stone foundations, still intact even after the mill burned to a cinder in the 1880s, protrude from the forest floor. She'd save the best tidbit for last when it would be too late for him to have a change of heart. Meanwhile, Birch's morbid curiosity egged her on to provide the lurid details of local lore which withstood the ravages of time.

Run-of-the-mill specifics originate with William Potter establishing the workplace in 1799. Expanding operations in 1813, he made his son-in-law, Peleg Walker, a partner. Whereas the Potters ran the mill by day, Peleg flitted about in his capacity of night watchman, making rounds with a lantern in hand. At daybreak, he'd ring the bell suspended by a rope, summoning the workers who lived in the nearby village.

For two fellows at odds, the arrangement seemed to work like a well-oiled machine for several years. Alas, a disagreement between Peleg and his father-in-law reached a crisis point in May of 1822.

Omitting long-winded verbiage, Etta brought her passenger up to snuff and got to the good stuff. "So, I guess those two had a serious falling out. Maybe Potter threatened to fire his son-in-

law. Rumor has it, Walker said they'd first have to remove the mill keys from the pocket of a dead man."

She paused for effect.

"Thus far, you've managed to get the hair on the back of my neck to stand at attention."

"Exactly what I wanted to hear. Well, one morning, the bell didn't ring. When the workers arrived at the mill, they found Peleg Walker hanging from the bell rope with his keys dangling from a pocket. Just like he'd threatened!"

Thrilled over inducing goosebumps, Etta pressed on with ghoulish relish. "Freaky enough, right? Just the beginning! All sorts of weird shit started happening after Peleg's burial. For a few nights, the bell still rang at midnight. Spooked, the Potters removed it. The next morning, the mill was running full-tilt boogie with the waterwheel moving in the opposite direction of the stream.

"Scared out of their wits, the villagers fled. With no one around to run the machinery, the mill closed down. Yet, eyewitnesses swore they'd seen Walker's ghost carrying a lantern as he made his rounds in the abandoned factory."

"Your wicked grin leads me to believe there's more," assumed Birch.

"You can count on it!"

Along Rams Tail Road, Etta took a right onto a dirt road and followed it to the end, braking the Citroen to a dead stop. She faced Birch, her eyes ablaze with mischief. "Chances are, on a moonlit night you'll see the ghost of Peleg Walker swinging his lantern through the ruins where we're going to have our picnic. Sometimes, at midnight, you might hear the toll of a bell."

"Oh, yeah? What are the odds of Walker showing up in the middle of the afternoon?" Birch ventured.

"Beats me! Guess there's only one way for us to find out," she declared.

***

Facing the woods, Birch and Etta settled down on a tarp she had spread out over the leaf-covered clearing surrounded by stone foundations. Hungry, they both rummaged inside their paper bags to remove the identical lunches Sal had prepared and packed for their outing. Each popped the pull tab on a can of root beer soda and took a swig before undoing the wrappers on medium-sized Italian grinders loaded with all the trimmings. Then, ripping open, snack bags of potato chips.

Birch made a show of picking out a few pepperoncini rings and flinging them toward the ruins. "Hey, if holy water and crosses can repel vampires, the heat in pepperoncini might keep Walker's ghost away."

Etta's cackles of laughter had a greater potential for scaring off the invisible night watchman if he lurked in the vicinity. "Or, maybe, you're scattering O-rings because you really can't take the heat and wouldn't admit it to my dad," she sputtered.

"So, now my reputation for handling hot stuff is at stake! I'll show you!" Birch sank his teeth into the torpedo roll and tore off an end segment of salami, mortadella, provolone, lettuce, tomato, onions and pepperoncini. The whole works marinated in oil and red wine vinegar. After swallowing what he chewed, his eyes watered. He reached for his can of soda and chugged.

"I'm not so sure you proved your point," chaffed Etta, jabbing him in his side with her elbow. She decided to keep their ongoing conversation light, conceding to Birch the right of way for changing lanes. Halfway through his sandwich, he did.

"Hey, just wondering. Do you still chum around with any of your old friends in the clique?"

Birch's probe struck a chord, sending her on a trip back in time to when her heart pined for him. "No. Our get-together at The Swirl was pretty much it."

"That's cool. In a way. Otherwise, I might've closed the subject I meant to bring up."

Puzzled and peeved, her voice rose in pitch. "What are you driving at?"

"Just that, if I'm going to put myself on the line, I wouldn't want my words to circle back to the in-crowd and bite me in the ass. My folks and Alison's parents play bridge every Wednesday night at our house. And, you already know the Perrys live around the corner from me. Too close for comfort, if you get my drift."

"I certainly do! You're insulting my integrity. If you're that much in doubt, why bother bringing up the subject at all? And, on cursed territory, for God's sake!"

"Maybe I'm paranoid, okay? For your information, my dad's an arch conservative with zero tolerance. Maybe I wouldn't have suggested we meet somewhere to get something off of my chest, had I not cared so much about you!" he retorted.

The ghost of adolescent memories triggered tears to roll down her cheeks. Finishing their lunch in silence afforded each of them a reprieve to compose themselves and collect their thoughts.

"Cross my heart and hope to die, your revelation is between thee and me. Forever. So mote it be," Etta pledged.

Birch kissed the bridge of her nose. Emboldened by Etta's word of honor, he peeled back the past, aiming to put it in

perspective for her. "When Alison phoned to tell me that a bunch of you were going to the ice cream parlor for a farewell party, I planned on showing up." He paused to let his words sink in. "Especially since she mentioned you had a crush on me."

Humiliated, Etta's cheeks burned from a betrayal of trust. Birch drew her in for a hug. "She didn't have to tell me. I already knew. All the more reason to get you alone, walk you to your car, and talk. Only I chickened out and made up a story about caddying."

"And, all these years I thought you felt indifferent toward me."

"Nothing could be further from the truth. I'm really sorry the smokescreen I hid behind gave you that false impression. Wish I had the courage to clear the air between us that day." He peered into her eyes with a soul-penetrating gaze and gave up the secret he'd regretted keeping from her. "I'm Gay."

In that suspended moment between them, Etta understood the importance of her reaction to his brave revelation, however taken aback by complete surprise. She didn't care to know when he first realized his sexual orientation. She didn't care to know if he was in a relationship. She only cared about letting him know the foundation of their friendship would withstand the ravages of time.

Etta's eyes glistened with fresh tears as she planted a kiss on his cheek. Neither of them said a word as they held onto each other for dear life, her head resting on his broad shoulder. If they'd heard the rustle of leaves several feet behind them, each may have thought it was the jackrabbit scampering across the clearing.

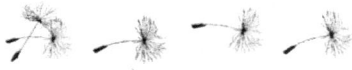

Certainly not Peleg Walker. Or, someone spying on them through the iron sight clamped on the barrel of a .410-bore shotgun.

Chapter 66

Suspicion:

For a small-game hunter, the .410 serves its master well. Shells minimal in size with less shot reduce damage to the meat, as opposed to a 12 or 20-gauge shotgun. To the point of a clichéd exaggeration, if he'd heard it once, he'd heard it a hundred times from both Grandpappy Wentworth and Mad Daddy Wayne. A bullet point well-driven when they'd granted their consent for Wyatt to take his first shot at backyard fauna on his eighth birthday.

Up to then, he trekked alongside them with their kill until they reached home. There, he'd break ranks and dispel pent-up energy running around and raising a ruckus with his brothers and sisters in the great outdoors. Going about their business indoors, Grandpappy and Mad Daddy soaked the critter in a pot of saltwater where it'd stay overnight to tenderize. The following day, his maw and grandmaw removed the bones. Setting the meat aside, they chopped homegrown vegetables to simmer in broth thickened with cornstarch.

Eyeing those two huddled together on a tarp, with a trigger finger itchy to squeeze, his mouth watered just thinking of redneck rabbit stew. To the best of his recollections, no one in his family ever got sick, despite the risks associated with consuming a varmint ridden with disease or parasites.

Of utmost importance he remain unheard and unseen, Wyatt allowed the plump jackrabbit crossing his field of vision to flee scot-free. There'd be others. Robins and sparrows too, during that forlorn summer.

He kneeled behind a low-lying entanglement of branches within three feet of his subjects of interest who appeared

oblivious to the sights and sounds around them. She, resting her head on that guy's shoulder. That guy's cheek grazing hers. Sure as shootin', he could crawl within a foot of two sitting ducks and kill two birds with one fatal shot if he had the mind to.

For all of his jealousy and seething fury, his adoration for Etta prevented him from carrying out an execution-style hit. Just as cautious in skulking away from the scene of an uncommitted crime to avoid detection, he exercised the utmost care to avoid snapping twigs or crunching dried leaves underfoot.

When he reached his pickup he'd had the foresight to park far enough away from Etta's Citroen, he turned the ignition key to the on position and moved the gearshift to neutral. Able to roll back several feet before starting the engine, he made a clean break from the Ram Tail Mill ruins.

***

Quiet Wyatt's still waters ran deep for Etta ever since he first laid eyes on her. That'd be the day she made her debut on the school grounds of Ponaganset High. In the same huddle with Obie and Tom, the only thing stopping him from joining his buddies in approaching her was Mad Daddy's deep-seated hatred for Sal Rizzio, founded solely on ethnic prejudice. The decision Wyatt lived to regret wasn't grounded in fear of recriminations from a madman. As matters stood, the bastard's foreseen and foretold death occurred the week of Independence Day that July preceding his senior year, freeing the rising generation of Coles from tyranny.

Rather, wariness mired Wyatt in the sludge of stagnation.

A decent young man, he harbored none of the elder Coles' intolerance. Wyatt thought he didn't stand a chance with her because of coagulated bad blood between their dads. An ill-

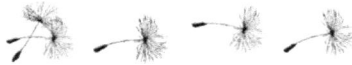

conceived conclusion based solely on an error in judgement, wool-gathered moss.

Fact check: Sal never found out who shot up the deli.

Chief Bretton thought it best to let the cur he cowered lie in his own excrement. Fist agreed, lest Sal put his life on the line from the likelihood of firing up his temper to confront a dangerous man on booby-trapped turf at the fringe of society.

***

So, on that first day of school, upholding an impressive academic track record, Wyatt conducted a quick study of Etta from afar. A sharpshooter who seldom missed a moving target, he sized up the new girl's compatibility for hitting it off. Had he acted on the courage of his conviction to beat a path to her alongside Obie and Tom, the odds were in his favor to spark and hold Etta's interest at first sight and forevermore.

He owned the slow and deliberate swagger of a cowboy. Lean and muscular, he presented a fine package in tight, flared corduroys. A strong jawline conveyed assertiveness, an automatic turn-on for Etta. A lazy grin. Covetous green eyes. One other selling point for jockeying to the front of the crowd was that his longer, unrulier variation of the mop-top in tawny blonde, hit the neckband of his shirt collar.

Instead, he held back on the basis of assumption and blew an opportunity of a lifetime. Who knows? Ignited, they might have set fire to the rain. Preferable to brandishing a firearm when he did.

Could've. Should've. Wyatt would have plenty of time to mull over the what-ifs behind bars, an unforeseen destination ascribed to impulsive and irrational behavior.

***

302

On those occasions when Wyatt and Etta crossed paths in the school corridors, she stood apart from the throng of students hustling to their classrooms before the warning bell rang. Besides her dazzling beauty and distinct ensemble of the day, she radiated confidence and charm. Attributes which attracted Wyatt to her in the first place, held his heart hostage.

Indistinguishable to Etta as most seniors she had nothing in common with academically or socially, she traipsed through her junior year as though Wyatt never existed. In the wrong, Wyatt saw no point in striking up a conversation with someone he thought would rebuff him on account of associating the Cole name with mud. So, for his own well-being, he redirected his romantic feelings toward Iris Fenner who became his steady girl throughout the remains of their last year in high school.

***

As runner-up, Wyatt couldn't do much better than Iris, although he tested the waters aplenty after graduation. No longer tethered to the yoke of Mad Daddy's oppression, he left the confines of Foster to lap up the life of an outdoorsman, fishing and hunting in Sebago, Maine, and frequenting the local dives.

The vitality of his psyche and soul restored from the change of scenery, Wyatt headed back to the green grass of home the following spring. Submitting to the realization Iris possessed the desirable traits of an ideal wife—attractive, trustworthy, selfless, and pleasant—he pursued her in earnest without the ardor befitting a suitor.

Comfortably numb with the humdrum turn of events in adulthood, Wyatt filled out an application for full-time employment at the sawmill, and aced the follow-up interview. Hired for the job of shipping transports, he'd truck lumber to home improvement retailers in the tri-state area.

303

Until the company owned his soul, and before he took a knee for popping the question to Iris, Wyatt intended to stretch out the summer by viewing the lay of the land he dearly loved through a gun-sight.

***

Setting foot on Breezy Hill, a prehistoric, architectural site, Wyatt crouched behind greenery, concealing himself from prospective deer filing in to feed on lush growth in the infancy of summer. Within the realm of possibility, a doe with her fawns or a young buck. Peering through the gun-sight on a 12-guage shotgun for surveilling the surroundings, his eyes lit up when the muzzle aligned with Etta Rizzio, sketching at a distance.

The mere sight of her swept aside the tangle of cobwebs he'd woven to entrap his desires. Released from captivity, infatuation triggered his heart to beat faster and caused him to feel weak at the knees. His skin felt clammy. Not wanting to startle her at the risk of inciting a combative reaction against a sworn enemy, Wyatt cleared out.

Throwing away another now-or-never moment, Wyatt convinced himself he'd get one more shot to sort things out with her before the season tapered off.

Third time's a dream come true. Maybe not:

Prelude to making his dream come true, Wyatt spotted the two-toned Citroen hunkered in place, its suspension system in high position to provide clearance on rough terrain. His heart leaped with joy as the jauntiness in his step delivered him to the outer rim of the Ram Tail Mill ruins. There, he grotesquely twisted a startling discovery out of context through his supposition of suspicion.

When far afield of the ruins, and having exceeded the speed limit in his escape along roads leading home, Wyatt began to get a hold of himself. Corralling his disappointment and

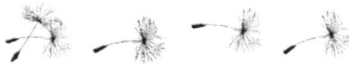

despair, he drew solace from foreseeing a future with Iris as his lawfully wedded wife. Of this, Wyatt kept reminding himself whenever his heart waged war against his sense of decency and fair play.

***

Swaddled in the security of their friendship, Birch and Etta reluctantly parted at the seam. In a joint effort to gather trash and fold the tarp, they wrapped up their conversation.

"Listen, Hot Stuff. I'll have you know, I purged you out of my system from schtupping someone who reminded me of you," she fessed.

Taking his cue from Etta, Birch picked up the pace to keep up with her line of thought. "Sounds like he made it worth your while."

"For the most part." Looking him straight in the eye, "The crux of the matter is, I'm totally hot for a guy I got off on the wrong foot with."

Put that way, Birch latched onto an image of Etta frozen in place by the car door, facing the opposite direction. "Not that guy loading the catering truck!"

Jabbing him in the side with her elbow again, "Yeah. That guy!"

Chapter 67

On a morning when the month of August started off on a clean slate, the windswept rain pushed open the front door of the deli with greater force than Keith Lawrence anticipated, throwing off his gait. If the elements weren't conspiring against him, he'd have been on his way to Brooklyn, Connecticut, impatient to wipe his reputable slate clean of a false charge. With time to kill, he'd have grabbed breakfast before showing up to settle the score at the agreed upon location down the road a ways from the Pleasant Dreams Motel, the source of his nightmare.

When Keith crossed over the threshold, water rolled off his weatherproof poncho onto the tile floor. Sal looked up from his base of operations in the public arena of his kitchen. "Look what the cat dragged in! Stay put so you don't flood the rest of the joint." He snatched a couple of fresh dish towels and rushed to the front, tossing them at his set-up man.

Untying the hood, and slipping it off, Keith raked his fingers through his head of hair to make himself more presentable. He then proceeded to towel-dry the sleeves and front of the poncho.

"Don't take this the wrong way," needled Sal. "But, on a day you have no business being here at all, what brings you in at this hour?"

Coming to grips with his jeans having gotten soaked from the knees on down to the cuffs, "I'm getting around to that. Mind if I have a cup of coffee, first? Black. To match my dark mood. Man, when it rains, it pours!"

Wrenching the poncho to the left and to the right, Keith managed to wipe most of the back. As Sal poured piping hot

coffee into a cup, Keith moseyed to the counter in his abrasion-resistant and waterproof cowhide footwear.

"This one's on the house. So, what gives?" asked Sal.

"I got a legal obligation to be somewhere in Connecticut, and the bike won't cut it in this weather. Can I borrow your car?"

Sal stroked his chin, deep in contemplation. Under ordinary circumstances, he would have handed over his keys to the Biscayne. But, he felt responsible for the recent pandemonium in the deli which gave Keith the wrong impression about Etta's romantic attachment to Birch. Seizing an opportunity to redeem himself, Sal came up with an alternate plan.

"Hey, beggars can't be choosers, right?"

***

While Keith stayed put behind the counter, taking tentative sips of the strong, scorching brew, Sal tested the limits in stretching the cord to the receiver from wall to wall. Out of sight, but not out of hearing range, he dialed home.

Abandoning her oatmeal, Etta got up from the kitchen table and picked up their phone's receiver on the second ring. "Dad, speak up if you expect me to hear what you're saying."

Still modulating at a hoarse whisper, "No can do. Keith's at the counter, soaked to his skin. And, desperate for a ride to Connecticut. A court appearance would be my guess. Use caution, but don't dawdle getting here."

"Wh-h-h-a-a?"

Sal cut her off. "Here's your chance to get on his good side. Even though he's the love of your life, promise me you won't elope with him just yet." Grinning from ear to ear, he walked the receiver to its base and hung up.

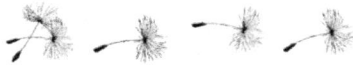

Etta pulled the receiver away from her ear and stared at it in disbelief before smashing an imaginative figment of her dad's skull into the cradle on the wall. Balling her hands into fists, she shrieked high-pitch indignation at the top of her lungs. "O-o-o-o-o-h!"

Having no other recourse, Etta threw on her hooded rain slicker and snatched the car keys off a hook by the phone. Sprinting from the front porch onto the driveway, the blustery weather railed against her hastiness to reach Sydney.

Chapter 68

Keith stepped out of the deli as soon as Etta pulled up to the curb. Of his own volition, he opened the door on the passenger side and slid onto the front seat. Face to face, each took in the other's dishevelment. He, staring at her tempest-tossed curls, fanning outward like Medusa's serpents. She, staring at his messy bedhead. For the sake of keeping the peace, neither vocalized their caustic thoughts, saving their breath for practical vocalization.

"So, just where in Connecticut is this courtroom I'm taking you?"

Raising a quizzical eyebrow, "Who said I'm going to court?"

Reciprocating a quizzical eyebrow, Etta conveyed her point.

"Well, I might have given your dad the wrong impression when I mentioned I have a legal obligation."

Etta jacked up the defrosters, put the gearshift in reverse, and backed away from the curb. Braking, she turned to face Keith. "Spin me in the right direction."

Assuming she knew her way to the highway, he instructed her to get on Route 101 and head west. "Take it slow. Shouldn't take more than twenty minutes to reach Brooklyn and drop me off where I need to be."

Turning left out of the parking lot, Etta glanced his way again. "Where's that?"

"To In the Gutter Bowling Alley." Forewarned by Etta's deliberate, deadpan expression, Keith intervened before her

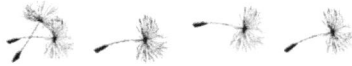

snide remark surfaced. "The case is being settled out of court. The location was mutually agreed upon for its convenience. Satisfied?"

Shifting her focus on the road ahead to the exclusion of much else, Etta dismissed the absurdity without a word of rebuttal. "Visibility sucks! Make sure you let me know the turnoff well in advance. Got that?"

"Yeah. We don't want to wind up in a gutter."

***

Hazardous driving conditions imposed an unspoken truce between two people who thrived on waging a war of wits. Hunched over the steering wheel, Etta bit her bottom lip in trepidation of hydroplaning on the slick roadway—and winding up in a gutter.

Keith leaned back against the headrest, staring out the rain-battered windshield through blurred vision. Lost in thought, and unmindful of the wipers sweeping at warp speed, he mulled over the fine mess his court-appointed attorney would get him out of, using the flimsiest evidence for leverage.

To begin with, time wasn't on Keith's side during the early Seventies. Until DNA fingerprinting first became available in 1988, the gold standard for determining paternity involved comparing blood types, a process which achieved eighty per cent accuracy.

Whether through cunning or conniving, his defense lawyer obtained information pertaining to the approximate due date of pregnancy for the complainant from her obstetrician's medical secretary. Counting backwards for an estimation of conception, the complainant's due date was at odds with the date on the motel receipt, which also coincided with Keith's handwritten entry in the ledger.

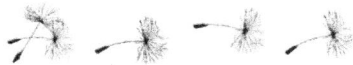

According to the projection cited in the medical record, the litigant would have conceived two months prior to engaging in consensual intercourse with the defendant. Only once, claimed Keith. The desk clerk, who identified him in the company of his attorney, attested Keith stayed at the motel just that one time.

All well and good. However, it didn't rule out the plaintiff and defendant having consensual intercourse on several occasions at different lodgings prior to their rendezvous at the Pleasant Dreams Motel.

So, going out on a limb, Keith's defense attorney enlisted the help of a private investigator for checking out the comings and goings at the bar where Keith had hooked up with the complainant. Diligent surveillance yielded touchy-feely photos of the plaintiff leaving the establishment with a different escort on two separate stakeouts.

Each image worth a thousand words of innuendo amounted to a pile of cheap shots at character defamation which did not, by any means, rule out the defendant fathering the plaintiff's unborn child. For the sake of argument, the plaintiff's own court-appointed attorney could poke more holes in their circumstantial evidence than a slice of Swiss cheese.

Nevertheless, Keith's legal counsel contacted the prosecuting attorney for the sake of making his own argument in suggesting the plaintiff drop the charge. Going with a strong gut feeling on the presumption of his client's innocence, he gambled against the odds, believing their angle of the truth would call her bluff and convince a deceptive opportunist to save face by settling out of court.

The gamble paid off.

Absorbed in thought, Keith came close to missing his cue for directing Etta off the two-lane, a faux pas with potential to incur her wrath. Affecting a lazy drawl to cover up his angst, he

dragged his words. "Take a left onto Dog Hill Road, about a half-mile ahead. Then another left, and a right after that. Far enough in advance for you?"

Etta dared to turn her head to the right, rolling her eyes for his benefit.

***

Pulling up to the set of double doors in front of the bowling alley, Keith could sense Etta's unease. No doubt, conjured by the seedy surroundings of fissures in the asphalt and peeling paint on the neon sign. He sighted his attorney's beat-up Ford Cortina in the lot and figured the others would show up soon.

Reluctant to leave Etta alone, he aimed to get her at a place with safety in numbers. Playing it cool, "Hey, why don't you head across the street to the diner and get us a table. You fly, I buy. As soon as the paperwork is taken care of, I'll be there in two shakes of a lamb's tail."

"Since I risked my life getting you to this hellhole—before you fly off the handle of that door, I think I deserve to know what you're settling out of court."

"Oh! Neglected to mention it, did I?" finding joy in getting her dander up. "A wrongful paternity suit."

Contrary to the reaction he expected, Etta's playful grin unnerved him. "Well! Look who's hot stuff, after all!"

Flying off the handle of the passenger door and slamming it, he stood outside the bowling alley until Etta pulled into a parking space across the street. Exiting the confines of Sydney, she flourished a coquettish wave to him during her mad dash to get out of the rain.

If Keith hadn't already surmised it from the start, he knew for sure right then and there, that any road Etta took, she'd find him.

312

Chapter 69

Led to one of the small booths without fanfare or finesse by a waitress who had nothing on Muriel, Etta slid onto the bench seat facing the door. A complete stranger to her surroundings, she settled back, conducting a subtle once-over of Hot off the Griddle diner and its patrons, while conveying interest in an open menu the fly-by waitress dropped in front of her.

Huddles of unpretentious folks like those who chowed down at her dad's deli spoke their mind without caring who heard them. The few heated discussions going on all at once drowned out the most recent song selected from one of the Seeburg Wall-O-Matic 100 Juke Boxes. Falling on deaf ears, Tammy Wynette's justification to stand by your man despite his infidelities.

Comforted by the ambience brought to light, she loosened up and scanned the various breakfast combinations listed on the left side of the worn laminate. Her stomach growled in wanton need of more than the bland oatmeal she'd consumed, leaving half to stagnate in the name of justice.

Etta took notice of the same stout waitress flouncing past her, heading further down the aisle with a tray on which a stack of blueberry pancakes tantalized her taste buds. Swayed, she closed the menu and eyeballed the glass door. The morning gloom had cleared and the rain had stopped, sparing Keith from getting drenched whenever he should cross the street to the diner. Savoring his renewed taste of freedom, she supposed.

She flipped over the upside-down cup on her saucer, and skated the green-banded ivory duo to the edge of the table, confident one of the efficient waitstaff would come pouring. The waitress under Etta's scrutiny barreled her way back,

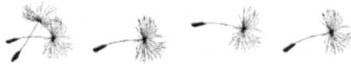

ditched the empty tray, and picked up a coffee pot off a warmer to extend the courtesy.

***

Adding the contents of two creamers to her scalding brew, Etta left no margin for spillage to squirt another. Reluctant to take a sip, she let the cup rest in its cradle while keeping watch on the door in anticipation of the only man she yearned to stand by and love.

After a short cooling-off period, Keith walked in, his eyes seeking Etta as her eyes sought him. As though under a spell, each became ensnared in the other's penetrating gaze. While he moved forward from threshold to booth, neither relinquished their starry-eyed hold on one another. To Etta, his jauntiness suggested a worrisome weight had been lifted off his shoulders. To Keith, Etta's curls spiraling in disarray enhanced her natural beauty without her seeming the wiser for it.

Sliding onto the seat across from her, Keith grabbed hold of Etta's hand, embracing it with both of his. Leaning toward her, their foreheads on the verge of bumping, he broke the news, "My nightmare is over!"

Etta placed her free hand on top of his. "Glad to hear your life is back on track."

Determined to put out a subtle feeler, he winked and replied, "Almost."

Picking up on Keith's innuendo, while trying not to hang onto the thread of ambiguity connoted from one word, Etta put out a subtle feeler of her own. She gently squeezed his hand, initiating the commemorative occurrence of two genuine smiles, broadening with mesmerizing sincerity rather than wry mockery.

A gravelly voice disrupted their trance. Disengaging from one another, Keith flipped his cup so Fran, the back-and-forth

314

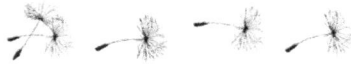

waitress he referred to by name, could honor his affirmative nod for coffee.

Etta addressed Keith, "I take it you come here often."

"Too often, if you ask me," Fran remarked. "But, not as much, lately," she added, slapping him on the back. "The usual?"

"Sounds good to me. The little lady might need more time to decide."

"Nope! I've had my heart set on the short stack of blueberry pancakes."

"You won't be sorry," vouched Fran. "You want a side of sausage or bacon with those?"

Etta no sooner declined when Keith contradicted her. "Sausage." Then, speaking to Etta, "Humor me."

Fran arched her brow at Etta. "For your information, his usual is scrambled eggs with home fries and two slices of Canadian bacon. In other words, it's more than enough to choke a horse." Satisfied, she got in the last word, Fran went about her business serving the rest of mankind seated inside Hot off the Griddle.

***

Not one to pass up an opportunity to seduce Keith if she hadn't succeeded already, Etta flashed a coquettish grin and trifled with him. "I believe you just had your way with me."

A badass chuckle indicated his receptiveness to play along. "I believe it was consensual, my dear."

His right hand reached for her left, their fingers entwining. Contingent upon giving Keith a piece of her heart, she had to know the answer to a burning question percolating in her mind for nearly an hour while she waited for him. "So tell me.

Assuming you *had* fathered the unborn child of your accuser during consensual sex, would you go the distance to pay child support?"

Fully aware of the gravity of a hypothetical situation Etta placed him in, and how his response could make or break them, he banked on the truth. "It goes without saying."

She gave his hand a squeeze. "Exactly what I thought. Fair and square. Like my dad! Although, I confess to protesting his fairness by throwing temper tantrums. Which makes him more of a square."

Keith shook his head in amusement. "Sal's a stand-up guy, all right. And, one helluva father I never had. My own cut out on my mom before I was born."

Fran showed up with their orders, hot off the griddle. Setting their meals in front of them, she replenished both coffee cups without their asking her to. "Is there anything else I can get for you folks?"

"I'm all set, thanks," said Etta.

"Not when there's more than enough food on my plate to choke a horse," teased Keith.

"Wise guy, ain't he!" retorted Fran, taking off to clear an available table and collect her tip.

***

Keeping small talk at a minimum to prioritize plowing through their breakfast, Keith strategized his next move. This, he accomplished while wolfing down food on his turf and maneuvering his fork to stab the sausage links off Etta's. Ready to put his plan into play, he fortified himself with a swallow of coffee. "Hey, seeing the weather has cleared up, how 'bout we

take a walk by Winsor Brook before dropping me off at the deli?"

Encouraged by the sparkle in her eyes, Etta's forthcoming response to his upcoming probe would determine if he'd retract his invitation or enact it. "Unless, of course, it would cramp your style with Hot Stuff."

Etta fortified herself with a swallow of coffee, having suffered cognitive whiplash from Sal's fatherly advice, the source of her most recent temper tantrum.

Here's your chance to get on his good side.

Recognizing Keith's jibe for its true intention, Etta weighed her words before replying. Not wanting to blow the chance Sal had given her, nor wanting to appear desperate, she took a nonchalant approach in delivering a smidgeon of the truth. "If you're referring to Birch, we're just friends."

That was putting it kindly after what Birch put me up to. Just thinking about what I've agreed to do tomorrow infuriates me.

Having no reason to disregard the cursory crumb Etta threw his way, Keith took it at face value and tabled his speculations. For now.

Chapter 70

Keith took Etta by the hand and guided her down the slippery slope toward Winsor Brook's ragged, scalloped edge. A misshapen pie crust characterized the contour of a shoreless perimeter for the 3.5-mile stream which fed into the Ponaganset River. Give or take a few yards on either side, Obie descended a similar line of passage to lay eyes on Keith's corpse.

Relentless rays emanating from the noonday sun had yet to evaporate a downpour's largesse on topsoil, or decrease humidity in the cloying air. Both encroachers bore the brunt of these drawbacks.

Brushing up against low-lying scrub oaks in their path, the branches retaliated by clawing at their arms and catapulting spurts of raindrops before snapping back into place. Tramping on spongy ground swallowed their footwear from sole to vamp. Worse, from working up a sweat, their jeans clung to their legs. Much worse, the substantial rainfall hosted an outbreak of blood-sucking mosquitoes feasting on every inch of exposed skin above their torsos.

"Man, where's a swat team when you need one?" Keith exhorted. "Let's make a run for the car!"

***

At best, their efforts approximated an uphill trudge along waterlogged terrain to reach the segment of Winsor Road where Etta had parked the Citroen. She picked up a twig from the woods abutting the road, and persisted in scraping away most of the muck smeared on her canvas sneakers. Her partner in grime used his handkerchief to wipe mud off of his distressed leather boots.

While they both leaned against Sydney's broadside during their purging of debris, Keith's determination to make headway with Etta resurfaced without an honorable mention of Hot Stuff. "By any chance, would you be interested in a rain check for dinner this evening? At my place."

While Etta appeared lost in thought, perhaps mulling over what intentions he had in mind, Keith smoothed the way. "I caught a couple of rainbow trout last night, gutted them, and put those suckers into a cooler with crushed ice. Since I was planning to grill them on the hibachi anyway, I thought you might like to join me."

Etta's uninhibited smile provided all the proof Keith needed for him to know he'd won her over. "Then, I'll expect you around seven. If you're ready to roll now, I'll show you where the cabin is."

***

Not much further ahead on Winsor Road, loomed the nondescript Rainbow Trout Cabins sign. Etta turned onto the gravel horseshoe which curved along the row of identical whitewashed cabins with their narrow front porches enclosed on three sides by handrails, bottom rails, balusters, and columns. Numbered in sequence, Keith pointed out his lodging at the end—number six. "It's not the lap of luxury, so we'll be dining at a card table in the kitchen or on the porch. Take your pick."

Promenading past Keith's lodging and following the arc back onto Winsor Road, Etta established her conditions. "I prefer the porch. But, only if you can guarantee there'll be no mosquitoes."

"Other than diverting them with smoke from the hibachi, I won't be held accountable for making any promises I can't keep," he mocked, counting on Etta to catch his devious implication. The upward arch of her brows indicated she had.

From there, they bantered throughout the seventeen-minute, left-right-left-right progression to the deli in Foster Center. "Since I really do prefer the ambience of a porch, I'll confiscate one of the tiki torches off mine."

"That'll work. Now, can you overlook plastic plates and utensils?"

"Meh. Allow me to do the honors of porcelain and heavy metal for two. Consider them housewarming gifts."

Keith rocked his head back and forth, acknowledging his windfall in the manner of a cocksure kingpin. "While I'm at it— your drink options are beer or cola. And, if you got any objections to baked beans on the side, be my guest."

Driving along the last right turn leading into Foster Center, Etta considered the matter. "Not sayin' I don't like what's on the menu . . ."

"I'm open to suggestions. Maybe you can come up with something that doesn't cause gas."

The two broke into uproarious laughter as Etta pulled up to the curbing in front of the deli and parked. Until the tide of mirth ebbed, they remained inside the vehicle. "I'm sure my dad will be happy to oblige. Especially after he gets *wind* of the skinny."

Another fit of laughter ensued as each of them opened their doors to step out of the car. Meeting outside the glass portal to Sal's domain before they parted ways, Keith kissed Etta on the cheek. "Later."

Etta sucked in a deep breath before entering the deli, bracing herself for her dad's proclivity to shoot off his mouth with reckless abandon. In a rare display of decorum, Sal held his tongue until she closed the distance between them.

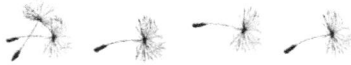

"Based on what I just saw, I'll assume you got on his good side. You're welcome."

Etta stretched over the counter to give her dad a peck on his cheek. Then, she placed her order for the evening meal, apprising him of the details. For once, Sal allowed his patrons to speculate the reason behind their guffaws without letting them in on a laughing matter.

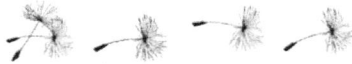

Chapter 71

Three round trips. Much to Sal's amusement.

Making himself comfortable leaning back against a lounger on the wraparound porch, he monitored his daughter's comings and goings as she lugged accoutrements from the great room to her car. He presumed, from the resonant slam of the trunk, she'd completed the final lap. As Etta sprinted up the steps to the front door, Sal called out to her before he lost further contact. "Yo! Tell me something."

"Dad, can it wait until tomorrow morning? I have just enough time to grab a shower and throw on fresh threads."

"A-a-h, so you are planning on coming home! That's all I wanted to know. Could've fooled me with all that inventory. I half-expected to see you carrying a hobo blanket stick over your shoulder."

Etta rolled her eyes in exasperation. Although they'd never admit their unspoken devotion to each other, Etta rummaged inside her heart to come up with soothing words. Stumbled upon, she bluntly delivered them, the way both preferred. "Expect it, the day I walk past you, towing the luggage Nonna and Grampa bought me for my getaway. Toodle-oo."

A-a-h, the tangerine Jet-Set luggage she'd gotten for Christmas. Conveyors of Etta's dream to hang her hat in Greenwich Village when she graduated from RIZ-Dee in three more years.

Deep in disturbing thoughts, Sal rubbed the evening stubble on his chin. As much as he dreaded his daughter braving it on her own in the heart of bohemia, he derived a measure of comfort from the deferment of time they had together, and

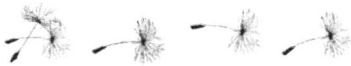

knowing she'd have the Tavershams at her beck and call when she flew the coop.

Then, on a whim, he invites a complete stranger into their home for dinner, sparking off fireworks. Ay-ay-ay!

Sal wondered if the thorn in his side he cherished so much was destined to follow in her mother's footsteps by trampling over the spoils of dreams in deference to letting love lead her astray.

***

While soaping, shampooing, and rinsing away the day's grime in the shower, Etta considered what to wear for a milestone occasion. She made up her mind in the midst of stepping out, drying off, smearing lotion over welts, and spritzing lavender eau de toilette on the erogenous zones of her neck and forearms. Comfortable in her own skin, and one with nature, she decided to complement the woodland setting in commemoration of her very first date.

The march of time took into account the futile crush she had on Birch. Followed by the fallow season at Ponaganset High where she avoided a glut of virile males dying to plow her. Hooking up in a dorm room with Sloan during her freshman year. Her mindset to forego the dating game until she met the Johnny Strabler type. Badass and brash, Keith Lawrence had the Wild One beat on both counts.

Letting her hair dry a bit before she pinned it up with her usual haphazard abandon, Etta first scuttled to put on her underwear. From there, she slipped into a pair of never-fail, denim cutoffs and one of her ruffle, off-the-shoulder peasant blouses in white to show off her summer tan. When thrusting her feet into a pair of beaded, leather flip-flops, she piled her damp hair onto her head and secured it with long bobby pins.

Without a backward glance in the mirror, Etta got her wiggle on and skedaddled out of the bedroom. Whooshing down the stairs, she rushed out the front door and bounded along the wooden steps. Hitting the pavement and hightailing it to Sydney, she stopped in her tracks to snap her dad awake from his snooze. "Yoo-hoo! Dad! I'm le-a-v-ing!"

Sal's eyes fluttered open. "Don't forget your way back home."

***

When Etta pulled up to cabin number six, she swerved onto the grassy patch in front of the entrance ramp to the porch, aiming to bridge the distance for delivering a meal on wheels. During the maneuver, she noticed the card table and folding chairs set up to the right of the doorway.

At the sound of tires crunching on gravel, Keith stepped out of his humble abode, shod in beat-up canvas sneakers without laces. He moved towards the car, brazen as ever, in a tawdry getup consisting of ragged jeans cut off at the knees, and one of his favorite T-shirts sun-bleached to a washed-out gray.

He muscled his way until he stood shoulder to shoulder with Etta who had just popped open the trunk. The glint in her eye suggested a wave of cynicism was about to hit him hard. "In your dinner invitation, you neglected to mention if there was a black-tie dress code, so I improvised."

Since fawning all over her figure-flattering attire would blow his cover, Keith preferred to fall back on his sense of humor along the same wavelength as hers. "Guilty as charged. Being a gentleman, I erred on the side of caution not to show you up."

At a stalemate for the time being, both preoccupied themselves with the contents of the trunk. The crystal stemware and bottle of wine poking outside the lid on the wicker picnic

basket, smote Keith with even more amazement and admiration for the remarkable woman beside him. Also striking a chord, the tremendous amount of labor-intensive effort she had put forth to turn a poor man's supper into an elegant dinner.

"Black-tie, be damned! Thanks to you, this meal is going to be up there with the best of 'em served at one of those fancy-dancy waterfront restaurants."

Etta's tug on his heartstrings grew stronger with every beat. Keith wanted nothing more than to scoop her in his arms and pledge his undying love and loyalty to her for the rest of his life.

A foolish move at this juncture, Keith scaled back the melodrama as he hefted the picnic basket out of the trunk. That's when he discovered the crisply folded linen tablecloth and matching napkins tucked away in a corner. Exerting the utmost control not to choke up, he funneled his emotions into barking out orders. "Other than setting the table and serving the sides, you're to park your duff for the rest of the evening."

Touched by his chivalry, and overcome with emotion, Etta suppressed the urge to dissolve in tears. Turning away, she opened the back door on the driver's side. "Does your ultimatum take effect before or after I carry up the tiki torch?" Grateful she hadn't forgotten or reneged on taking along an insect repellant, especially after their bombardment with bites.

"Effective immediately. Step away from your vehicle, empty-handed. Now, start walking!"

Hoisting the picnic basket over his shoulder, Keith allowed his guest a head start up the ramp and onto the porch. After setting the basket down near the table, he backtracked to fetch the table linens and tiki torch out of the car. With utmost expediency, Keith clamped the torch into place directly across from their dining area. Meanwhile, smoke curled upwards from

the cast-iron hibachi grill squatting on a flagstone at the other end. A telltale sign the olive oil he'd rubbed on the grates had started to burn off.

Confident the fired-up charcoal was hot as medium-hell, he sped things along. "I hope you're hungry because I'm ready to go all out searing rainbow trout."

"Starving! I'll have the table set, plates filled, and wine poured in two shakes of a lamb's tail."

Keith made his way to the threshold, eager to raid the fridge for two thawed trout, ten to twelve inches in length, the best for eating. "Where've I heard that line before?"

***

Manning their posts, each did their part in preparing dinner. Etta spread her white linen tablecloth over the scuffed and stained vinyl surface of the card table. Folding each napkin into a silverware roll, she inserted a fork and butter knife. Further delving into the picnic basket, she withdrew two porcelain plates pilfered from Momma's wildflower dinnerware service for four, seldom used after she passed away. Etta placed the dishes at opposite sides of the table, and put the rolled napkins to the left of each.

Delving into the depths of the basket once more, she retrieved two plastic containers and a serving spoon. Prying off the stubborn lids, she set them aside and ladled pasta salad and marinated porcini mushrooms onto both plates.

"Ready or not, here I come!" announced Keith.

If Etta had paid Keith any mind during his twelve minutes of flame, she surely would have marveled at his culinary dexterity. As it were, she missed out on his flick of the wrists when it came to coating the trout with olive oil, seasoning them with salt and pepper, then drizzling the juice of a squeezed lemon over both pieces. Unbeknownst to her, he grilled their

fish over direct heat for a few minutes to get a good sear, secretly admiring the grate marks, before flipping them to cook through.

Showmanship aside, Etta already found Keith smokin' hot, with or without forge play. "Perfect! I'm about to light a candle."

Chapter 72

Using his grilling fork, Keith slid both pieces of fish off a serving dish onto their plates, landing each into the void bordering portions of marinated mushrooms and pasta salad. Nearing sunset, the flame flickering from the jar candle Etta had rested on a trivet at the center of the table, illuminated Winsor Brook's bounty. "I'm s-oh glad you cut the heads off those bad boys!"

"Pulled out the entrails too, and used an old toothbrush to clean the blood vein running along the spine."

"E-w-w! Way more than I care to know!"

"Would've affected the taste if I didn't."

Keith disposed of the serving dish by placing it on the decking outside the doorway. The simple act enabled him to bend both elbows for accomplishing a chivalrous deed. "Allow me." Scooting over to Etta's side of the table, he pulled out the folding chair to seat his date.

She waited for Keith to seat himself across from her. Their eyes locked in a gaze tempered with yearning. Etta broke the trance. "Goes to show you, clothes don't bring out the gentleman in a guy. It's attentiveness."

His impish grin surfaced. "Believe me, there's plenty more attentiveness where that came from."

Arching her brows in playfulness, "The crook of your arms?"

"I plead the fifth not to incriminate myself."

"Legal jargon from someone who settled out of court in a bowling alley."

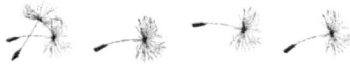

Keith raised his wine glass, reaching upward and outward. Etta, in turn, duplicated the gesture, closing in on his glass with hers for a clinking. "Here's to plenty more," toasted Keith, certain his guest understood what he suggested without needing to grimace for emphasis.

***

Unlike patrons at a fine-dining establishment sublimed by elegant décor, Etta's formal layout did little to enhance their etiquette in each other's company. Her sincere compliments to the chef dispensed with, and his rave reviews for the trimmings emoted, they dug into virgin terrain heedless of manners.

Spurred on by hearty appetites, they used their forks like a shovel and inserted the whole utensil in their mouth. Rather than avoiding topics related to sex, politics, and religion for the sake of decorous propriety, nothing was off limits. Instead of sipping their white wine, they gulped it down to quench the thirst brought on by rigorous discussion which fell on the deaf ears of vacant cabins at close range, typical for a weekday.

Etta refilled their glasses, which left just enough in the bottle to replenish one more. The unrestrained flow of conversation leading from one subject to another reinforced their like-mindedness in harboring liberal and devil-may-care attitudes. By the time they scraped the last remnants of food off their plates, their looseness of tongue opened the door for revealing to each other intimate details one doesn't share with just anyone.

Hanging on Keith's every word about his childhood and adolescence, she blinked back tears when he'd confided his single mom's desperate decision to marry for the purpose of establishing a stable home environment, didn't work out for him. During the few times his mom had the gumption to intervene on his behalf, she bore the brunt of a black eye. A broken jaw ended her willingness to negotiate a full pardon or

leniency with a browbeating stepdad who doled out corporal punishment at the least infraction.

When Keith turned eighteen, strong enough to kill the bastard with his bare hands, he took off. She stayed. "Enlisting in the army, I traded a lesser hell for the napalm of Vietnam. Pure hatred for my stepdad steeled me to spray the V-C with bullets from a semi-automatic. No matter how many I blew away, the spittin' image of his face was imprinted on theirs."

Keith grabbed hold of the wine bottle, removed its cork, and tilted his head back to guzzle the remains. Slamming the empty on the table, he proclaimed, "After my deployment, I drifted aimlessly from place to place for a couple of years. Left to my own devices, I went hog wild with the women I met in bars. That paternity suit was a wake-up call for me to get my life on track. For starters, looking for a job at the sawmill."

"Otherwise, you might have given Foster the slip."

"Possibly. Maybe fate brought me here. Being a set-up man for your dad and a barker operator at the mill have kept me on the straight and narrow. Turns out, while holing up at Winsor Brook, I discover how much I enjoy fishing. It clears my head."

Not sure whether the timing was right for him to tell her how he felt at the moment and for all eternity, the wine unfettered his inhibitions and he poured his heart out. "Then, when I first laid eyes on you in your dining room, you got under my skin—in two shakes of a lamb's tail. Because of you, I'm in no hurry to leave."

"Even though I accused you of *possibly* being a serial killer?"

"That outburst is what fanned my fire!"

Up until Keith's disclosure, she'd kept her feelings for him caged inside her heart longer than she could bear. Without

330

finesse or forethought to modulate her candor in a civil tone, she blurted, "I don't ever want you to leave!"

Generated by the heat of passion, a spontaneous combustion occurred. Both leaped from their chairs and lunged toward each other from across the divide, causing the table linen to bunch and come into contact with the candle flame.

Enclosed in an awkward embrace, their lips smashed, tongues clashed, and teeth gnashed as plates shifted and collided beneath them. The disturbance caused the liquidated wine bottle hovering on the edge to tumble onto the planks. One of the empty wine glasses toppled onto porcelain, shattering and spewing shards, some of which pelted them during the trajectory.

The sound of tinkling glass and a stinging sensation broke their magnetic hold on one another, discouraging further manifestations of ardor. The blazing fabric emitted an odor of burning hair, bringing them to their senses and provoking initial reactions to the aggressive flare-up. Keith yelled an expletive. Etta gasped in shock.

Thinking on her feet, she grabbed hold of the tablecloth's overhang and wadded it, pouncing on and snuffing out the yellow flames produced when natural fibers catch fire. Keith picked up the serving dish by the door and proceeded to retrieve those byproducts that survived the detonation of wantonness. "I'll be right back with a broom and wastebasket to clean up another fine mess."

"I may as well wash and dry the spoils of war while you're busy. I can always take a rain check for parking on my duff."

"Sure! Be my guest." Keith held the door open for Etta to enter the sparsely furnished cabin. After setting the serving tray on the kitchenette counter, he opened one of the cupboard doors under the sink to grab a bottle of detergent and a dishpan.

Putting his arm around Etta's waist, he drew her near to him and initiated a lingering kiss. "By the way, I have no intention of ever leaving."

***

The bane of torrential rain, pesky mosquitoes, an accelerating fire, or dubious assumptions pegging Hot Stuff a rival suitor, could not dissuade him from pursuing Etta. In fact, the unjustified suspicion he drummed up only served to inflame his determination. Such were Keith's rebounding thoughts during his janitorial recovery mission on the porch.

More regrettable to him than failing to consummate their love as a follow-up to the evening's hairpin turn, the missed opportunity for Etta to disclose her life-changing moments to him, as he had to her. From her lips. From her point of view. Sal's briefing about her mother's heartbreaking death, divulged during one of their bull sessions before a catering delivery, didn't cut it for him.

Despite the tough veneer she maintained, he surmised Etta's still waters ran deep, cresting with sorrow and vulnerability. Nearing the end of his disaster relief efforts, Keith's thoughts fell into place. Whereas their lovemaking might scratch the surface in gaining her trust, he reckoned time and patience would bring Etta around to realize he'd walk the wire for protecting her from life's hard knocks.

Keith mopped beads of sweat off his brow with the back of his hand. *I can scratch off tonight in going the distance anywhere with her! Just as well, for my own safety.* Owing to reporting for work before sunup and operating dangerous machinery, he'd adopted the habit of going to bed early. He needed his wits about him to avoid maiming a finger or hand during the process of removing bark, knots and foreign matter preparatory to the peeling process.

Etta washed and dried the scant amount of dinner artifacts in a jiff, relieved Momma's plates hadn't sustained any chips or cracks during the debacle. While Keith's labor-intensive chore detained him on the porch, she opened both cupboards above the sink. Their emptiness substantiated her hunch he swigged from bottles and scraped his meals off of paper or plastic when left to his own devices. For no particular reason, she chose the one on the right to store the glass, serving dish, and plates for future candlelit dinners. So she hoped.

Their romantic interlude brought her to a fork in the road she hadn't anticipated, obsessed with pulling up stakes to transplant herself in Greenwich Village. Keith's kiss shook her grounded foundation, displacing a time-honored, ideological construct. Flustered, she held her conflicting thoughts in check, focusing on tomorrow.

Just as well nothing happened tonight, given I have to rise and shine earlier than usual in the morning. Owing to accepting Birch's invitation to attend a charity match at Triggs Memorial Golf Course in Providence. Thinking the fire may have been a blessing in disguise, it eliminated a poor excuse for leaving Keith high and dry, and pouring salt onto a sore point of his named Birch.

Then again, I wanted to go the distance with him.

Locked in their own rationale for seeing the evening come to a close, a kiss sealed their promise to get together Saturday afternoon without an end of the day in sight. For peace of mind, Keith insisted on following Etta home, trailing her on his bike to the base of her driveway. True to the rebellious image she credited him for, he took off in badass fashion, serenading her with a deafening roar from the Harley's loud pipes.

If her dad had dozed off in the great room while watching television, Keith's boisterous departure guaranteed to wake him with a start and incite his sarcasm. She parked herself on the edge of the sofa by Sal's outstretched legs. "Hey, Dad! How's it going?"

Without lifting his head from the pillow, "Was that your prince taking off for his castle on horsepower?"

"None other. He wanted to make sure I got home safe and sound."

"I'd expect nothing less for my daughter."

Speaking in a wheedling tone, "During your man-to-man talks, have you been priming Keith to be on his best behavior?"

Sal grinned. "What do you think?"

Rather than storming out of the room in a huff as usual, Etta got up and walked over to her dad, bending forward to plant a kiss on his forehead. On her way to head upstairs to her room, she turned and looked him in the eye. "Dad, your crowning achievement is seeing through people. Without a doubt, whatsoever, you knew Keith was no serial killer when you first met him."

Sal's eyes watered in acknowledgement of his daughter's rare compliment. "I also happen to know you two sticks of dynamite are perfect for each other."

Chapter 73

The scattered incidents about to occur would contribute to havoc wreaked for the long haul in one way or another.

Muttering self-recriminations under her breath, Etta began to get dressed, none too pleased with herself for allowing Birch to exploit their friendship. Having wrested control away from him by imposing sanctions he never saw coming, truth could prevail after all.

She slipped into a preppy ensemble which served her well during the charade of temping at the pro shop. Chosen with an eye for conservative restraint, the outfit would play a role in pimping her a poseur. Birch's dad, one of several attendees sponsoring the charitable event at Triggs, looked forward to meeting her, courtesy of his son's hype. As a last resort, contingent upon Mr. Hansford bringing it up, Etta agreed to back the pretense she and Birch started dating soon after running into each other at Foster Country Club. Since his old man considered himself an elitist, having a son who rubbed shoulders with Oliver Taversham's granddaughter would get Birch off the hook until he achieved his objective.

The mere thought of doing Birch's dishonest dirty work, however short-term the delusion, put her in the same foul mood his original plan had fomented. Short-term because Etta sabotaged the execution of its tailpiece.

***

Things soured between two friends before her first date with Keith. Voicing objections with vehemence over a burger and fries at a local joint on Birch's turf in the East Side, Etta let him have it. "You've violated the code of friendship by

expecting me to go along with something that flies in the teeth of my ethics!"

Surmising she was about to lower the boom on their friendship by severing ties after fulfilling their duplicitous covenant, Birch placed a forefinger against her lips to silence further denunciations. "My dad's been badgering me to find the right woman and settle down. I can't bring myself to tell him the truth because of his open hostility toward homosexuals. Fearing his reaction, I'm desperate!"

"That's where I come in."

Wounded by Etta's dispassionate iciness, he bowed his head in shame. Steeling himself to look her in the eye, he persevered. "I know my putting pressure on you to sell yourself short is an imposition. But, it's part of my harebrained scheme to strike out on my own in Provincetown."

Witnessing Birch's distress, she toned down her sarcasm a notch. "This, I have to hear."

He omitted telling her what she already knew about Provincetown. A coastal resort town at the extreme tip of Cape Cod, it had a significant Gay population. What he did go on to explain, upset her even more and brought on a wave of nausea.

"Seeing I handle the books for my family's mop-and-pop appliance shop, I've been embezzling a little here and there to finance my break."

Privy to the color draining from Etta's face, and the shock overtaking her features, Birch surged ahead, hoping to salvage a thread of his shredded decency. "My plan includes leaving behind an IOU." Perceiving no change in her complexion during the aftershock, Birch thought it best to plow through. "I'll add something to the effect that I'm hitchhiking cross-country, but will make good on my promise to settle my debt by wiring payments to him through Western Union."

336

What Etta managed to say before standing and walking out on Birch, drained the color from his face and left no doubt whatsoever their friendship hit the skids. "You're beyond cruel! For worrying your parents to death! And, for using me to aid and abet your pathetic scheme! I'm giving you the benefit of two days after the golf match to come clean to them."

His shoulders sagging, Birch appeared to shrink before her eyes. From her perspective, he had sunk to a new low. "You're to call me after it's done. When things cool off, I'll stop by the store and apologize to your dad for my involvement."

Further shying away from his verbal antagonist, Birch buried his face in his hands. While invisible to him, Etta delivered her ultimatum. "Whether you blow me off, or lie, I intend to hit the ground running at Hansford's Reliable Appliances."

Etta's turnabout did nothing to stem the tide of Wyatt's irrational plan of action, or Keith's unfounded speculations until his dying day.

***

On her way:

While taking the turn onto North Road a little after half past eight, she missed Keith's phone call during his morning break. Thrust into the role of arbitrator, Sal relied on his gut feelings for steering their conversation.

"Left the house? Where does a lady of leisure go at this hour?"

Put wise that his daughter deliberately withheld information from Keith the night before, Sal rationalized he could keep the peace if he told him Etta went off on a sketching jaunt. No matter how practical or reasonable, lying wasn't Sal's strong suit. He preferred to allocate the truth on a need-to-know basis.

"On her way out the door, she mentioned attending some golf match."

Enough said. Hip to whose set of balls Etta would feast her eyes on, Keith stewed in silence. Sal wangled his way inside Keith's head. "Believe me, for whatever reason, she doesn't want to be there. Hemmed and hawed. Stomped her feet." Pausing for effect, Sal added, "Mano-a-mano, you got nothing to worry about."

***

Etta's bad taste for burgers and fries led her to suggest Italian comfort food for their midday meal to roll out Saturday's date. They ended up at Angelo's on the Hill, a stone's throw from the Capisci Deli. Despite Keith's temperament of a wild man—*Fee-fi-fo-fum, I smell the blood of a fellow Englishman*—he stilled his resentment toward Birch, the figment of a nonexistent foe fighting him for Etta's affections.

Etta stilled her own resentment of Birch while nibbling her way through their appetizer of breaded and fried calamari topped with hot pepperoncini rings. Every bite haunted her with memories of the afternoon they'd spent in each other's company at the mill ruins where Birch introduced her to his skeleton in the closet.

Keen on meeting Etta's skeletons, Keith led with his chin while they made short work of their meatball parmigiana grinders. "If circumstances in your life had been different, I wonder if you'd have given me the time of day."

Finished with chewing and swallowing a mouthful, Etta sipped cola through a straw, mulling over the cards destiny had dealt. Stalling to get her bearings, she quipped, "Meaning? My dad has told you stuff."

"Only about transferring you out of some *upper crust* school after your mom died. He didn't use those exact words.

338

They're mine. He also didn't mention how much he regretted doing it, but I could tell."

Thinking back to her dad's tactless maneuver, she chuckled. Seeing the puzzled expression on Keith's face, she backtracked to that point in time, and filled him in. Replaying the conversation between father and daughter, both of them burst into laughter over Sal's audacity to snoop inside her wallet for her Social Security card and make light of it.

Turning serious, Etta grabbed hold of Keith's hand to address his presumption as best she could without getting bogged down. "As for my dad's high-handedness, he did me a favor. Away from the *it* girls, I lived up to my potential of a hippie chick. My mother also taught me well through her example to make the best out of living in Foster. During school summer vacations, we'd venture to unexplored frontiers for our art. She'd write poetry. I'd sketch. Rainy days were the best because we hunkered down together to watch old movies."

Etta took another bite from her half-eaten grinder. Keith tore into what little remained of his. Hanging on every word, he didn't want her reminiscing to end, though she had yet to explain what she saw in him. Before polishing off the rest of her meal, Etta broached the subject head-on. "I'll have you know my requirements for the ideal man are based on the lead character in one of Brando's films. Since you outdid my expectations, that's reason enough for me to give you the time of day. And, then some."

Mistrust of Birch set aside, for now, Keith felt he'd hit the jackpot for winning her heart. Beaming with pride, while keeping his ego in check, "It better not be Stanley Kowalski!"

"Not on your life! I'll tell you when I'm good and ready."

The waitress placed their tab in the middle of the table, prompting Keith to navigate their date. "Would you like to take in a movie, or head to the cabin?"

She grinned, deflecting a suggestive gleam in her eye. Parroting Sal's overused one-liner, "What do you think?"

Chapter 74

Standing within a hair's breadth of each other inside the spartan living quarters of cabin number six, they engaged in pleasurable preliminaries previous to sowing the seeds of their love. Keith removed the hairpins from Etta's tousled upsweep. A shake of her head loosened unruly locks to cascade past her shoulders. His breath hitched from the allure of her beauty and the spellbinding scent of lavender her body heat radiated.

Etta raked her fingers through Keith's long waves. When he put his arms around her and leaned his forehead against hers, she swooned upon catching a seductive whiff of musk aftershave.

Both ablaze with wantonness, Keith crushed his lips against hers. The scorching of Etta's flesh sent electrical impulses through her psyche, soul, and hot-to-trot spots. Anticipating their heated exchange escalating to a Valkyrian dance, Keith broke off their kiss. Purely for carrying out tactical maneuvers.

Staggering in each other's arms, his voice raspy with ardor, "I don't trust the legs on this contraption to withstand an undertaking of this magnitude."

He yanked the pillow and quilt off the collapsible bed, pitching Sal's housewarming gifts to the floor. Etta knelt, folding the duvet in half to fashion a thicker pad for cushioning their sexual escapade. Keith crouched down, cupping her face in his hands. "Now, where were we?"

Etta moved her mouth toward his, hungering for much more than their appetizer. Slipping the tip of his tongue through her parted lips, their kiss deepened. An accelerant for burning their bridges behind them, there'd be no turning back from the inferno consuming both. His loins, girded for action. Her cavern

walls, saturated and engorged, were primed to receive Keith's bounty. Throbbing with excitement, they succumbed to the internal flames of desire burning for one another.

Working in their favor for muting the prospective sound of grunts, moans, and squeals, the occupant in cabin number five was hosting a redneck-rowdy keg party outdoors. Already in progress when Keith and Etta showed up, they had declined an invitation to attend. Navigating their own ground fog under the influence, the revelers paid them no mind.

***

Tempest-tossed from their all-consuming jam session, they crash-landed and simmered in passion's bittersweet surrender. Cradled in each other's arms, Etta laid her head to rest on Keith's chest. Coiling one of her curls around his finger, Etta looked up at him with eyes misted over. "Brando in the role of Johnny Strabler."

"What about it, darlin'?"

"I'm telling you that you're my Johnny Strabler."

"The outlaw biker?"

By her own volition, Etta opened the door for him to penetrate her innermost reaches. Keith's eyes misted over and he tightened his hold on her inside his arms. She kissed the tip of his nose. "My Wild One!"

Chapter 75

Ever protective of Etta, Keith suggested she should set out for home no later than ten, and he'd trail behind her on the Harley. Dissuading the few drunken hangers-on sprawled across the lawn next door from directing any lewd remarks toward *his* enchantress, Keith grandstanded an overt display of affection as Etta tucked herself in place on the driver's side.

***

Unbeknownst to Etta, Keith, or Sal, the tag end of August laid the groundwork for desolation as symptoms, suspicions, and speculations became ensnared in a vortex at Sal's Italian Deli.

As for symptoms, Etta had experienced abdominal cramping, bloating, and tender breasts for the past two months. Surefire signs of an approaching period, hers was not forthcoming. She dismissed the possibility of a pregnancy. After her breakup with Sloan, she went through a dry spell up until entering a monogamous relationship with Keith. Backing up her line of thinking, the Wild One slipped a rubber on each time without fail, considering his recent shakedown in a paternity suit. Not wanting to set off a false alarm by mentioning any of this to Keith, Etta promised herself she'd call her gynecologist in a few days if the dam hadn't breached her floodgates by then.

Also worrisome, working up the nerve to tell Keith, while figuring out just how to tell her dad, that she'd quit. No longer interested in resuming her studies in September, Etta met with an advisor and completed the necessary paperwork for withdrawing from the A-list design and art school she'd attended for two semesters. Without a pang of regret, she turned

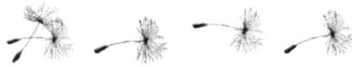

her back on an institution with its Ivy League connection to Brown University.

Her life-altering decision also aligned with dropping the hammer on relocating to Greenwich Village. Sure, Keith may have trailblazed unwitting intentions for her to veer off the yellow brick road, just as her dad had inadvertently altered her mother's course of action. Even so, throughout the stretch of summer on her solo sketching ventures hither, thither, and yon, Rosalia's ethereal presence trickled into her soul, inciting a major breakthrough.

Treading both familiar and untapped sites on their fishing ground, Etta came to realize the surroundings of Foster sharpened her artistic talent by grounding her in practicality. Preferable to floundering in the fantasy of chasing elusive rainbows inside an academic bubble destined to burst from discontent. Then, factoring in her wealth begetting wealth, she had no ambition for seeking structured employment in the design industry.

A freethinking bohemian, she enjoyed setting out for the wilds of Foster whenever and wherever the spirit of adventure led her. Purveying her finished pieces to local shops, Etta donated all proceeds to a charitable cause. Without the encumbrance of furthering her education, she'd have the precious gift of time to create more art and peddle her wares.

***

Keith splurged on booking a lavish room at Providence's upscale Biltmore Hotel. A once-in-a-lifetime extravagance that went against the grain of two outdoorsy individuals, he paid through the nose for the novelty of making love to Etta in comfort on a double bed. Cuddled in each other's arms, flesh on flesh after a bout of Saturday afternoon delight, the release of love hormones enhanced feelings of intimacy and trust between them while entangled in the sheets.

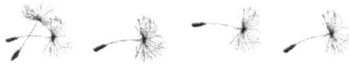

Still hooked on a feeling, Etta unburdened her soul, laying out the reasons behind her decision to quit her studies. "So, I don't ever want you to blame yourself for my judgement call." Pressing her forehead against his, "But, you've everything to do with my giving up Greenwich Village."

Even though Keith understood the artistic and altruistic rationale for her change of plans, he had no dog in Etta's fight for self-justification. However, he did have a claim staked on her territorial jurisdiction. Stroking her stubborn curls which defied submission, "Darlin', that's what I'd call taking the moral high ground."

In the time remaining, they took advantage of room service and breaking ground beyond their wildest imagination on the four-poster bed.

***

Cutting it close, Etta braced herself to tell Sal on Sunday evening after he arrived home from work. Better late than never. Better late than sooner in the day when he was full of vim and vinegar. She'd wait until he showered and sprawled out on the sofa before mentioning what she surmised her dad already suspected when she fell hard for Keith. Unbeknownst to either of them as he shouted to her on his way out the door that morning, Sal wouldn't be coming back home.

***

As for suspicions, Wyatt's became the tail that wagged the dog. His romantic obsession with Etta overrode his commitment to Iris whom he'd strung along past the prime of his promise to marry her. Straining their relationship with vagueness, and withholding an engagement ring she'd grown weary of expecting, Wyatt severed ties before things turned hostile between them. He summoned all the decency his Maw instilled in her sons, breaking the news to Iris with a gentleness Mad

Daddy Wayne and Grandpappy Wentworth didn't know from nothing.

With Iris out of the picture, Wyatt could implement the simple plan gathering moss ever since he stumbled upon Etta and her companion at the factory ruins. A mirthless chuckle burst forth. *Nuzzling nudged me to take a bull by its horn.*

A God-fearing man, thanks to Maw, he chose Sunday to confront his bull-headed nemesis at the deli Mad Daddy had vandalized. Back when Wyatt was knee-high tall to the juniper berry shrub his daddy plucked berries from to flavor his gin. Pure and simple, Wyatt would show up at the deli just before closing time.

Anticipating resistance before he could make a plea for ending the grudge between both families, Wyatt came up with a foolproof idea. To get the owner's undivided attention, he'd point the barrel of a 1969 Colt Python 357 Magnum, the Rolls Royce of revolvers, right between Mr. Rizzio's eyes.

He salivated, anticipating the taste of victory in the sweetness of Etta's kisses.

Chapter 76

The Closed sign didn't deter Wyatt from trying the door which yielded to his tug on the handle. Even better, the man he wanted to see was in plain sight. If the door had been locked, and the proprietor nowhere to be found, he would have tapped on the glass with the butt end of the Python to produce the necessary acoustics for smoking his quarry out of the kitchen.

No telling what might have happened on the other side of the door if he hammered it. Just thinking about the possible outcomes caused his upper lip to twitch, animating his mustache.

For instance, spooking his future father-in-law to run for cover and call the police. Worse than that, grabbing a firearm, shooting him, and asking questions later.

So far, so good. In like Flynn, Wyatt advanced toward Sal who stood in front of the dining side of the counter, holding onto a mop with a death grip.

Wyatt reckoned he had a few more swings left in him to finish the job.

The soles of Wyatt's leather ankle boots left a trail of muddy, outback footprints on the slick tiles behind him. It pissed off Sal to no end. About to lay into the schmuck, Wyatt pulled the revolver from the side pocket of his jacket and, according to plan, aimed it dead center at Sal's forehead.

The man who put up with all of Etta's histrionics over the years didn't scare easy. "After you get what you came for, I suggest you remove all trace evidence on your way out before I call the police. Unless, you're planning on knocking me out cold or killing me so I can't sic the law on your ass."

Sal's intuition told him this schmuck wasn't after money, so he took perverse pleasure in making him feel uneasy. Wyatt turned sideways and spared a wary glance along the path of his size 11 footprints. "Sorry, Mr. Rizzio. No worries. I'll clean up after myself."

Momentarily distracted from the script he'd worked out, and rattled at the notion of killing a human being, Wyatt shuddered as he took back his lead. "Sir, I'm not here to rob the place or do you any harm. This is the best method I could come up with for you to hear me out. I'm Wyatt Cole."

Sal didn't flinch, leading Wyatt to believe he struck a nerve. "Mr. Rizzio, chances are you still hold a grudge against my family ever since my dad shot at your window ages ago. Well, he's six feet under. Wouldn't you say it's about time to put the past behind us and declare a truce between the Coles and Rizzios?"

Floored by the shocking revelation, Sal's features contorted into a grimace. Finding his voice, "Until now, I never knew. Back then, I was assured it would never happen again. It didn't. So, I moved on. I suggest you do the same by turning around and mopping your way out the door."

His mind blown to pieces, the jagged shrapnel of regrets perforated his heart. Regret for all those missed opportunities to chat up Etta in the halls at Ponaganset High as a means to becoming inseparable sweethearts. Regret for not approaching Etta the day he came across her on Breezy Hill. *Within the realm of possibilities, they could have been married by now.*

So overwrought, Wyatt stood frozen in place, processing his anguish. Heavy-hearted, and losing strength in his right arm from bearing the weight of the revolver at a lofty position, he lowered his aim. Moistening parched lips with his tongue, he fought back stinging tears on the verge of spilling over his lower eyelids.

Still not convinced he should put the revolver back to bed inside the side pocket of his jacket, Wyatt groped through his darkest hour.

"Well, I'll be damned! Here I came to patch things up for the right of way to ask your daughter out on a date. I've carried a torch for her since high school, but always held myself back because I thought you'd forbid us to see each other."

The muzzle of a gun levelled at his chest prevented Sal from administering a pull-in man-hug followed by a couple of quick slaps on the back. "Listen, Wyatt. I've lived with my daughter long enough to know she's a handful for any man. And, seeing life can be time-sensitive to what we want, consider yourself lucky she's taken up with someone else."

Having waited this long and come this far at the sacrifice of his pride, Wyatt had nothing left to lose but Etta. He couldn't walk away just yet. "Mr. Rizzio, with all due respect, Etta could do a whole lot better than the golden-haired retriever I'd seen her with. I really think I have a shot at getting somewhere with her if I try."

Dumbfounded by the second delusional disclosure, Sal struggled to find the right words to correct his captor's misconception without provoking a hair-trigger response. In their taut state, the ear-splitting slam of the back door threw both of them off guard. Wyatt's finger jerked the Colt's trigger. Smooth and light, it required minimal pressure for the projectile to exit the muzzle. A bullet barreled into Sal's sternum at point-blank range, entering his heart. Blood from the damaged aorta flooded his chest and lungs, drowning him within seconds.

Shock from the blast flashbacked Keith to enemy territory in Nam, spurring him into action. Nimble and quick, he darted out front. One glance at Sal, a sitting-duck leaning against the counter, bleeding out onto the bib of his white apron, confirmed his worst fear. Gone. An ashen complexion and the all-too-

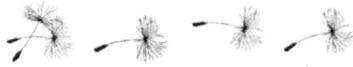

familiar slightly open, watery eyes he'd seen after a fresh kill of friend and foe in the rice fields or jungle forests, stared him in the face.

Ashen, but very much alive, the shooter had collapsed to the floor. Folded into a crumpled heap next to Sal, his eyes projected a vacant stare. The fact that he hadn't scrammed struck Keith as odd. Discovering the weapon nearby, Keith kicked it out of range and dashed to the phone.

Keeping his eye on Sal's murderer, prepared to tackle him and snap his neck, if warranted, he dialed 911. Straight to the point, Keith stated his emergency, providing the address and his slant on what went down at Sal's Italian Deli in the life span of a minute. In his mind, a botched robbery where Sal resisted and got plugged for it. Until law enforcement arrived at the scene, he made it clear that a former sniper in the United States Army could hold his own.

Distraught over Sal's demise, and beside himself over how to break the news to Etta, an anguished bellow jolted his focus back to the killer.

"N-o-h!"

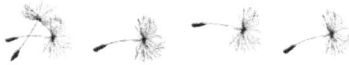

Chapter 77

Keith narrowed a wary eye on the gunslinger, renewing his resolve to wrestle him to the ground if he tried to make a break for it. To the contrary, he stayed put. Just as distraught as Keith, but for his own reasons, Wyatt revived his verbal assault. "You got it all wrong! I didn't come here to rob the joint. Or, to kill Mr. Rizzio. I jumped the gun when the slam of the door spooked me!"

***

Roving in the vicinity of Boswell Trail, Patrolman Obediah Smith gloated in the gloaming of the dashboard lights on his cruiser. Only twenty more minutes to go before his shift ended. A Sunday night guarantee, Muriel had set her hair on rollers and went to bed, shoring up on beauty sleep to dazzle the diner's early morning customers.

Although he still considered themselves newlyweds in their honeymoon phase, Muriel dashed his desire to get lucky more times than he cared to recall. Even with luck on his side, the tremulous act involved skinny-dipping into frigid waters where Muriel's calculating falsetto propelled him to a rapid climax. Besides the other subversive tactics she employed to shorten the romp, or avoid it altogether, he could swear his wife went out of her way to look unappealing to him.

At 8:46 p.m., Obie received an incoming call on his two-way radio.

During the '70s, calls to Foster's patrol officers were dispatched from either Rhode Island State Police Headquarters. Or, the Scituate Police Department, the origin of his summons from a dispatcher he'd become well-acquainted with.

"Respond to Sal's Italian Deli on Foster Center Road. The caller—slash—employee reported a fatal shooting of the proprietor. Suspect on premises, subdued by caller. Sending backup and medical examiner."

Obie, on the force less than a year, and still green around the gills, felt sick to his stomach when he heard the devastating news alluding to Etta's father. Squelching emotions from surfacing, Officer Smith responded with the professional decorum his department instilled in him, and which he demanded of himself.

"Copy. And, Kendall, would you mind calling my house to let Muriel know I'll be detained on the job?"

During a leisurely patrol around town, Obie might have covered the 3.1-mile stretch from Boswell Trail to Foster Center Road in six minutes. Flooring the gas pedal, he'd cut his time in half without any vehicular interference on the dark, deserted road.

***

Dimwitted in comparison to Etta, Muriel beat her to the punch when it came to plying flattery for furthering her own interests, whereas her bestie played it straight. Small talk lowered the drawbridge for persuading the police dispatcher to disclose her husband's destination, however close-mouthed he remained on providing further details.

Muriel never had a problem filling in the blanks to suit herself. Considering it her moral obligation to share vital information, she dialed the aggrieved party. The ringing of the phone startled Etta who had dozed off on the sofa after coddling severe stomach cramps with a hot-water bottle.

Drowsy, she shuffled barefoot to the kitchen and picked up the receiver. Muriel's chilling words jolted her wide awake.

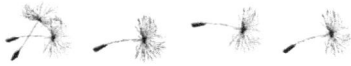

"Thought you should know that Obie was just dispatched to the deli. Most likely, responding to a burglary."

Without so much as a reply, Etta dropped the earpiece, leaving it dangling and swaying by its cord. Turning a deaf ear to Muriel's shrill entreaties, she grabbed her car keys off the peg on the wall and snatched her shoulder satchel off the countertop. Shoving the screen door open, Etta stepped into a pair of thong, terry slippers she kept on the porch by the threshold. Not the best choice of footwear to run amok in, by any means.

Hoarse, though ineffective in reaching out to Etta, Muriel surmised she'd taken off for the deli. Without an unprecedented care in the world for appearing in public with her hair in curlers, and cinched inside a bathrobe, Muriel decided she'd head there too.

***

Delirious and barely coherent, the shooter regurgitated bits and pieces to his keeper before the heat turned up. The name, Wyatt Cole, didn't register with Keith, but what he'd first mentioned, hammered his conscience. Then, and until the day he died, Keith blamed himself for Sal's murder, convinced he pulled the trigger, not Wyatt, whose gunfire resulted from an involuntary reflex action.

Consumed with grief and guilt, Keith tuned out Wyatt's rambles about his father's ethnic hostility toward Sal and the false assumptions of a feud. Then, Wyatt hit pay dirt. "So, carrying a torch for his daughter since high school, I told Mr. Rizzio she could do much better than the golden boy I saw her chumming with. I only came here to make peace and get permission to pursue Etta. Understood?"

Slipping away from his own existence, Keith turned a deaf ear to Wyatt's next round of babbles in an attempt to make

sense out of his jaw-dropper. *Hot Stuff!* Revving his mind in reverse, Keith slammed the brakes when he arrived at the scene of locking eyes with Etta in the parking lot of the deli just before she and Birch took off together. Shifting gears, his brain powered him forward, driving his train of thought to Etta attending a recent golf match at Birch's invitation.

Was there more to Hot Stuff than Etta let on? Now, this Johnny-come-lately turns up out of the woodwork to stake his claim on her.

Keith's thoughts accelerated at a high rate of speed, propelling him to the edge of a cliff. The precarious position he found himself in prevented him from turning back to the life he and Etta had once shared. Hurling to rock bottom, the tentacles of turmoil squeezed his innards as he envisioned his own downfall.

None of that other shit is going to matter when Etta finds out I brought on her father's death and she disowns me.

As the flashing turret lights on top of a police cruiser came into view, Keith retched the remnants of veal & peppers on a torpedo roll Sal had fed him before he rolled out of the lot to a catering gig.

Chapter 78

Given the situation, Officer Smith entered the deli with his service revolver drawn, caught unawares by the stench of vomit. Canvassing the area in front of him while stepping forward, Obie took it all in, doing his utmost to retain a poker face. The alleged weapon at the periphery of the crime scene. Torrential hemorrhaging from the deceased. Based on what Muriel shared with him about her best friend, the employee blotting his face with a handkerchief had to be Etta's flame.

Obie squinted his eyes to better ascertain the identity of the shooter slumped in front of the counter. None other than Wyatt Cole. The same guy he hung around with until they went their separate ways after high school. Stunned, he never pegged Wyatt for taking after his old man. Somehow, the gruesome scene in front of him didn't reek of cold-blooded murder. *Gawd!*

In the context of conducting a criminal investigation, Obie began to read him the Miranda rights. Wyatt interrupted, weary and skunked. "Come on, Obie. Cut the bullshit and cuff me. The weapon you spotted coming in will have my prints all over it. You'll find gunshot residue on my hands and clothes. Only, I never came here to rob or kill anyone."

The wound in Keith's psyche stung in anticipation of the salt Wyatt would rub in it from retelling his story. A wild-eyed Etta burst into the deli, rudely interrupting Wyatt's monologue approaching the juncture of disclosing Keith's official role in offing Sal.

***

Sighting the runnel of blood pooling around Sal, she froze in place at the edge of the threshold, held hostage by shock.

Defying the weakness overtaking her body, she surged ahead on shaky limbs. Wondering what the hell she was doing here, a tightening in his chest and a surge of adrenalin juiced up Keith to charge toward Etta to stop her from advancing any closer to where her dad lay.

Losing control of her mobility in slippers ill-equipped to support her wobble, Etta slipped on grains of sand in the configuration of a footprint. Unable to steady herself on her feet, she fell backward and bashed her head on the tiles. The spill knocked her out cold.

At wit's end, Keith yelled, "Get a rescue vehicle here!"

Meanwhile, hurtling himself back to Vietnam all over again, he reverted to incidents of head trauma he'd encountered on the battlefield. Working with what he had in front of him, Keith slipped Etta's satchel off her arm. Bunching the fabric underneath to keep her head and shoulders slightly elevated, he became aware of blood running down her inner thighs.

***

Obie's backup arrived on site within minutes of the secondary mishap. In a heightened state of awareness, the senior officer entered the premises, absorbing the temporary micromanagement of mayhem implemented by the responding rookie who drew the short end of a stick right before going off-duty. Proceeding to secure the compromised crime scene with tape around the perimeter, Obie and those in the throes, other than Etta, gaped as though a Martian tried the door.

Muriel got as far as the first row of tiles, shivering in her timbers from Obie's withering glance. In as civil a tone he could muster through clenched teeth, "This is an active crime scene. Please see yourself out."

Part Four - Covering Ground

Chapter 79

Obie's one and only homicide investigation, if you could call it that, fell short of protocol for interviewing multiple witnesses and pursuing a fugitive at large. Nipped in the bud, Foster's bloody murder coincided with harboring his first fantasy of eliminating Muriel, or wishing her dead. Preferred methods for putting an end to his misery involved laying hold of either a sharp, pointed instrument to inflict multiple stab wounds, or a striking implement for delivering several blows to bash in her skull.

Irking him to no end, Muriel's impertinence to inveigle privileged information and peddle it to Etta. As though baiting her friend to show up at the deli wasn't reason enough to pistol whip Muriel to death, she had the audacity to materialize at a crime scene.

His seething anger approaching its boiling point, Obie suspended his indignation in concession to the paper shuffle of gathering information from his subjects. Sitting behind a desk at the station, he obtained independent formal statements from both Wyatt and Keith, documenting their corroborating testimonies. At face value, both narratives supported the evidence seized at the crime scene.

Just before dismissing his guilt-ridden eyewitness, Obie felt compelled to digress even if Keith couldn't buy into it. "The slam of a door didn't kill Sal Rizzio. A bullet fired from the revolver Wyatt Cole aimed at Sal put a hole in his chest, whether premeditated or accidental."

***

Dog-tired with enough menace left in him to chew Muriel out when he arrived home, his fury would have to simmer on a

back burner until he got there. A patrolman thrust into the role of homicide investigator, he set out to notify the next of kin in person at Rhode Island Hospital where Etta had been transported.

Obie had a hunch he'd find Keith Lawrence there, and caught up with him in the vicinity of the front desk. Dead on his feet and looking the worse for wear, Keith slurred his recap of what he had just found out. "As a precaution, they're keeping her overnight because the signs and symptoms of a concussion may not appear for hours. No visitors allowed."

"Under the present circumstances, I'll flash my badge for leverage. Etta deserves to know what happened to her father. Go home. You look like shit and stink to high heaven. I'll tell her you were here."

"Maybe so. But, you look like something's sticking in your craw."

"It's that obvious, heh?"

"Very! You oughta try fishing for what's ailing you."

"I'll take your suggestion under advisement. One of these days."

A running start for their lifelong friendship, Obie never got around to taking Keith up on his offer.

Keith omitted mentioning the internal probe on tap for Etta in the morning. What was neither here nor there for an officer on duty, reeked of utmost importance to him, considering the night's air strikes. Punch-drunk from fatigue and baseless brainwork, he staggered to his Harley in the parking lot and kick-started the engine.

As the wind whipped Keith's locks of hair all the way to Winsor Road, it also kicked back the odor of dried puke on his T-shirt. Numb to his own stench, he weighed the possibility of a

miscarriage where the odds were stacked against him for having anything to do with making a baby.

***

At the risk of pushing Etta to the brink, Obie entered the room. No sense leaving her in the dark by putting off formal notification until morning. Convinced, she'd want the hard-nosed approach, Obie fortified himself to speak as he gazed upon her tear-streaked face contorted with anguish.

***

Etta's fitful night's sleep associated with episodes of sobbing and dozing on and off, eliminated the nursing staff from having to awaken her when they checked in periodically. In addition to ruling out the inability to wake up, she showed no symptoms of slurred speech, numbness, or decreased coordination. Etta's restlessness and highly agitated state had everything to do with her father's murder.

Chapter 80

Stoked by the incredulity factor, bad news had traveled with high velocity by sunrise. Artie Dufresne's live news broadcast outside the crime scene at 11 p.m. set a rolling buzz in motion which had paralleled the widespread sensation created on May 19, 1822 soon after workers discovered the body of Peleg Walker hanging from the bell rope at Ram Tail Mill.

Hungover from lack of sleep due to grieving and brooding, Keith showed up for work and fell in line to punch in. Talk of Sal's murder committed by one of their blue-collar bros had spread like sawdust blown from an industrial fan.

His boss took one look at Keith and confronted him at the time clock. "Hey, you look like death warmed over! You're not fit to operate machinery, so if you know what's good for you, you'll take today off without a dock in pay to get your head screwed on right. Now, beat it!"

***

Keith dozed off in fits and starts on the folding bed. A restorative nap out of the question, Keith left the cabin mid-morning. Anxious to find out where things stood with Etta's physical condition and emotional state, he straddled the Harley and drove to a pay phone in Foster Center.

Gazing in the direction of the deli, he beheld the Citroen parked out front. He hit on the crazy angle at which Etta had abandoned it in her haste to charge through the door. A lump rose in his throat as he gazed at the Closed sign which portended the end of a thriving business built on a faraway dream and the hard work it took to come true.

Responding to Keith's inquiry without dispensing any medical update, a nurse at the front desk merely informed him of the patient's pending release at noon. Counting on a girl's best friend keeping bedside vigil until discharge, and danged sure she'd bring Etta home, he pressed the nurse to summon Muriel to the phone. Keith dropped another dime into the coin slot while he waited.

With the speed of lightning, tragic news had reached Muriel's boss at the State Line before she called in to say why she couldn't come to work. On tenterhooks with Obie, she sought safe haven away from him at the hospital, and fared no better with Etta who blamed a short-sighted phone call for putting her there.

Keith kept it brusque and brisk. "Hey, Muriel. Tell Etta I'll meet her at the house."

"She's been asking for you."

Hedging a bet with himself for entrusting Muriel with spilling the beans on the subject of Etta's pelvic exam if he brought it up, Keith picked her brain. Muriel's audible sigh led him to drop another dime in the coin slot. "Etta's hemorrhaging was due to a ruptured ovarian cyst caused by endometriosis."

"What the hell is that?"

Muriel responded with greater clarity than she ever could when held accountable to answer on-stage pageant questions. "It's a condition where tissue lining the uterus grows outside of it. In Etta's case, the tissue formed on one of her ovaries and produced a cyst that burst."

During a rare occasion of exercising good judgement, Muriel stopped herself short of saying anything more to Keith, leaving it for Etta to share the rest if she so chose.

***

362

Keith took off for North Road and parked his Harley in the vacated spot at the bend in the driveway reserved for Sydney. Until Muriel and Etta showed up, he made himself comfortable sprawled on a lounger at the back end of the wraparound porch. His face welcomed caresses from the late-summer sun which granted temporary respite from the previous day's chilling aberration.

The sound of tires crunching gravel announced Muriel's slow uphill ascent. Keith scrambled to his feet and arrived at the crest as Muriel braked. The handle on the passenger side relented to his tug. When he leaned in to unfasten Etta's seatbelt, she threw her arms around his neck and sobbed into his chest.

Muriel got out of the car and came around to the other side, holding Etta's shoulder satchel and the plastic bag containing her soiled clothes. Ready to pawn them off on Keith when those two let go of each other, Muriel averted her eyes away from their spectacle of intimacy which triggered a level of discomfort much worse than Obie's tongue-lashing tirade.

Short-lived sustenance for Keith's tormented soul, both relinquished their grip on one another. Helping Etta out of the passenger seat, he took a gander at the boxy blouse and baggy, above-the-knee plaid shorts Muriel had loaned for her homecoming. The grim turn of events prevented him from making a wisecrack.

Instead, with arms outstretched, he got hold of Etta's things and tucked them to one side. Putting his left arm around Etta's waist, at the ready to assist her climb along the few steps to the front door, Keith took over. "Thanks for everything, Muriel. I got this. Go home and get some rest."

Knowing full well the haunting refrain of self-guilt, he abstained from blaming Muriel for endangering Etta and putting

her in the hospital. He presumed her husband had already hauled her over the coals.

Her voice weak, Etta echoed his sentiments. "Resting is exactly what I'm going to do because I can barely stand. For the last time, you're forgiven. Now, go home, Muriel."

Muriel's lips quivered in reaction to the iciness in Etta's voice. Having dismissed her best friend, she dangled her house key in front of Keith. His arm around her, they trudged to the top step where he turned the key inside the lock. He followed her in and closed the front door behind them, shutting out the world.

Chapter 81

After placing her belongings on the kitchen table, Keith felt awkward standing by empty-handed while awaiting direction. When Etta spoke, the ambiguity of her words threw him off-base. "I'm going to crash on the sofa for a bit. Then, we'll talk."

For sure, they had a lot of ground to cover, and that's what worried him. Careful in choosing his words, Keith avoided an outright mention of the deli. "Why don't I . . . uh, head out to pick up your car? I'll rustle up some grub for us at the State Line. Later, if you're up for it, we'll take a ride to get the Harley."

Preoccupied in thought, Etta nodded absent-mindedly. "The car keys are in my handbag."

"How do burgers—medium-well with the works—and, an order of fries sound?"

"Yeah, sure." Food, of little consequence to her, Etta started sobbing again. "How could a guy I'd never given a second thought to in high school, and never crossed paths with since then, be so delusional as to confront my father at gunpoint and cost him his life?"

Keith felt the color drain from his face as Etta collapsed against him. Holding her tight against his chest, he stroked her quirky curls and felt the goose egg on her scalp. While her face was buried in the fabric of his being, he jumped the gun. "Darlin', Wyatt never meant to shoot your dad. My slamming the door behind me unnerved him." As tears rolled down his cheeks, Keith preached self-damnation. "I all but killed your dad when Wyatt fired that bullet."

Etta freed herself from Keith's hold. Shaking her head back and forth, choking back a residue of sobs, she admonished him. "Obie told me how it went down, and that you blame yourself. Wyatt is solely responsible. Not you! Please don't torture yourself over this. I couldn't bear to see you suffer. And, neither would Sal who thought the world of you."

Keith brushed away his tears with the back of his hand. Etta lifted up the straight edge of Muriel's button-down blouse to swipe at her trickles. Excusing herself to lie down, Keith seated himself at the kitchen table, gathering his wits about him before rummaging inside Etta's satchel for her car keys.

Dredging the keys from the bottom of her bag, he also came up with carbon copies of hospital paperwork and an information leaflet about endometriosis. Seizing the opportunity of privacy to familiarize himself with certain female troubles beyond what Muriel explained, Keith skimmed through the leaflet. Having gotten a general idea of the condition, he rubbed the scruff of his neck while mulling over what Muriel left unsaid:

Endometriosis can affect fertility. Increase the risk of ovarian cancer. May require surgery.

Ready to take off for the deli, Keith folded the leaflet and placed it face down on the table. He stood up from the chair and picked up Etta's car keys. That's when his eyes lit on *Ectopic Pregnancy*. Tottering on his feet as he delved further, he began to wonder which way the wind blew. *Was the growth outside the uterus which caused Etta's heavy bleeding a fertilized egg? Or, was the growth which burst and caused heavy bleeding an ovarian cyst?*

Slumped forward as though punched in the gut, his mind took a turn onto a dark road overshadowed with the doom and gloom of Birch Hansford. Groping in the darkness, he tried feeling his way by messing with his head:

366

Could be, when Etta and I started seeing each other, she was at least eight weeks pregnant. Could be, she didn't know and thought her period was late. Could be, even if she did know, Etta wouldn't burden me while the dust my lawsuit kicked up had yet to settle.

Picking up on Muriel's neediness, she'd do or say anything Etta told her to. Or, from what I'd put together, Etta could scramble the facts and Muriel would be none the wiser.

Could be, I misread all the mixed signals. After all, Etta did tell me that she and Hot Stuff were just friends. She has too much integrity to lie.

Not sure if he suffered the effects of self-inflicted or self-defense wounds, Keith straightened up. He let himself out the screen door, careful not to slam it behind him so he wouldn't disturb Etta. *Had I thought to use good manners when shutting a door behind me at the deli, Sal would be alive.*

Chapter 82

When Keith let himself in through the back door, Etta had gotten around to setting the table with placemats, plates, silverware, and one too many glasses. "A Narragansett for me, if you have any left." Every now and then, he and Sal would mellow out on the porch, tossing back lager from a local brewery.

Etta grabbed a cold one from the fridge and tossed the can to him. He flipped the tab and quenched his thirst while she unloaded burgers and fries onto plates. "Well, let's have at it! I'm starving, after all!"

Needing no further coaxing, Keith pulled out the chair aligned with his placemat next to hers and seated himself at the head of the table. "How do you think I felt smelling this stuff on the way?" Catching sight of her feeble smile gladdened his heart.

Both demolished their charbroiled burgers and crammed down their crispy fries without an afterthought of dousing them with vinegar or ketchup. Engrossed in making short work of their meal, they abstained from initiating conversation between bites.

With nothing left to chew, and much to lose, Etta nibbled at the heart of matters. "Think you could stick around tonight?"

Keith's eyes lit up. "I planned on it. Packed a change of clothes even though I assumed you'd want nothing more to do with me."

They leaned into each other and nuzzled. Etta's eyes glistened with tears as she took another nibble. "Well, this is

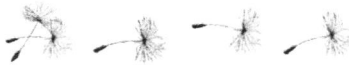

going to be awkward. Giving you a heads-up that I'm not hinting at marriage. But, all the same, you ought to know."

Wired from his beer intake, qualms and second thoughts rushed to the forefront of his brain, causing him to feel lightheaded. Noticing the change in Keith's demeanor, and realizing her words must have sounded like a trap, Etta got on with it. "You never mentioned where you stand on the subject of fatherhood, other than denying it. Since endometriosis can increase my risk for ovarian cancer, the attending physician strongly recommended I have a hysterectomy."

Thinking anything he'd do or say could be held against him, Keith hung his head in limbo during her pause for effect. His inner voice took advantage of the deafening silence by plowing him under with information he retained from the leaflet. That is to say, an ectopic pregnancy can occur on an ovary. Keith rubbed his temple relative to the throbbing thought which gained on him. *Therefore, the surgical precaution doesn't rule out a miscarriage, does it?*

Etta's next bite-sized tear set off a spontaneous reaction which defied checks and balances on his part. "My barrenness is your one-way ticket out, if you need it."

"Hey, aren't you getting way ahead of yourself? I'm still recovering from a guilt complex for Sal's murder. You ought to know the thought of losing you over it nearly destroyed me. If it's all the same to you, we'll deal with whatever lies in our future, one day at a time. I'm not planning on going anywhere without you. Now, what do you say, we head out to pick up the bike?"

Reaching out to him, a flood of tears streamed down her cheeks. Keith held onto her, absorbing her pain as he overturned his own conflictions which paled in comparison to their need for each other. To ask her anything about Birch, now or later, would undermine her platonic spin on past history and violate

their trust in one another. Even though, at times, the shadow of a doubt would haunt his thoughts until death had befallen him, moving forward together mattered more to Keith than any of their human frailties.

***

Before the days of reckoning swept them along the opposing currents of events, they took the evening in stride. Home after their errand, Etta took Keith by the hand and led him to the sofa where they cuddled in each other's arms, adrift in their own sea of tranquility.

Slumped against him and on the verge of drifting off to sleep, Keith bestirred her from falling into a deep slumber. "Darlin', seeing as you have some mighty storms to weather in the days ahead, let's get you to bed for the night."

Ticking off the tip of the iceberg in her mind, knocked Etta for a tailspin of a tizzy. *Funeral. Selling the deli. Surgery. Court hearing.* "First, I'd like a bath to calm my nerves," she quavered.

Flashing a glimmer of devilry in his eyes, "I can help with that."

***

While Etta fetched her babydoll pajamas from the bedroom, Keith started drawing a hot bath next door. Out of curiosity, he picked up the bottle of lavender bubble bath from a corner of the tub and removed the cap. Inhaling the earthy, floral fragrance evoked sensuous images of Etta. The aromatic fix put him in a romantic mood coinciding with her grand entrance, wrapped inside a towel. Befitting the deplorable state of affairs and the trauma her body had undergone, he treated Etta with reverence rather than ravishing her when she dropped her covering.

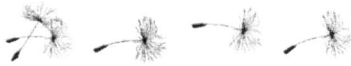

As the tub filled, Keith poured two capfuls under the running water and ran his fingers through the liquid beneath the tap to increase the volume of suds. Satisfied with the depth and amount of heat generated, he led Etta by the hand into the tub.

Settled in, she flashed him an impish grin. "Let's see how good you are at working me into a lather."

Keith stripped his shirt off and delved into caressing her skin with soap suds on a washcloth. Serenaded by murmurs of contentment, he progressed to shampooing her hair. Draining the tub while running both faucets to rinse her off from head to toe, he admired his canvas in squeaky-clean pink.

Just as he guided Etta into the tub, he grasped her hand to help her stand. Keith blotted her hair and patted her skin dry with a bath towel he grabbed from one of the shelves mounted on the wall. Hooking her arm into the crook of his elbow, she stepped onto the plush rug in front of the bathtub. "A gal could get used to this, you know."

His eyes twinkled with mischief. "If I'm going to live up to my reputation of the Wild One, it'll be a twosome another time."

"I'll hold you to it," she said, slipping on her babydolls.

"Considering you're tuckered out, get to bed. I'll be up after I shower and shave in Sal's man cave."

Etta put her arms around Keith's neck and brushed her cheek along the stubble of his face. Keith stroked the back of her neck. As they pulled away from their hug, they gazed into each other's eyes before sealing the evening with a lingering kiss.

"Darlin', taking into account when my shift starts, I may be gone before you wake up in the morning. Your grandparents will never know you had an overnight guest."

With a glint in her eye, Etta set him straight. "They will after I tell them. It won't faze Tavvy and Nonna in the least to find out we're shacking up."

Chapter 83

A mite before sunrise, the Tavershams let themselves in using their own key. Despite their four-hour commute from Brooklyn, Tavvy stepped with verve into the great room, towing two suitcases behind him. Ready to move heaven and earth for his granddaughter, he prioritized putting first things first.

"Honey Bun, if we're going to cover ground, would you mind tending to today's first order of business while I put on a pot of coffee?"

Humoring him, "On the double, mio caro." Viola stroked his cheek and kissed his forehead. "I'll head up to nudge her awake."

***

Following a brief indulgence of hugs and in-person condolences, Nonna and Etta whipped up a breakfast of scrambled eggs, bacon, and toast to fiddle with the strong coffee Tavvy poured into their mugs. Not one to dawdle, Tavvy got down to bedrock while their eggs were still hot.

Picking each other's brain to plan a civil funeral ceremony similar to Rosalia's, they agreed upon skipping an obituary and death notice to assure the presence of attendees by invitation only. Expressing her intent on asking Mr. Doyle to deliver the eulogy, Etta aimed to call him right away.

As for the bitches who'd gotten in touch with her about a month ago to share news of Joan's second marriage, Etta decided to spare herself the daunting task of calling them. She didn't have the stamina to announce the gruesome details of her dad's demise, nor deal with their reaction. Instead, she proposed

recruiting Muriel for contacting Helen, who in turn, would telephone the others.

Scattering in different directions, each had their work cut out for them. Nonna stayed behind to clear the table and wash dishes while waiting for Tony to swing by so they could ride together to the deli. There, they'd deplete the inventory in the fridge and freezer to prepare a full-course, family-style meal for an intimate funeral reception at home in the dining room.

***

Both Tony and Viola primed themselves before entering the deli which staked its claim on Sal. Reassuring one another they'd be paying their highest respect in honoring the man and his life's vocation by working in his kitchen, Tony unlocked the door. As they crossed over the threshold, Viola consecrated their presence, making a sign of the cross and addressing their mission with reverence. "Cooking for a solemn occasion where family and friends gather together to honor the dearly departed is an expression of love."

"Amen to that."

While underway with preparations, Viola had the foresight in suggesting they put together several dinners for Etta to store in the freezer to tie her over during her post-surgery convalescence. "We'd better make each serving a double," she said, twitching her eyebrows at Tony.

Quick to deliver a comedic response, he chipped in, "The set-up man set himself up pretty well with the boss's daughter, didn't he?"

Nonna poked him in the rib with her elbow. "At breakfast she *may* have mentioned how crazy in love she is. Her grampa and I can't wait to meet him."

"Sal took a liking to him right away. So did I. Keith's an up-front kind of guy! Hey, if he can go toe to toe with Etta, he'll

374

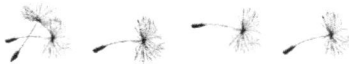

have no problem standing his ground against the likes of Tavvy."

Viola crossed her arms and tapped her foot, rattling off the names of Rosalia, Sal, Etta, Tavvy, and Keith. After a deliberate delay, she asserted, "Another alpha in the pack!"

***

Planning Sal's wake at the funeral parlor, Tavvy and Etta forged a silent partnership. Out of keeping for the tenacious tycoon used to conducting business, he kept his trap shut. When appropriate, he nodded his approval and rubbed Etta's back as she made her wishes known to the director.

Gaining ground on their way to the florist in Tavvy's Cadillac, he maintained his silence while attuned to his granddaughter's mood. Irritated by her grampa's laid-back temperament at a time when she needed him to put his foot down, Etta dished it out. "You know, I could have used a little guidance in there while groping my way through the dark!"

A cautious driver, Tavvy focused on traffic in the city of Providence, keeping his eyes straight ahead. Nevertheless, Etta caught his impertinent grin. "Hogwash! If you needed advice, you would have asked for it. You let your heart do the talking, and did right by your dad without my getting in your hair."

"Sorry I mistook your silent treatment for neglect rather than respect," she replied with sullen resignation.

Tavvy pulled over to the curb in front of Petal Perfect. Turning off the ignition, he faced her. "Other than an Aspidistra that fends for itself in our apartment, when it comes to horticulture, I'm a blooming idiot."

She grimaced at her Grampa's pun. "Okay, you're off the hook. Based on my dad telling anyone who'd listen I'm a thorn in his side, he's given me something to go on."

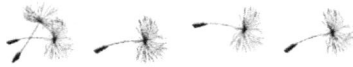

Shaken to the core over an old friend's passing, Fist delivered the eulogy with a slight tremor in his voice. He began his tribute at the point where their friendship broke ground inside the Capisci Deli. "Fed up with driving all the way to Providence for a decent sandwich, I convinced Sal to buy into his dream of owning a deli when the beauty shop in Foster Center went up for sale."

The small gathering seated inside the funeral home for Sal's wake listened with rapt attention, moved to tears and chuckles over Fist's recollections. The one exception, Lois Doyle. She attended to keep the peace with her husband and to feign sympathy for her daughter's best friend.

Drowsing in her chair, she stifled a yawn and shifted her gaze to the white floral arrangements flanking the mahogany casket. Poring over the splendor of a standing spray of roses and a wreath featuring roses surrounded by lilies, she was unable to find fault.

H-m-m. No doubt, Oliver Taversham footed the bill for the whole kit and caboodle to bury a commoner who married into money.

For lack of anything better to do while sitting in a padded, viewing chair, Lois preyed upon Etta's mourning attire. She considered the black, drawstring-waist dress with its handkerchief hem a trite too informal for a solemn occasion. And, the white rose pinned in her hair, tacky.

Her daughter, on the other hand, dressed the part admirably.

Heeding her mother's advice to silence her carping, Muriel wore a navy blue suit with a white, high-neck, bow blouse.

At the conclusion of Fist's moving farewell speech, the pallbearers rose to carry the casket to the hearse for the

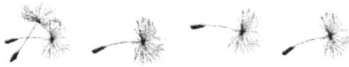

graveside service at the cemetery: Keith, Tony, Obie and fellow officer, Ray Patterson. Taking advantage of everyone's leave-taking, and taking Fist by surprise, Lois murmured her change of plans to him.

Approaching Muriel, she sweet-talked her daughter into implementing the idea which surfaced when her feet hit the floor that morning. "From here on out, your father will have to ride with you and Obie. I'm driving myself home to nurse this god-awful migraine in bed."

Glad to be rid of her mother, Muriel went along with the ruse and twisted the knife in an old wound inflicted by their dirty secret. Linking arms with her dad, she beamed, "Obie and I get to have you all to ourselves for most of the day."

***

Miles to go before I sleep.

Although Rosalia skimmed over the details of her courtship with Sal, Etta latched onto content shared during their jammies sessions. Especially when her mother's eyes lit up with dreaminess. Rummaging through those memories, Etta salvaged Momma's account of how her dad developed a keen interest in the poetry of Robert Frost. So mote it be written on his half of the headstone alongside *Love at first bite!*

Little did Etta realize Sal had spoken those words to Rosalia leading up to her conception in the back seat of a Woodie wagon.

***

Taking solace in one another's company at the dining room table over which Tony presided, pleasant conversation fell in place. Those who knew Lois harbored their voiceless gratitude for her absence as they basked in the glory of delicious food and companionship.

377

Etta livened the tempo when she complimented Joan on her radiant glow. Helen and Gloria needed no further encouragement to rag on their sister bitch's newlywed status in front of everyone. While most of those at the table had been accustomed to forks in the road detouring to impropriety, Fist, Muriel, Obie, and Ray took all of the bawdiness in stride.

"Why shouldn't she have a glow?" led Helen. "The old gray mare got someone to muck out her stall."

When the roaring laughter subsided and the beet-red flush to Joan's face began to fade, Helen faced down Etta. "What about you? When everyone leaves and you're alone in this big house, who's going to look after you?"

Glowing, Etta leaned in toward Keith. "The stable boy who mucks out *my* stall."

Chapter 84

All eyes were glued on the stable boy in the hot seat, awaiting what Keith might have to say for himself. Not one to overlook a four-leaf clover blown his way, Keith chose to capitalize on the opportunity to air his intentions. Only too cognizant of Etta's independent streak, he hadn't pressed his luck in suggesting he take up lodging to see her through surgery and recovery just yet.

Now, he could put his objective on the table and get the backing he needed from those in Etta's corner if she kicked up a fuss. Nodding at Helen, "Seeing as you brought it up, I've been meaning to discuss some kind of living arrangement until Etta's out of the woods. But, that can wait. Today, it's all about giving Sal his due."

Tony stood and raised his glass. "To Sal!"

Following the lead of Sal's right-hand man, everyone rose and lifted their glass for a round of Italian *Saw-lutays*, *Cheers*, and *Here Heres* before sipping their wine. Propriety had reasserted itself. Sincerity prevailed.

***

The Tavershams could rest assured Keith embodied the stand-up guy Sal and Tony pegged him for. Confident Etta was in capable hands with plenty of provisions to see them both over a hurdle, the doting grandparents decided to cut their stay short by a few days to grant them peace and quiet.

But, only after Tavvy sealed a deal with a handshake. "Keith, as soon as you find out the outcome of her surgery, you're to call us without delay. Understood?"

From that day forth, Etta and Keith established a life together one day at a time, without any foreseen formality of matrimony. Taking precautions so her caregiver wouldn't feel saddled with her, Etta played it coy when suggesting he extend his stay beyond her recuperation period.

Snuggling together under a throw on the sofa toward the end of an abstinence advisory to forego sexual intercourse for six weeks after her full hysterectomy, Etta brought up the subject. "By any chance, have you given a thought to freezing your butt off inside a drafty cabin when late autumn and winter roll around?"

Hoping Etta had rolled out the red carpet for him, Keith kept up the charade, affecting his lackadaisical drawl. "Pulling up stakes off-season has crossed my mind. Figured there's still time for me to hold out on making a move before my short-term lease here expires."

Responding in kind, Etta walked her fingers along Keith's chest and neck, stopping at the vertical cleft in his chin. "With the exception of your fishing gear, most of your belongings are here. I'm offering you permanent occupancy with a non-binding clause. This way, there's an escape hatch if one of us ever needs it."

Keeping his wits about him while beaming with elation, Keith added his own terms of agreement to their verbal contract. "Providing we split living expenses fifty-fifty. That's how it has to be if I'm going to take up residence with a filthy-rich chick."

"If you insist."

As though they'd written wedding vows promising to stay together through thick and thin, Keith and Etta consummated their open-ended arrangement with flesh-on-flesh contact. Each moved their lips toward the other's and used their tongues to caress and explore.

Hoarse with unbridled passion after their tender moment, Keith murmured, "I'm counting the days until I can muck out your stall."

***

Etta tallied their graphic countdown on a magnetic memo pad adhered to the fridge. Six celibate days remained on the home front.

On that sixth day as Etta sorted through the mail while Keith showered, sloughing off the workday's sawdust down the drain, she came across a delivery which unnerved her. With trembling hands, she broke the seal on an envelope stamped with the name and address of the state correctional facility. Wyatt Cole was being held in custody there pending his sentencing approximately sixty days from the postmark date.

She slid the lined loose-leaf paper folded in thirds out of its carrier pigeon and pored over the contents.

Dear Etta,

I don't expect you to forgive me for my rash decision which resulted in your father's death. I can't forgive myself for all the pain I've caused your family and mine. Other than my own selfishness and crazy obsession, I had no reason to believe my reckless behavior would win your heart.

I want you to know how sorry I am for what I've done. There isn't any punishment harsh enough to ever lessen my guilt for taking your father's life.

Sincerely,
Wyatt Cole

Etta never expected to feel any compassion for the man who murdered her dad. Wyatt's effort to convey genuine remorse and take full responsibility opened her heart a crack. Just as any maximum prison sentence could not expunge Wyatt's guilt, his penalty would not diminish her sense of loss. Still holding the letter in her hands, she contemplated the ethics of justice.

Not one to hold grudges, Sal's tolerance and easy-going nature bestowed Etta with the guiding principles she needed to cover murky ground. When the roar of running water had subsided, Etta cried out, "When you're dry, there's something I want you to read."

Chapter 85

At his arraignment, Wyatt Cole entered a "knowing and intelligent" guilty plea. In confessing his own guilt under oath, and signing a form waiving his legal rights of due process, Wyatt kissed his keister good-bye. He forfeited his right to counsel, his right to a jury or bench trial, and his right not to incriminate himself.

During the wane of August the wheels of justice moved swiftly to prosecute a self-convicted criminal. The consequence of putting the screws to himself had subjected Wyatt to a "Judges Remand". While detained in custody at the ACI, he would be treated as a sentenced prisoner until his hearing in ninety days.

As customary, the judge requested a pre-sentence report. The contents of which had the power of persuasion to influence his decision in modifying a sentence based upon: nature of the crime, character background, prior convictions, and whether the defendant had expressed remorse during the intervening time. That report would be the only fair shake extended to Wyatt who was up a creek against an overzealous prosecutor in the judicial backwater.

***

Putting aside the gruesome details of a tragic scenario, Etta pivoted from Wyatt's candid letter and her dad's tendency to give folks the benefit of a doubt. Contrition and compassion governed the words she penned in a letter to the sentencing judge. In her closing statement, Etta implored the court to err on the side of mercy.

***

On the cusp of Thanksgiving, Etta and Keith arrived at the Licht Judicial Complex sprawled along Benefit and South Main Streets in Providence. There to attend Wyatt's sentencing hearing, they stood inside Superior Court's main hall, a vestibule of marble. Perusing the directory for whereabouts of the courtroom, they established their bearings for locating Room 8.

Etta and Keith entered the stately chamber, in awe of its grandeur. Gold leaf embellished the ceiling and wood-paneled walls of hand-carved mahogany adorned with Roman-Georgian columns. They seated themselves on upholstered chairs in the front row of the spectator section.

To their left, at the opposite end, Wyatt's maw and his sister sat, looking uptight. Other than his sister, Earline, and a couple of deadbeat brothers, the Cole clan had left Rhode Island. Pulled up stakes after Mad Daddy croaked, eager to distance themselves from all the scuttlebutt kicked up by the legacy of Foster's legendary roughneck. Good enough for Wyatt who didn't want his kinfolk showing their faces in court. Earline promised him she'd look after Maw who had suffered and sustained damage from a heart attack at the tipping point of his father's illness. That's all he asked.

A railing with a swinging door separated the gathering from the well of the court. Two counsel tables were situated at the back of that well. The prosecuting attorney occupied the plaintiff's table, the one closest to the jury box. Bushy-browed and endowed with a crown of white curls, the victor radiated confidence in his custom-tailored suit and somber tie. The bespectacled, snowy owl struck Keith as a sock-it-to-him kind of guy.

The clerk, a pale young man, entered the picture in his late thirties. Fading in the background of his light gray suit, he sat on the side of the judge's bench, opposite the witness stand.

The court reporter who coiled her hair in a chignon with wispy tendrils trailing along the back of her neck, looked to be in her forties. That morning she dressed herself in the businesslike attire of a skirt and open jacket in matching beige with a white blouse underneath. Settled in her designated chair near the witness stand, she appeared ready to capture the words of a legal proceeding.

Those assembled waited in stifling silence for the defendant to arrive from the slammer. Disallowed privileges afforded unconvicted individuals prior to sentencing, Wyatt was treated as one of the prison's own. Each day he donned a khaki uniform which he found well-suited to his guilty conscience. Time served would factor into his sentence. That amounted to a chip off the old cell block.

***

Breaking up the blank stares of the spectators, Wyatt's escorted entrance in prison issue. Associate Justice Harold E. Klein, who had read the pre-sentencing report, allowed the defendant in his courtroom without the restraints of a belly chain, handcuffs and leg shackles he wore during transport. The concession amounted to a fig leaf of freedom, considering the sheriff's deputy keeping an eye on him carried a Taser, baton, handcuffs, and pepper spray.

Must have been the sight of her favorite son in uniform which caused frail, fragile Madelyn Cole to whimper and ram her face against her daughter's shoulder. Wyatt's sweeping gaze across the front row lingered on Maw and Etta, bringing on a pained expression visible to all.

Figuring on Golden Boy accompanying Etta, a flicker of surprise crossed his features when he saw Keith there instead. Ushered to his seat behind the defense's table, Wyatt had a few minutes to mull over this startling discovery before the judge came in.

As directed by the bailiff, all rose when the judge entered the courtroom. *By outward appearances, a man who paid his dues*, thought Etta, taking in the long-serving official's regal bearing and mane of white hair tied in a ponytail. "This Court with the Honorable Judge Harold E. Klein presiding, is now in session."

Formalities out of the way, Judge Klein moved proceedings along at warp speed for getting to the finish line of the *State of Rhode Island and Providence Plantations vs. Wyatt Cole*. "This sentencing process takes into account the nature of the crime, outcome of the crime, impact on the victim's family, and the defendant's profile. Factoring in all of the above, this Court imposes a sentence it believes appropriate to the crime charged, according to law. There is nothing in the defendant's background to suggest any previous criminal conviction or tendency. There is nothing to indicate he may be a repeat offender . . ."

Tears pooled in Etta's eyes. If only Wyatt had struck up a conversation with her in high school. She could have easily been smitten with his tawny brawn. Even if the flirtation resulted in one date and they went their separate ways, none of this other stuff would have happened. Her dad would be alive and Wyatt wouldn't be sitting in a court of law.

Sensing Etta's suffering through the perspiration in her palm, Keith squeezed her hand. Etta leaned into his shoulder. Convinced a film she watched with Momma cultivated her love for Keith before she met him, Etta could not imagine giving a piece of her heart to anyone else.

". . . Gleaned from the Court's observations and the defendant's guilty plea to accept full responsibility for an unintentional homicide, without malice aforethought,

committed in the performance of an unlawful act with criminal negligence involving a firearm . . ."

Pausing for effect. ". . . It is the second form of involuntary manslaughter, which based on the unlawful act theory in Rhode Island, called misdemeanor manslaughter and considered a felony in the state of Rhode Island, that a felony punishment for this crime is deemed appropriate. Will the defendant please rise?"

All during the judge's warm-up, Wyatt gnawed on a bone of contention. That, for all of the illegal distilling Mad Daddy and Grandpappy conducted on their property. For all of their gun trafficking. For all their hate crimes. They managed to evade the law. Here I am, a law-abiding citizen. And, because of one boneheaded decision, my felony conviction will follow me wherever I go for the rest of my life.

Although his knees threatened to buckle, Wyatt stood on his feet to take his punishment like a man.

"The Court hereby sentences the defendant, Wyatt Cole, to fifteen years at the Adult Correctional Institution, ten years to be served by him in a Minimum Security Prison with the remaining five years to be suspended."

***

At the bang of a gavel, the sheriff's deputy rose to his feet and proceeded to escort the defendant out of the courtroom. Maw's burst of tears and Etta's sorrow tore Wyatt's heart to shreds. Preparing to exit the courtroom themselves, Keith stood aside while the women exchanged comforting hugs.

Chapter 86

In the aftermath of crime and punishment, other groundbreaking developments occurred. Fist Doyle, persuasive in convincing Sal to purchase a defunct salon and convert it to a deli, proved just as influential in expediting the sale of a vacant property. The spin of a Rolodex yielded the phone number of Les Barnaby, the go-to realtor he contacted to get in touch with Etta.

Barnaby's listing in the classifieds capitalized on Foster Center's business potential. The building's strategic location enticed a prospective buyer looking to establish a fitness center in town. In need of a personal loan for a down payment, Les Barnaby highly recommended Gordon Doyle for a square deal. Through mutual cooperation, two businessmen had formed a profitable alliance over the years.

Location presumably inspired the generic legal name, Foster Fitness Center, a breeding ground for Muriel's plausible suspicion of Obie and widowed Carolyn Farnum working up a sweat inside and outside the gym. The fitness center also provided fertile ground for cultivating a budding romance between castaways, Iris Fenner and Tom Holden.

If it weren't for news media coverage depicting Etta Rizzo the catalyst of a capricious crime, Wyatt's jilted lover might never have discovered the hurtful truth. And, Tom? Always spurned whenever he tried to get off the ground with an elusive butterfly, he suffered the consequences for busting his chops to pursue Etta.

Perchance, vulnerability drew Iris and Tom to each other. During their from-here-to-eternity journey through life together, both kept their deepest secrets to themselves. Whereas Tom

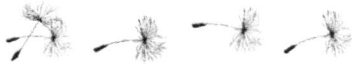

knew Wyatt had made a fool of Iris, his wife never knew she played second fiddle to yet another man love-starved for Etta.

***

Closing in on six months of living together, Keith suggested, rather than proposed, legalizing their arrangement. In the midst of sponging Etta in the surrounds of a lavender-scented bubble bath, he drawled, "Darlin', what are we waitin' for? Let's get married."

Peering at him through steam clouds swirling around them, she replied with affected indifference, "Offhand, I don't see any reason not to."

The Wild One let out a whoop and holler, stripping off his jeans and undershorts. He vaulted over the apron of the bathtub into the deep. Scooting himself in place across from Etta, they maneuvered their slippery bodies to partake in water sex.

***

Within two weeks of obtaining their marriage license, Etta and Keith tied the knot. One of Fist's cronies, a former probate judge, officiated their wedding at the office of Doyle Savings & Loan, LLC. On neutral territory without the presence of Lois to defile it, Gordon Doyle stood in for Sal. Honored to do so, he locked arms with Etta and presented her to Keith.

After a brief exchange of vows, Keith slipped a braided, white gold wedding band entwined with Etta's birthstone amethysts on her left ring finger. In turn, Etta slipped a brushed silver band with *The Wild One* engraved inside, on Keith's.

Muriel and Obie witnessed the nuptials, adding their signatures to the license after the ceremony. That day the bond of matrimony joined four friends together in sickness and in health; for better or worse. Till death would they part.

Nine months after Muriel's miraculous conception, she gave birth to a son. Overriding her mother's objections dramatized with crocodile tears, Etta and Keith Lawrence attended Ethan's baptismal christening, assuming their obligation to serve as godparents.

***

From their marital day forward, Keith and Etta loved and cherished each other. For richer, rather than poorer, both remained grounded in sensibility and lived frugally despite their vast wealth. They understood the importance of maintaining their connections to the simple pleasures in life which brought them self-satisfaction. Keith took to fishing on weekends, holing up in cabin number six. As often happened when holding a line in the muddy waters of Winsor Brook, he was taunted by two nagging thoughts imprisoned in his soul.

Etta took advantage of Keith's absence by ramping up her sketching excursions and adapting her pen-and-ink impressions to colorful masterpieces. The perfection which paid off in sales at shops, galleries, and festivals benefited her charitable causes.

Having sown enough wild oats burning up the road on a Harley, Keith sold it and drove Sal's Biscayne. Ugly as all get-out, the behemoth got him to work and back. The roomy trunk accommodated his fishing gear and a cooler packed with ice. When keeping the Chevy in running condition outweighed its reliability on asphalt, Keith bought a pickup. His mode of transportation until he departed from this world, the Wild One drove his trucks into the ground before he'd consider getting a new one. Soon succumbing to a death rattle in the engine, Keith was about due for another pickup on the day he died.

On the flip side, Etta mollycoddled the Citroen. Semi-retiring Sydney, she took the Fat Man out for an occasional spin, preferring to cover ground in a jeep when the going got tough.

While doing time for his crime in a facility of the state prison complex, Wyatt marinated in the error of his ways. With hours on end at his disposal, he found comfort in reading the Bible and extracting meaning from scripture. Faithfully serving time alongside him, the Good Book showed its age in accordance with dog-eared corners and a weakened spine. Its reverent handler underlined favorite passages and scribbled notes outside the page margins. Although Wyatt repented for his folly over and over again, he couldn't forgive himself. Etta's pardon in the letter she'd written to Judge Klein had no discerning effect.

Moving on as best he could, Wyatt enrolled in several correspondence courses, studying his way to earn a bachelor's degree in forestry. Becoming more in tune with the forest ranger's role of preserving natural habitats, Wyatt swore off hunting and possessing guns of any kind. During his sixth year of incarceration, Maw's heart failed her for the last time. Her passing severed his emotional ties to Foster.

When released from prison four years later, he emerged a more grounded man than when he entered. Heading to Juneau for gainful employment as a forest ranger, Rhode Island disappeared from his range of vision long before he approached the Alaska-Canada Highway in Dawson Creek, British Columbia. Trying not to let the hum of his tires drive him batty, Wyatt listened to country music. Pacing himself along the thirteen-hour stretch, and allowing for an overnight motel stay, he arrived at his destination in two days.

In the course of time, Wyatt married a divorcée who waitressed at the sports bar & grill where he unwound at the end of the day. After a few platonic get-togethers, Wyatt tested the waters, coming clean with his hard-luck story. Encouraged by

his honesty, she lowered her guard and apprised him of a checkered past fueled by drug addiction.

When romance took root, they decided getting hitched was the logical thing to do. Affection for one another, rather than an all-consuming love, formed the basis of their union. Drifting off to sleep on the first night of their formal arrangement, Iris wangled her way into the marital bed, drawing a logical conclusion for him. *"If you had married me when you should've, Sal Rizzio would still be alive."*

Until the day Wyatt died of natural causes in old age, he condemned himself for Sal's death, and suffered from the internal damnation of laying a guilt trip on an innocent bystander who slammed a door.

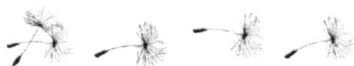

Part Five - Shifting Ground

Chapter 87

As days of yore receded and conceded to the present, mechanical diggers and hydraulic hammers shifted ground for digging burial plots.

Ever feeling the pinch of her parents' premature mortality, Etta considered Nonna and Grampa's longevity a blessing until they reached the pyramidal summit of their eighties. Then, old age conferred the cruelty of excess suffering before granting them a merciful death.

Detected too late due to nonspecific symptoms of weight loss and lack of appetite, Viola succumbed to pancreatic cancer. Granting him a cooling-off period to mull over a practical move, Tavvy rejected the notion of renting or selling his brownstone to take up permanent residence with Etta and Keith. "Dash it! Last time I stayed at the homestead, I don't recall seeing any sidewalks for a stroll."

A routine the Tavershams engaged in most evenings after dinner, Tavvy refused to give up the ground on which he worshipped Honey Bun ever since the day they had met. No less stubborn than usual on a frigid January night, he dismissed the doorman's winter-watch advisory urging him to forego venturing onto the icy sidewalk. "Spare me the tommyrot! I'm nimble as Fred Astaire."

Tavvy skippered the length of one Brooklyn block before slipping and making a hard landing on his tailbone. Fractured on impact, the spill immobilized him in his bed, necessitating round-the-clock care. Incapacity, which led to pulmonary congestion and pneumonia, claimed Tavvy's life within six months of his wife's passing.

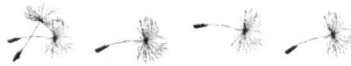

Among the keepsakes and largesse Etta inherited after the brownstone sold for a pretty penny, she adopted her grandparents' Aspidistra. By rule of green thumb, the houseplant had flourished for twenty-five years or thereabouts under their devil-may-care auspices. The cast-iron genus with a legendary reputation to surpass fifty years of age from blatant neglect motivated Etta to safeguard her grandparents' living relic.

Striving to foster the Aspidistra's longevity, she subjected the slow-growing species to conditions which would kill most other housebound plants. Preferring shade, she placed her potted protégé on a stand set slightly back from a north-facing window in her studio to shield it from direct sunlight. Blocking Keith from advancing any further with a watering can, she admonished him. "Don't come any closer. You'll end up killing the plant with kindness by saturating its soil. In the interest of the Aspidistra's welfare, please allow the plant wiggle room to fend for itself."

Plying his dry wit, "Is that what it told you?"

Keeping a straight face, "Implied rather than expressly stated."

***

On the seamy side of town in the hush of night, a gap-toothed and stringy-haired vagabond of slim build, pulled back the lid on a dumpster. Lithe and limber from exercises in survival, the former cougar who morphed into a haggard crone from years of hard living, dropped into the pungent pen. On all fours, she began a methodical search for commodities to trade with her homeless homies, or to sell at a recycling center. Abetted by a streetlight, she sifted and sorted through the upper crust of late-hour discards from restaurants and shops on the verge of closing, adding this and that to her plastic bag.

Digging deeper, her bare hands uncovered a corpse, warm to the touch. From having pickpocketed a fair amount of stiffs in blind alleys, she was dead certain this sap with a fatal gunshot wound to the head, winked out less than three hours ago. Making light work of tugging a wallet out of the front pocket on his jeans, she filched a thick wad of bills and stashed the cash inside the waist of her panties.

Of no use to her, she left his license and credit cards intact. Submerging an arm up to its shoulder, she gave the wallet a decent burial before scrabbling her way out of the dumpster. Dropping to the ground, she scuttled to her cardboard vestibule under a bridge, anxious to count her blessings away from the prying eyes of other squalid squatters.

On morning break having a smoke, a college-grad dishwasher standing out back of the Fast Eats Diner, happened to glimpse a body freefalling from the dumpster into a waste hauler. Ditching his cigarette, the moonlighting playwright made a scene to overcompensate for the front loader's engine roar. Planting himself on the driver's side of the truck, he hollered and performed a few jumping jacks. His antics got the trash collector to open his window.

***

All because a wallet containing an ID had parted company with a corpse, John Doe had been refrigerated at the morgue to delay decomposition during the waiting game of obtaining a name. The coroner had charted the homicide victim's teeth and fillings to compare with dental records of missing persons. Typical, the process of zeroing in on who's who could take from six to eight weeks.

At last, the match made in hell paired up with Dean Doyle. Identity established, the medical examiner's office notified the next of kin. Not the least bit surprised his cuz met a violent end, the coroner could only provide how he died, not why someone

plugged him. Saddened, Fist booked a flight to Mississippi, dead set on arranging a decent burial for Keen.

Local authorities speculated Doyle's demise had ties with the doings of Biloxi's Dixie Mafia. An unsolved murder, no one was the wiser Keen botched an attempt to fulfill a contract killing. His intended mark turned the tables on him, disposing his body further south from the crime scene.

If Lois had half a brain, she'd have jumped for joy over despicable Dean's knick-knack paddywhack. In a nursing home, swimming toward the deep end of dementia, she required vigilant care. Incontinent and unable to speak or make herself understood, Lois was trapped in her own cesspool of polluted, convoluted thoughts. Together, Muriel and her daddy made their daily pilgrimages to visit her out of obligation rather than devotion.

Granted a few years of reprieve from the degradation of Lois rolling over to the far side of their bed every night to avoid physical contact, Fist died alone peacefully in his sleep from sudden cardiac arrest. Cutting the ground from under his wife's feet by two years, Muriel kept up the daily drudgery of visiting her mother because Daddy would have wanted her to. At her bedside when Lois expelled her last breath, Muriel walked away with the everlasting impression of her mouth twisted into an ugly grimace as death claimed a dark soul.

And, since Uncle Reggie erased his carbon footprints to wherever he had fled, no one knew if he paid the devil his due. Regardless, he had the bad habit of showing up in Muriel's head uninvited, scaring the hell out of her every time.

***

The bitches, Etta's surrogate aunts, still held their ground at the time of Keith's death. True to their word before parting company at Rosalia and Sal's wedding, they honored their pact

to keep in touch on a regular basis. Technological advances increased their frequency of contact through the ease of digital communication.

Less surefooted, Helen hobbled as a consequence of the sprain to her ankle. Stumbling over her youngest great-grandson's toy in the middle of the night, she toppled and turned her ankle in the fall. For the healing period of three to six months, she used crutches to get around. During that interval she beat a home intruder to a bloody pulp with the bottom portion of a crutch, making it clear she hadn't changed horses in her midstream eighties.

Drawing last month's telephone conversation with Etta to a close, she got in the last word. "When I got through with that prowler, he didn't have a leg to stand on!"

***

In the round-robin of phone calls, Joan added more to Helen's story after she and Etta had depleted their arsenals of mundane musings.

Joan, whom Helen dubbed Seward's Folly after her fall. "What was I thinking that day I strong-armed you into coming home with me to Nebraska? I never dreamed you'd settle in Seward, too close for comfort. Spoiled my grandkids and great-grandkids rotten, you did! That toy car I tripped on may as well have had your name written on it."

Joan reached inside her purse and withdrew a duplicate, handing the miniature, metal replacement to Helen. "John-John told me you crushed the other one."

Helen heaved a sigh of exasperation. Tears welled in her eyes for a soul sister who remained pure as the driven snow despite the mud slung at her. She held her arms out in an open invitation to hug Joan. "You're incorrigible!"

"Feeling guilty for the toy I bought that ended up in harm's way, I offered to wait on her hand and foot. Plying her trademark huff-and-puff, she turned me down."

"Never mind me. I've got a husband to do that. Turn your fanny around and focus on stoking the home fires with husband number two."

"What did you expect from Helen?" teased Etta.

Tears welled in Joan's eyes for a soul sister who covered her tracks of compassion with gruffness. "Nothing less from a protective mama bear."

***

Motoring along the National Scenic Byway of Historic Route 66, Gloria had checked in with Etta. On a nostalgic toot to recapture the spirit of their carefree cruise all those years ago in a '47 Mercury convertible, she and Lenny decided to kick asphalt in their more accommodating SUV. Questioning how many years he and Gloria had left to get up and go, the retired doctor and his missus planned their great escape to Steinbeck's land of hopes and dreams, strewn with relics from the original highway's glory days.

"I'm in Conway, Texas. No, I'm not kidding!" Gloria allowed Etta a moment for her whereabouts along their westward movement to sink in. "We just pulled into the lot of a fast-food joint, so thought I'd seize the moment to say hello."

"What's to see in Conway?"

"*Saw.* We just left the Bug Ranch. We were told it's still a popular place to visit even though the poor buggers are falling apart. You and Keith ought to get out of Foster and take a cross-country road trip."

Going along for the ride, she lied. "I'll mention it to him. Meanwhile, you and Lenny have a safe trip."

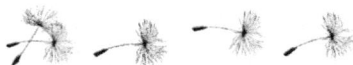

In view of the fact that she and the Wild One had become content creatures of habit in their rural habitat, Etta did not foresee a nomadic getaway in the near future. Nor, did she expect the Aspidistra to outlive either one of them.

Chapter 88

Wilted from all of the negative energy expelled during her tossfest and tirade, Etta fell into a deep sleep after setting Obie straight about Muriel. Dead to the world upon smashing her head against the pillows propped at one end of the sofa, sensory deprivation inoculated her against Obie's chemical warfare to expunge every trace of casserole carnage in the cuckoo's nest. Throughout his scouring the kitchen's entire surface area, to the denouement of locking the door behind him in the wee smalls, she hadn't moved a muscle.

***

Seeing the light of day:

Sunlight streaming through the windows at the back of the great room jolted Etta awake at full throttle. Thrusting herself to an upright position, her face contorted as pain riddled her lower back. Taking in the surroundings of last night's campground, she struggled with the logic of her sleeping arrangement. Bewildered for a few blinks more, a whiff of her body odor banished any lingering brain fog. Like smelling salts, her rankness revived the horror of what had occurred—and, what must have occurred at the same time Keith drowned.

A guttural cry escaped her throat, releasing slags of misery and anger which lay dormant in the pit of her being while in the arms of Morpheus. Wailing her outrage, Etta grappled with vilifying or vindicating Keith due to impaired judgement wrought by implication.

Damn you, Muriel!

Finger-raking her hair, she ruffled through loose strands of a ratty upsweep snagged with flecks of fossilized casserole. She

bristled at her filth and glowered at the clock on the wall by the staircase which stared her in the face.

"I'll lock up on my way out, and come back around nine to help you with the funeral arrangements."

With not much more than an hour before Obie showed up, Etta sprang to her feet, regretting her haste. Fully awake and in command of her faculties, the sudden movement put things in perspective by aligning the mishap of falling on her butt with that of banishing Muriel and cheesing off in the kitchen. Favoring her lower back, Etta dragged her feet along the stairs to the top of the landing, determined to draw the bath Muriel had so rudely interrupted.

***

Before purging herself of vileness, Etta shuffled into the bedroom where she peeled off her clothes and removed bobby pins from a stale bun. From the top of a bureau, she grabbed her portable audio player.

When the notion had originally struck her fancy, a ding-dong pissed away the afterthought of fetching it. The idea of tapping her favorite song to enhance the mood-setting candles she'd lit around the bathtub held appeal. Aphrodisiacal tipping points she had foreseen sending her over the edge while fingering her vulnerable spot and fantasizing Keith's loving touch.

No such luck!

Etta limped into the adjoining bathroom. Flinching, she knelt on the scatter rug in front of the tub, placing the electronic device on its soft nap. Determined to sort through her ambivalent feelings toward Keith in a setting which hosted many romantic interludes, she stretched forward, crying out in pain as she turned both faucets, favoring hot.

Foremost in her mind, as steam clouded her vision, the foreplay of Keith's marriage proposal. Nostalgic flashbacks obliterated conscious awareness of filling the tub, or drizzling lavender-scented bubble bath into the raging swirls of water. Etta tapped the play button. Steeling herself against another jab of pain, she climbed over the rim and lowered herself into the hot water, hoping the heat would loosen her stiffness.

Leaning back against the tub, soaking, she closed her eyes, funneling Janis Joplin's raw delivery bemoaning an all-consuming love. The emotional shivers in "Piece of My Heart" nourished Etta's wanton soul. A song she associated with the Wild One underpinned how she'd given him a big piece of her heart right before they set the night on fire during their first date.

Her man. Most often, unshaven. Always rough-hewn. His overall broodiness and badassery attracted her to him in the first place. Had she overlooked an underlying discontent which predisposed him to stray? Up until Muriel put a bug in her ear, she never had a reason to question Keith's faithfulness.

Swabbing herself squeaky clean with a vengeance, her body shook with convulsive sobs as she pieced together segments of their lives. Throughout her mental sweep, she saw the ever-present light and heat flickering in Keith's eyes whenever he looked at her. Heeding the vibrations in her soul, Etta reached out to him in the thick of crying.

"Pl-ease forgive me for ever doubting you!" Catching her breath, "I recognized you were the love of my life the day we first crossed paths. There's been no one else, before or since. And, never will."

Pouring a generous amount of shampoo into her cupped hand to finish her cleansing ritual, Etta lathered her scalp. She felt a deep warmth radiating from her heart chakra. No doubt in her mind, Keith's reverberating love energy. Feeling an influx

of peace wash over her, she sighed and whispered, "I love you, my Wild One. For all eternity and beyond. So mote it be."

***

Feeling a bit more limber climbing out of the bathtub than she had climbing in, Etta rubbed a fluffy towel over her body, then commenced blotting excess water from her hair. Padding in the buff to her bedroom, she heard the front door click. Following on its heels, a booming voice, comforting in its familiarity. "Hey! I got us bagels and coffee."

"I'll be down as soon as I throw on some clothes."

Chapter 89

A cleaner and calmer version of her former self arrived in the kitchen. Still wet behind the ears, her hair hadn't spiraled out of control just yet. There, she discovered Obie spreading out their breakfast on rattan placemats at opposite ends of the farmhouse table, the setting for yesterday evening's dissension.

Funny, Obie must have arranged the pair as a finishing touch before he hightailed it home.

The scuff of her house slippers on tile diverted his attention away from the table. Encircling her in a bear hug, Obie detected the lilting scent of lavender he loved to embrace. Relinquishing his hold, he gave Etta his seal of approval. "Gawd, what a difference a day makes! Last night, I could have used a clothespin to pinch my nose."

The rebuke earned him a humorless smile and counterblow. "I see you had the good sense to cover up your hideous legs."

"Fair enough." Too tired to elaborate on his raw deal, Obie didn't mention how the khakis chafed his wounds with every move. Changing the subject, "Hope you're game for bacon, cream cheese, and scallions on your bagel."

The enticing aroma of coffee and appetizing smear of fixings on their bagels caused her empty stomach to rumble from hunger. "Good choice."

He removed the coffee cup lids and pitched them into the barren liner of the wastebasket. "There's your invitation to sit down."

In unison, Etta and Obie slid the tucked-in chairs out from under the table and seated themselves. Barehanded, they tackled what lay in front of them.

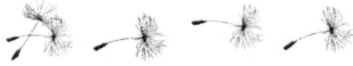

Cramming down their food in reverent silence, Etta couldn't resist the temptation to bite the hand that fed her. "Didn't Muriel make your breakfast this morning?"

Caught unaware by a distasteful subject, Obie looked up, still chewing the chunk of bagel he'd bitten off. Since he had whittled the bagel to a nub held between his thumb and forefinger, Etta gave him the grand opening he needed in the nick of time. All because neither of them had put the elephant stuck in their craw to bed last night.

He chased an audible swallow with a gulp of coffee and used his napkin to swipe at splotches of cream cheese on his upper lip. He didn't succeed at wiping the sheepish grin off his face.

Red-faced, he fessed up. "Other than making a pit stop at home to drop off an empty casserole dish under her nose, I spent the night elsewhere. After this morning's unannounced return to hell's kitchen, I left with my stomach running on empty." Obie anticipated she'd ask where he sought refuge, offering him the perfect lead to steer Etta in the direction he wanted her to go.

"Did she tell you what happened?" Etta asked, reaching for her coffee.

Sidetracked, he rubbed his clean-shaven jaw. "If Muriel had any intentions of leveling with me, which I highly doubt, my ass-whooping took the wind out of her sails, and then some." He bottled up the provocation for their skirmish.

Either Etta didn't catch, or didn't care where he spent the night. Regardless, he had to get her there.

"So, as a result, I holed up at the Rainbow Trout Cabins with the woman Muriel saw Keith with at Chelo's. Judith Grant. Judy. A lovely gal."

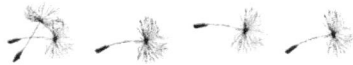

As though Obie punched her in the gut, Etta spit a mouthful of coffee into her napkin, choking on the bean juice still lodged in her throat. Taking advantage of her incapacity to speak, and worried he might not get a word in edgewise once she recovered, Obie soldiered on in a hurry.

"She and Keith weren't having an affair, if that's what Muriel led you to believe." He whipped out one of the extra napkins from the paper bag in the middle of the table, and used it to rub the sweat off his forehead.

In a hoarse voice thick with emotion, Etta rasped, "You didn't have to tell me. I drew my own conclusion while coming clean in the bathtub. I hadn't expected your specifics, that's all."

Blown off course by her admission, Etta's change of heart spared him from tampering with evidence of Keith's marital fidelity. Prepared to go the added mile, he would have regurgitated a remnant from one of the many conversations shared with a hard-ass on the porch while chugging beer. *"My woman's never given me any reason to stray."*

What he replied to Keith had no bearing on navigating today's narrow strait.

"That's great, kid! It's always best when faith leads you to believe an undisputed truth someone tries to discredit." Now, for nudging her in the right direction. "Before you plan Keith's funeral, I strongly advise you to call on Judy. For one thing, Keith's nemesis is in her freezer."

Knocked off-kilter by an allusion to Keith's drowning, she covered her face with her hands and wept an outpouring of sorrow. Flustered, Obie fussed with clearing his placemat and disposing trash, conceding a few minutes for Etta to channel her grief. Facing the sink with his back toward her, he buckled at the knees when she spoke.

"If *you* spent the *night* with *J-o-o-d-y*, why couldn't you bring me Keith's trophy yourself?"

Gawd! If she only knew the round trip that poor bass made from Keith's reel to his Escape's wheels all the way to North Road, and right back to Winsor Brook where it got hooked.

Stiff in the legs, Obie lumbered from the sink to his seat across from her, raring to button down the situation between them. "I could've. But, leaving Keith's bass with Judy is the ace up my sleeve for getting you to see her. Today. Soon."

Put off by Etta's stone face and unvoiced intentions, Obie took advantage of the standstill to redeem himself in her eyes. "Just because I spent the night at Judy's place doesn't mean I slept with her. After having it out with Muriel, I couldn't bear staying under the same roof. Other than circling back to your place, there was nowhere else for me to go at that hour."

Chapter 90

Safe haven:

Tired and battered to the bone when he arrived at Judy's chalet, a persistent round of knocks rousted her out of bed from the second floor. Groggy, she listened on the other side, doing up the snaps on her cotton duster to cover a short nightie. Processing Obie's abridged version of what led him to go on the lam with only the clothes on his back, she relented. Unlocking and opening the door, she stepped aside to accommodate a man of strong build toting Keith's ice cooler.

The rancid odor of body sweat and stinky cheese prompted her to show him to the bathroom where she procured a disposable razor and spare toothbrush from inside the cabinet under the sink. He didn't balk when she offered to drape one of her husband's bathrobes over the outer doorknob for him to slip on when he finished showering. Before stepping inside the stall, he dropped his filthy garments on the threshold for her to dump in the washer.

***

Cinching his bare bottom inside tight-fitting Tartan plaid, Obie materialized in the homey front room, its ambience a welcome departure from Muriel's anathema of strait-jacketed décor. Judy was waiting for him with a tube of antibiotic ointment in her hands.

"We can do this the easy way or the hard way," she suggested.

Smarting from the burning sensation in his lower extremities, he fired back, "I didn't know there was an easy way."

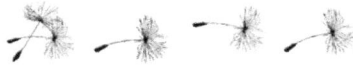

"What I meant is, what would be easier for me. If you stretch out on the sofa, it will be. Plus, you won't have far to fall asleep when I'm done."

Clamping his mouth shut to prevent profanities from escaping, his legs thrashed as she applied a thin layer of salve on the canvas of his ruptured skin, and covered a few repeat offenders with bandages. The tears welling in his eyes hadn't sprung from pain, but from a tenderness he'd never known from Muriel's fingertips. He refrained from sitting up and cupping her chin in his hands to caress her lips with his.

Before Judy padded up the wood-grain open-riser to her bedroom, she told him what he needed to know and mentioned cooking breakfast later on. Obie declined her tempting offer, mulling over her groundbreaking announcement without yammering his disbelief.

Anxious to get rolling, he let her in on his immediate plan to snooze a few hours before heading back home to change, then checking in with Etta. He thought it only fair to let her in on his spur-of-the-moment brainchild. "Ruling out cabin number six for battening down the hatches while I figure out a permanent living arrangement, I'll set up camp in my spare bedroom until another vacancy turns up.

"But, I'll be back this evening to return the bathrobe and pick up my duds. If you can stand my company, I'd like to take you to dinner. Knowing Etta the way I do, she'll have me working up an appetite from trying to convince her to come by your place."

"As long as it's not Chelo's."

***

So, cavorting like a perv on the prowl, belted inside a bathrobe with plenty of leeway to expose his paraphernalia, Obie sprinted from his vehicle to the walkway of interwoven

concrete pavers which led him to his source of angst. He fumbled with unlocking the door to the enclosed breezeway. Once inside, he jammed the second key in the lock of the door feeding into the kitchen, jiggling it to do his bidding. Thrust forward by its sudden opening, he stumbled onto the battleground where he had discharged his loose cannon.

He stepped in the direct line of Muriel's icy glare. Sitting at the table, dressed in street clothes and sipping her morning coffee, she was poised for a confrontation. "Well, look who's back!"

Ill-tempered from all of his ordeals, Obie strived to fend off her ire, postponing any talk of moving out or filing for divorce until they could muster an ounce of civility toward each other. "I happened to be in the neighborhood, so thought I'd stop by to make myself presentable."

Partway along the staircase, Muriel waxed suspicious and malicious, throwing a dirty-martini fit. "Is that Keith's robe you're wearing? Ever since biology lab, you've wanted to get into Etta's pants!"

He had at that. The best-laid plans to get laid had gone awry because of Etta's fixer-upper fiasco. Dismayed how last night's incendiary explanation for his whereabouts hadn't penetrated her thick skull, he turned, loath to face his shrew of a wife for accosting him and for maligning her best friend. *A grieving widow, for Gawd's sake!* Furthermore, he doubted Keith owned a bathrobe, comfortable romping around in his own skin.

"No, it's not."

Picking up his pace to reach the master bedroom, Obie held his ground, ignoring the magnitude of Muriel's aftershock. "If not Keith's, it belongs to Carolyn Farnum's dead husband,

411

that's who! Just how long have you and that harlot been making whoopee?"

Muriel never had a shortage of women from the Dark Ages of their past to foist upon him.

Chapter 91

Annoyed with Etta's reluctance to reply, Obie fidgeted in discomfiture under her stern scrutiny from across the table. When ready to take him on, she weighed in. "A quick recap, if you please. I'm to put off making funeral arrangements for the sake of picking up a fish held in custody by a woman of interest to you and Keith, whom neither of you slept with."

"You got that right." Still noncommittal, he pushed. "Keeping your best interest at heart, there's more. But, it's not my place to elaborate."

More? That's an understatement! Other than mentioning the handyman repairs and sprucing up he did for the property owner, Keith omitted biographical particulars beyond widowhood. She never asked. Today, she intended to ferret out his well-kept secret.

Etta sighed. Not sure where she and Muriel stood after wanting to strangle the life out of her, she felt indebted to the teenager who turned her life around after Momma died. Perhaps the time had come to revoke Muriel's secret in the slim hope of salvaging the shreds of her marriage.

Etta probed. "Should I agree to head over there, what do you intend to do in the meantime?"

He hadn't thought that far ahead. Grateful she'd considered his proposal, Obie played it by ear. "If it's okay with you, I'll sack out on the sofa until you get back."

Leveraging her upper hand, "Tell you what. I'll see Judy if you agree to go back home and smooth things over with Muriel."

Knocked off his pins by her audacity to barter for a lost cause, he got up to help himself to a can of beer, thankful Keith had stocked the fridge. Sitting back down, he pulled the tab and took a long slug of local brew.

"No can do. I bore the brunt of her pistol-whipping this morning." *So did you!* "I've made up my mind to pull the plug on our farce of a marriage. In the past six months or more, I can count on the fingers of one hand the number of times Muriel let me have my way with her. When a cabin other than Keith's becomes vacant, I'm going to lay low there while riding out the tide of our divorce."

He guzzled the rest of his beer, crushed the can, and pitched it into the wastebasket. Etta lowered the boom, pulling out all the stops. "Before you cozy up to Judy any more than you already have, I think you should know why Muriel hasn't been an eager beaver all these years."

"W-w-hoa!" he decried, lunging forward. "You're way out of line, sister!"

Obie's menacing outburst did nothing to deter her betrayal of trust. "I'm going to give it to you straight. When Muriel was five her uncle molested her—fingering and tonguing her sweet spot. Coerced, she returned the favor, slurping his manhood. When she got the nerve to tell her mother, Lois didn't swoop up Muriel in her arms and cover her face with kisses. Instead, she browbeat Muriel into keeping it a secret from Fist, who surely would have killed him if he knew."

Obie clocked out of the present and jettisoned himself to the Dark Ages of his past. Specifically, Etta's high school graduation party where the sight of Carolyn Bettencourt spiked memories of his senior prom and skyrocketed his libido. Aroused, he spirited Muriel away from the party and into the Citroen, pressuring her for more than gratuitous necking and hand jobs.

414

While Etta pontificated, the sweat poured out of him as he recalled Muriel's mind-blowing blowjob, so out of whack for her. Mind-boggling! After all these years, Etta just force-fed him Muriel's childhood trauma, the underlying reason behind her reluctance and ill-disguised revulsion toward his sexual advances.

"Fist bought the cover story his wife told about her brother's hasty departure. He disappeared for good without a forwarding address. Dead or alive, he's ever present in Muriel's mind. Never recovering from her molestation, top that off with Lois brainwashing Muriel into believing moral women endure, rather than enjoy sex."

Etta's crash course on Muriel was too much for him to digest all at once. He felt his stomach slam the brakes on mixing and grinding, shifting its contents in reverse at fourth gear. Obie dived for the wastebasket. Dropping to his knees, he retched until he'd cast out every morsel ingested at breakfast. Purged, he sat back on his haunches, shuddering at the thought of Muriel not being able to cast out her demons. Far be it from him to bring up a sore subject that wouldn't change things between them.

Etta came up from behind and placed her hands on his shoulders giving them a squeeze. *Too little, too late. Regardless, Obie deserved to know what he'd been up against all these years.* "Hey, big fella. I'll be running along to see Judy. The sofa is all yours."

415

Chapter 92

At the risk of taxing Sydney's old joints on rutted backroads, Etta got behind the wheel of her Wrangler. Lowering all the windows to finish air-drying her damp hair, she set off on a windswept, 7-mile drive to Winsor Road. Turning onto North Road at the end of her driveway, she headed northeast toward Balcom Road. During the 13-minute pilgrimage to Keith's sacred ground in the wilderness, Etta's woolgathering led the way, veering her further from the primary purpose of retrieving his bass and weekend belongings.

After two miles of bumpety-bumping on uneven surface, she took a left onto RI-94 N and addressed Keith as though he sat in the passenger seat. "My Wild One, I promise to fulfill your wishes by scattering your ashes over Winsor Brook as you would have scattered mine."

Taking a right onto US-6 E, Etta wrangled over a matter dear to her heart. Somewhere along the 1.6-mile stretch before hanging a left onto Rams Tail Road, she arrived at her decision to wait until after the funeral to contact the bitches. *At their age, I refuse to push their limits for getting here by fair means or foul. It'd be just like them to live up to their principles under any circumstances.* She cringed at the thought of Helen hobbling her way around, accompanied by Joan, an overprotective nursemaid. *And, there's no way I'll put the brakes on Gloria and Lenny's second honeymoon.*

Etta turned left onto Danielson Pike, bearing right where it became Winsor Road. A few minutes later, she drove past the property sign and onto the gravel horseshoe which meandered along the row of cabins. Instead of following the curve to the end, Etta parked in front of the chalet, turning the key to the off position and removing it from the ignition.

416

Looming large through the windshield, Keith's pickup on the fringe of cabin number six. Tearing up, "My Wild One, Obie and I will see to your truck."

She clutched the steering wheel as a means of fortifying herself to stanch the flow of tears before meeting Judy. Detached from matters of inconsequence, Etta stepped out of the Wrangler, unaware the wind had whipped her hair into a voluminous frenzy.

***

Approaching the front door, Etta felt more composed, attributing the dramatic shift to Keith's spiritual presence alongside her. Halfway between forging ahead and doubling back, Judy exited the chalet and walked toward her, exuding warmth and compassion from every fiber of her being. Apart from their physical similarities—*and, holy smoke, honey-blonde hair pinned up in a slipshod bun*—Etta felt a soulful connection with this complete stranger. The vibes in their viselike hug, however brief, led Etta to believe Judy felt it too.

No introductions needed, Judy expressed her condolences. "I'm so sorry for the loss of your husband. After my own passed last year, Keith started doing odd jobs around the place and we became good friends." Hesitant, she added, "Nothing more."

Etta ceded a reassuring touch to Judy's arm. "I figured out as much on my own. After the damage was done."

"Gosh, that's a major relief! When Obie showed up at my door, he scratched the surface of a three-way entanglement. The stink clinging to him backed up his story, all right."

Shamefaced, Etta owned up to her initial breach of trust. "When I followed up on a friend's insinuation by phoning Keith and got no answer, I went berserk without probable cause. Obie,

bless his heart, pulled an all-nighter, picking up after me when I sacked out."

Judy rubbed Etta's forearm, bequeathing an understanding smile. "Love makes us do crazy things." Changing course, "If we don't move inside, we're going to wilt under the blazing sun."

Etta followed her host into the cozy front room outfitted in an eclectic mix of shabby-chic furniture and retro effects manifesting the idiosyncrasies of time-worn fabric and indelible scars. She took up Judy's offer to make herself comfortable, choosing to sit on the overstuffed armchair by her Wild One's duffel bag. "Thank you for gathering Keith's belongings. Obie mentioned you owe me a bass."

Judy chuckled. "That I do. If you'll excuse me, I'll only be a few minutes rounding up refreshments."

***

During a breather of sipping iced teas garnished with slices of lemon, and munching on egg biscuits, Judy took charge. "Tell me something. Did you and Keith prefer a serving of bacon or sausage with your eggs?"

Thrown by a query of trivial importance, "Come again?"

"Humor me, if you will." Judy slid open a drawer on her side of the coffee table positioned in front of the sofa on which she sat across from Etta.

"Either one worked for us. Why?"

Judy removed, from what Etta could tell, a document of some sort. "Keith had a doozy of a surprise he meant to share with you at breakfast this morning. My guess is you might have served bacon or sausage with cheesy egg casserole."

Embarrassed, Etta shrank into the cushion. Judy oriented the paperwork right-side up and handed it over to her. Without

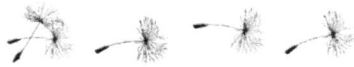

her reading glasses on, Etta squinted to decipher its typewritten context of legal import. She scanned property information about the Rainbow Trout Cabins which included its address and type of dwelling. Her eyes popped from shock when she reached the final section pertaining to financial particulars and terms of a private sale. Keith Lawrence's standout, squiggly signature rocked her reality check.

In a tremulous, croaking voice, "I take it this is why Obie pressured me to see you."

Judy nodded. Respecting Etta's fragile and frazzled state, she inched forward. "Worn out from caring for Doug during his last few months, and devastated when he left this world, I wanted nothing more to do with this place. When I put it on the market, Keith got squirrely over possible defamation of the property's character. He thought the two of you were ready to downsize in your golden years. Maybe move into the chalet until both of you came up with other plans for your new forever home in cabin six. Surprise!"

"That's for sure! Years ago, when my grampa passed, I gifted Keith half the money fetched from the estate. He deposited it in a savings account. Never touched a penny of it, priding himself on being self-sufficient in his own right." Etta's lip quivered. "After all this time, he finally put his money where his heart always felt at home." She wept without restraining herself, and dug out a tissue from the pocket of her jeans to absorb her tears and blow her nose.

Judy rose from the sofa, allowing Etta some privacy to compose herself while she went back into the kitchen and delved inside the fridge. At the counter, she removed the rind from a honeydew melon and cut the flesh into several slices, wrapping prosciutto around each one.

Determined to prolong the visit, she needed to detain Etta long enough to get one other thing off her chest, all the while debating whether or not to let it fall by the wayside.

Chapter 93

Judy set a pile of napkins and her decoy platter of reinforcements on the coffee table. By all outward appearances, Etta had pulled herself together. In contradiction, her eyes reflected a mournful soul. While reluctant to inflict more heartache, Judy decided in favor of rubbing salt in a fresh wound. *Damn it, if the shoe were on the other foot, I'd want to know. Thank goodness, Doug was an open book. Perhaps that's why I've taken a shine to Obie. He's up front. What you see, is what you get.*

Covering up the tracks of her guilty conscience, "Help yourself while they're cold."

"Italian-style hospitality at its finest! This was one of my dad's signature appetizers served at his catering events. Pairing cured meet with fruit is supposed to boost the immune system."

"Then . . . buon appetito! Since Obie insisted on leaving before daylight, he missed out on breakfast. Not one to fuss for myself, I saved the good stuff for us. Provided that you showed up, of course."

Etta picked up a napkin to cradle the piece she took hold of.

Judy buckled down to business. "As Keith kept to himself, we barely spoke to each other until my circumstances changed. In need of a handyman to keep up with repairs, he and I trumped up a convenient business arrangement and friendship."

Etta maintained her silence and kept a straight face, a devious ploy meant to extort a tell-all. It worked.

"Pouring my heart out to Keith may have encouraged him to blow the whistle on what had been eating away at him for years." On pins and needles, Judy rubbed the back of her neck,

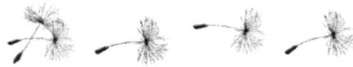

a nervous reaction borne out of viewing Etta's stiffened demeanor. "I got the impression he bore the brunt of what troubled him because of his love for you."

Etta's ears perked. *Be careful what you wish for. Curiosity killed the cat, and all that.* Uncertain how to continue, Judy stalled.

Harsher than she intended, "Please. Don't hesitate on my account. By all means, finish what you started."

Approaching the watershed moment of her declaration, Judy went the distance. "To begin with, Keith couldn't let go of blaming himself for your father's death."

Upset, Etta wrung her hands. "His guilt was the silent killer I couldn't foil no matter how hard I tried."

"He told me as much." At that point, Judy gripped the edge of the coffee table to brace herself for delivering the final blow. "There's a matter I practically begged Keith to take up with you. He refused because he thought it reflected poorly on him, and he didn't want to rock his marriage."

Pinning herself against the backrest of the armchair, Etta waited for the thunderbolt to strike.

"Going against the grain of his better judgment, he questioned the diagnosis of your medical emergency." In full view of Etta's facial features frozen dumbstruck, Judy felt queasy.

Etta reclaimed her ability to speak. "For mercy's sake, what did he question without daring to ask?"

"Given the timing and precautions he admitted to taking, Keith couldn't help wondering if your friend had gotten you pregnant and you suffered a miscarriage." Judy slumped against the sofa cushions, waiting for the psychological debris to hit.

Birch. Putting the fear of God in him, she'd given him no choice in the matter for disclosing his sexual orientation to his dad. Turns out, for all of Mr. Hansford's Gay-bashing and badgering his son to find a suitable wife, the admission hadn't caused irreparable damage between them. Birch worked off his debt and held up his end of Hansford's Reliable Appliances. He never embarked on that cross-country trip he had no need to take.

In her eyes, Birch redeemed himself and they tried to patch up a friendship which had lost cohesiveness. Bowled over by Keith, and spending more time with him, she and Birch drifted apart. Last she heard, via Blackstone Boulevard's gossip outreach, Birch and his partner settled in Palm Beach, living an idyllic life making the rounds of posh golf courses.

Etta snapped back to present-day reality confounded by the past. *Keith was right. Had he questioned my diagnosis, or second-guessed the nature of my relationship with Birch, I would have disclosed his homosexuality. Doing so to dispel Keith's doubts, he'd have lost more ground than he could have possibly gained. Like losing my respect. Heaven knows, I nearly lost my own self-respect for questioning his faithfulness. In the long run, some things are best taken on faith.*

Said out loud for Keith's benefit on the other side of the veil, even though Etta felt he'd already read her innermost thoughts, "My friend and I never engaged in any sexual activity. And, my diagnosis was correct." Recasting their conversation, "With lots of ground to cover, I should go."

"And, I should get Keith's bass ready for the road." Thinking it tacky to throw in the rainbow trout, Judy left it that.

"While you're busy, I'll pick up after us."

***

423

When they had secured Keith's cooler in the Wrangler's cargo hold, Judy touched upon matters with Etta before she got behind the wheel. "I'll get the details for Keith's memorial service from Obie at dinner tonight."

Torn between her loyalty to Muriel and her compassion for Obie, she nodded her head without commenting on their get-together. She embraced Judy in a quick hug.

"One more thing. If you could give me a little time to get my bearings before moving out, I'd really appreciate it."

On shaky ground ever since Keith passed away, Etta found her footing. "Please take all the time you need. It's what Keith would have wanted." Arching her brow to emphasize irreverence, "Should heart's desire overrule your original plan, you're welcome to stay rent-free."

A hairsbreadth from crying, Judy's bottom lip quivered. "I'm still going through the grieving process, but I'll keep an open mind and consider your generous offer if I have a change of heart."

"I've only just begun coming to terms with my grief. But, I look forward to going ahead with Keith's plans to set up shop on this side of heaven."

***

Close to home, Etta pulled over onto the brush along Balcom Road. Contemplating a new home for Keith's long-in-the-tooth truck, it gave her an excuse to call Muriel while out of range from Obie. This seemed an opportune time to find out if their friendship withstood the blows she had dealt it.

Unwilling to add to the raw sewage Uncle Reggie and Lois had already dumped on Muriel, Etta pushed off as though her huckleberry friend's well-meaning connivance never occurred. "Hey, Muriel. I thought I'd give Ethan the right of first refusal to take Keith's truck off my hands. I know it's seen better days,

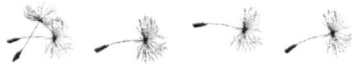

but what are a few dents, scratches, and body rot to a landscaper looking to expand his business?"

The lilt in Muriel's voice suggested she had snapped up the lifeline Etta tossed her way. "I can't imagine him turning down your generous offer. I'll let him know."

One step forward, two steps back. "U-m-m, when I questioned Obie again this morning, he denied any funny business with you. Ruling you out, I narrowed down his outside interests to Carolyn Farnum. He had nothing to say in his defense."

W-h-a-t? Did Muriel just say that? A carbon copy of her mother's way of thinking. If Obie follows through on his plan to escape the loony bin, Muriel will need someone to lean on. Nobody else is qualified to cope with the extent of her dysfunction. She's family. And, one twisted sister, at that!

"Muriel, perhaps your second unfounded accusation left Obie speechless. Things aren't always what they seem."

Muriel thought better of asking Etta if she happened to come across the lid to her baking dish.

Epilogue

Things aren't always what they seem.

Opting for direct cremation, Etta arranged a brief and simple memorial service to honor Keith, prioritizing a private observance at the funeral home. On the surface, Muriel and Obie looked like any older adult couple who had grown indifferent toward each other, rather than two peas about to split from their pod. Presenting a united front, they sat together to pay their respects at a vigil comprised of three people until Judy walked in and made it four.

Since neither Obie nor Etta brought Muriel up to speed on Judy's tie-in with Keith just yet, both women harbored false assumptions about each other. Still under the impression Judy was Keith's paramour, Muriel's eyes narrowed in distaste, thinking she had some nerve to show up.

Going by Obie's unvarnished truth about his marriage, Judy thought Muriel's eye daggers targeted her for providing him a safe haven away from her. When, in fact, Obie hadn't bothered to set Muriel straight about Carolyn just yet, or where he'd spent the night.

The warmth of Obie's discreet gaze counteracted his wife's frosty reception. Anyhow, Judy thought it prudent to maintain her distance from him for the time being.

***

Things have a way of working out.

Divorce forged a strong friendship between Muriel and Obie because it put an end to sexual contention. It also didn't hurt letting Muriel think she gained the upper hand in the

426

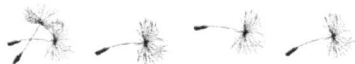

financial settlement when Obie transferred the title of their property to her.

Becoming his own man, and being loved back by someone he loved, revitalized Obie. He and Judy embarked on a life together in her chalet, pulling their own weight by contributing financially to the upkeep of Etta's fishing ground. *One of these days, I'll give Keith what for by slipping on a pair of waders to press my luck with his rod and reel.*

***

When it came time for Etta to pull up stakes, she entrusted her log home on North Road to a non-profit organization dedicated in providing a retreat for women recovering from sexual abuse and domestic violence.

After adding a second floor and implementing extensive renovations on the ground level to accommodate year-round occupancy, she moved into cabin number six. The Aspidistra accompanied her and took up residence where the sun doesn't shine in the common room off of the kitchen. In keeping with her way of life, Etta converted one of the upstairs' bedrooms into a combination art studio and gallery for displaying Keith's bounty from Winsor Brook, which included his last strapping bass.

The other five cabins continued to provide lodging off the beaten path for fishing enthusiasts. Etta carried on with her sketching pilgrimages around town. Since home is where the heart is, she found comfort traversing the fringes of Winsor Brook, feeling close to Keith on the parallel side of his universe.

Until sometime tomorrow, my Wild One. So mote it be.

Every so often, the sound of tires crunching along the gravel horseshoe outside cabin number six alerted her to Muriel's arrival in tow with a freshly baked cheesy sausage-and-croissant casserole.

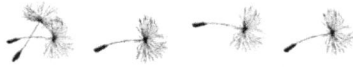

About the Author

Multi-award winning author, **Eva Pasco**, a lifelong native Rhode Islander, integrates local setting in her lit with grit. Weaving historic events, geographic landmarks, and regional culture into the fabric of her storytelling, she blurs the lines of demarcation between fact and fiction.

Tapping into significant issues impacting the lives of women, Eva's novels emphasize character-driven plots propelled by flawed and feisty females over forty.

Should you find yourself reluctant to leave the rustic town of Foster, there may be a vacancy at Rainbow Trout Cabins on Etta's fishing ground.

All of the author's published works are available in eBook and paperback at Amazon via **Eva Pasco's Amazon Author Page:**

http://www.amazon.com/author/evapasco

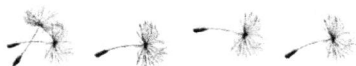

Contents

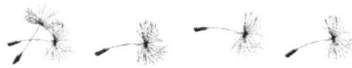

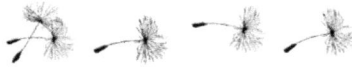

Made in the USA
Las Vegas, NV
21 December 2021

39112378R00243